S0-ADP-800

ROSALYN ALSOBROOK

TIME STORM

PINNACLE BOOKS
WINDSOR PUBLISHING CORP.

PINNACLE BOOKS are published by

Windsor Publishing Corp.
475 Park Avenue South
New York, NY 10016

First Printing: July, 1993

Printed in the United States of America

Special Thanks

To Dewayne Razier of Woodvale Heights for all the useful information about his neighborhood. He was very tolerant of this inquisitive stranger. To Robin at the Johnstown Flood Museum for allowing me to peruse the archives at my leisure. To the rangers at the Johnstown Flood Memorial who answered my endless stream of questions concerning the area. To the Upshur County Library for locating the books I needed when I needed them. To Nurse Deanna and Dr. Stu Patty of Illinois and a "special" thanks to author/nurse Patricia Rae Walls of Dallas for verifying emergency room procedures for me.

I'd also like to thank my editor, Alice Alfonsi, and my agent, Ruth Cohen, for their constant support during this project. And finally, I'd like to thank my family for their continued patience: my husband, Bobby; my oldest son, Andy; and my youngest son, Tony.

Author's Notes

At 4:07 on the afternoon of May 31, 1889, the thriving city of Johnstown, Pennsylvania, was washed away by a 35- 45-foot mountain of debris-packed water traveling approximately 40 miles per hour. The South Fork Dam, just over 14 miles upriver, had finally broken and had sent over 20,000,000 tons of water crashing down the steep, narrow valley below.

Because of recent rains, the two swift-running rivers that formed a point near the business district of Johnstown had already overflowed, though that was a common occurrence since the city had been built on a floodplain. Every spring flood water swamped those businesses nearest the rivers.

But by noon on that particular Friday, Johnstown already had two to seven feet of water filling its streets, which was said to be "the worst flood in recent memory." By 3:10 P.M., the time the faulty dam finally gave way, even the residents in those neighborhoods that had never flooded before were busy preparing their houses for high water. Few people headed for the surrounding mountains where they would have been safe because hardly anyone believed there was any real danger of the earthen dam finally giving way.

Of the 30,000 people thought to be in the valley

that day (due largely to the Memorial Day celebrations held the day before), 2,209 did not survive the onslaught. Some drowned immediately; others were caught in the tons of wreckage that jammed against the old stone bridge below town. Most of those trapped at the bridge were either crushed by the weight of the wreckage or they burned to death when the oil-soaked rubble suddenly caught fire. The burning pile of debris at the bridge worked like a second dam, forcing the water to form a new lake over Johnstown. The high water delayed the efforts to rescue those who were stranded but had somehow survived.

Although *Time Storm* is clearly a work of fiction and the characters exist solely within my imagination, the events involving the Johnstown Flood of 1889 are presented as accurately and honestly as possible.

Chapter One

JoAnn Griffin sat on the large rock beneath a bleak gray sky with her shoulders slumped, feeling more responsible than ever for her parents' deaths.

The temperature was 42 degrees, unseasonably cold for late March. Dark clouds blocked the midday sun and provided dismal contrast to the flowering dogwoods and the newly budded oaks below. JoAnn had spent most of that morning seated on the large flat rock staring morosely across a small, shaded pond that had been a delight to her in childhood but now was haunted with the grayer images of her youth.

The wooded haven, canopied by the entangled limbs of native trees, had been a favored hideaway during JoAnn's earlier years. The refuge was nestled in the secluded woodlands just north of her parents' land, at the very edge of Woodvale Heights, only a few miles northeast of Johnstown, Pennsylvania. It had always been the perfect place for spending hours of uninterrupted contemplation.

Today was no exception. A thick scattering of dogwoods and several smaller trees growing on the mountainside had sprouted the first of their springtime blossoms. Sprinkled beneath the more massive trees were large yellow and dainty white wildflowers that jutted through the thick patches of winter-faded grass. All around, early sprouts of Virginia creeper peeped from beneath the dead foliage. But JoAnn was too lost to her brooding thoughts to notice yet the early burgeoning of nature's palette.

Grief-stricken, JoAnn's attention had centered on what she should do with her life now that her parents were gone. Because of their recent deaths, the only family she had left were two unmarried aunts living in Texas. She had no brothers. No sisters. No nieces or nephews. And certainly no children of her own. Never had she felt more depressed — nor ever more alone.

Desperately, she tried to sort through a tumbling array of thoughts in an effort to place her pain-filled emotions into better perspective. There had to be a *reason* for her parents' deaths. A reason other than the obvious fact *she* had been unable to save them.

"There *has* to be a purpose to all this," she wailed. "God would not take them without first having a logical reason." But for the life of her, she could not figure out what that reason might be.

During the past several hours, JoAnn had become so lost to her gut-wrenching thoughts, she barely noticed the late winter storm as it rumbled across the sky from the north. She had neither the inclination nor the energy to pull her mind away from the torturing realization she was not the competent doctor she had thought.

"Why couldn't I save them?" Her voice was so strained it could barely be heard above the wind kicking through the leaves. "Why, when I'd needed my medical training the most, did it fail me like that? Why did I struggle through all those years of mind-staggering work and obtain all that education when it didn't even help me to save my own parents' lives?"

Her whole body trembled while she closed her eyes against the sharp pain that forced the breath right out of her. What kind of doctor was she? Did she choose the wrong profession all those years ago? Was it possible she really was *not* cut out to be the trauma doctor she had always longed to be? Or any other doctor for that matter. And if *that* was true, what could she possibly do with her life now? Except for a career in medicine, she had no other vocation to fall back on.

A now-familiar ache coiled through her stomach and left her with a cold, hollow feeling — a void she was not certain could ever again be filled.

To keep her tears from falling, she drew in a long, deep breath, held it several seconds then slowly released it. How she hated tears. Still she found it impossible to blink away the moisture or in any way alleviate the powerful feelings of guilt and helplessness that engulfed her. If only the hurt would go away.

Still hoping to keep the tears at bay, JoAnn tossed her head back and blinked several more times. Strange, until two weeks ago she had thought of herself as a very competent, self-assured doctor. But now all she had were doubts.

The sharp, bitter-cold wind rustled through the tall trees overhead and drew her attention. She was surprised to see how threateningly dark the sky had become. Her first thought was to hurry toward her car parked on a small rise just the other side of the narrow earthen dam; but the approaching thunderstorm suited her mood. Tilting her head back further, she let the brisk wind tug at her long dark tresses. The smell of approaching rain reached her senses.

11

A slight chill cut through her lightweight clothing but not enough to make her bother with the sweater she carried. Instead of slipping the bulky white garment over her shoulders, she hugged its thick softness to her breast while she watched the dark, towering clouds tumble threateningly above the swaying treetops. Shifting her weight forward, she kept her face toward the wind, invigorated by its strength, believing there was time yet to make the short run to her car before any rain fell. Even so, she slipped a hand into her skirt pocket to find her car keys and have them ready.

When brief flashes of lightning illuminated a boiling patch of the dark clouds off to the north, she brought the keys out of her pocket and cupped them in her hand. The low, demonic rumblings that followed drowned the clattering of a coal train that past through Woodvale far in the valley below. She shivered when the ominous sound clamored past, haunting the dreary heavens with its baleful discord.

Judging by the time delay from flash to thunder, the storm front still lay several miles away. Even so, JoAnn stood and brushed the back of her dark blue linen skirt with her free hand. Yet she did not head immediately for her car. Instead she stared with momentary fascination at the powerful display nature provided both above and around her.

Suddenly, another bolt of lightning gave a deafening crack. Startled, she screamed. Clasping a hand against her chest, she sucked in several quick breaths before looking to see if any damage had been done.

"What the—?" Her eyebrows notched with immediate concern when she noticed a mass of black smoke only a few hundred feet away. A strange acrid odor,

12

which smelled something like hair burning, accompanied the smoke.

Quickly, she cupped her hand over her nose then noticed something extremely odd about the boiling mass of smoke. The formation itself was an ever-changing mixture of dark blue, gray, and black that originated about a foot off the ground. From where she stood, it looked like the balloon of smoke billowed out of *nowhere*.

Huge, fat pillars of dark blue and gray twisted to form a large, black cloud that hung low in the air. Yet very little of the billowing mass escaped into the actual environment. It was almost like the bizarre accumulation of smoke and ash was somehow being drawn back into itself, as if lured by some strange midair gravitational force.

Unable to detect what exactly had caught fire yet wanting to help keep the blaze from spreading, JoAnn hurried toward the thick, swirling mass. Prepared to beat out the flames with her sweater, she squinted as she tried to peer into the thick, curling haze. She was as curious to know what held the strange smoke suspended above the ground as she was to find out what had caught fire. But even when she stood within several feet of the twisting mass, she could not determine a logical reason for there to be any smoke. There was nothing there to burn. It was as if the air itself had caught fire; yet there were no visible flames. No heat. Just a foul-smelling pillar of smoke.

With the worst of the storm passing to the north, JoAnn gave the strange apparition her full attention. Cautiously, she draped the sweater over her left arm, then stretched her right hand outward to touch the churning wall of smoke with the tips of her fingers.

Almost expecting to feel its strange movement, she watched with growing fascination while a cool, dark vapor eased along her hand then slowly curled around her wrist, luring her closer. When she leaned forward to accommodate, the hand disappeared. Oddly, the smoke did not seem quite thick enough to obscure her entire hand yet that was exactly what it did.

Since the haze had not yet caused her any physical pain, and with her curiosity peaked beyond normal, she slipped her entire arm into the peculiar wall and was further intrigued when it, too, appeared to vanish—right up to her shoulder. Staring at where her arm should be yet seeing nothing but swirling gray smoke, she then tossed her sweater over her shoulder and reached her other hand inside the gently twisting cloud to feel for the first arm. She wanted to assure herself it was still there.

Although she could no longer see either arm, she still felt them. Believing the disappearance was due to some strange optical illusion caused by the smoke, she played with the uniqueness of watching her hands and arms disappear and reappear for several more seconds before lifting her foot and taking a large, bold step forward, an action that put her completely into the swirling, dark mist.

While taking the step, it surprised her to discover she had to lift her other leg several inches to pull her foot over some unseen obstruction and into the smoke. It was then she realized the strange aperture had a physical shape. She could not make out the form by merely looking at it; still, she detected an uneven boundary when she touched the soft, cushiony edge with her fingers.

Finding it odd that she could touch something she

14

could not see, she then applied pressure to the inner rim of the oblong-shaped opening. It gave slightly to her touch; yet when she placed her hand on any other side of the unseen circle, she felt nothing. Her hand passed right through. It was as if this strange configuration had only an inner boundary.

By continuing to use touch, JoAnn soon discovered the top of the smoking hole hung approximately seven feet from the ground while the base was only about six or eight inches off the ground. The width varied from four to five feet across, being slightly larger near the base, and it felt as if the thickness was little more than a fraction of an inch.

Having stepped all the way into the smoldering circle, she was surprised that the smoke did not burn her eyes. She was able to watch, amazed, when the first part of her body disappeared from her sight yet was there waiting for her as soon as she had crossed through the smoke completely.

At first, the unusual configuration held her full attention and she continued to play with the peculiar illusionary effect. Gradually, her attention was drawn to her surroundings and she noticed several changes. The temperature was suddenly much warmer and the air no longer smelled like burning hair. There also seemed to be a lot more trees around her than before.

Slowly she scanned her surroundings. One delicate eyebrow arched while the other remained flat when she realized that not only were there *more* trees, but they were not quite as wide nor quite as tall as they had been. Most of the trees that surrounded her now appeared to be fairly young trees, but not so young they could be mistaken for freshly planted.

The next startling thing JoAnn noticed was that the

pond had completely disappeared, as had the large, smooth rock she had used for a bench. Instead, a small creek now wove through the area, its yellow-brown water rushing rapidly toward the Little Conemaugh River, less than a mile away.

Blinking with further confusion, she next noticed that the grass which had just moments before been withered and white from a lingering winter had suddenly perked and turned bright green in places. There were also twice as many wildflowers as before, probably because there was twice the area for them to grow with the pond suddenly gone.

Her face furrowed with a bewildered expression when next she glanced around for her car and noticed it, too, was gone. Yet she had not heard the engine start nor had she heard it drive away.

An eerie feeling washed over her, causing goose bumps at the back of her neck and across her upper arms. Then her gaze was drawn to the bright splashes of sunlight that trickled through the rustling leaves overhead.

What had happened to the storm? And why were there so many more new leaves than before as if spring had taken a sudden leap forward?

On top of having lost everything else, was she now losing her mind? she thought frantically.

JoAnn became further unnerved when she noticed the gentle sound of rain falling somewhere in the distance. Seconds later a few scattered drops penetrated the smoke and splattered at her feet. Yet there was not as much as a wisp of a cloud overhead.

Alarmed, she pressed her palm against her cheek, expecting to find it hot with fever, but it was as cool as ever.

16

Had she become so overcome by her grief and feelings of guilt that her mind had suddenly decided to rebel against reality by choosing to hallucinate instead? Or *was* this real?

It was while she further contemplated the absurdity behind all these changes—too puzzled and too fascinated by how real it all seemed to be yet frightened—that she heard a dog's incessant barking and what sounded like a horse running toward her from somewhere in the northeast.

Curiously, she glanced in the direction of the sounds and saw what looked like a narrow, curving dirt road layered with bark and wood shavings only a hundred yards away.

"Where'd *that* come from?" she asked aloud, certain the road was not there earlier. Yet it was there now, clear as the day was sunny, winding through the woods barely a football field's length away. And coming toward her at a very dangerous speed was a sleek white horse with a gleaming black carriage bouncing precariously behind it. From what she could see of the small openstyle carriage, it had been painstakingly restored but was now in danger of being completely destroyed.

It was not until the vehicle rounded a sharp bend then headed directly toward her that she noticed a man with gray hair slumped in the front seat. The large black dog crouched beside him barked wildly in a frantic attempt to wake the man. A few hundred yards behind the clattering contraption, JoAnn saw a second man riding a large black horse at breakneck speed. He had leaned forward to aid the horse's agile movements while he tried desperately to catch the runaway horse.

17

The carriage continued to jostle and bounce along the rutted road causing the driver to roll off the seat onto the floor while the rider behind him slowly closed the distance. JoAnn watched, awestruck, while the carriage first banged across a small wooden bridge then quickly approached another sharp bend in the road only a few dozen yards from where she stood.

At the bend, the horse cut too close to a roadside tree and with the rider nearly ninety feet behind, the carriage slammed against the tree and splintered into pieces. The impact sent both occupants into the air. The dog struck the ground first and yelped with pain while the man tumbled over and over in the dirt. The horse continued racing along the curved road, still dragging a large mangled piece of the carriage behind.

With a doctor's quick reflexes, JoAnn dropped her car keys and sweater, then hurried to help. She arrived at the injured man's side just seconds before the rider brought his horse to a dust-swirling stop nearby. She noticed immediately how oddly these two were dressed. Although the injured man wore black and the other man just now swinging his leg over the horse's back wore dark gray, they both had on the same sort of strange, square-cut suits with pocketed vests and skinny black neckties that looked like they were made out of a thick ribbon of some sort.

Watching the uninjured man while he dropped lithely to the ground, she decided his gray suit and square-toed boots looked like something Jarrod Barkley might wear when dressed for a special gathering in the old television series "The Big Valley." Even the man's dark brown hair was styled a little like Jarrod's, combed away from his face with a slight forward curve. But the facial features themselves reminded her more of someone else: Kevin Costner, the star of that Robin Hood video she had recently rented. From what she could see of the approaching man through the dust, he could easily be the handsome actor's double.

It occurred to her then that perhaps these *were* movie stars, or a couple of movie star doubles. Perhaps she had unwittingly stumbled onto a movie set. But when she saw no cameras, no crew, and when the older man from the carriage did not jump up and dust himself off so one of the stars could come in and take his place, she knew it was real. Someone had to save this man and with no other doctor present, that someone would have to be her—whether she felt suited for the task or not.

After only a moment's hesitation, giving no thought to her pantyhose nor her brand new navy blue skirt, she dropped immediately to her knees. The earth felt damp and cold against her skin. But with no time to worry about her own discomfort, she bent forward and examined this strangely dressed man. Because he had been unconscious even before the accident occurred and because of his near-blue coloring, she decided he suffered a heart attack.

The dog, uninjured by the crash, now sat only a few feet away, low on its haunches, growling menacingly. It was as if the animal was warning her to be extremely careful with whatever she did; yet he did nothing to prevent her from actually touching the man. Apparently, the dog sensed she was there to help; but even so, wanted her to be alert and cautious.

Within the next few seconds, the handsome rider had looped his reins around his saddle horn and hurried to her side.

Panic-stricken, Adam Johnson's pulse hammered at a maddening rate while he tried to elbow JoAnn aside so he could have a better look. He had already prejudged her to be a *sporting woman* from one of the many saloons in the area, mainly because of the indecent cut of her skirt — barely below her knees — and the dark blue and black face-coloring painted across her eyelids and her brown hair draped loosely over her shoulders. Because of that, he wanted her out of the way.

But JoAnn refused to budge. There was no time to allow a layman a moment to poke and prod. Because the injured man was obviously well into cardiac arrest, she had to start immediate cardiopulmonary resuscitation. Despite the brief opportunity she'd had to examine him, she had yet to find a carotid pulse nor any evidence of breathing. That meant no oxygen was getting to the brain. Time meant everything.

Within seconds after the younger man had attempted to push JoAnn aside, the growling dog transferred his focus from her concerned expression to the man's and the deep growl became suddenly more distinct. If there was to be a physical brawl, this dog intended to be in on it.

Sensing the animal offered her no real threat and not caring if the man did or not, JoAnn again reached for the pulse point at the hollow of the injured man's neck. She hoped to feel a throb, however faint, but when she found none, nor any new signs of breathing, she realized she had to put life over limb. She could not afford to lose any more valuable time and did not try to stabilize his neck or secure his back against possible spinal injuries. Pushing aside any earlier worries of incompetence, JoAnn shoved her sleeves above her

20

elbows then she rolled the victim onto his back.

"Please, sir, move away," she said in a stern voice. "I need more room to stretch this man full length."

Not responding to her command, the younger man continued to crowd her while he futilely attempted to wake the injured man by rubbing and patting his face and neck. She became angry. She was not used to having her directives ignored.

"Are you by any chance a doctor?" she asked in a sharp tone, knowing no doctor would be dressed the way this man was dressed.

"No, but I—" he attempted, but his answer was cut short.

"Then get out of my way. Don't you understand what's happened here? If I don't preform CPR on this man right away, he will die." She knew, technically, he already *was* dead. Still there was a slight chance, he could be revived.

Adam refused to be bullied and watched, horrified, when the deranged woman suddenly reached down and tugged the hem of her shamefully short skirt several inches above her knees. She then tossed one slender leg over the man's waist and shifted her weight on top of him.

Not knowing what this CPR was and wanting to stop the foolish tart before she did something to make the situation worse, he grabbed her by her shoulders just as she had balanced her weight on her knees and had reached for the man's shirtfront. Thinking her plans were to ransack his pockets, he thrust her sharply aside.

"That man happens to be my father!" he shouted angrily, furious that this perverted woman would do something so vile to what was obviously a dying, if not

21

already dead man. "Leave him alone!"

"But he *needs* a doctor," she reasoned with him, unaware she had failed to announce herself as such. Again, she attempted to straddle the victim. She wanted to position herself directly over the heart. When the onlooker again grabbed her by her shoulders to shove her away, she instinctively dipped her head and bit his hand until she drew blood. She was determined not to lose any more precious time. There was a life at stake.

"Madam, he *is* a doctor," the young man clarified, his teeth clenched against the sharp pain while he continued his struggle to pull this demented woman away. If his father had to die, he wanted him to do so in peace — with the quiet dignity the man deserved. "And at this time of day he is probably the *only* doctor around for several miles," he added, knowing the other doctors would still be in Johnstown taking care of patients, which is where his father would be if he had not suddenly decided to take the day off. Which was something the man had not done in almost a year. Remorsefully, he wondered if his father had known he was dying and had taken the day off so he *could* die in peace.

"But that's not true. *I* am a doctor," she said, having given up biting him to try again to reason with him. She now understood why this man behaved so irrationally. This was his father. He was as afraid of losing him as he was angry with her for interfering. "I may not be the best doctor this area has to offer, but I *do* have a medical degree and I know how to give CPR."

"You're no doctor," he muttered, his lips pressed tightly against his teeth. It angered him more to know she considered him that gullible. Although he continued to hold her by her upper arms, determined to keep her away, he lessened the pressure slightly.

"Not dressed like *that* you're not. Granted, there may actually be such things as women doctors these days, but you, my dear, are definitely not one. You look a lot more like some fancied-up saloon girl to me." He then narrowed his steely blue eyes and glared at her through his thick dark eyelashes. His fingers retightened their hold through the thin material of her blouse just before he suddenly shoved her away again. The sudden force caused her to fall over on her side. "Just what is it you're after here?"

Saloon girl? JoAnn looked at him, bewildered. Thinking that odd terminology for a man of the nineties, she glanced down at her clothing, which to her seemed rather discreet. Because of her mourning, she wore a simple straight-line navy skirt that ended just below her knees and a loosely fitted sapphire-blue, long-sleeve blouse with a modestly cut V-neck. While she hurriedly righted herself, she wondered what was so "fancy" about such a conservative outfit. It covered a good two-thirds of her body in demure shades of blue. She then wondered if he thought her dressed brazenly because he was one of those Amish people she had read about. He was certainly dressed the part.

"What I'm *after* is the chance to save this man's life!" she replied stubbornly, then sat forward and shoved him back with unexpected strength. "And I don't care what you think of the way I'm dressed or whether or not you believe I am the licensed doctor I say I am." She resumed her preparations for CPR by hurriedly loosening the man's tie and popping open his shirt just enough to expose the front of his chest. "I am damn well going to save this man's life!"

23

Temporarily stunned by her coarse language and the determined way in which she had just shoved him aside, he watched with a rumpled brow while she hastily straddled his father's abdomen again. He was too stunned by her bizarre behavior to comment when she next placed one hand on top of the other, locked her arms, then leaned forward until her shoulders were positioned directly above her flattened palms. After that, she began a strange ritual of pushing down on his father's chest with short downward thrusts, performing what she claimed to be "See-pea-are."

He was further bewildered when after about twelve sharp poundings on his father's chest, she suddenly leaned forward, grabbed his father by the cheeks then kissed him directly on the mouth. He blinked, unable to believe what she had just done. Did this insane woman think herself some magical princess?

By the time she had finished with a series of noisy kisses and had sat erect again, his father's lips had lost all their color. Adam realized the true hopelessness of the situation and remained paralyzed from the numbing fear that resulted from having lost his father. He watched helplessly for several more seconds while the woman repeated her odd manipulations. Then he pulled himself out of the sorrow-induced daze. Again he thought his father deserved to be left alone and grabbed her by the arms to renew his attempts to stop her.

"Get off of him." His blue eyes glinted with a combination of hurt, confusion, and pure anger. "Leave him alone."

She again jerked free from his grasp and, still thinking the man was Amish or Quaker — or from some other religious order that did not believe in medical

24

intervention—she lashed out impatiently, "I have no intention of letting this man die! I don't care who you are or what your beliefs may be. I am a doctor and I am *not* going to lose another life."

As frustrated as she was angry, she immediately resumed CPR. Without glancing to see how he may have reacted to her emotional outburst, she commented in a calmer voice something she should have mentioned earlier, "This man needs an ambulance. Get to a phone and call 911."

"You mean a *tele*phone?"

Stressed to her limit, she answered in a tone so harsh it sounded barely above a growl. "Yes, of course I mean a *tele*phone. What other kind of phone is there? How would you propose we get a call through to 911? Carrier pigeon?"

"But the only telephones around here are in Johnstown and a couple in South Fork." He gestured to the wooded mountainside surrounding them. "In this terrain, the ride to either place would take at least an hour and it would take yet another hour for the ambulance to make it back out here."

JoAnn exhaled sharply, trying to keep her temper in check. She knew none of what he said was true, but decided this man lived so far in the past he probably would not know how to use a telephone even if she directed him to one. He was obviously one of those people who had refused to allow such conveniences as telephones and electricity into his life. If only she knew how she had gotten separated from her car, she could use the cellular phone. But as it was, she had no idea where the car might be; she would have to make do with no ambulance.

"Do you at least know how to perform artificial respiration?" she asked, starting to panic. Her arms already felt the strain from the constant pumping. She needed help if she hoped to last long enough to save this man; and save him she must because, deep inside, she believed that saving this man's life might partially atone for not having been able to save her own parents.

He lifted an eyebrow at such a peculiar question and for a moment believed that perhaps she really was a doctor. Staring at her dumbfoundedly, he slowly shook his head. "I don't even know what artificial respiration is."

Frowning when she realized he spoke the truth, JoAnn wondered where this man had attended school. She thought *everyone* knew how to perform emergency respiration. Even most children understood the basics. Hadn't this man ever even taken a health class? Just how backward could he really be? It was then she realized he had probably been taught at home like so many of those children were. He had undoubtedly learned only what his parents wanted him to learn, and first aid was not part of his education.

Without pausing in the procedure, she asked, "Have you watched what I've been doing to your father's mouth?" She did not wait for an answer. "By pinching his nose and keeping his head tilted back to help hold his mouth and his trachea open, I've been able to keep him breathing artificially by forcing puffs of my own breath into his lungs. But I need to conserve more of my energy and concentrate on pumping his heart at a more consistent rate. I need for you to take over the breathing part for me."

When he looked at her, skeptical and obviously confused, she quickly added, "All you have to remember is to seal your mouth over his and give him a long, full breath, then pull away and count quickly to three before giving him another, then another. After three such breaths, pause long enough for me to make about ten chest compressions then breathe again. We'll keep it up until I say stop."

While he took over the breathing, JoAnn continued to pump the victim's chest at quick, regular intervals. The fear of losing yet another life caused her to thrust the heel of her palm against his lower breastbone harder and harder, until suddenly the man gasped and took a breath on his own.

JoAnn felt so relieved, she forgot that she still straddled the man. With tears in her eyes, she bent forward to check the pulse point first at his throat then at his wrist. *She'd done it.* She had saved the man's life. She was no longer a *total* failure.

The old doctor's face registered immediate surprise when his blue eyes fluttered open and he discovered a beautiful young woman hovering over him, one slender leg braced on either side of his hips. He blinked with further confusion when he noticed her skirt hiked well above her knees and her long brown hair streaming down around her shoulders in wild, careless abandon. He next noticed the tree limbs above them and realized he was out in the woods somewhere lying on the ground.

While he tried to decide why this woods nymph would be on top of him, she suddenly leaned forward and set about feeling his head with her fingertips, then hurried to examine his neck, arms, and legs, almost as another doctor might. To make the situation all the more peculiar, while she repeatedly pressed her fingertips into his flesh, she muttered constantly to his son,

27

who for some reason knelt off to the side looking as if he had just seen a ghost.

Returning his attention to the young woman, he yelped and winced when she suddenly pressed against a particularly painful spot at the base of his skull.

"Don't do that. It hurts." Because she was a woman, he kept the words *like hell* to himself.

When she then reached into his torn shirt to examine his ribs, obviously looking for possible breaks or pockets of fluid, he realized what she was doing and quickly brushed her hands away. "Don't do that either. I'm ticklish."

He pushed himself into a seated position and winced again at the dull throb pressing against the base of his skull. A distant whirring sound filled the back of his head. He hadn't felt this badly nor this disoriented since that morning after his fiftieth birthday celebration when he had consumed too much alcohol. And that was eight years ago!

"But you could have further injuries," she insisted. With his heart pumping again, several of his cuts had filled with blood. Fortunately, none of them were deep enough to cause much concern.

"If I do, I'll find them," he stated emphatically. He blinked several more times then proceeded with his own examination for broken bones, cuts, and abrasions, aware by the debris around them he had somehow wrecked his carriage. "Looks like I do have several cuts and contusions, and even a few abrasions but no broken bones. Nothing serious."

With hands still shaking from the overpowering relief that left her feeling both physically weak and yet extremely exhilarated, JoAnn finally pooled enough strength to stand. Letting out a prolonged breath, she straightened her skirt and brushed the dirt from the knees of her torn pantyhose.

Adam also stood, feeling so grateful to this woman for what she had done that he was quite willing to overlook the shameful cut of her clothing, even though the skirt revealed a goodly portion of her legs and had a daring six-inch opening up the back seam that allowed occasional glimpses of her lower thighs. Forcing his gaze back to her face, he smiled, then extended his hand to thank her and introduced himself as Adam Johnson and his father, Dr. Park Johnson. He smiled wider still when she then tried to introduce herself as Dr. JoAnn Griffin. She truly wanted him to believe she had a medical degree of some sort.

"Miss Griffin, I do want to thank you for saving my father's life," he said. Even though he still doubted the fact she was a full-fledged doctor, she *had* saved his father's life and the evidence of his appreciation glimmered from the shining depths of his silvery blue eyes.

"Then you don't plan to hold what I did against me?" she asked, aware many a doctor had been sued after having forced medical care on someone who held such strict religious beliefs. When she looked at his face to judge his expression, she was surprised to see he was at least six-foot-two. For some reason she had not expected him to be quite that tall.

"Why would I hold it against you?" He looked truly puzzled then realized she was upset because of his earlier behavior.

His smile widened until it formed several deep, curving indentations in his cheeks and revealed a set of remarkably white teeth. Her next thought was that he would make a perfect model for toothpaste commercials and for the first time, JoAnn was aware of

29

Adam as a man—a very virile, very *attractive* man. It was while she continued to stare into his smiling face she was again reminded of Kevin Costner. Especially at the corner of his eyes where several tiny laugh lines had formed, lines that drew her attention to the uncanny color of his eyes—so startlingly pale they looked more silver than blue.

"I assure you, I am deeply grateful." He spoke in a deep, beckoning voice. "I'm sorry if I hurt your feelings by what I said earlier; but you have to admit you don't exactly look like a doctor." He glanced down at her skirt, then at her legs. His eyes widened when he realized just how much of their shapeliness was bared to his view. "Most women—especially those claiming to be doctors—wouldn't traipse around the woods partially dressed like that."

JoAnn felt too emotionally drained to argue, even against such an incredibly archaic manner of thinking. Instead, she shook her head tiredly while she continued to stare at the tall, handsome man. Again, she noted the width of his broad, masculine shoulders and the unconventional cut of his clothing. What an unfortunate waste of manhood to have one who looked that extraordinary—even dressed as strangely as he was— living such a painfully restricted life.

The sound of a wagon coming from the same road as the carriage had come drew her attention away from Adam, albeit reluctantly.

Having left her sunglasses in her car, she squinted to get a closer look at the clattering vehicle as it stirred a faint trail of dust. She thought it peculiar that the driver of the wagon was just as oddly dressed as the other two men, though not in a dark, square-cut suit. This man was dressed for hard work. He wore a long-sleeve, khaki-colored shirt along with a pair of dark brown trousers, brown square-toed boots, and brown leather suspenders. She wondered if a whole colony of these extremists had moved into the area without her parents ever being aware. Certainly, they would have mentioned something like that to her had they known.

JoAnn watched while Adam waved the wagon to a stop. She was not surprised that he and the driver obviously knew each other, nor was she surprised by how easily the driver was convinced to set aside a part of his load long enough to transport his father to Adam's house.

"There's no need for all that," Park protested, then attempted to stand only to be ordered to stay put by the other men. "Let him keep his load." In the several minutes that had passed since his accident, his head had cleared and he'd concluded that he had merely been shaken. "I may have taken a bad lick, but I'm not so injured that I have to be hauled around like so much freight. I'm perfectly capable of sitting on the seat beside Glenn Burt there. It's not as if I'd have to go very far. Your house is the next one up the road. We should be there in a matter of minutes."

"Still, I don't want to take any chances," Adam responded while he continued to help Glenn unload a small section of his wagon near the back. When they had cleared an area that looked large enough, he returned to his father's side and without giving him another chance to protest, slipped his arms beneath him. "The wagon is ready. All you and that dog of yours have to do is lie down in the back long enough for Glenn to haul you to the house. And after you arrive, you will go right to bed where you will stay until I can send for Doctor Lowman. I want to hear *him* tell me

31

there are no serious injuries."

It was while Glenn and Adam were convincing Park to lie in the back of the wagon with the large black labrador retriever that JoAnn first suspected something was extremely wrong about the whole situation. It was something more than the strange way these men were dressed or their unusual speech patterns, which were clearly not from around Johnstown; it was the items this man carried in his wagon that made her suddenly wary.

Inside the bed, stacked beside a small pile of untreated lumber that had not been unloaded, she noticed several different sized barrels made from fresh wood and marked in bold black letters to be carrying such goods as sugar, flour, cornmeal, salt rock, and cheese. There was also a large wooden crate filled with dark metal cans and bulky fruit jars that sported handwritten labels. Beside the crate was an old-fashion steamer trunk in such immaculate condition it looked as if it was brand new.

While the two men did what they could to make the doctor and his dog comfortable, her attention was drawn from the strange contents in the wagon to something shiny on the ground. She bent for a closer look and discovered it was a small coin of some sort that had obviously fallen from one of the men's pockets. It was either brass or gold and looked like no coin she had ever seen. But the oddest thing about this coin was the date: 1885.

"Have one of you lost this?" she asked, aware the coin had to be very valuable. It was over a hundred years old and in mint condition.

"Thanks," Glenn responded reaching automatically for the coin, then patted his shirt pocket as if checking for more. "I guess I really should have put my change in my trouser pocket but I was in a hurry."

"But that can't have come from your change. That's a valuable antique coin," she said, thinking he should put it in a separate pocket so he did not accidentally spend it as part of his regular money. But the man had already turned his back to pick up a black leather satchel that had been flung from the wreckage and did not hear her. Nor did anyone else. They were too busy making sure the doctor and his dog were comfortable.

"I already told you," Park muttered, his face drawn into a craggy frown while he folded his arms over his chest and stared angrily at the patches of sky showing through the trees. "I'm not all that hurt."

"That may be, but you will still follow my orders," Adam said with exasperation. He placed the satchel Glenn handed him into the wagon. "And you *will* lie there and let Glenn take you on to the house where you promptly will be put to bed." He narrowed his steely gaze to emphasize his words. "And that is all there is to it."

JoAnn waited until Park had ceased his muttering before offering a suggestion of her own. "Why don't you forget taking him to your house and take him to the nearest hospital instead."

"Hospital?" Adam's eyebrows arched with uncertainty. "Why would we take him to the hospital? Hospitals are for the severely injured or dying. Like he just told you, he's not all that hurt. There are no broken bones, no bad cuts."

"Still, his heart is not all that stable. I think it would be wise to let the hospital run a complete battery of tests on him. He needs an EKG, a CAT scan, and probably half a dozen X rays to double-check that there are no broken bones. There could be a hairline fracture or other traumatic injuries he has not yet felt. Truth is, your father nearly died and it really would be best for him to be admitted into a hospital where he can have the proper tests made and be closely monitored for the next several days."

The three men looked at her questioningly then at each other. "Do you have any idea what she's talking about?" Adam asked his father as he raked his hand through his dark hair.

Park propped on his elbows and returned his son's curious stare. "I haven't a clue."

The three again looked at each other questioningly, as if wondering if this woman was a few bricks shy of a load before Park finally asked, "Missy, just what is an EKG and why would I need one?"

Again his questioning gaze darted to Adam, who shrugged and glanced curiously at Glenn, who also shrugged and looked at Park, who eventually shrugged and returned his attention to JoAnn. His face twisted into a peculiar frown as he suddenly noticed her dust-caked clothing.

Aware they were trying to form an opinion of her, JoAnn felt an unaccountable urge to take a tiny step backward. Judging from their deepened expressions *and* by the way they kept looking down at her clothing as if almost embarrassed by her choice of apparel, JoAnn realized she was as much an oddity to them as they were to her. Immediately she joined that fact to the other differences she had noticed earlier: from just a few minutes ago all the way back to when she had first stepped through that strange wall of smoke.

Slowly she concluded—that as preposterous as the idea seemed—she had somehow entered into a different time period. But rather than attempt to explain the unexplainable and risk raising further suspicions from them, she answered that last question very carefully.

"Oh, its just a test some doctors like to run. I guess it's not all that important." Especially if it did not even exist yet.

"Then if it isn't all that important, I think we'd better be on our way," Adam said, already headed for his horse with long nimble strides. "Glenn, you head on. I'll be right behind you."

Just as he swung his body easily into the saddle, JoAnn finally found the courage to ask her question. "Before you go, would you mind telling me what day it is?" Even though she really did not believe it possible, she had to know for sure.

Adam gathered the reins in one hand, then furrowed his forehead while he thought. "I *think* it's March twenty-seven. I *know* it's a Wednesday."

The March 27 fit, but it shouldn't be Wednesday, it should be Friday. Wednesday was the day she had finally asked for her eight-week vacation and that was only two days ago. "Are you sure it's Wednesday?"

"Well, considering yesterday was Tuesday and tomorrow is supposed to be Thursday then, yes, I feel pretty certain that today is a Wednesday." One dark eyebrow rose high above a glittering blue eye while the other remained low and cautious. "Unless someone came along while I wasn't looking and changed the order of things."

JoAnn thought about that. Someone very well may have. "Tell me something else. What year is it?"

Both of Adam's eyebrows shot upward as he looked at her with renewed doubt. Perhaps she was partly deranged after all. She certainly talked as if she might be, what with all her peculiar suggestions and odd phrasing like: getting a *double check* at the hospital and having his father *monitored*.

"Unless I miss my guess," he said, looking at her cautiously, "it is still Eighteen eighty-nine and will be for three more seasons."

1889?

Suddenly JoAnn's heart twisted, causing a sharp, cutting pain to pierce her chest.

Her whole body felt weak.

Chapter Two

JoAnn blinked, stunned by such an absurd response. She refused to believe such a thing could be true. Even so, a foreboding chill tumbled down her spine, lifting the tiny hairs at the back of her neck. With a sudden feeling of panic, she scanned her surroundings, eager to find something, *anything*, to prove him wrong. But she saw nothing to confirm the twentieth century.

Could such a thing be true? she wondered. But then again how could it? How could she have slipped into the year 1889? How could anyone? Things like that just didn't happen.

"Are you sure?" she finally asked and turned her troubled gaze to his. Already trembling inside, she studied his expression carefully, hoping to find a reason to believe this was all just one big, elaborate, practical joke. Something her colleagues had cooked up to help her forget her other troubles for a while.

"Am I sure about what?" He looked thoroughly mystified.

"About the year. About it being Eighteen eighty-nine."

Adam's brow dipped low while he tried to decide

37

what was wrong with her. Just a few minutes ago she had seemed perfectly rational, in complete control of her faculties. Now suddenly she didn't even know what year it was. "Of course I'm sure. If you want to follow me to my house, I can show you a calendar that will prove the date."

Aware by his baffled expression he spoke the truth, or at least thought he did, JoAnn's insides coiled tighter, making it hard for her to breathe. It felt like a huge, oppressive weight had fallen on her and now wanted to squeeze the life right out of her. "No, that won't be necessary."

As was her habit whenever she was upset, she lifted her fingertips to play with a thick strand of her long brown hair while she thought more about what might have happened. She remembered the strange coin dated 1885 and the fact the driver of the wagon had assumed the coin had fallen out of his regular change. She also remembered the eerie feeling she'd had when she had quit playing with the smoke and noticed all the changes around her, including the sudden disappearance of her car.

As impossible as it seemed, a time-conversion of some sort must have occurred when she stepped through that peculiar patch of smoke. It was the only explanation she could come up with, even as unrealistic as it seemed.

Glancing from Adam's puzzled expression to his outdated clothing to the strange-looking saddle on his horse, her blood turned icy cold, causing her whole body to ache with the sudden awareness. *It had to be true.* Somehow she had left the twentieth century and traveled over one hundred years into the past.

Suddenly she was fascinated by the sheer absurdity

38

of it all. She had somehow been transported more than an entire century back in time. But almost as abruptly as the fascination for what had happened emerged, it died when she considered the very frightening, very *real* prospect of having become totally and irreversibly insane.

But just as frightening was the thought of *not* being insane. That would mean she was *indeed* in the year 1889. Even more frightening: what if she were trapped in this previous time period forever? What if there was no way to return to her own century?

Horror-struck, she glanced at the area where she had last seen the smoke. Another sickening wave of apprehension washed over her when she realized the air had cleared.

There was nothing left to indicate where that hole had been. *Nothing.*

"Miss, are you on foot?" Adam asked, thinking she looked a little lost and a lot frightened, unaware there was good reason for her to be both. "You look a little disoriented. Do you need a ride somewhere?"

JoAnn looked at him with a peculiar expression, still too frightened and bewildered by what had happened to understand what he had said. All she knew was that he had spoken and now awaited a response. "What did you say?"

"I asked if you needed a ride somewhere."

"Oh, no, thank you." Again she stared at the area where the dark hole had formed. If only she could spot a tiny wisp of smoke. Or a burnt edge of the opening. *Anything* that might direct her to the proper spot. "I can walk back to where I want to go."

Or at least she *hoped* that proved true.

"Then I'd better be on my way," he stated and

glanced curiously in the same direction. He wondered what she had found so distracting about the small grassy clearing. "I really should try to get to the house before Father does so I can warn Doris."

Thinking Doris must be his wife, she nodded understandingly, but at the same time she wondered why it disappointed her to know he was married. This man wasn't even from her own time period for goodness sake. Why should she care if there was a woman in his life? "Yes, I imagine she would want to be forewarned."

He again looked at her troubled expression then toward the sunny spot where her attention kept straying. Other than a huge yellow butterfly flitting among the wildflowers, there was nothing in the area to draw such deep scrutiny. "Thank you again for what you did for my father."

"It's what I'm trained to do," she responded automatically, no longer paying attention to her own words when she turned away from him and started toward the clearing. "Just see that he stays in bed for the next few days and avoids any strenuous activity for at least a month." It was such a pat response for her when dealing with heart patients, she did not realize she spoke it. Her thoughts and fears were focused on finding that hole.

Adam stared after her a few seconds, contemplating what she had just said, then gripped the leather reins tighter in his hand and quickly nudged his horse into a steady trot. He did not have time to worry about this half-crazed woman, no matter how beautiful or helpless she looked. He had to make sure his father obeyed his orders and went straight to bed and stayed there until Dr. Lowman had a chance to examine him.

40

Only vaguely aware that Adam had left, JoAnn continued toward the grassy area where she remembered the hole to have been, certain now that the strange wall of smoke had been her entry point into the past and that the freak flash of lightning had had something to do with the hole's formation.

Squinting while she carefully scanned the sun-dappled area, she tried to detect even the slightest trace of smoke. But there was no evidence at all. Not even a charred edge. Nor ashes scattered on the ground.

Terrified to find nothing that might help, her throat constricted and her breath came in short, painful bursts. A hard, throbbing ache centered in the pit of her chest and grew larger and stronger with each beat of her heart. How would she ever find her way back to the present if she could not locate the hole? Every muscle in her body constricted and every breath became an effort. Then suddenly she glimpsed a flash of bright light from inside a tall clump of grass several yards away.

Her heart filled with hope when she hurried closer and spotted her car keys and her rumpled sweater lying in the tall grass. She remembered dropping them immediately after the accident, knowing they would only hinder her attempts to help.

Unwittingly, she had marked the opening. That is if it was still there.

Relief washed over her making her whole body feel warm and liquidy as she hurried closer and discovered the hole still existed. Although the opening was not visible to the eye, she had eventually located the hole by thrusting her hand forward until part of it disappeared from sight. Then by using touch, she established exactly where the perimeter was.

41

Eager to return to her own time and afraid something might yet prevent her from actually accomplishing that goal, she snatched up her sweater and keys then closed her eyes and prayed fervently as she lifted her foot and stepped back through the hole. Her skin tingled with renewed anticipation when she again noticed the abrupt change in temperature. It was much cooler on the twentieth century side and again there was the faint smell like burning hair — that is if she really had returned to her own time.

Still afraid the transference might not have occurred as hoped, JoAnn's breath caught and held at the base of her throat until she opened her eyes again. Relief washed over her when she noticed that everything was soaking wet, including *her car*. Slowly, she released the trapped breath as she clutched her sweater against her breast. The sky was dark again and a large broken limb floated in the middle of the pond, indicating a rainstorm had indeed passed through. It obviously had not been a dream. Yet the thought of having traveled back in time was still very hard to accept.

Emotionally overwhelmed by what had happened, JoAnn felt dizzy. Tucking her sweater beneath her arm, she bent forward, braced her hands on her knees, and took several deep breaths to fill her sudden need for oxygen and steady her frazzled nerves. Although the strange incident was now over and she was safely back in her own time, she remained shaken and out of breath. Physically, it felt as if she had just made a wild, desperate run for her life when in fact all she had done was step lightly through an invisible hole.

Still thoroughly confused by what had happened and still very much in awe of the fact that it *had* happened, JoAnn retained just enough forethought to

42

mark the spot. First, she again laid her keys and sweater in front of the hole then hurried to gather enough rocks to build a small, permanent mound. After making certain the rocks marked the appropriate spot by sticking her arms into the hole and watching them disappear, she picked up her things and hurried toward her car. She wanted to tell someone about the incredible incident that had just occurred.

Thinking of her trusted friend, Dr. Jean Gallagher, she slipped into the low seat of her new '92 Corvette and reached for her cellular phone. She bit into the tender flesh of her lower lip in an attempt to hold back her excitement while she hurriedly pressed the appropriate numbers. But before she had all the numbers punched in, she realized it was not the sort of thing she should *tell* her friend. It was more the sort of thing she should *show* her. No one, not even Jean, would willingly believe anything quite so bizarre without absolute proof. And why should they?

Not wanting to chance being doubted and not certain she knew the right words to convince her of the truth, JoAnn set the telephone back down and slipped the key into the ignition. But before actually starting the engine, she had already developed doubts of her own—doubts concerning her sanity.

Needing to prove to herself that she was indeed of sound mind and had not become so grief-stricken over the loss of her parents that she had started to hallucinate, she put the keys back into her skirt pocket. After quickly tossing her sweater behind the seat, she returned to the small pile of rocks.

Unaware she had approached from a different direction and not knowing that could make a difference, she was unable to find the hole at first. It was not until

43

she discovered the opening had a one-way entry that she was able to step through and prove her sanity.

The first thing she looked for after having felt her way back through what was obviously a stationary opening was her car. Again, she found that it and the small man-made pond beside it had disappeared. Again, it felt much warmer on this side and again there were twice as many trees, though smaller. When she spun around to have a better look at her surroundings, she spotted the carriage wreckage still scattered beside the narrow, bark-covered road. The fresh lumber and the large sacks of grain Adam and Glenn had unloaded just minutes earlier were still stacked nearby.

Amazed by the sheer incredibility of what had occurred, she tried to decide just who, besides Jean, she should entrust with this exceptional knowledge. She knew it had to be someone responsible enough not to misuse or in any way abuse the unique opportunity this time phenomenon presented. She also realized that whomever she did finally tell might think her daffy if not downright deranged should she not be able to find the opening again to prove what she had seen. It was possible this strange hole was not the stationary entity it seemed to be. If that proved true, it could easily drift away before she returned.

And even if it did not drift away—even if it proved to be held in place by earth's gravity—there was always the possibility that whoever she confided in might want to take advantage of the opportunity and experiment with time by purposely altering some event from the past just to see if it caused changes in the present.

"But what if those changes to the past produced *adverse* affects in the present?" she wondered aloud, trying to work everything out in her mind. "What if those changes ended up altering peoples' lives in ways they should not be altered?"

No, whoever she told, *if* she told anyone, that person would have to be someone she trusted implicitly. Someone who would promise not to share her secret with the general public and also promise not to meddle with history in any way—just observe. It seemed far too likely that if anyone attempted to alter what had once been the natural order of things, even in the slightest way, those modifications could set in motion an endless series of reactions that would echo through time forever. A progression of reactions that could never be turned back, with outcomes no one could possibly foresee; adverse effects that could cause disastrous results in her own time.

Chewing her lip while she thought more about what could happen should the information fall into the wrong hands, JoAnn realized that before she dared tell anyone, even her trusted friend Jean, she should consider the consequences more fully. She should act responsibly and take the time necessary to research this intriguing phenomenon of time displacement. She should find out exactly what effects tampering could have on both the people in the past as well as those in the present.

JoAnn felt it was possible if not downright probable that even the simplest modifications made to even one person's life while exploring in the year 1889 could result in permanent, unwanted changes in the 1990s. It was her responsibility to study the probabilities of cause and effect before she or anyone she might tell decided to take advantage of this unique opportunity.

A tight knot formed in her chest with that last thought.

What would be the far-reaching consequences of having saved Park Johnson? He was a *doctor* for goodness sake. By having added months if not years to a doctor's life, she had undoubtedly generated hundreds if not thousands of changes to future lives. And with each little change having the capability of provoking another change and yet another, the series of repercussions could be infinite. Dr. Johnson would now be around to help save lives that might otherwise have been lost.

Her eyes widened while her stomach slowly tightened into a hard, sickening coil. He could now save people who might otherwise have been destined to die. The resulting widows and widowers would then never meet much less marry the people they may have otherwise been destined to marry. Which meant they would no longer bear the resulting children who would not bear *their* resulting children. If that was true, hundreds of people in her time would never exist.

She gasped with further horror. What if the *reverse* were true? What if Dr. Johnson somehow bungled his treatment of a future patient and allowed a man to die that another doctor might have saved? Again all his future descendants would never exist.

Next, branching into an entirely different line of thought, what if the results of her visit into the past had already been calculated into the future? What if her visit into 1889 was something already accounted for because it had already happened? Was it possible she had been *destined* to make this link between present and past?

JoAnn had become so lost to the perplexing notions

that before she found the presence of mind to step back through the hole and into the present, she heard a soft, rustling noise and turned to find out what had made it. The white horse that had been involved in the accident had returned. He had lost the last remnants of the carriage in the short time she had been gone and his back leg was now coated with bright red blood.

Because the rocks she had stacked earlier were still piled on her side of time and of no use to her here, she took a minute to mark this side of the opening by quickly gathering more stones. Rather than return to her car for her medical bag, afraid the animal might run away again in the time she was gone, she quietly removed her half-slip to use as a tourniquet and eased closer to the animal. While talking to the horse in low, soothing tones, she bound the gaping wound tightly enough to stop the bleeding temporarily.

Remembering that Park had said something about Adam's house being nearby, she decided it should not take very much time to return the injured horse to its owner. Quickly, she checked to reassure herself that the hole had not moved in the time since the accident then led the horse by his tether strap in the direction the others had gone. She felt that as long as she stayed close to the road and hurried, she should be able to find her way back before dark.

As it turned out, that next house down the road was nearly a mile away. JoAnn was glad she had chosen to wear a pair of comfortable pumps that day. She would have hated to make that long trek along a bark-covered, rutted road in a pair of high heels.

When finally she came to the small driveway that turned toward the next house, she was surprised by the grandeur. The house reminded her of those imposing homes where the wealthy landowners always lived in most of those old western movies. Only instead of being set on an open plain or along one side of a teeming river, this particular house was set in the middle of a steep, sloping field with tall, massive trees circling at a distance. It was a large, three-story white-stuccoed brick home with oversized black shutters standing guard beside lofty windows and tall, black columns stationed across a wide, L-shaped veranda that shaded the entire front and part of one side.

The house was centered in an immaculately kept yard with several flower gardens and dozens of ornate trees planted all around. Several other white buildings with black trim lay scattered across a large area behind the house. Beyond the outbuildings were three large sloping pastures dappled with tiny wildflowers and enormous green trees. The closest meadow had about a dozen horses grazing lazily about while another pastured twenty or so cows. The third meadow had no animals in it at all but was knee deep with dark green grass.

Off to the right, near the other side of the house, she noticed a large area of freshly tilled land surrounded by a charming split-wood fence, probably destined to be a vegetable garden. Another fence, made from rungs of black ornate iron and anchored in fat columns of white brick, circled the front yard. The place reminded her of one of those elegantly restored Victorian homes in the historical districts of both Johnstown and Pittsburgh, only this one had the added benefit of a lot of land. Obviously, Adam Johnson was a man of considerable wealth for his time.

Still studying her surroundings, JoAnn led the horse down a long, narrow drive paved with small gray and white stones. When she came to the end of the drive, she tied the injured animal to a small post, then quietly opened a tall pedestrian gate that let her into the front yard. She walked up to the huge double front doors, knocked, then stepped to one side and waited patiently for someone to answer.

A few seconds later, one of the doors swung open and a short, stocky woman with bright red hair, wearing a full-length dark blue dress beneath a crisp white apron peered out expectantly. Her green eyes widened when she caught her first glimpse of JoAnn. Quickly, her gaze dipped to take in her scanty attire then shot back up to better examine her face.

"May I help you?" she asked in an accent that was definitely German.

Aware now why her manner of dress seemed so odd to these people, JoAnn wished she had returned to her parents' house and changed into something a little more appropriate for the time period, but realized all she had was one floor-length summer dress and knew it was too late to worry about that now anyway. Smiling, she gestured toward the injured horse with a backward sweep of her hand.

"Yes. My name is JoAnn Griffin and I have brought Doctor Johnson's horse. The animal returned to the wreckage about half an hour after everyone else had left. I'm afraid he's pretty badly injured."

"You the one who helped to save Doctor Johnson's life?" the woman questioned, her German accent obvious. Frowning deeply, she stepped out onto the front veranda to have a better look at both JoAnn and the horse. "You the voman who claims to be a doctor?"

49

"Yes, I guess that's me," JoAnn answered. She did not want to come across sounding vain though she knew she had saved the man's life and was indeed a doctor. "And now I am the woman who has brought back his horse."

Eyeing JoAnn's skimpy clothing with continued caution, Doris took several steps backward until she was again inside the house, though still facing her. It was obvious by her wary expression, she did not believe JoAnn was a doctor—nor a person she wanted inside the house. "You vait here. I'll go tell Mister Adam that you have brought his father's horse."

While JoAnn waited patiently out on the veranda, she glanced about at the immaculate gardens and the different outbuildings and wondered just what this Adam Johnson did for a living. Surely his wealth had to come from more than raising what little livestock he had. But she realized there could be other livestock in other pastures she could not see. For all she knew, he could own half this mountain if not all.

Seconds later, while she still contemplated the source and depth of Adam's wealth, he appeared in the doorway. It was obvious by the furrowed brow, he had not expected to see her again.

"Doris just told me that you brought Traveler back," he commented, then pulled his gaze away from hers to search for the horse.

JoAnn made a quick mental note that the Doris he spoke of earlier was not his wife after all. Doris was instead the red-haired housekeeper. She also made a mental note that he had been quick to shed his coat, vest, and tie; and had also unbuttoned the top three buttons of his shirt. That made him a man who enjoyed his comfort. It also made him a man who looked exceptionally appealing and at complete ease with the world.

Swallowing hard, she tried not to stare at the small expanse of dark body hair peeping through the opening when she responded. "That's right, I have. But I'm afraid the animal is seriously injured. Something sharp must have sliced into the back of his leg when your father's carriage smacked the tree. I did what I could to stop the bleeding but he still needs a lot more care. The wound needs to be cleansed and bandaged. If it isn't, it will undoubtedly become infected and instead of healing like it should, you will end up right back at square one. Or worse."

When Adam stepped outside to have a closer look at the horse, he noticed the makeshift bandage and the thick layers of dried blood. He nodded and smiled as if he finally comprehended. "So, you are an *animal* doctor. When you first told me you were a doctor, I thought you meant a *people* doctor. I didn't realize you meant you were a veterinarian."

JoAnn bristled at such a close-minded remark. He was obviously far more prepared to think of her as a veterinarian than a licensed medical doctor. But although such antiquated, chauvinistic notions were every bit as annoying to her as they had been earlier, they were a little more understandable now that she realized he really *was* from the past, not just someone trying to hold on to it.

Again she experienced a moment of awe over the realization that she was truly in the year 1889 and she tried her best to keep a civil tone. "Oh, but I *am* a 'people' doctor. It just so happens I work for a large hospital in Pittsburgh."

She decided not to bother naming the hospital since

51

she did not think McCain General existed back then. Or is that back *now*? she thought with a perplexed scowl.

It was hard to decide whether to think of the events occurring around her as being a part of the past or a part of the present. In a way, they were both.

"If you work in Pittsburgh, then what on earth are you doing way out here?" Adam asked, already headed for the horse. "Why we are nearly a full day's train ride from there." Leaning forward after he rounded the fence, he unwrapped the tether strap from the post and indicated JoAnn should follow them to the stable. Meanwhile, he wondered if her being from a city the size of Pittsburgh was the reason she talked so strangely. Did all folks from the city say things like *smacked into a tree* and *to square one?*

"I'm on sort of a vacation," is all she was willing to admit, trying to be as honest with her answers as possible. She did not want to lie to these people, but at the same time she did not want them to think her completely insane.

Fortunately, Adam did not ask any more questions until they reached the stable, then his questions pertained to the horse's injuries.

"How bad is the cut?" he asked and quickly dropped to one knee to remove the makeshift bandage. Holding the satiny material of the bloodstained slip in his hands, he looked at the lacy garment questioningly. The material was so thin, he could practically see through it. Despite himself, he wondered what sort of woman chose to wear such flimsy underthings.

JoAnn misread his wide-eyed expression. "I realize it is not all that absorbent, but it was all I had at the moment," she explained, also kneeling as she took the bloodstained garment from him and quickly cast it aside knowing she would never wear it again. When she then noticed the fresh bandage on Adam's hand, she wondered what he had done to himself in so short a time, then she felt a sharp twinge of guilt when she realized the source of his injury. Obviously she had caused a lot more damage when she bit him than she had intended. It was then she remembered having tasted blood.

"Sorry about your hand," she said, aware an apology was in order. "I didn't mean to hurt you. It's just that you were getting in the way and I was running out of time."

"I know that now," he admitted and offered another of his heart-stopping smiles, which stretched full width across his ample mouth. "But at that particular moment I truly thought you were half deranged."

She could well imagine why. They had no way of knowing the benefits of CPR back in the year 1889. But rather than get into a discussion about a procedure she would rather not divulge, she quickly returned his attention to the horse's leg. "As you can see, the cut is pretty deep. It will take a couple of months for that to mend. Until it does, you'll want to keep the cut clean and bandaged. A cut that deep can easily become infected."

"I'll get the carbolic acid. It should be back there in the same cabinet with the liniment and bandages," Adam said, then quickly stood. When he returned from the back of the stable, he held a folded cloth soaked with the clear liquid in one hand and a clean roll of cloth in the other. "Here. You do it. I get a little squeamish when it comes to open wounds like that. I guess that's why I never followed in my father's footsteps. I don't like the sight of blood."

Smiling, JoAnn accepted the cloth and carefully scrubbed the damaged area while Adam held the horse's leg stationary. When she then took the bandage from him and slowly wrapped the narrow strip of cloth around the leg, her hand accidentally brushed against his, causing a sudden fiery jolt to shoot through her arm. The physical response surprised her and she suddenly became more aware of the fact he was a very handsome man.

Though she tried to repress the strong inner reactions, her body continued to respond abnormally to whatever brief touches they shared, causing her to feel both exhilarated and discomfited — and greatly relieved when a slender boy dressed in baggy cotton pants and bright red suspenders suddenly appeared from the back of the stable and came to stand beside them.

The inquisitive lad, who was fairly tall but looked to be no older than eleven, was introduced to her only as George and offered a much wanted distraction. His questions were endless.

"How bad hurt is he?" the boy wanted to know, his brow dipped low with concern.

"Bad enough he shouldn't be pulling a carriage for a couple of months," Adam answered.

"At least." JoAnn put in, aware now that she had cleansed the wound that the cut had gone to the bone.

"How long that bandage got to stay on that leg?" George then asked, bending at the waist and watching JoAnn's movements with a careful eye while she continued to wrap the leg, studying how she did it.

"This particular bandage should be left in place only a couple of days," JoAnn answered. "At that time, someone should replace it with a fresh one."

"Why?" He squatted so he could watch her better and pushed his shaggy blond hair back out of his face with the back of his hand. "Seems to me that's a perfectly good bandage there. You've done a fine job of puttin' it on, too."

"Thanks, but changing it regularly will help keep infection out of the wound."

"What's infection?" He glanced around as if expecting to see something in the air he hadn't seen before.

Knowing how bothersome George's quizzing could be, Adam quickly rested a hand on one of the boy's shoulders. "Quit asking so many questions."

"Why?" he wanted to know, looking at Adam earnestly.

Rather than answer that, knowing it would only lead to yet another question, then another, he simply shook his head and tousled the boy's hair with his hand. He then returned his attention to JoAnn just as she brought the last part of the bandage around and pressed it into place.

"I need the clips," she said and glanced at his hand for the metal pieces needed to anchor the bandage in place.

"Clips?" he asked, again looking puzzled.

"You know, those metal stays that help hold the bandage in place."

He shook his head, indicating he had no idea what she meant.

"What about a roll of surgical tape then?"

Again he shook his head. "Never heard of it. I guess I don't keep up with the times around here."

JoAnn nodded, knowing it would be impossible for him to keep up with *her* time when that time was still a good hundred years into the future. "Then how do I keep this bandage from coming loose? Tie it?" Then, aware that was the only way, she loosened the last loop of the cloth and tucked the end under so she could indeed tie it in place. "There. How's that?"

"Looks like a pretty good job to me." George tilted his head to one side as if that might help him judge. "You a veterinarian?"

JoAnn looked at the boy then at Adam and answered, clearly rankled. "No, I am a *people* doctor."

"You?" He asked in a high-pitched voice then stood erect again and looked at Adam for verification. "Is she really a people doctor?"

"That's what she says." Adam said, also standing. He looked at her oddly. "And it could be true. She is the one who saved Father's life."

"*Her*?" George again looked at JoAnn as if he could not believe she was a doctor. "A *people* doctor?"

"Like father, like son," JoAnn muttered as she, too, stood and brushed the dirt and spotted remnants of hay and horse hair from her skirt with the backs of her hands. When Adam then looked as if he had not fully understood that last comment, she explained. "Your son here seems to have the same narrow-minded views about women that you do."

"Oh, but George is not my son. He's Doris's son. He and his older brother, Cyrus, work for me. They help out by taking care of the livestock," he explained, then smiled down at the boy. "Though I wouldn't mind having a son like him someday."

George grinned at the compliment and straightened his shoulders proudly. "Then you'd better quit all your dallyin' and get yourself married to that Miss Constance. Before too long you'll be too old to even think

56

about havin' yourself any children, and that Miss Constance ain't about to wait around forever."

Adam raised an eyebrow questioningly. "And what do you know about Miss Constance?"

"Just that you see more of her than you do any of your other women friends," he said with a slight shrug of his slender shoulders as if it were a common fact. "Mama says that woman has got her bonnet set for you, whatever that means. She's also seen you two kiss. Told Aunt Christina all about it."

Feeling a little uncomfortable to know his housekeeper discussed his personal life that openly, Adam quickly dismissed the subject by returning their attention to JoAnn. "Since you seem to be through here, we may as well head on back to the house so you can wash the blood off your hands. George, here, will stay behind and see that the harness is removed and the horse properly bedded."

"I would like a chance to wash," she agreed, wondering why Adam seemed so reluctant to discuss this Miss Constance of his, or was it simply the idea of marriage that had made him so eager to change the subject. Her eyebrows perked into a questioning frown while she followed him through the stable door, across the yard, and up the painted black stairs that led to a large back porch that obviously doubled as the laundry area. For some reason JoAnn did not like the idea of Adam marrying someone named "Miss Constance."

"You can wash in there," Adam said after he opened a small door to the left and indicated a dimly lit bathroom that held a tall, footed bathtub, a small porcelain sink, a tiny wooden vanity with an oval mirror, and a funny-looking metal contraption near the ceiling that she guessed to be a hot water heater of some sort.

"Thank you," she said, then hurried inside to do just that. She was too accustomed to having clean hands to let them stay sticky a moment longer.

"Speaking of thank yous, I don't think I remembered to thank you for returning the horse and seeing to it his leg was properly treated." Adam leaned heavily against the door frame while he watched her take the large cake of soap and vigorously scrub the blood from her hands and wrists. "How much do I owe you?"

"Owe me?" She looked at him, puzzled. "Why nothing. I did it as a favor."

"But I feel I should do something to repay you. If not for saving my father's life, then at least for taking such good care of his horse. That horse means a lot to him and you worked hard to save the leg — and it was definitely something I didn't want to do." His pale blue eyes cringed at the thought.

"Okay," she relented, thinking quickly while she patted her hands dry with a nearby towel. "If you want to repay me for having returned and bandaged the horse, then let me have one more look at your father before I leave. I think I'd rest a lot easier tonight if I knew he was okay." She still thought they should have taken him on to a hospital where he could be watched more closely, but remembered that idea had not set well with them.

Adam shrugged, thinking that was the least he could do. He stepped back and gestured toward a door that entered into the main part of the house. "He's in one of the guest bedrooms upstairs. I'll show you. But you may as well know, I've already sent Cyrus into

58

Johnstown for Doctor Lowman. They should be back about dark."

"And who is Doctor Lowman?" She headed in the direction he had indicated, glad they planned to have a local doctor look at him. She'd feel better about leaving if he was in another doctor's care.

Adam caught up and walked along beside her while he explained about Doctor Lowman. "Doc Lowman is a neighbor and a very close friend of Father's. They work in the same hospital, but their private clinics are in separate buildings. Father has a small office just down the street from the new hospital while Doctor Lowman's office is still in his home over near the park. Of course they both make calls as far east as South Fork and as far west as Sang Hollow. Sometimes Father has been known to go as far as New Florence or Lilly to see a patient."

"Then your father doesn't live here with you?" She glanced around at the spacious house.

"No, his home is in Johnstown, over on Main Street, very near the city park."

"You live here alone?" she asked, thinking the house a little extravagant for one person.

"Well, Doris and her two sons live in the five rooms provided for them at the back of the house; but yes, other than those three, I am usually here alone."

She studied her elegant surroundings with further interest. The house was a veritable showplace, everything perfectly placed, as if an interior decorator or a set designer had just finished with it. Even so, the house still held a certain warmth, a certain feeling of home.

"You mean this beautiful house is all yours?" She looked into his blue eyes curiously. "What do you do for a living? Rob banks?"

Adam chuckled. "No, but I am on the board of one. Fact is I'm a vice president of the Morrell State Bank."

"Then you are a banker?" She nodded, thinking that explained it. Everyone knew bankers made good money.

"Not exactly. I'm a chemist and a geologist for the Cambria Iron Works. But I have a second cousin, also named Adam Johnson, who lured me into banking several years ago. He's now the president of the same bank where I'm vice president, which makes for a lot of confusion."

"But how do you have time for your jobs with both the iron works and a bank and still manage to take care of this house and all the livestock you have here?"

Again he shrugged, causing the gap in his shirt to widen that revealed more of the lightly haired, muscular chest she had been trying valiantly to ignore. "I also teach part-time at the Morrell Institute."

JoAnn fell silent while she absorbed that new information. No wonder Adam was not married. He had no time for a wife. With all he did, she wondered how he ever found the time to be with *Miss Constance*.

"How long have you been teaching?"

"Since 1883, about a year before Daniel Morrell died. They wanted someone to teach geology and chemistry and because that is something I happen to know a lot about, I was chosen. In the past I have taught as many as three nights a week, but right now, I teach only one night a week."

JoAnn nodded, remembering Daniel J. Morrell from her history classes in high school as well as from area lore. Daniel Morrell was a local legend, so much so his name was still linked to several businesses in the

60

Johnstown area. He had been the innovative ironmaster that helped bring the valley's lifeblood, Cambria Iron Works, out of a temporary slump back in the mid-1800s and, while doing so, made the company into one of the largest, most progressive Bessemer steel plants in the United States.

"When do you find time to sleep?"

Adam laughed. "Don't let this place fool you. Because I now grow mostly timber and hay, and have cut back considerably on the amount of cattle and horses I produce, this place practically takes care of itself. In the summer, I do have to take on a few extra part-time workers and I have to spend more time up here; but during the winter, Doris's two sons are all I need to help take care of this place."

When they reached the top of the wide, mahogany staircase, JoAnn hesitated. The hallway branched off in three different directions. Rather than chance heading the wrong way, she waited until Adam had stepped ahead of her and indicated they should turn left.

Aware the house was far larger than she had first thought, she purposely held back a step so she could more easily follow. Eventually, they arrived at a bedroom she suspected stood near the front of the house. Inside she saw Park resting against a large pile of bed pillows, a dark scowl on his face. But that scowl lifted instantly when he noticed he had company.

"How do you feel?" she asked, headed directly for the bedside, careful to step around the black labrador retriever lying on the floor near the bed. Obviously the dog rarely left his master's side.

"A little weak I guess," he admitted, then tossed back the covers as if he intended to stand. "And like someone hit me in the chest with a hundred-pound

61

weight."

When he swung his legs over and attempted to sit up, Adam rushed forward and placed a restraining hand on his father's shoulder. "You are not getting out of that bed. Not until Doctor Lowman tells me it is okay for you to do so."

Again Park scowled. "You're worse than your mother, God rest her soul."

"And he's right," JoAnn injected sternly. "That was a pretty serious accident. You have a head injury to consider. You should listen to your son. You should also get out of those clothes and into something more comfortable because I suspect you will be in that bed for quite some time."

Tenderly Park lifted his hand to touch the area hidden beneath his thick gray hair and frowned when he realized the swelling had yet to go down. "Oh that? That's just a little bump." He glanced at her with a raised brow as if daring her to dispute his judgment. "Nothing to worry about."

"That may be true, but you still need to stay in that bed." She then glanced at Adam. "Do you have any strong rope? It appears we may have to tie this man down."

"I'm sure we do," Adam said, already taking a step toward the door.

"Oh, stay put. You know that won't be necessary," Park muttered, then glowered while he sank against his pillows. But when he pulled his gaze off Adam and looked at JoAnn again, a sparkle of amusement entered his blue eyes. "I'll behave myself."

Adam's eyebrows arched at how readily his usually strong-willed father had surrendered to this woman's demands.

When JoAnn then reached forward to feel for Park's pulse, as much out of habit as anything, Park grabbed her arm and looked at her wristwatch with immediate fascination. "Where'd you ever find a timepiece you can wear on your arm like that?"

"In Pittsburgh," she answered honestly, wondering just when wristwatches became fashionable. "They seem to be all the rage. Even men wear them."

"Men? Wearing bracelets?" He frowned. Clearly he did not want to believe such a thing. "Is that where you're from, Doctor Griffin? Pittsburgh?"

"Yes," she answered, aware he was the only one who had yet to use her title when addressing her. "I have a small apartment near the hospital where I work. And please, call me JoAnn. All my friends do," she told him while she held her fingers against his wrist long enough to check his pulse rate, glad to find it as strong as it was. When she lowered his arm back to the bed, she turned her attention to the improved color of his skin.

"An apartment? Isn't that kind of a small place to be raising your children?"

"I don't have any children. I've never been married."

He seemed pleased to have that bit of information. "Must not have a steady beau then either."

"Why do you say that?" She turned her brown eyes to meet his inquisitive blue.

"Why else would you be out wandering around in the woods all alone like you were? What were you doing out there anyway?"

"Just having a look around," she answered vaguely, not about to try to explain the truth to either of them, especially when she did not quite believe it herself. She was relieved when Adam stepped forward to add

63

information of his own.

"She's on a vacation."

"On vacation?" Park looked first at Adam then at JoAnn. "Visiting friends in the area?"

"No. I don't know anyone in this area." *At least not in this century.* "I recently suffered a death in my family, two deaths actually, and I just needed to get away and have a little time to myself."

Because she was a stranger to him and because she was dressed so oddly, Park willingly accepted her as being someone from the city just passing through. "Where are you staying?"

"Nowhere in particular," she answered evasively. She wished he would stop asking so many personal questions. It made her feel awkward to give so many answers with double meanings.

"But where are your belongings?" he wanted to know, wincing his right eye as if the bump on his head had suddenly caused him a burst of pain.

Rather than shock Park with the truth, aware it was not likely he would believe her anyway, she quickly invented a story of having rented a carriage to take her from Johnstown to East Conemaugh, where she had hoped to stay for a few days before catching a train back west. She claimed that soon after she had left the livery a man jumped into the rented carriage and forced her at knifepoint to drive into the country where she was promptly robbed of both her belongings and the carriage.

Adam leaned one well-muscled hip against the intricately carved footboard while he listened to the story. He did not accept her words as readily as his father obviously did. But because he saw nothing to be gained by trying to prove her a liar, he kept his opinions to himself and allowed her to continue her strange tale.

Obviously feeling sorry for her pitiful circumstances, Park reached out and took her slender hand in his, making her feel guilty for having had to lie. "You've had a terrible experience, my dear. Just terrible. Imagine having everything stolen like that. That's why I think you should stay here with us for a few days. At least until you have a chance to wire back home for enough money to replace your lost clothes and buy a train ticket."

"I can't do that," she said, startled by the kind invitation.

"Why not? There is certainly enough room and, since I am being forced into complete bed rest and total boredom, I would enjoy having someone as pretty and bright as you to talk with. Besides, I'd like to hear more about this CPR procedure Adam told me about."

"But I can't impose like that," she continued, not about to accept such an invitation, no matter how tempting. She had to get back to her own time.

"Why not?" Park wanted to know. "After all, you saved my life. We owe you something." He folded his arms across his chest, coughed once as a result of the pressure against his sore ribs, then thrust his chin forward to show his determination. Without offering Adam as much as an inquiring glance, he added, "You've already admitted you don't have anywhere else to go. You are staying here with us for a few days and that, my dear, is that!"

Chapter Three

"But this is not your house," JoAnn reminded Park. With so little time to think, she was unable to come up with a more logical reason to decline his invitation to stay there. She had already admitted having nowhere else to go.

"If you're worried about Adam. Don't be. He doesn't mind." Park turned his gaze on his son. "Do you, Adam?" He lifted his eyebrows as if truly expecting an answer, but did not give Adam time to speak. "Besides, he often invites his friends to dine at my house without mentioning it to me until they are at my very door. It's an understanding we have: what's his is mine and what's mine is also mine." He grinned. "But I'm usually willing to share. Besides, there's plenty of room here." He moved his arm in a wide sweeping gesture. "Why there are three empty bedrooms on this floor alone."

Although JoAnn knew it would be far more prudent to return immediately to the twentieth century, the idea of staying a night in the year 1889 was just too tempting to resist. Intrigued by such a bizarre phenomenon and aware she was still in her first week of the eight-week sabbatical the hospital had granted her, she considered taking advantage of the exceptional opportunity.

Her friends expected her to remain sequestered away at her parents' house until she had come to terms with her grief and put their personal affairs in order. If she were gone just the one night, she would probably not even be missed. No one would ever need know her secret. And knowing she could return to her own time that following morning as easily as that afternoon, the temptation to stay and see what it was like finally overcame her.

Experiencing a night in not only another place but a whole other century could be just the diversion she needed to lure herself out of the dark mood that had shrouded her since her parents' deaths.

What was it her closest friend, Jean, had said? You need to find *something* to help get your mind off that horrible night. And because Jean was one of McCain Hospital's highest acclaimed and highest paid psychiatrists who specialized in drug dependency and stress management, she should know how best to deal with grief and its resulting bouts of depression. It was Jean who had eventually convinced her to ask for the eight weeks off.

"Well, if you are absolutely sure your son won't mind," JoAnn commented. She glanced at Adam to see his reaction and felt a little annoyed to see no apparent response at all. He merely stood off to one side, leaning casually against the rounded post of the footboard, as if he cared little how the conversation ended.

"Of course he doesn't mind," Park quickly assured her, then reached out to take her hand again. "If I know Adam, he's probably looking forward to having someone else around during my next few days of forced convalescence if for no other reason than to help keep me company. While you are busy telling me all about this new CPR procedure and what life is like in Pittsburgh these days, he can be off tending to his stock or working on some of his paperwork." He tilted his head slightly forward and spoke in a soft voice, as if telling JoAnn some well-kept family secret. "This poor fellow is always behind on his paperwork. A terrible procrastinator when it comes to picking up his pencil or studying someone else's reports."

"That's true enough," Adam muttered. Having heard his father's whispers, he scowled. Paperwork was indeed the least liked part of both his teaching and banking jobs. At least at Cambria Iron all he usually expected to do was make a weekly oral report to the ironmaster. He was thankful that John Fulton did not like having his desk cluttered with a lot of unnecessary paper. If John felt an incident or an idea was important enough to be written down, he'd call his secretary in to take a few notes, something Adam truly appreciated.

"Well, then, if you're sure I won't be in the way, I guess I could stay for one night," she agreed, although she had no intention of filling Park's ear with too many medical facts while there and had no idea what Pittsburgh might be like in the year 1889.

She smiled when Park let go of her hand to place his arms triumphantly across his chest and felt as excited over the prospect of discovering what life had been like back in the late eighteen hundreds as she felt hesitant. Although eager for the adventure, she worried that something might happen between now and the following morning that might prevent her from returning home.

"*One* night?" Park shook his head firmly, causing his

hair to tousle on the pillows behind him. "I won't hear of it. You will stay right here until the arrangements have been made for enough money to be sent to purchase your train ticket back home."

Adam studied Park's pleased expression for a moment and wondered why his father did not simply advance her the money she needed right now. Knowing it would be the easiest solution, he narrowed his gaze and studied his father's cheerful countenance a moment longer.

For some selfish, illogical reason, his father wanted JoAnn there for the next several days and Adam could easily guess why. His father was an incurable matchmaker determined to have grandchildren one day. He was also not terribly fond of his son's present choice in companion, Miss Constance Seguin. But in all honesty, neither was Adam.

Although he usually enjoyed her company, Constance did have a way of getting on one's nerves on occasion. She was extremely beautiful and poised, like someone from a famous portrait — *when her mouth was closed*. When not, she had the most annoying tendency to prattle forever about the most inconsequential matters. And if ever angered, Constance had a tongue that could slice a person in half.

Her conversations usually focused on the most current fashions coming out of Europe, or the latest play to hit town, or what one of her friends had had the audacity to wear to the latest ball which many times bored Adam to tears. Still, being with Constance Seguin was preferable to being with someone who did not talk at all and a grand sight better than being with his former lady friend, Patricia White — especially after having discovered Patricia had never truly divorced her husband. At least he had no doubt that

69

Constance was indeed a widow.

After the fiasco with Patricia, he had visited Constance's husband's grave himself, just to be sure her story rang true. He wanted no more irate husbands coming out of the woodwork eager to off his fool head.

Although Adam was attracted to beauty like any man, he was practical enough to know Constance could never completely fulfill his needs. His hopes were one day to find a woman with far more admirable qualities than those possessed by Constance Seguin. He wanted a woman who was not just beautiful and willing to meet his needs. He wanted a woman who was also honest, reliable, and able to hold an intelligent conversation. But not since his wife's death had he found one who exhibited all those traits; and until he did, he would make do with Constance.

Certainly, he did not need to get involved with a woman like Miss Griffin; a woman who told such incredible tales while walking around in such peculiar clothing. Someone so far removed from reality she could not even remember the year.

But his father *had* made one valid point. If there was the slightest possibility she could keep his father entertained while she was there then she was welcome to stay a few days. Past experience reminded him what a poor patient his father could be.

"I'll go downstairs and tell Doris to have fresh bedclothes put on one of the beds," Adam said. Pushing himself away from the footboard, he headed toward the door with such slow, agile movements, his actions temporarily drew JoAnn's attention. He reminded her of a sleek cat of prey when he walked.

"Tell her to put JoAnn in that bedroom across the hall," Park called after him. "It's really the nicest guest room you have and it will put her closer to me."

70

And closer to *me*, Adam thought, wondering if his father realized how obvious that suggestion had been. The guest room across the hall was not only next to his own, but because his wife had planned for the room to be used for a nursery, it was also connected through a large inner door.

"I'll see what I can do," he muttered and glanced back at his father with one perfectly arched brow. His blue eyes glimmered with intent.

If Park noticed his son's silent warning, he did not show it. Instead, he patted the side of his bed and returned his attention to JoAnn. "While he's doing that, you come sit beside me and tell me all about this new CPR procedure they've come up with. Who developed it?"

Conscious now that any premature knowledge from the future could result in serious and unwarranted changes in the past — permanent changes she had no right to initiate — JoAnn did sit on the bed beside him, but was purposely evasive while she explained some of what she had done to save his life. She did not tell him how his heart had stopped completely nor that he had been clinically dead for several minutes before she started her attempts to revive him. Still, he found it fascinating that she had thought to put her own breath into his lungs.

"You know a few years back I read something in the *Universal Medical Journal* about a European doctor who used such a procedure successfully, but I've never really had a call to use it. Not too sure I believed in it. Always wondered how such a thing could work. How can receiving air that already has had all the oxygen taken out by one set of lungs help a man who has already stopped breathing start again on his own?" He wrinkled his brow. "Or is it simply a way to force the lungs to reflex and start working again on their own?"

Relieved to learn that artificial respiration had already been developed, therefore she would not be introducing something that did not yet exist, JoAnn explained readily. "Oh, but one person's lungs do not take all the oxygen out of the air. Lungs take only what that one person needed, plus that part of the breath still in the windpipe right after a breath has been taken is still fully oxygenated."

"Because it never reached the lungs," he commented, having realized the reason on his own while nodding appreciatively over what she had told him. "But how is it you know so much about it? It's not something that's been in any of the medical journals is it?"

JoAnn shrugged and admitted, "I learned about it in medical school. It may not be in the medical journals right now, but it was in my textbook." Then rather than get into a long discussion on modern medicine, knowing that a lot of what she could tell him was well beyond anyone's knowledge in 1889, she quickly changed the subject. "As was the information that a patient should try to get all the rest possible right after having had a heart attack."

"Is that what I had?" he asked, studying her closely. His expression was suddenly very solemn. "A heart attack?"

"Although you should wait and hear what your own doctor says, yes, I think you had a heart attack. And when you slumped over as a result of that heart attack, your dog must have started barking to wake you which startled your horse into a dead run, which is why you had such a serious carriage accident."

"So I owe this big sore spot on the back of my head to Shadow do I?" He glanced at the sleeping dog and lowered one eyebrow to form a good-natured frown. "See if I ever take him for another ride in the country." He then fell silent for a long moment before he glanced at JoAnn again, his thick white eyebrows drawn into a questioning expression. "Just where did you go to medical school?"

"New York," she said, thinking that would be the logical place for a woman of the 1880s to have gone for her medical education. She knew that most of the smaller universities during that time still did not allow women in their classrooms.

"Then that explains your clothes," he said, nodding again, as if suddenly understanding what to him had to seem very eccentric. "Very progressive place that New York. How long did you live there?"

"Just long enough to work my way through medical school," she said, still keeping her answers as evasive as she knew how.

If she wanted a chance to know these people better, she did not dare tell the truth. Why frighten them away by trying to convince them of something she had a hard time accepting herself—that she had come there from another century?

"How long have you been a doctor?" Park asked, curious to know more about her. "To tell you the truth, you don't look old enough to have finished your residency much less all those years of college."

"I'm thirty-four and have been a licensed doctor for a couple of years now." She was pleased by the way his eyebrows shot up with disbelief. She had long since passed the point of wanting to appear older, even to impress others in the medical community. Now that she was in her midthirties, it felt nice to be thought of as younger.

"And you work for a hospital in Pittsburgh?"

"Well, right now I have a temporary leave from the hospital. I recently lost both my parents and am having a very hard time adjusting to the loss." Amazingly, she had managed to say that without tears. Perhaps her jumbled emotions were finally settling. "Because of how poorly I was handling their deaths, it was suggested I take eight weeks off." *Strongly suggested,* not only by Jean but also by Dr. Ruby Steed, the hospital administrator. JoAnn was making too many mistakes in the emergency room, mistakes neither she nor the hospital could afford to have made.

Adam returned at that moment, one eyebrow still raised as if he doubted everything she said. "And so you decided to take those eight weeks and travel the state?"

JoAnn turned, not realizing he'd come back. Pressing her hand to the base of her throat in a reflexive gesture, she saw the skepticism in both his expression and his voice and wondered just how much of her story he did not believe. Did he at least believe the parts that were true or did he think every word was fabricated? "I decided everyone was right. I needed to get away. To think about the changes I now have to face — and to get my parents' affairs in order. Not only was I their only child and their main heir, but I was also appointed executrix to their estate, small as it is."

"Oh? Did they live around here?" Park wanted to know. His face lifted with renewed curiosity.

JoAnn thought about that. The answer could be given either way and still lean toward the truth. Yes, they had lived just over the next rise — in *her* time; but, no, as far as those in the year 1889 were concerned, her parents were not even born yet. The peculiarity of the situation became more obvious with each question Park asked.

"No," she finally answered, afraid Park and Adam would wonder why they had never heard of them if she answered yes. "They lived much farther away. Like I said earlier, I was really just passing through when the carriage I'd hired and my belongings were suddenly stolen. I still tremble when I think of that horrible man leaping onto the seat beside me with that knife pointed at me."

She tried her best to looked frightened by such a memory when what really frightened her at that moment was the fact that Adam obviously did not believe her. There was also the tiny nagging fear that when she returned to the hole tomorrow morning, it might not be where she had left it — though she could think of no logical reason for it to move. It had not moved during those first few hours, therefore it stood to reason that it would still be there when she returned. If it was going to remain fixed in space while the earth rotated away from it, then it would have immediately shown evidence of such.

"My but you've had a trying day," Parks said, shaking his head sympathetically while he studied her troubled expression. "I think we should send Cyrus back into town as soon as he's returned with Lowman and ask him to report the theft. Maybe they can catch the man and return your belongings."

Believing such a report could cause little harm since she would be gone by the time they realized she had made up the incident, and knowing to resist the idea would make Adam doubt her all the more, JoAnn quickly agreed. "Perhaps I *should* notify someone, but I don't think it has to be tonight. By the time Cyrus returns with your doctor, he will be too tired to make a return trip. Tomorrow will be soon enough. Besides, right now all I really want is a chance to freshen up."

She smiled inwardly when she noted what a true master she had become at changing the subject.

"Freshen up?" Adam asked. He blinked once then looked at her questioningly.

"Yes, you know. *Freshen up.* Perhaps I could take a damp cloth to my face and—" she paused, trying to find a discreet way to express the rest of what she needed to do. It had been seven hours since she had left her parents' house. "And, ah, use the *facilities.*"

"The facilities?" Still Adam did not understand what she wanted.

Annoyed that he had yet to catch on, she finally sighed and said it as plainly as she knew how, "I need to use the bathroom."

"Oh, you want to take a full bath," Adam said, nodding that he finally understood, though he still wondered why she had not just come right out and said what she wanted.

"Among *other* things." She tapped her foot impatiently and wondered what phrases these people used to express taking care of their private needs. Then remembering that Park was a doctor, she sighed again and without looking at either of them, added, "And if you don't mind, I *also* need a place to urinate."

"Then why didn't you say so?" Park said, grinning at how awkwardly she had handled the situation. It amazed him how intelligent and sophisticated she acted one minute and how timid and naive she acted the next. "What you want to know is where to find the privy."

JoAnn wrinkled her nose. *The privy?* Didn't that mean an outhouse? Why would they bother with the inconvenience of an outhouse when they already had indoor plumbing?

"Yes, of course, that's what I meant," she said,

reaching up and playing idly with a strand of the brown hair that had fallen over her shoulder. "Where *is* the privy?"

"It's downstairs. Just outside the same door we entered earlier," Adam quickly supplied, also grinning. He wondered why a woman who dressed in such bold clothing and who had actually cursed at him earlier had shown such difficulty in asking for use of the privy. "Come with me. I'll show you."

JoAnn followed in silence. Remembering the old two-holer that had stood outside her great-grand-mother's home when she was a small child, she wondered just how sane her decision to stay had been. Just the memory of how rancid the small wooden structure had smelled and how that hard, splintered seat had felt against her tender flesh made her shudder. She decided it would be wise not to take in much liquid while still in the year 1889.

"There you are," Adam said, effectively breaking her thoughts only moments after they had stepped out onto the back porch. He gestured toward a closed door that had been cut two inches shorter than the door opening.

Much to JoAnn's relief, the privy was not a tiny wooden structure out in the yard like she had feared. It had been built as an add-on to the house right behind the bathroom where she had washed the blood off her hands earlier.

She stepped closer and frowned when she opened the door and peered inside. The room was dark and looked to be about the size of a small coat closet. It had no window to allow extra ventilation and no place to wash her hands afterward.

"Thank you," she said with little enthusiasm, not bothering to look back at Adam while she quietly

77

stepped into the room.

By the time she had finished fumbling around in the dark with her clothing and had found the small porcelain and wood toilet, she was coated with a fine sheen of sweat, which made pulling up her torn panty hose when she was finished next to impossible, though she tried.

In a fit of frustration, she tugged them off and stuffed them into her pocket, then shoved her bared feet into her shoes. When she finally came out of the tiny room, her hair was damp and she was surprised at how cool the following rush of air felt. What she wouldn't give for a room full of air-conditioning about now.

"Are you ready for that bath?" Adam asked, having waited outside for her for what had seemed an extraordinarily long time for what was to be done. He glanced curiously at the bulge in the side of her skirt and wondered what it could possibly be. There wasn't anything inside worth stealing.

"Yes, please," she answered eagerly, although not too pleased at the thought of having to put the same clothing back on when she was through.

Adam gestured toward the bathroom, then stepped inside. Quickly, he dropped open a small window high in the wall at the back of the room and then one directly over the door before he left JoAnn. "I'll be in my study if you need me for any reason. When you're finished, find Doris. She will then show you to your room."

He studied her a few seconds more before he turned and promptly left.

JoAnn lingered in the tall, footed bathtub a little longer than was necessary. It felt so good to have a long, cool bath, especially after all she had been through that day. Still the bath could not last forever and, although she did not look forward to putting on dirty clothes, she knew she had little choice. Her other clothes were all back in the twentieth century.

When she stepped out of the water and patted herself dry, she wondered about that last thought: *back in the twentieth century.* Shouldn't she think of the twentieth century as a time forward instead of backward? Still that was the way she saw it. As something she had left behind that awaited her return.

While putting her clothing back on and bending to slip her still damp feet into her shoes, she realized she would not be able to stay more than the one day, even if she wanted to. By morning, her clothing would have taken on a definitely foul odor.

Even if she rinsed the blouse and her undergarments in soapy water and hung them out to dry, the skirt was dry clean only. She seriously doubted that these people had the proper cleaning solvent for such a garment.

With that thought still in mind, while she followed the short, stocky housekeeper upstairs, she explained she would be there only the one night. It felt somehow reassuring to know she had made up her mind. She would not stay longer than that. With no change of clothing, nor the proper night clothes, she would not be easily convinced to continue this charade come morning. Knowing the odor her clothing would have by then, it was highly unlikely she would go against reason a second time — no matter how tempted she was.

When the housekeeper neared the area of the house where JoAnn and Adam had left Park resting an hour earlier, JoAnn noticed his bedroom door was closed.

As if sensing her question, Doris gestured toward the door and explained. "Doctor Lowman is in there now."

JoAnn looked away to keep from grinning when she heard loud muttering through the closed door. Evidently the two doctors did not agree on their diagnoses. She was reminded of Drs. Edison and Weathers: two thoracic surgeons from McCain General who rarely agreed completely on their diagnoses or prognoses; yet they remained the best of friends and championed each other's causes.

"Supper will be in an hour," Doris said, pretending she had not noticed the bickering sounds from the closed room while she stepped back and allowed JoAnn to enter the guest room across the hall. Following her inside, Doris headed for a tall, ornate cabinet across the room, moving with unusual grace for a woman so large.

"When Mister Adam is here, he likes supper to be served promptly at seven," she informed without glancing back, obviously used to doing whatever was needed then getting on to something else.

"When he's here?" JoAnn wondered why on earth he would ever be anywhere else. If she had a beautiful home like this, far away from the tumult of the city, she would spend every spare moment there. "Why? Where else does he stay?"

"Mostly he visits at his father's house on Main Street in Johnstown proper," Doris supplied with a thick German accent. "Especially on those nights he teaches. Between his duties at the institute, those at the bank, and those at the iron mill, he does not have time much to spend out here. He comes out on the veekend from time to time, but spends most his veekdays in town. Normally, he leaves the everyday running of this place to myself and my sons." She

80

straightened and smiled proudly. "He trusts us to do vhatever needs to be done. The only reason he is here today is because his father had vanted to take a day off and sit idly in the country."

"But I don't understand," JoAnn said, glad Doris proved to be so talkative. "Why does Mister Adam work so hard and take on so many different jobs? It seems pretty obvious by this beautiful home and all the land that surrounds it that he is not exactly hurting for money." JoAnn then realized that she had been the same about her work. During the past two years, she had become what Jean termed a "chronic workaholic," allowing nothing to interfere with her career. Jean, who forever analyzed every situation, had claimed JoAnn's compulsive devotion to her career was because subconsciously she did not want the time nor the opportunity to develop any new male-female relationships, not after that disastrous affair with Thomas Rourke.

Which could be true.

After having found out that Tom was engaged to marry someone else—even though he had vowed his undying love to her—she was too devastated by the betrayal to ever want to fall in love again. He had exploited her by manipulating her deepest emotions. He had promised her the happy-ever-after she wanted and she had believed him. But what she had ended up with was the pain and humiliation found only in the grimmest of realities. Falling in love just was not worth the emotional risk.

But JoAnn had not realized the serious risk involved when she'd first met Tom while still attending the University of Chicago. All that registered in her mind was that he was tall, handsome, and extremely confident of both himself and his future. For JoAnn it had been love at first sight. They'd had so much in common: music, movies, similar career goals. But after a year and a half of what she believed was a strong, giving, love-filled relationship, she had discovered a letter from the "girl back home" and was horrified to learn he had courted them both during that time.

When confronted with the truth, Tom had willingly admitted he was engaged and that he had every intention of marrying the other girl whom it turned out was his wealthy though not quite as beautiful childhood sweetheart. He'd had no intention of ever marrying JoAnn, which was why he had so carefully avoided the subject during their courtship.

It was Jean's theory that because her relationship with Tom had ended in such an abrupt and painful manner, JoAnn now subconsciously refused to become *that* emotionally involved with anyone else. Which was true. As a means of self-preservation, she was determined never again to allow herself to be that vulnerable with anyone. The possibility of ever again suffering such a gut-wrenching devastation and humiliation was what helped her to keep her private emotions buried deep inside her. Love had proved to be too much a gamble, and the risk of opening one's heart was not worth the horrible pain that could follow.

But Jean was right. After the bitter breakup with Thomas, JoAnn immediately immersed herself in her studies and later in her work. And until a couple of weeks ago when fate stepped in and suddenly shook her priorities, she had become so aggressively dedicated to her chosen field, she had unwittingly allowed her medical career to become her whole life.

Was that also what Adam was trying to do? Hide in

his work? But from what could Adam possibly have to hide? His life appeared about as perfect as a person could hope during such an outmoded time period. True he was not as mega-wealthy as some of the mining, railroad, and steel tycoons of his time, but he had everything a man of his era could want.

With her attention again drawn to the unique trappings around her, she watched Doris pull open the tall cabinet and reach inside. She came out with a white towel and face cloth which she set beside a tall pitcher and basin on a nearby vanity.

The bedroom was like something out of an old John Wayne movie, made of dark woods, whites, and bright yellows. The bed was a cumbersome-looking thing, waist high with a thick yellow and white bed cover that draped with elegant folds to the floor. Delicate veils of white netting trimmed with tiny yellow ribbon were gathered at the corners of the canopy and tied to the ornate bedposts with shimmering yellow sashes.

The main furniture, which included both a bedroom suite and a small sitting arrangement, looked to be hand carved and glistened from years of careful care. It gave the room an air of quiet dignity. The plasterwork ceiling stood a good twelve feet from the gleaming wood floor and dangled a tall crystal candelabra from a sturdy gilt chain. The three doors in the room looked to be at least seven feet tall and were painted stark white like the walls, with ventilation windows above two of them.

Doris pulled open a small drawer inside the narrow wooden vanity and took out a large white chunk of soap much like JoAnn had used when taking her bath. Using both hands, she broke it in two then set the larger half on the small porcelain tray beside the pitcher and returned the remaining portion to the drawer. She then glanced around the room to see if she had missed anything important before she finally answered JoAnn's question.

"Yes, Mister Adam has been like that—vork, vork, vork—ever since the death of his beloved vife, Dorothy. Nothing or no'vone slows down that man."

"Wife?" JoAnn asked, surprised. "Mister Adam was married?" After having discovered Doris was the housekeeper and not his wife and then hearing his stable boy tell him it was time he settled down and take a mate before he was too old to have children, she had promptly dismissed any thought of his *ever* having been married. Perhaps that was because she wanted him never to have been married, although she had no idea why it should matter to her one way or the other. He was from the past.

"Back vhen Mister Adam vas but a young man of twenty-five, barely a year after his dear mother departed this vorld, he married a beautiful lass with hair golden and the greenest eyes a person would ever hope to see. Her name vas Dorothy Ellen Freeburg. She vas an authoress and a poet. Vhat lovely vords that voman could vrite." Doris then fell sadly silent, as if mourning the young woman's memory.

"But she died?" JoAnn prompted her to continue. She wanted to learn more about this part of Adam's life, surprised that perhaps he did have something in his past worth hiding from. Perhaps the loss of his wife was why he, too, had immersed himself in his work. Suddenly, JoAnn felt as if they had a common bond. They had both loved and lost; but at least he had lost to death, not to another person with more to offer than mere love.

"Yes, she did," Doris answered solemnly. "Died of something called the cholera back in Eighteen eighty-one—despite Doctor Johnson's efforts to save her. Such a sad day that vas." She shook her head then turned her glimmering green eyes to meet with JoAnn's questioning brown. Her rounded cheeks quivered when she continued. "She vas seven months along vith vhat vould have been the young couple's first child. T'vas all looking forvard to the little babe, ve vas. T'vas a traumatic experience for Mister Adam. It took him years to overcome the pain though he still has his dark moods come September."

JoAnn guessed that was when the deaths must have occurred, sometime in September. Feeling sudden remorse from having learned this new bit of information about Adam, she asked, "And what about Doctor Johnson? He obviously lost his wife, his daughter-in-law, and his future grandchild all within about a year."

"True, he did. But he controlled his sadness much better than Mister Adam. He vas back to acting his old self vithin a couple of months. I guess that comes from being a doctor. Doctors are able to cope with death more easily than most folks."

Not really, JoAnn thought sadly and wondered how long it would take *her* finally to come to terms with her parents' deaths. Years like Adam? Or just months like Park? If only she could get beyond the gnawing feeling that their deaths were in some way her own fault. If only her mother had not died in her arms—while she was so powerless to save her.

Blinking rapidly to keep back the tears forming at the outer edges of her eyes, JoAnn quickly pushed such painful thoughts aside. "And neither man has ever remarried?"

"No, neither man ever found anyone to replace those they loved so dear," Doris answered with a sad shake of her head. "But enough about such dreary matters. I have supper to finish." She was almost to the hallway door when suddenly she spun about, causing her dark green skirts to swish about her ankles. "By the by, Miss Griffin, it might do you good to know that this room vas to be the nursery. That is vhy you have a door that connects directly with Mister Adam's bedroom." She nodded toward a tall door to the right. "Don't vorry that there is no lock. Mister Adam rarely comes in here. Even though the babe's furniture vas removed years ago, the room still holds too many sad memories for him."

Without turning to watch Doris leave the room, JoAnn pulled her gaze from the door she had thought opened to a closet to glance again at the rest of the room and saw the gaily decorated bedroom in a sad new light. It seemed odd to be told that other people had suffered devastations equal to if not worse than her own.

Morosely, she wondered if Dr. Johnson had felt in any way responsible for his daughter-in-law's early death. Doris had mentioned his attempt to save her. Surely it had crossed his mind that another doctor in another place with a clearer mind or with more advanced skills might have been able to save her when he had not.

JoAnn could fight her tears no longer. Tossing herself across the massive bed, she wept bitterly, unable to push the haunting memories away.

Chapter Four

More than two weeks had passed since the horrible incident, but to JoAnn it still felt like it had happened just hours ago. To her, it was as if Jean Gallagher had just stopped by the doctor's lounge to say she was headed home for the evening after having completed her rounds early.

"I should still be awake at eleven o'clock when you get off," she'd said and closed her purse after pulling out her car keys. "And since it is Saturday and neither of us has a date tonight, why don't you stop by and we'll split a pizza or something? I know how you hate to cook, being as undomestically inclined as you are. And if you don't stop by my apartment for pizza, you'll probably end up just going on home and popping a frozen dinner of some sort into the microwave. Besides, we haven't had much chance to visit lately."

"That's because you are always out with what's-his-name Boswell," JoAnn retorted with a teasing grin, knowing it annoyed Jean to have John's name forgotten. "Why don't you and your latest significant-other have plans tonight? Don't tell me there is already trouble in paradise with you two. You haven't even dated him a full year yet."

"He had to fly to Dallas on business and won't be back until Tuesday," Jean responded with a pretty pout. "So how about it? Want to split a pizza and gab for a while?"

"Only if you can remember to order jalapeños on my half," JoAnn warned with a purposeful lift of her eyebrow. Jean was notorious for forgetting that she liked jalapeños on her pizza, probably because every now and then one accidentally found its way onto her half and when it came to anything spicy hot, Jean was a definite pansy-mouth.

"Oh, and I just bought that new Mel Gibson movie. You know, that one you told me you never did get the chance to go see," Jean added. "We can watch that if you want."

"Spending a couple of hours in your apartment with Mel Gibson sounds good to me," she answered with a quick, off-centered grin. "But I'll have to leave around two or three because I promised Tony I'd come in and cover for him tomorrow afternoon. His brother, Andy, is finally getting married and Tony has this strange notion that simply because he's the best man, he has to be there."

"Imagine that," Jean countered with a laugh.

"Problem is, whoever scheduled us this weekend obviously didn't think Tony's being there was quite that important."

Dangling her keys from the tips of her perfectly manicured fingers, Jean started toward the side entrance. "That's my JoAnn. Always taking on everyone else's problems, even when it means extra work — which it usually does."

"That's just because I'm such a generous, kind-hearted soul," JoAnn called after her with a melodramatic wave of her hand, wondering why the word *patsy* came so quickly to mind.

She watched until Jean had stepped through the glass door marked EMPLOYEE ENTRANCE: EMERGENCY then turned and headed back into the lounge where she popped open a now lukewarm can of diet Coke and settled into a fat, gray vinyl chair with the latest copy of *Rescue* magazine. Having trained herself to listen for reference to her name only, she tuned out the paging system as well as any bits of conversation from the endless procession of doctors and nurses that came in to refill coffee cups or buy soft drinks from the machine. Instead she refocused her attention on the article she had started earlier.

At the moment patient traffic was slow in what she and her colleagues jokingly referred to as the "front lines." But with Saturday night only a couple hours away, the pace would soon increase considerably. Being the main pit doctor on duty, she knew that from around eight o'clock until eleven when her shift finally ended she would be on her feet constantly giving orders and seeing to a steady stream of patients with everything from simple indigestion to serious cuts, broken bones, internal injuries, heart disorders, strokes, gunshot wounds, and drug overdoses. Saturday nights were notoriously chaotic in Emergency Services at McCain General.

But it looked like this Saturday night was to get off to an especially early start because at about six-thirty, the red light came on in the lounge which brought her to full alert. She heard her name called just as she bounded out into the hall and hurried toward the entrance.

Seconds later, when she neared the front, she heard

89

the distant wail of a siren which meant the ambulance was only blocks away. She was met halfway by a short and always scowling Nurse Walls. While clutching her ever-present clipboard, Nurse Walls quickly informed her and the nurses who had also responded that Emergency had three accident victims en route as well as one burn victim. The three accident victims were due to arrive any minute and the burn victim, a small child who had tipped a pan of hot grease over on himself, was also en route and due to arrive in eight to ten minutes.

She tapped the clipboard with the end of her pencil then went into further detail. "Two of the accident victims are very seriously injured. Both have unstable vitals. The third has a possible fractured arm but otherwise seems all right. All three are Caucasian in their mid to late fifties. Two male. One female. Because the two who are seriously injured were not wearing their seatbelts, there are massive head and internal injuries. Both are unconscious. The female also has a deep cut in her right arm. Sliced nearly in two. Up near the shoulder. Hanging on by a flap is how Terry put it. Appears she's also a heavy bleeder."

"Better get Doctor Owen down here," JoAnn responded immediately, knowing they would need his expertise.

"Already paged him," Nurse Walls said as she pushed a few stray curls off her forehead with the backs of her fingers then returned to her notes. Nurse Walls was forever pushing her springy white curls away from her face because they refused to stay beneath her starched white cap. "Paged the lab and RT, too," she added unnecessarily. It had become automatic for her to contact Respiratory Therapy and the laboratory when patients this serious were in-coming.

"What about the burn victim?" JoAnn asked, already headed for the sink to scrub.

"Caucasian. Male. Four years old. First, second, and third degree burns over about thirty percent of his body. The grease adhered to the skin along his right shoulder and arm. He has not yet gone into shock. Still screaming his little head off according to Henry Brooks."

"And with good reason. Page Philip Burns." Ironically, the burn specialist at McCain General was named Burns.

"I've already done that, too. And since this same boy was in here just last week after supposedly having fallen out of his parents' mobile home and cutting his face, we already have a blood type for him so I have the whole blood on standby."

"A frequent visitor?" As she snapped her gloves into place, she made a mental note to look for signs of child abuse.

"I plan to keep a close eye on that one," she responded with a knowing nod. "When a kid's only four years old, he can't very well watch out for himself."

JoAnn smiled, grateful that Nurse Walls was so perceptive and efficient. "Anything else?"

"Just that the accident victims are here," Nurse Walls said and turned toward the gleaming pneumatic doors just as they hissed open.

The loud sirens cut at almost that same moment but the red lights continued to dart across the far wall with annoying regularity. Seconds later, the paramedics and aides wheeled the first of the three accident victims into emergency. At that same moment, Dr. Owen crashed through the ER doors from the inner corridor, his white coat flapping behind him while he demanded to know what happened. Dr. Owen was a tall, imposing man, a fourth-generation surgeon who took his work very seriously.

By the time the two gurneys had been wheeled inside, Drs. Mack, Edison, and Weathers had also arrived from upstairs, each shouting for his favorite nurses. Soon everyone was ready for whatever was about to happen — or so they thought.

The two patients being hurriedly wheeled past the admitting nurse had sustained such serious head injuries, JoAnn did not at first recognize them.

"Take these two on in. Start a line on each," she said, not taking time to do more than give them a quick glance. "Get that woman typed, stat. Looks like she's going to need whole blood and plenty of it." She then turned to wait for the third victim. When she watched him stumble in on foot, escorted by a policeman instead of being wheeled in on a gurney, she realized they had another drunk driver on their hands. Seeing that the drunken man's life was in no immediate danger, she ordered him to sit in one of the chairs near the admitting office and wait. She then hurried into the trauma area to help with the other two.

"Chris, you are in charge of the man," she said to Dr. Edison as she rounded the eight-foot curtain that separated the two patients. "I'll take the woman."

Turning her attention to her patient, she wiggled her way in among the nurses, doctors, and paramedics to check the carotid pulse. "Where's the lab tech and RT? They should be here by now."

"Lab tech is here," one of the nurses told her as a young man in a white lab coat rounded the curtain and set his tray nearby. "RT is on the way."

It was not until she had reached for a pair of scissors to cut away what remained of the woman's bloodied clothing that she realized just who it was they had. Her heart gave a painful leap when the recognition struck her full force.

"Oh my God!" For a moment it felt as if her main airway had twisted shut. There was so much pain she could not breathe.

"What's the problem?" Dr. Owen asked. He stood just behind her curious to know why she had frozen. Not wanting to waste valuable time with a patient who had already lost a critical amount of blood, he reached around and took JoAnn's scissors then abruptly nudged her aside.

JoAnn finally sucked in a needed breath then followed it with several.

"That's my mother," she said, unable to pull her gaze off her mother's swollen and bloodied face. Upon hearing her own words, her stomach constricted with such force it felt as if someone had struck her with a board. Having been effectively shoved aside, she turned and without taking into consideration the contamination to her gloves, she pulled back the curtain to have a quick look at the other victim. Her hands curled into tight fists, knotting the curtain while a white-hot scream welled inside her.

"Th-that's my father," she wailed, her voice so strained it had sounded foreign even to her.

Dr. Owen hesitated only a second before cutting away the last of the woman's clothing then dropping the bloodied wad into a nearby bucket. Meanwhile, Dr. Mack pulled back both eyelids and checked the pupils for response to light while the lab tech drew his first syringe of blood.

"Then maybe you'd better sit this one out." Dr. Owen glanced at her only briefly while he removed the ice pack the paramedics had provided. He quickly unwrapped the severed arm to view the damage. JoAnn was the only one to cringe at the bits of mangled flesh hanging from the tear.

Dr. Owen reached immediately for the bottle of Zephiran to rinse the area. "Wade and I can handle this one," he told her then glanced at Dr. Mack who was already writing notations. "Can't we, Wade?"

"Sure. But by the looks of that arm, we do have our night cut out for us." His voice had come across more hopeful than his expression.

JoAnn forced herself to face Dr. Owen again then took several deep breaths while she focused on her mother's swollen face instead of the gaping tear in her arm. Her mind reeled in a half-dozen different directions, unable to latch on to any one thought for long. "What could have happened?" she asked of no one in particular. "When I talked to Mom yesterday, she didn't say anything to me about driving over to Pittsburgh tonight. This is Saturday night. They should be home, watching rented movies and eating popcorn. Why are they here?"

Although she really had not expected an answer to that last question, she got one.

"A drunk driver veered into oncoming traffic and struck their car head on," one of the paramedics explained while he continued to work the ambu bag, still waiting for the RT to arrive and take over. "It happened so quick, these two probably never even knew what hit 'em. Happened about half a mile from the ball park." He paused long enough for one of the nurses to respond to Dr. Owen's demand for a blood pressure reading then continued, "The man had on a Pirate ball cap. Maybe they had decided at the last minute to take in the game."

"But why weren't they wearing their seatbelts? They always wear their seatbelts," JoAnn asked, looking from face to face, hoping for an explanation she knew was not to come.

No one had time to offer any guesses. Now that the clothing had been cut away, the blood taken, and the IV's started, it was time to go to work. Every second was vital.

"Nurse Sobey, two grams Mannitol, 20 percent, stat," Dr. Owen shouted as he tossed a bloodied towel out of his way then glanced again at JoAnn. "Since she's your mother, you have your choice. You can re-scrub and come in with us as an observer or you can wait out here and help Chris and Richard work with your father." By now the burn victim was being wheeled into the trauma area, screaming and flailing his arms and legs. "Or you can stay here and see to the kid."

"I'll go in with you," she answered without hesitation. She knew from the seriousness of her mother's injuries there would be a need for more than two doctors in OR. She turned to look at her father. Drs. Edison and Weathers were already bent over his limp frame, working to stop his bleeding while one of the two respiratory technicians who had just arrived slipped an oxygen mask into place. She fought the urge to go over and reassure her father, knowing he was still unconscious and would never hear her anyway. Instead she hurried to follow Dr. Owen.

Even though Dr. Lawrence Owen was unquestionably the best vascular surgeon at McCain General,

95

JoAnn wanted to be in the room when he and Dr. Mack operated. While the nurses and technicians rolled her mother and all the auxiliary equipment toward the operating room, she ordered Dr. Edison to take charge then followed Drs. Owen and Mack into the scrub room. "Larry, be honest with me. What do you think her chances are?"

"To be honest? I really don't know," he answered. "But I'll do everything I can to save her. You know that."

She took a deep, shuddering breath to help collect her thoughts. "I know you will. We all will."

Because it was an emergency situation and because even after her mother had been placed on a recovery system, she continued to lose blood at an alarming rate, JoAnn was allowed to assist within minutes after the operation got underway.

Despite everyone's speed and efficiency, progress crept at a snail's pace. Tempers became short and Dr. Owen's demands more frantic. "What's the B/P now? Pulse? Damn! That's too low. We need to get that B/P up to ninety or she's going to crash!"

"Doctor, she's fibrillating!"

"Start CPR! Now!"

Dr. Mack immediately began the cardiac massage, stopping every several seconds to check the cardiac monitor. But rather than show the good steady heart rhythm they needed, the jagged indicator line grew more and more shallow.

Despite everything done to keep JoAnn's mother alive, she died just four hours into the operation. JoAnn was standing beside her, holding the dear woman's face in her hands, pleading with her to live when she eventually flatlined. After continued attempts to revive her and with all hope finally gone, JoAnn admitted their defeat then hurried out to see what she could to do help her father only to learn that he, too, had died at about the same time as her mother.

Suddenly both her parents were gone and she was alone. Alone with the knowledge that neither she nor her colleagues had been able to save either of them. Losing them like that, while under her own care, had destroyed whatever confidence she'd had in herself as a doctor, to the point she could no longer perform her duties in ER effectively. Suddenly, she felt inadequate not only as a doctor, but as a human being in general. She had failed. Failed the hospital. Failed her own parents. And because she'd failed, she'd begun to think of herself as a total fraud and soon she questioned every decision she made.

During the following weeks, she became so grief-stricken and felt so emotionally drained, she was unable to function as she had. She almost allowed another patient to die due to her own bumbling inaction. Finally, she accepted the fact she had a problem that desperately needed to be worked through and decided to take Jean's advice. She requested the full eight weeks.

She had hoped that while performing her duties as executrix to their will—seeing that everything was done exactly as they would have wanted—she would be able to make good use of that time alone and work her way past all those painful feelings of inadequacy and guilt. But thus far, nothing she had done had helped dull the horrifying memories from that night. Living in their house, surrounded by their things, eating at their table, and sitting in her father's favorite chair had only intensified her pain.

JoAnn rolled over in the huge bed and stared at the underside of the bright yellow and white canopy while fat tears of anguish rolled down the sides of her face and into her hair.

Nothing had changed. Nothing would *ever* change.

She had failed.

And her parents were dead because of it.

Shutting her eyes against the pain that drove through her heart like a stake, she rolled over and sobbed silently into her pillow until sleep finally overtook her.

JoAnn awoke the following morning groggy from having slept fifteen fitful hours without waking and was immediately confused by her unfamiliar surroundings. Where was she? Why was she still dressed except for her hosiery and shoes? And why did her eyes and face feel so heavy and swollen, as if she were just getting over a cold or had been crying all night?

Lifting her head off the pillow, she blinked in a futile effort to clear her head while she looked at the room more closely. Her thoughts were still too fogged with sleep to remember what had happened. It was obvious she had seen the room before because nothing about it surprised her; yet she had no idea where she was.

Not remembering where she was or how she came to be there gave her an eerie feeling, and when such simple facts did not immediately come to her, panic set in. Her heart hammered with a burst of fear knowing the sort of personal trauma she had suffered recently could easily cause sudden lapses in memory. Perhaps she didn't *want* to remember, which might also explain why she felt as if she'd been drugged.

Something terrible had happened and her mind was working hard against remembering.

She glanced at the room again, then at her dirty riddled clothing.

What had happened to her?

She splayed her left hand against her breastbone while she sank back into the pillows and tried to decide what to do. Did she dare leave this room when she had no idea who or what was out there? What if the reason she did not want to remember was because danger awaited her outside?

While she lay there frozen with indecision, a deep, rich male voice came through the netting of a nearby open window and said something about a gate latch. She immediately remembered *Adam*. His smiling face came to her as a complete, compelling image, and after having recognized his voice, the rest of what happened came back to her in a bewildering rush.

Although trauma may very well have helped block the initial memory of having been transported back in time, she knew she had not been drugged. She felt so tired and ragged because she had cried herself to sleep again. But with such a beautiful display of sunlight spilling into her room from the east, she was lured from her more morbid thoughts and was able to put aside the painful memories associated with her parents' death—at least for a while.

She smiled when she realized just how mistaken she had been. She was not a prisoner in this strange place. She was a guest. A guest in Adam Johnson's home. *A guest in the year 1889.* The thought of that both thrilled and terrified her, causing her adrenaline to shoot through her and bring her wide awake. Her circumstances were again clear, though still a little bewildering. Aware the time switch was true and not something she had dreamed—she really *was* in the year 1889—JoAnn sat bolt upright and tossed back an unfamiliar yellow and white afghan.

While continuing to visualize Adam's distinctively handsome features as well as the magnificent era in which she now visited, she wondered why no one had bothered to wake her. Because of the downward slant of the sun rays through her windows, it had to be well into morning. She glanced at the clock. It was nearly nine. She had slept through supper and right through the night.

Ready to get on with her morning, she hopped from the oversized bed and padded across the carpeted area of the floor toward the small vanity with the slender porcelain pitcher, where she hoped to find fresh water both to drink and wash her face.

On the way she stumbled over a tall, enameled bucket and knew by the strange shape it had to be a chamber pot. She blinked when she realized it had not been there before. Neither had that afghan. Nor the folded nightgown at the foot of the bed. And her shoes had still been on her feet when she'd fallen asleep, not on the floor beside the bed. She was sure of it.

Someone had come into the room during the night and taken care of her comforts. She felt strangely ill at ease when she wondered if her nighttime visitor had been Adam. Had he come into her room while she slept? She glanced at the door that joined her room to Adam's, relieved to find it still closed. But was it closed all night? He could easily have come in and gone out, gently closing the door behind him, and she would be none the wiser.

She felt more uneasy when she realized that not

only had a chamber pot been brought in without her being aware, it had been brought in for her convenience. There was only the one toilet for this entire household and it was downstairs, on the back porch.

Such a luxury, she thought with a wrinkled nose, glad she hadn't had anything to drink nor eat since that previous morning and wouldn't have to use the awkward-looking thing. With any luck she would be able to hold off entirely until she had gone safely back into her own time.

Using just two fingers to grasp the wooden and wire handle, she quickly set the bucket out of her way, glad that such inconveniences were not to be a permanent part of her life. When she returned to her parents' house there would be not one but three bathrooms awaiting her use.

Aware she had no makeup with her and that her clothes looked very much like the bed she had just slept in, she splashed her face with cold water to ease the heavy feeling around her eyes. She then gently patted her face dry, hoping to leave part of the makeup intact. To her chagrin there was practically none to be saved around her eyes because of all her tears.

Leaning toward the oval-shaped mirror that was part of the vanity, she did what she could to rake the tangles from her long dark hair by using just her fingers. Since she didn't have a hair blower or a styling iron, nor the electricity to use either, she was glad most of the curl had held from the morning before.

As soon as her hair looked halfway presentable, she returned to the side of the bed and shoved her bare feet back into her shoes, then hurried downstairs, eager to experience as much as possible in the short time she had left. She would want to be back in her car before dark. That gave her about eight hours.

Having slept through last night's supper, JoAnn was very hungry and very pleased with the tantalizing aroma that came from the dining room as she hurried down the stairs.

With the delicious smell of smoked ham and fresh bread to guide her, she located the dining room with very little trouble and was a little surprised to find Dr. Johnson seated at the table feasting on a huge pile of fried ham and eggs. Of all things for a man with heart trouble to eat! Of course there was no way for him to know the devastating effect such food might have on his already damaged circulatory system. Cholesterol did not become a major concern until the latter part of the twentieth century.

Her first thought when she entered the room was to warn him against such food, but she realized he would want to know more about the ill effects of cholesterol and he would also want to know how she had come by such knowledge. Rather than try to explain medical findings not yet known in the year 1889, she decided to let him enjoy his meal instead.

"Ah, glad to see you're finally awake," Park commented with a generous smile when he spotted her from across the room. He started to get up but then thought better of it and gestured to the empty seat across from him instead. "I'd greet you properly, but Lowman thinks I need to take things a little easier for a while. He seems to have it in his head that I had a heart attack of some sort yesterday."

"I wonder where I heard that diagnosis before?" she asked, also smiling. Seeing the other place was already set, she did not hesitate accepting his unspoken offer

102

to dine with him and hurried toward the chair. "And what was his prognosis?"

"He seems to think I'll recover enough to go back to work if I'll just agree to take it easy for the next couple of weeks and give my body time to get over the shock of what happened. He also told me not to be running in any foot races—as if there was a chance I would."

JoAnn suspected Dr. Lowman had told him much more than that. "And did he have anything to say about that nasty little lump on the back of your head?"

Park winced as he tenderly touched the spot. "Just that if I didn't obey him and take it a lot easier for a while, he'd give me another one just like it."

JoAnn laughed. She liked this Dr. Lowman. "Good for him." Resting her hand on the chair Park had indicated, she glanced to see where Adam would sit. There were no other places set. "Are you sure I should sit here?"

"Of course. Adam's the only other person who would possibly be eating in here and he had his breakfast two hours ago," he said with a reproachful shake of his head. "My dear child, it is nearly nine o'clock."

So? JoAnn thought, thinking nine a respectable hour for breakfast, especially on a morning she didn't have to go in to work. "What time does he usually eat?"

"Six-thirty. Just like I normally do. But today, for some reason I didn't awake at my usual hour. I guess it was because of all that medication Lowman made me swallow last night." He rolled his pale eyes for emphasis. "You'd think he had his own pharmacy the way he kept handing me bottles. When I first opened my eyes this morning, I was so muddled by the aftereffects of all that medicine, it was as if I was in another world."

JoAnn certainly knew that feeling. She wondered now if her own morning grogginess had been something more than the result of having overslept. Perhaps it was an aftereffect from having traveled through time — something like jet lag. "I hope you didn't try to take those stairs alone in that condition."

"No, I had Adam walk with me," Parks admitted. "After all, I am a doctor. I know better." He chuckled as if finding humor in that. "And you know what remarkable patients we doctors make. I'm sure you're the same way when you're sick, always following every order no matter how inane."

"Of course." JoAnn smiled, glad at least *someone* in the year 1889 had accepted the fact she was a doctor. She knew Adam and Doris would not be so easily swayed. "What all are we having for breakfast? I'm starved."

"As well you should be, having missed supper. When Doris went upstairs last evening to see why you were so late coming down for supper and found you sound asleep on top of your bed, she just couldn't bear the thought of waking you. She said you looked exhausted." What he didn't mention was that Doris had also claimed that she looked as if she had been crying.

"Then Doris is the one who took such good care of me," she said, feeling oddly relieved it was not Adam. "I must thank her."

"Yes, Doris is the resident mother hen. Rather than wake you from such a sound sleep, she decided to toss some covers over you then left a food tray beside your bed in case you woke hungry."

"Food tray?" She did not remember seeing a food tray.

104

"She took it away earlier this morning when she went in and saw you hadn't touched it. Decided by then it would be too cold."

"She was in my room twice?" She wondered why she hadn't heard anything. Although she knew she had missed a lot of sleep lately, had she really been *that* tired? So tired she had not heard Doris moving about her bed?

"Actually she was in there several times. Once to cover you. Once to take you the food. And several times to see if you'd ever wakened and eaten so she could take away the dishes," he explained while he reached for a small brass hand bell that sat off to his right. "Doris can be quiet as a mouse when she wants to be. Downright spooky when you consider how large that woman is."

He then rang the bell and several seconds later a swinging door opened and the smiling object of their conversation stuck her head into the room. Through the door, JoAnn noticed she had on a long, dark-green dress similar to the one she had worn the day before with a starched white apron that covered much of the front. She wore her long red hair in a neat twist at the back of her head.

"You vanted something?" she asked, but when she saw JoAnn had joined him, she did not wait for his response. "Glad you are avake. I have a nice plate of ham, rice, and eggs on the varming shelf vaiting for you." She then disappeared to return seconds later with JoAnn's plate and a tall glass of milk.

JoAnn was surprised at how much food had been piled on her breakfast plate. There was enough to serve a small family. Even after having eaten her fill, she had more than half a plate of food left. Groaning from having overeaten, she pushed the plate back and watched while Park continued to put away large bites of ham, rice, and eggs. She wondered how any man could eat that much and remain so trim and decided he must have a very active metabolism.

"Is that all you plan to eat?" Park asked, looking at her with disbelief. "After having missed that meal last night?"

"There's only so much room in my stomach," she admitted, then gave her middle a sound pat before leaning forward to rest her hands on the table. Now that she had finished eating, she felt fully revived and she wondered what she should do next. She did not want to waste a minute of what time she had left in 1889 by sitting around staring at a half-filled plate of food.

"Fact is, I think I've eaten far too much. Maybe I should take a short walk outside to work off some of this stuffy feeling." She wondered if Adam might still be outside or if he had left for Johnstown already. Not knowing if he worked regular hours or shift work at the iron mill, she had no idea what time he would have to leave.

"Don't go just yet," Parks said and lifted his hand to stop her. "I'm expecting a special delivery from town any minute."

"What sort of special delivery?" she asked, wondering what that had to do with her. Did he want her to carry whatever it was to his room for him? Why couldn't Doris or one of the boys do that?

Park pulled his gold watch out of his vest pocket and snapped it open. "You'll see. It should be here any time now." He glanced from the watch to the door and frowned. "Most of the stores on Market Street open at

106

seven o'clock and it is nearly nine now. And I told him to be there right at seven."

"What stores?"

Before he could answer her a loud knock sounded somewhere near the front of the house and Park's worried frown melted into catlike satisfaction. "There it is now."

Chapter Five

"There what is?" JoAnn wondered if she should follow when Park hurriedly pushed his chair back and headed out of the room. Afraid he might still be weak and light-headed, which could cause him to fall, she, too, pushed away from the breakfast table and followed him down the hall.

Ahead, near the front of the house, she saw Doris standing aside, holding the left side of the front door open while a young man dressed in baggy black pants and a waist-length black jacket brought several fat boxes into the room and set them on a nearby table. He made three trips before he finally accepted a coin from Park and left.

Grinning like a young schoolboy, Park hurried to open one of the larger boxes. "Let's see what Lowman picked out."

He looked pleased when he lifted open the box and pulled out a long turquoise-blue dress made out of a material that rustled. He held the bulky garment against himself as if it might be intended for him.

"Yes, that should do nicely," he said, glimpsing at her with an excited glimmer in his blue eyes, then

108

hurriedly set the dress aside. Eagerly, he opened the next box. "Let's see what else he picked out for you."

"For me?" JoAnn asked then looked at the garment he had just cast aside with sudden apprehension. He expected her to wear that thing? Why there was enough material worked into that one garment to cover a king-sized bed. She'd swelter in an outfit like that.

"Yes, of course these are for you. They are far too small for Doris and not the style I usually wear." He peeked into yet another box and arched his eyebrows before looking at her. "I couldn't very well let you go around wearing those same clothes day after day." Glancing back down, he pulled out all manner of undergarments from the box and glimpsed each one only briefly before shoving everything back into the box and slipping the lid back in place. "Not after you saved my life the way you did."

"But you shouldn't have gone to all this trouble." She felt suddenly guilty. "Especially when you know I plan to leave here this afternoon."

"It was no trouble." He shrugged. "Lowman owes me a favor. He was more than happy to make the purchases and have them sent out. And although I don't want to alarm you, I truly doubt you'll have the money you need for your train ticket by this afternoon. Even if you sent a wire right away, it would still take a few days for that large a draft to be verified and forwarded. Meanwhile, you have to look nice."

"And a bit more respectable," Doris muttered just loud enough for only JoAnn to hear.

"What was that?" He lifted his thick white eyebrows when he turned to look at her, as if suspecting her to have done something out of line.

She stiffened but bravely spoke her mind. "I was

just thinking how much better for Miss Griffin to dress a little more—ah, conventionally vhile she is here. Those clothes of hers may be fine for Pittsburgh, but they are not good for vearing around here," she said. Then as if aware she may have just insulted a guest, she quickly added, "I think she vill look very beautiful in that pink one." She nodded toward a skirt and jacket combination Park now held. "It vill bring out the high color in her cheeks, don't you think?" She hurried forward to gather as many of the items as she could carry. "Come, I vill help you put them on to see if they need altering."

"But—" JoAnn tried to think of a reason to protest, knowing how hot she'd be in all that clothing, especially by that afternoon when the temperatures would likely climb into the upper seventies or lower eighties. Then deciding it might be worth the discomfort to dress up in authentic period costume while she was there, she shrugged her shoulders and stepped forward to help Doris carry some of Park's purchases upstairs. Park followed with the rest.

"I hope they fit you. I told Lowman you were about the size of his wife but not the same height so he would have a pretty good idea what size to buy. He promised to take his wife with him to pick out everything so he would not only find the right size but would be sure to get *everything* a woman your age would need, including a pair of new walking boots."

He nodded toward one of the boxes he carried to indicate she would find her new boots inside. "I felt so sorry for you, having had your belongings stolen that I decided I should do something to rectify the matter." He walked ahead of the other two to set the boxes he carried on the bed. "Besides, I owe you something for saving my life yesterday."

110

"No you don't. I just did what I'm trained to do," she explained as she set her boxes beside his. She noticed a peculiar expression on Doris's face, as if not quite sure what to think of their conversation. "It's what *any* doctor would have done," she said, stressing the fact she was one, too.

Why it bothered JoAnn that this woman obviously doubted her credentials was beyond her, but it did. She felt it was time these people grasped the fact that a woman could be just as qualified to become a doctor as any man. True, she herself might not be the most competent of doctors—or her parents would still be alive—but that didn't mean all women were that incompetent.

"Still, you saved my life and this is the only way I have to repay you." He gestured again to the garments and boxes scattered across the unmade bed. "I will now leave you two to your dressing. I'll be right across the hall resting. Let me see when you're finally dressed."

"And you remember to take off your boots before climbing into that bed," Doris warned with a sharp wag of her finger, sounding more like a nagging wife than a housekeeper. She waited until Park had closed the door before she reached into the pile of garments and pulled out something made of white cotton and eyelet lace edged with white ruffles. She handed the funny-looking garment to JoAnn then turned back to the bed to search for the next piece. "It seems a little odd to be helping a voman do her dressing again." She paused to think about that. "There hasn't been a voman around here for such as that in nearly eight years."

Not wanting anyone to discover she had no idea what to do with such unusual-looking underclothes,

111

JoAnn draped the white garment she had just been handed over her arm and smiled complacently. "There's really no need for you to bother yourself with this. I'm quite used to dressing myself. After all, I do live alone."

Doris's green eyes widened with astonishment as she set what was obviously a summer nightgown off to the side. "You don't have yourself a husband?"

"No. No husband. Never saw much need for one," she answered, though in truth she had come very close to marriage several years ago. Or so she had thought.

Doris's head tilted to one side while her eyebrows pulled together, evidence of her sudden concern. "And you don't live vith your parents or some other relative?"

The mention of her parents gave JoAnn a sharp, painful tug, but she managed to keep the emotion from her voice when she answered. "My parents died very recently in an accident and the only other relatives I have are my mother's two half-sisters who now live in Texas." She paused to think about what she had just said. Truth was, her aunts Jacque and Nicolle wouldn't move to Texas until the years 1976 and 1977, which technically were eighty-seven and eighty-eight years into the future.

"And since your parents' deaths you haven't been able to find anyone to live vith?" Doris looked truly concerned while she pulled out yet another undergarment and handed it to JoAnn. This one had laces along one side and something that felt like strips of metal or hard plastic sewn into the body of it. "It must be very frightening to live alone."

"Not too frightening," JoAnn assured her, remembering now how uncommon it had been for an unmarried woman to live alone.

112

The ache that had tightened her throat and speared her heart at the mere mention of her parents' death gradually subsided while she decided just how to explain her situation. "I live in an apartment building with lots of other people who also live alone. Most of us work at the same hospital so we tend to look out for each other."

"Oh, that means you can valk to vork together," Doris said, nodding as if she saw the wisdom of such an arrangement.

Knowing it would undoubtedly blow this poor woman's mind to be told that even though the apartment building was only four blocks from the hospital, most of them drove themselves to work in their own self-propelled automobiles, JoAnn also nodded. "That's right. We can walk to work together whenever we like just like we can walk to the store together if we want. So you see there really is very little danger in my living alone."

Doris paused with yet another undergarment in hand and looked at JoAnn curiously. "But vhat do people think of a young beautiful voman such as you living all alone like that?"

JoAnn blinked, feeling odd that Doris had referred to her as a beautiful woman. True, she was not gag-awful ugly; still she had never really considered herself knock-'em-dead gorgeous either. But then Doris didn't have glamorous women like Linda Evans, Whitney Houston, or Connie Sellecca to compare with. Perhaps measured against the women Doris knew, the women of 1889, she *was* beautiful.

Her eyebrows arched at the absurd notion of being considered anything beyond pleasant looking and a smile slowly stretched across her face, shaping two dimples on either side of what she had always consid-

113

ered a far too generous mouth.

Too bad she couldn't stay in this intriguing year 1889 long enough to find out what it might be like to be considered truly beautiful. It would certainly be a pleasant change.

"People don't really think that much about me living alone. Lots of women live alone in the city." She glanced questioningly at the white garment Doris had just handed her. That made three undergarments thus far. Just how much was a woman expected to wear under those monstrosity dresses. "It really is quite common."

"Still, I'd vant someone living vith me," Doris said, her eyes wide and expressive. "If it veren't for my boys being here and Mister Adam coming by from time to time to check on matters, I'd be frightened to death of living out here all alone." She then smiled and her expression relaxed. "As it is, I have my strong son, Cyrus, and my feisty son, George, here to take care of me. You never know vhat sort of vagrant vill come tramping through the mountainside at night."

"And I have my best friend, Jean, to take care of me," JoAnn assured her, then wondered what Jean would have to say about this strange adventure she'd happened upon. She knew it would take an awful lot of convincing to get her friend to believe her enough to go searching for some invisible hole that a lightning bolt had supposedly burned into what had otherwise been an undetectable time barrier. It would take even more convincing to persuade her to step through the hole and find out what the world was really like back then. Knowing how fascinated she would be by this place, JoAnn set aside any earlier worries and could hardly wait to share the experience with her.

"I should stay at least long enough to help you vith

114

your corset," Doris said, breaking into JoAnn's meandering thoughts while she reached for the laced garment that felt like it had metal strips sewn inside. She continued to hold on to that garment while she draped everything else across the foot of the bed. "It is too much trouble to get into one of these on your own. *I know.*"

JoAnn eyed the garment with sudden interest. "That's a corset?"

"Of course. Vhat did you think it vas?" Doris turned it over in her hands as if trying to figure out what had caused her not to recognize something so common.

"Well then you can set that thing aside. I doubt I'll wear it." Nothing bothered her worse than tight clothing.

"But if you don't vear a corset, you von't have the attractive twenty-inch vaist a young voman like you is supposed to have," Doris reminded her.

Twenty-inch waist? Who was Doris kidding? She hadn't had a twenty-inch waist since she was fourteen.

"Forget it," she responded and took the offensive garment from Doris and tossed it to the far side of the bed. "I'd much rather breathe."

Doris's green eyes twinkled with amusement. "But vhat if you don't fit into the dresses othervise?"

"Then I won't wear them." After all, it was not as if she were doomed to wear her present outfit forever. She could change into a fresh outfit that evening when she returned home. "True these clothes are a little rumpled and don't smell particularly pleasant, but I happen to like comfort." She also liked keeping her circulatory system open and a good supply of blood flowing to her brain. With that thought, she wondered if the reason why so many women in the past swooned so often was because their corsets had been pulled too

115

tight. It was an idea worth considering.

"Vell, then if you're sure you von't be needing me, and since I have everything all laid out for you anyvay, I'll go on downstairs and start my preparations for lunch. Mister Adam likes to eat sharply at noon."

"Does Mister Adam live his entire life around such a set schedule?" JoAnn wanted to know, thinking it a little rigid to always dine at seven, breakfast at six-thirty, and lunch at noon.

"He does vhen he's out here," she replied, already headed for the door. "Though I doubt he follows as strict a schedule vhenever he stays with his father. Doctor Johnson never knows vhen he'll arrive home to take his meals. Vhen Mister Adam stays there, he usually vaits to eat until his father comes in from seeing the last of his patients. That sometimes is as late as nine o'clock." She paused with her hand on the latch. "Except of course on the nights Mister Adam's teaches at the Institute or on the nights he escorts Miss Constance to dinner or to the theater or out to some other fancy frolic."

JoAnn wrinkled her nose into an irritated frown. There was that name Constance again. "Just how serious is the relationship between Mister Adam and this Miss Constance I have heard so much about?"

"As serious as it has been vith any voman since his vife died," she answered quickly, although she didn't look all too pleased. "He's been calling on her off and on for over a year now."

JoAnn did not yet understand why it bothered her so to know Adam dated a woman named Constance. It wasn't as if she had any personal feelings for him. Still, just knowing he had a special woman in his life with a stodgy name like Constance caused an annoying ache to settle over her. "Your son, George, seems to think Mister Adam should marry this Miss Constance and have children."

"George just vants Mister Adam to have reason to spend more days out here. Mister Adam is very good to George vhen he's here. Spends time vith him. I'm afraid my young son thinks of Mister Adam as the father he lost vhen he vas just a babe. They are very close friends. I think George also believes that if Mister Adam vas finally to get himself a vife, he and his new bride vould then move out here to live like they do in those books he reads at school — happy everafter." Her expression hardened. "My son does not understand that a voman like Miss Constance vould not be happy everafter living out here vith no one to talk to but the animals and the servants. She'd vant a house in town vhere she could go shopping vith her friends vhenever she vanted."

So that was why Doris didn't seem all that happy about the relationship between Adam and Constance. She viewed Constance as a spoiled city girl who could end up changing everyone's way of life for the worse. "Well, perhaps theirs is just a temporary relationship. Perhaps they won't actually decide to marry."

"It's none of my business if they do," Doris said with a sudden lift of her chin. She tried to sound unconcerned when she pulled the door open then stepped quietly out into the hallway. "Oh, there's a hairbrush and comb in the vanity. And a toothbrush, and a small can of tooth powder. Call through the vindow if you need me. I'll be out in the summer kitchen. It's too hot these days to cook in the small room downstairs."

"Don't worry, I won't need any help," JoAnn insisted, although she already wondered what some of the garments might be. "I'll be down to let you see the first outfit after I've let Park have a quick look at it." After all, she was a fairly intelligent woman. She should be able to figure out what went where. "I'll see you in a short while."

Little did she know how long a short while that would be.

Several times JoAnn became so frustrated she wanted to scream aloud before she eventually had enough ties tied and enough hooks hooked to look presentable. By the time she had finished putting on most of the clothing Doris had left behind for her, the corset and one of the two double-wrap petticoats had been tossed under the bed, well out of her sight. It was bad enough she had to wear five layers of cotton and wool snug against her waist, but to add all that extra underclothing had asked too much of her. As it was, she could hardly move.

If she had had more time, she would have simply rinsed out her original undergarments, let them dry, then put them back on and forgotten all this other garbage. Not only did she have on a pair of split bloomers that bagged to just below her knees that she had first tried to put on as an undershirt, she had on a pair of thick stockings, a camisole, an ankle-length petticoat with a ton of ruffles near the floor, a plain skirt made of a lightweight pink wool lined with cotton and an overskirt made of a much heavier and darker pink wool that draped in neat folds and covered two-thirds of the original skirt.

In addition to all that, she also wore a long-sleeve white blouse that buttoned in the back and had several layers of starched white ruffles sewn across the front and around the cuffs. Over the blouse she wore a thick woolen jacket that covered everything but the ruffles. There was also a heavy bulk of material sewn into the

118

back of the skirt that made sitting virtually impossible. The darts and seams in the jacket and blouse had been placed in the most peculiar places, making the garments practically immobile. To lift her arms above her head, she had to bring her elbows forward first, which made arching her back or flexing her shoulders to relieve tension an impossible task. She had no doubt this garment had been designed by a man who secretly hated women.

JoAnn frowned with further annoyance when she tried to take a few steps in the heavy garment. It felt like she was moving around in a full suit of armor. She could not imagine having to wear a corset and yet a second full-length petticoat under all this. Suddenly, she held a whole new respect for the women who survived the 1880s. They had to have had superhuman strength just to get around in their clothing.

But at least the clothing provided her was clean and it made her look more a part of the time period. When she glanced at herself in the full-length mirror that stood in the corner of her bedroom, she had to smile. She looked like something out of an old Hollywood movie. With most of her eye makeup gone from having cried herself to sleep and much of her face makeup washed away, she barely recognized herself. It was like staring at a stranger — *a stranger from another time*.

Cocking an eyebrow, she lowered her chin in a very seductive manner, aware this stranger in the mirror looked somewhat beguiling. "Scarlett O'Hara, eat your heart out."

The only thing killing the overall effect was her hair. It was a shame she didn't know how to shape her massive locks into a thick pile of ringlets at the back. As it was, the best she could do was brush it thoroughly and tie the length back with a rose-colored ribbon she had found in the same drawer with the brush. At least that kept the thick tresses off her neck.

She next turned her attention to her feet. Although the boots were the right size, JoAnn wasn't used to that type of footwear and chose to slip back into her pumps instead. Beneath long skirts that brushed the floor when she walked, it didn't matter to her that the slender dark-blue shoes looked ludicrous with such heavy white stockings. At least she wouldn't have to worry about getting blisters from leather rubbing against her ankles.

After deciding against the little hat made of pink satin with dangling strips of black and white lace, JoAnn grabbed the pink satin and lace folding fan and headed across the hall to Park's room. She slipped it into her skirt pocket along with the car keys she had just transferred from her old skirt rather than chance them being found. She was certain the tiny fan would come in handy before the day was over, what with no air-conditioning to keep her cool.

"May I come in?" she asked after she found Park in bed wearing wire-rimmed eyeglasses, reading. Without waiting for his response she stepped inside and for some reason felt compelled to curtsy when he lifted his gaze to look at her clothing.

"Now that's more like it," he said with a broad smile while he took in the beauty before him. His blue eyes sparkled with genuine admiration. "You are truly beautiful."

JoAnn's smile widened. For the second time that day, she had been called beautiful. She wondered how many more times it would take before such praise finally went to her head. "Thank you. I have to admit, I do feel beautiful in this dress." Which was true. De-

120

spite the awkwardness, she did feel somewhat elegant if not downright regal wearing such a gown. It was not unlike the feelings she had felt as a child whenever she'd played dress up in her mother's favorite clothes.

"Makes me wish I was about twenty years younger," he said with a playful wink. "Has Adam seen it yet?"

"No. No one has seen me in this but you."

"Not even Doris?" His wrinkled brow let her know that puzzled him.

"No, but that's because I sent her on downstairs with the promise I'd come out to the summer kitchen and show it to her when I finished."

"Then you are headed downstairs?"

I'm going to attempt it, she thought, aware how awkward taking those short, steep steps would be while wearing such a heavy, restrictive garment. "Yes, I'm headed down just as soon as I leave here."

"Good. Then you can give Adam a message for me," he said, his blue eyes widening with a sudden thought — eyes very much like Adam's. "Tell him that I am feeling much better now and would like to sit outside for a while. Remind him that because of Doctor Lowman's orders I'll need him to walk with me down the stairs just in case I become light-headed enough to fall. Personally, I don't think I will, but Lowman's from an old school of worriers and thinks I might."

"And you very well might," she reiterated with a smile, glad to hear Adam was still there. "I'd be happy to give Adam your message. A little sunshine might do you some good. Where is he?"

"Probably in his study by now." Park glanced at the tall, ornate clock that stood on his mantel. "Even though he's decided to stay here and keep a close watch over me for the next few days, he'll have work to do. He's already sent Cyrus into town to bring back

121

more of my clothes and a few files he thought he'd need from the bank," Park paused, then looked dutifully apologetic. "I'm afraid we forgot all about you needing to send a wire to Pittsburgh. But perhaps Cyrus will be back in time to make a second trip before the telegraph terminals close. You could also send a message to the sheriff telling him about that man who robbed you at the same time."

For some reason his apologetic expression looked more put on than genuine when he then added, "So I guess that means you'll have to stay here with us awhile longer."

"But I can't," she started to explain only to find her words fall on deaf ears.

"Tell Adam to hurry. I'm tired of being cooped in this bedroom. His study is behind that large door just to the right of the stairs. If it's closed that means he's definitely in there. Even though it cuts off some of the ventilation, he likes the door closed when he works."

Aware Park did not intend to listen to any of her excuses anyway, JoAnn sighed softly.

"On the right when going down or coming up?" she finally asked. All she knew thus far was where the back door and the dining room were.

"Going down. The parlor is on the right when coming back up. If he's not in his study, he might still be out at the stables."

"I'll find him," she assured him, eager to do so. She wanted to see if Adam thought her as beautiful in the new attire as Park obviously had.

After leaving Park's room, she paused momentarily at the top of the stairs then lifted the grand tonnage of skirts as high as her ankles and carefully made her way to the first landing. There she paused to check her hem in a full-length mirror which had obviously been provided for just that purpose. By releasing part of the material she held, she adjusted the distance of the hem from the floor to where she could safely move about without revealing that she wore a pair of twentieth-century pumps beneath her nineteenth-century skirts.

When she arrived at the door to the study, she paused again to make sure her outfit was in place, then took a deep breath to steady her nerves and knocked lightly.

Chapter Six

"Come in," came that deep, masculine voice through the heavy wooden door.

Feeling absurdly giddy, JoAnn lifted her chin to match the regal feeling the dress gave her then turned the handle and stepped quietly inside. When Adam did not immediately look up from his work, she considered just standing there and watching him for a while, but realized he would eventually attribute her interest to more than how attractive he looked with his dark hair fallen forward across his forehead.

Wetting her lips in anticipation, she spoke in a softer tone than usual. She wanted to sound every bit as feminine as she now felt. "I have a message from your father."

When her voice finally lured Adam's attention from his paperwork, his blue eyes rounded with immediate surprise. Her breath caught and held at the base of her throat while she waited for him to speak.

Now that she stood before him, she feared he was about to find fault with her new clothing instead of complimenting her as Park had—though it really shouldn't matter to her what Adam thought. Especially when it was so hard to think of him as being real—hard to think of *any* of this as being real, mainly because none of it was happening in *her* time, in *her* world.

Yet at the same time it was just as hard to think of a man that virile and that attractive as being anything but real. She took another deep breath and held it in an attempt to quell the unbidden thought of what it might be like to know Adam more intimately.

"Where did you find those clothes?" he asked, his bewildered gaze centered on the dark pink material that hugged her curves in all the best places—truly puzzled yet definitely pleased. It was not an outfit he had ever seen so it could not have been found among Dorothy's things still in the attic and it was far too small and colorful to ever have belonged to Doris.

"Your father bought it for me," she explained, wishing Adam would do or say something to let her know whether he liked it or hated it. She detected nothing from his startled expression but the fact he had not expected to see her dressed like that. "Seems he sent the money with Doctor Lowman last night, who in turn bought the clothing early this morning and had it sent directly here so your father could surprise me. Your father said it was his way of thanking me for my help yesterday." When Adam continued to do little more than stare at her, unblinking, she finally asked, "Do you like it?"

"Yes, I do like it," he answered honestly. "It is very attractive." His gaze roamed from the soft pleats near her shoulders downward to take in the way both the jacket and skirt snugged her waistline then flared again over the gentle curve of her hips. The ruffles that jutted through the front of the jacket in perfect white folds lured his attention to the rounded swell of her breasts.

"I gather your father didn't tell you about any of this," she said, pleased by the way his inquisitive gaze continued to roam over her. The outfit definitely did not repulse him.

"No, he didn't mention a word of it. But then my

father is very good at keeping such secrets from me," Adam admitted. Without taking his gaze off her, he slowly rose from his chair and rounded the desk toward her. Although he had thought her beautiful in the peculiar clothing she had worn the day before, today she was breathtaking. Suddenly, he sensed a very real danger in his father's obvious scheme to throw them together. "And you say Doctor Lowman picked this out?" Oddly enough, he had never given Dr. Lowman credit for having such good taste.

"Well, it's my understanding his wife selected it, but Doctor Lowman was the one responsible for seeing to the transaction itself, then sending it on out here so I'd have it this morning."

"Everything? What all did he buy?" Adam continued to stare with amazement and appreciation, aware of the delicate color the rose-colored garment had brought to her high cheeks. With those dark, almond-shaped eyes fringed with such long, black eyelashes, that tiny upturned nose, and the type of mouth that beckoned to be kissed, she was a true beauty.

"He purchased two complete outfits for daytime and a white cotton gown to wear at night," she admitted, aware his attention was now focused on the movement of her mouth. A slow warmth crept along her neck and prickled her skin, causing tiny bumps of apprehension to scatter across her arms and shoulders. She looked away long enough to bring the strange stirring back into control. She realized she hadn't felt that strong a reaction to a man since she first met Tom Rourke then cringed when she remembered how ill-fated that relationship had been. "I don't think your father quite believed me when I told him I would only be able to stay the one night. I think he still hopes to change my mind by convincing me to stick around a little longer."

Adam's eyebrow shot up at the unusual terminology,

but because he had understood her meaning he did not question the jargon.

"That's because my father is a man with an extremely kind heart and realizes you have no place else to go right now and no means to get there," Adam explained, although he did not believe either of those to be the real reason his father was so determined to keep her there. His father saw a possibility of interesting him in some woman other than Constance Seguin, at least for the next few days.

Reluctantly, Adam had to admit his father's scheme had promise because now that he had seen JoAnn in this new outfit, he was definitely interested. Despite her strange manner of expressing herself that sometimes lost him, and her inability to remember such minor details as the day of the week or the year, she had definitely attracted him. Perhaps it was the simple way she wore her hair—long, soft, and unencumbered. Or perhaps it was those overly large, almond-shaped brown eyes surrounded by such incredibly long lashes that lured him; or maybe it was simply the reluctant way she smiled when something pleased her. Or it might even be the way everything around them seemed to fascinate her, as if she were experiencing life for the first time. But *something* about her had captivated him. Truth was, he could not remember being quite that physically attracted to any woman, not since his wife's death eight years earlier.

He moved a few steps closer, drawn toward her as any man would be drawn toward a woman of such flawless beauty. "And to tell you the truth, my father is also a little selfish. He wants to have someone different around to keep him company while he's convalescing." Adam smiled inwardly, knowing *different* was an appropriate word for describing JoAnn Griffin. "My father loves to meet new people. I realize it might be asking a bit much, considering all you have already done for us; but couldn't you stay for a few more days? It would make my father's recovery so much easier to bear—for *all* of us." His gaze studied hers while he awaited her response. "He likes having you around."

Judging by Adam's intense expression and the deep, rich quality of his voice, *he* liked having her around, too. At that thought, a burst of exhilaration shot through her, causing every nerve ending to come alive with the heady realization she had somehow attracted a man as virile and as handsome as Adam. "But I can't stay. I already told you that."

Adam would not be swayed. He wanted her to stay. "Why can't you stay? At least for a few days? You've already admitted you don't have to return to work for a while and you have no family waiting for you at home. Is there somewhere else you have to be during these next few days?"

"Well, no, but—"

"Is someone expecting you? Someone who might become very worried should you not arrive there soon?" He bent forward an inch so he could better see her expression when she answered. If there was a special man in her life, he wanted to know it now. "Because if there is someone who will worry or might become angry, we should send him a wire and explain what happened. Explain why you have been delayed."

Aware there was only one person who might know she was gone and that was Jean Gallagher, she answered that question honestly. "There is one friend who might worry if I don't return home soon, but that friend is a she and not a he." She nodded her head knowingly. "There are only so many times she will listen to the same message on my machine before deciding there's trouble."

"Listen to the what?" He had followed her conversation up until the mention of a machine but now she had lost him again.

128

JoAnn's eyes widened when she realized what she had said. "Did I say listen? I meant read. Read the message I left for her. My friend is the type that if she doesn't hear from me every few days, she starts to worry about me, especially now." Fact was Jean had called her just that morning before, encouraging her to get out of the house for a while, get away from her parents' things long enough to put her mind on something else. It was Jean who had encouraged her to seek the refuge of the pond.

"Then we will send this friend of yours a telegram telling her not to worry," Adam said with a still cautious expression, glad to learn there was no man eagerly awaiting word from her but troubled by the way she would say one thing when she meant another. Such abrupt changes made it hard to keep up with the conversation.

He shook his head and wondered why the truly beautiful women in the world were usually either dull-witted or in some other way unstable. "Just as soon as Cyrus has returned with the bank files I need, I can send him right back into Johnstown with a message for your friend and another to send along to your banker. Cyrus would then see to it that both messages were dispatched this afternoon."

A lot of good that would do, she thought, her lips pursed into a short, flat line. It was unlikely that a wire sent in the year 1889 would ever reach a friend living in the year 1992. "But what if my friend doesn't receive the message?"

"You'll only be here a few days at the most. By the first of next week, your bank will have had enough time to send a verification for the money you'll need to return to Pittsburgh." Why he was suddenly so dead set on convincing her to stay was a mystery to him, but that was exactly what he wanted. There was just something about her that made him want to know her better.

129

"But I can't possibly stay here through the weekend," she argued, frustrated that she had yet to convince anyone of her very real need to leave. Her stomach knotted at the notion that something unforeseen could happen and force her to stay in the year 1889 forever. It was best not to press such fate by lingering in the past too long.

If only she could tell them the truth, then they would understand just how important it was she left — or *would* they? Before they could possibly understand how truly important it was for her to return, she would have to convince them of something she hardly believed herself, that a freak storm in the year 1992 had formed a small passageway in time and she had been fortunate enough — or unfortunate enough depending on how one viewed the situation — to be there when it happened.

She thought more about how she should classify this strange twist in fate. As long as she eventually returned to the twentieth century safe and unharmed, she was willing to view it as fortunate. After all, being in such a fascinating place, seeing how others had lived in another time had helped take her mind off other matters. Although it frightened her to a certain degree, it was definitely an adventure not afforded many. One that was very hard to turn down.

"But why can't you stay through the weekend?" he encouraged in that deep, silky voice of his. His gaze permeated hers, luring her from her previous thoughts. "A few more days shouldn't matter that much."

"The reason I can't stay any longer is —" she started, but no rational explanation followed. How could it? This was not a rational situation. What could she tell him? That she could not stay because she wanted to hurry back to the twentieth century; because she wanted to get back to air-conditioning, curling irons, microwave ovens, comfortable clothing, peanut-butter M&M's, and diet Coke? He already had doubts about her. What would he think of her then?

Finally, an honest answer came to her. "Because I'm out of place here."

"Why do you say that?" he asked, looking puzzled. "Has someone here made you feel unwelcome?"

"No, it's nothing like that. It's just that I'm a city girl. I'm not used to being out in the country like this."

"A city girl?" he repeated, thinking that an unusual way of putting it, especially when she was clearly and in every way a *woman*. "What's the trouble? Is the quiet bothering you?" Aware of how close he now stood to her, he smiled, then lifted a finger, unable to resist the urge to touch her cheek. He had to know if she was as warm and as soft as she looked.

JoAnn's eyes widened at the unexpected sensations his touch created and she realized it was not the *quiet* that bothered her. His touch had actually caused gooseflesh to pop out along the back of her neck and upper arms, making her skin feel oddly alive.

Afraid he might be able to read her thoughts and would know she had not been completely truthful, she pulled her gaze away. "I guess that's it. I'm used to a lot more noise, a lot more activity."

Adam, too, had experienced an explosive sensation after having touched her; but he recognized the feeling for what it was and did not let it bridle any attempt to touch her again. Outlining his lower lip with the top of his tongue while he concentrated on her tantalizing beauty, he gently trailed his finger down the side of her cheek again and continued to speak in a low, convincing voice. "You'll eventually grow used to the quiet. Please don't disappoint my father by leaving too soon. If you go now, he'll worry about you. Worry that some other terrible fate will befall you before you arrive back home. And all that worrying won't help toward his recovery one bit."

"But I can't stay," she tried again, wishing he would

just accept the fact. When she brought her gaze to meet his again, she had hoped that might help convince him; but looking at him again had turned out to be a dreadful mistake. There was something in the tilt of his head and the beseeching expression on his face that made her want to please him. When she spoke again her voice held far less determination than before. "I just can't."

"Can't you?" he asked, aware by her tone that her resolve had weakened. He reached out to touch her cheek a third time.

In gentle response to his tender touch, JoAnn closed her eyes briefly. She knew she was about to say something she might eventually regret but the words came anyway. "I guess I could arrange to stay one more day. But tomorrow I really will have to leave."

"But your bank couldn't possibly have your money transferred here by tomorrow, not even if we had remembered to send a telegram early this morning," he pointed out, hoping to win her with logic. "This is already Thursday and the banks always close early on Saturday and don't reopen again until Monday. Looks like you really have little choice but to stay with us until at least the first of next week." Even as he spoke he wondered how he would ever explain this beautiful woman's presence to Constance. But then again, he thought she might not have to know.

With his father suddenly so ill, perhaps she would understand if he simply sent a note with Cyrus explaining that their plans for the weekend would have to be canceled. He could suggest she go on to the theater Saturday night with her friends or her aunt and uncle. He would not have to mention JoAnn at all. It was not as if he and Constance had a verbal agreement to see no other people. "And please stop worrying that you will be in the way. My father was right, there is plenty of room for you here and I can certainly afford to have an

132

unexpected house guest or two."

That was true enough, JoAnn thought with an inward sigh and realized it might be nice to stay a while longer, especially with Adam there. Her pulse rate shot sky high at the thought of getting to know him *better*. She wondered what it would be like to have his strong, athletic arms around her, holding her in a passionate embrace. Her body shivered in response though the room felt suddenly extremely warm. She then shook her head and wondered what had become of her usual common sense. Had she left the practical side of her brain back in the twentieth century, allowing only the adventurous side to travel with her? She should not allow herself to be in any way attracted to him. It would not be fair to him and it certainly would not be fair to herself. She had to keep her priorities straight.

Rather than respond to Adam's suggestion she stay through the weekend, knowing she was not thinking all that clearly at the moment, she quickly changed the topic. "Oh, before I forget, your father sent me down here to find you. He wants to go outside for a while and needs your help. He told me he's feeling much, much better this morning, enough so I guess he's decided to get out there and soak up a little sunshine."

"Soak up a little sunshine?" Adam repeated questioningly. One eyebrow arched while he placed a hand at the small of her back, as if he expected her to go with him to Park's bedroom. "You do come out with the most unusual sayings."

Unusual? JoAnn wondered when the expression had come into use. Obviously at some point after the year 1889. Because she was not a professional linguist, she decided it might be best to refrain not only from mentioning objects and theories that might not have existed yet in the late 1880s but also refrain from using any modern-sounding expressions.

"I'd go upstairs with you," she said, already searching for an excuse to get away from his overpowering presence. Just the warmth of his hand pressed against the small of her back caused her blood to race at a ridiculously high rate. "But I promised Doris I'd come out to the summer kitchen and let her see how the dress looked on me just as soon as I was ready. She's probably wondering what happened to me."

"Of course," Adam said, but with very little enthusiasm and relinquished his hold when they stepped out into the hall. He watched with a curious expression when she then hurried off in the wrong direction. "Both kitchens are on the other side, near the back of the house," he called to her and shook his head, thinking her the most disoriented person he'd ever known. She had no clear concept of time or direction.

JoAnn turned and smiled a polite thank you, feeling as awkward from not knowing which direction to go as she did from knowing his gaze was on her. She swallowed hard, then spun about, hurrying to distance herself from his studious gaze.

Mainly because it was what Adam and Park both expected, JoAnn penned a brief note for Cyrus to carry to the nearest telegraph office. In it she asked that sufficient funds be sent in her name from the First National Bank of Pittsburgh to the Morrell State Bank in Johnstown.

Although JoAnn ran the very real risk of being exposed as an imposter when the bank reply claimed not to know her, she hoped that would not happen for days. Meanwhile she would enjoy what time she had left while in the late 1880s in every way she could. She was quite aware that this had to be an opportunity afforded very few.

But to avoid an angry confrontation with Jean later, she decided to return to her car long enough to leave a

134

message for her announcing she was safe. If anyone discovered her gone, it would be Jean; and since JoAnn really wasn't up to talking with her on the telephone right now, for fear she might sound more like a babbling idiot than a woman who had just had the phenomenal experience of stepping back in time, a note left in the open would have to do.

Later that afternoon, after convincing first Adam then young George that she would be perfectly safe walking through the woods alone, despite her earlier encounter with a robber, she headed for the clearing where she had left the piled stones.

Relieved to find the hole in the time barrier still intact, she slipped her keys out of her pocket and hurried to her car several hundred yards away. After opening the door and slipping inside, she dashed off a quick note on a prescription pad. "Jean, I'm on an adventure you would not believe. Don't worry about me. I'm safe."

Because she had left her purse at her parents' house, which was nearly a mile away, and wanting to return to Adam's before anyone became suspicious or worried, she scrambled through the glove compartment, hoping to find a compact or a bottle of makeup, or even an eyeliner pencil. To her chagrin, all she found was a lipstick that had melted until it was a useless mass of cranberry pink clogged in the cap. Sighing, she glanced into the rearview mirror and decided she could last a few more days without makeup.

Putting the note on the dash where it could be found by anyone searching for her car, JoAnn grabbed the bottle of aspirin and a tube of hand lotion she kept in the glove compartment, knowing she could make good use of them. But rather than risk having her keys discovered by someone in the past, because her keys did not look anything like the ones they used, she quickly locked her car, then hid the keys in a nearby clump of weeds.

She lifted her woolen skirts high and hurried back to the time opening and the other side of time. Aware she had been gone nearly an hour and had promised them her walk would be a short one, she lifted up the bulky skirts and jogged back to Adam's house.

When the house came into view, she dropped the heavy skirts and slowed to a rapid walk. About halfway along the drive, she noticed two large carriages near the front gate with their drivers standing under a nearby tree and realized Adam or Park had company. Thinking it wise not to burst in on everyone unannounced, and aware she was sweating profusely from having jogged nearly a mile in such a stifling outfit, she hurried around to the back door and quietly slipped inside. By the time she had made it to the main stairs, the heat trapped beneath her heavy clothes was unbearable, making her feel dizzy.

Without looking in any direction other than straight ahead when she rounded the foot of the stairs, she lifted her skirts just enough to place her foot on the first step then cringed when she heard Park call her by name.

"JoAnn, there you are." His voice came from inside the parlor. "I was wondering what happened to you."

JoAnn glanced toward the sound and saw Park and several other people seated in a small grouping of chairs and sofas positioned near a huge set of open windows at the front of the room. Fortunately, they sat at such an angle they could not have seen her hurried approach to the house which might have been hard to explain. And just as fortunate, because he was seated in a small armchair that afforded him a partial view of both the windows and the hallway with Shadow asleep at his left, Park was the only one to see her hesitant reaction.

Knowing he might question the plastic aspirin bottle and the small tube of hand lotion, she quickly tried to slip them into the small pocket hidden within the folds of

136

her skirt only to discover there was not enough room because of the folding fan. With nowhere else to put them, she curled her hands around each in an attempt to conceal the items before she headed into the parlor.

"This is the young lady I told you about," Park said, glancing at his guests then back at JoAnn while she continued toward him. Although he did not attempt to stand, he extended his hand to her in a warm greeting. "She's the one who saved my life yesterday."

When JoAnn entered the room and could see the entire group, she noted that Park had five visitors. Three women of varying ages lounged on a large blue and white tufted sofa and two men who looked to be about Park's age sat in winged chairs off to either side. While Park continued to extend his hand, the men stood and bowed gallantly toward her.

Aware Park expected her to accept his proffered hand, JoAnn's dark eyes widened with alarm. How could she ever explain the peculiar plastic containers to these people?

Thinking quickly, she placed both hands behind her and looked first at Park then at his guests apologetically.

"I'm so sorry, but I've just come in from petting Adam's horses," she said, unaware the others in the room had taken immediate notice of the way she had referred to Adam by his given name, which in that time indicated a *close* friendship. "I really should go up to my room and wash my hands." Thinking that the perfect excuse to leave, she took her first tentative step toward the door. "I'll be right back."

Just before she turned to hurry out of the room, she glimpsed the women still seated on the sofa and caught the youngest one's glower of pure animosity. While she hurried to the stairs, JoAnn knew instinctively she was about to have the misfortune of meeting Adam's "Miss Constance."

137

Suddenly it was very important to her that Constance think her a fair rival, though in truth she was no rival at all. JoAnn waited until she was no longer in sight of the door, then practically flew up the stairs to her bedroom. Hurriedly she made a few repairs to her hair, frowning at the tiny ringlets determined to frame her face, undoubtedly caused by the dampness from her skin. But rather than try to force the tiny curls into place, knowing without hair spray they would not stay, she decided they looked rather a part of the time period and left them alone.

Because her clothing was also still damp from her run back to the house, and aware clinging clothes were not at all attractive, she slipped her fan out of her pocket and popped it open. She did all she could to fan herself dry while she also dabbed at the perspiration along her face and neck with a cool, damp cloth.

By the time she felt comfortable again, the last remnants of her makeup were gone. Remembering a scene from *Gone With the Wind* or some such movie, she bent toward the mirror and quickly pinched her cheeks, then pressed her lips together to give them color before she headed back downstairs, walking as gracefully as the heavy dress allowed.

Although she knew she had kept them waiting well over fifteen minutes, she decided not to offer an excuse for the length of her absence. Instead, she entered the room smiling and headed directly toward Park, this time accepting his hand warmly. She felt Constance's malicious gaze cut into her back even before she turned to greet Park's guests with a gracious nod.

"The two gentlemen standing are longtime friends of mine," Park said as a way of introduction. "The tall one is Richard Goodman and the balding one with all those scruffy whiskers hanging from his jaws is Shawn Davis. Richard is a vice president at the same bank as Adam only Richard works there full time so he can be sure they don't mishandle any of his money. Shawn owns several restaurants in town."

JoAnn stepped forward to accept their proffered hands, starting with Richard then moving directly to Shawn. She made mental note of the fact that neither man actually shook her hand like she had expected. They merely took hers into both their own and gently squeezed it.

"So very pleased to meet you," she responded and smiled sweetly while she carefully avoided a glance in Constance's direction.

"Park here claims that you are a medical doctor of some sort," Shawn said. His expression indicated both uncertainty and admiration.

"Yes, I am," is all JoAnn provided him, not wanting to dwell on any topic having to do with herself, especially when she still held grave doubts concerning her abilities as a doctor. Even though she had saved Park's life, she still had to face the fact she had been unable to save her own parents.

"And it was a lucky thing for me she is a doctor," Park put in before Shawn could say something that might offend her, aware his friend had a definite knack for such as that. He then quickly turned his attention to the ladies. "And now that she's met you two old reprobates, I'd like to introduce her to your lovely wives: Carissa Davis and Sarah Goodman."

The two older women nodded in turn, letting JoAnn know that the plump woman on the left was Shawn Davis's wife and the gaunt woman in the middle had married Richard Goodman. Aware what was to come next, JoAnn then turned her attention to the younger woman beside Sarah, still certain Park would introduced her as Constance Somebody. Standing at an angle so the others in the room could not see her face

139

directly, she met the woman's hardened gaze with a look of obvious disinterest. She hadn't even spoken with her yet already she disliked her.

"And the pretty young lady on the end there is Constance Seguin, Shawn and Carissa's niece from Georgia. She's been living with her aunt and uncle for several years now."

"Ever since her husband, Aaron's, death," Carissa Davis provided, as if an explanation was in order.

Aware everyone, including Constance, was looking at her, awaiting a response, JoAnn nodded toward the young woman as cordially as she knew how and received a far less cordial nod in response.

I certainly guessed that one right, she mused while offering an indulgent smile to the group in general. The voluptuous little blonde with the hate-filled green eyes, the tiny upturned nose, and the word "arrogant" written all over her pretty brow was Constance.

JoAnn gave her one quick cursory look before turning away, but in that brief moment noted that Adam's "Miss Constance" wore her long hair in a splendid array of delicate curls high on her regal little head, probably to give the appearance of being taller than she actually was. She also noticed that Constance wore an outfit very similar to her own but pale blue in color with tiny insets of dark blue satin sewn into the jacket near the shoulders and around the pleated waistline. Judging by the size of everything else about her *ample* body, much of which was prominently displayed because, unlike her, Constance wore no ruffled blouse beneath her jacket, JoAnn decided the tiny waist Constance displayed was due to some heavy pulling on her corset strings.

Aware of the awkward silence, JoAnn felt she should say something either to Constance or to the group in general and tried to think of something engaging but had no idea what would interest people of the late

140

eighteen hundreds. Discussing the warm weather seemed rather inane. Fortunately, at that moment Adam entered the room and drew everyone's attention away from her.

"Sorry it took me so long, but I wanted to send this file back with Richard," he said while he walked across the thick carpet with his usual long strides. He handed the file to the taller of the two men. "Tell Saine I went over this in a rush because I know it is important we act quickly on this. That's why I want him to go back over my figures again before he agrees to the loan."

Before Richard could respond, Constance was out of her seat and headed toward them. She extended her right arm toward Adam with her pitiful little hand hanging limply at the wrist.

"Adam, darling, I thought you would never ever come out of there," she protested in a feminine voice JoAnn thought a bit overly done. The thick Southern accent she used had made her sound more like a small child than a grown woman. She glanced toward JoAnn with a meaningful lift of her chin while she quickly wrapped both her arms around one of Adam's, as if to designate ownership. "I've been waitin' oh-so long for a chance to talk with you about our plans for this comin' Saturday night."

Adam glanced at her arms curiously then at the cabinet-clock near the door. "I guess you didn't receive my message."

"What message?" When she looked up at him it was with huge, rounded doe eyes that made JoAnn like her all the less. What did Adam see in a woman like her? she wondered, but realized the answer to that when she again noticed the woman's ample curves.

"The message I sent with Cyrus a little over an hour ago." He again glanced at the clock. "I told him to stop by as soon as he'd delivered the other messages. He's probably knocking at your door right about now."

She looked again at JoAnn with a triumphant smile and clutched his arm tighter. "Oh? And what sweet little thing did your note say?"

"That if you really want to see that new play, you'll have to find someone else to take you. I won't be able to make it after all."

"But *why?*" She looked at him with such wide, unblinking eyes, JoAnn wanted to laugh. Clearly, Constance was not used to having someone break an engagement.

"Because I promised John Lowman I'd stay here and take care of Father for the next few days." He then glanced at Park. "He may not look it, but he's still pretty weak and he's had a throbbing headache ever since the accident."

JoAnn forgot Constance and looked at Park, worried. He had not mentioned the headache to her.

Knowing it might embarrass him to be examined in front of his friends, especially by her, she fought the urge to rush over and gently probe that injury on the back of his head. If the swelling was still there, he should go immediately to a hospital for closer observation. Home care could accomplish only so much.

"But why can't Doctor Lowman come out here and take care of your father himself?" Constance asked with a pout so childish it made JoAnn want to roll her eyes in response.

"Because he does happen to have patients other than my father," Adam said and sounded a little annoyed at her selfishness, though his face revealed nothing of his emotions. "But then just because I can't leave here for the next few days doesn't mean you have to give up your chance to attend the opening of that play." He then looked to Shawn beseechingly. "Perhaps your aunt and uncle will take you, or perhaps you can convince a few of

142

your friends to join you. I'll provide the tickets for however many friends you'd care to invite."

Constance studied his face for a long moment then cut her gaze to JoAnn. When she did, her pitiful, little-girl expression dissolved into a look of pure female malevolence. "Why don't I ask Miss Griffin to join me? I could send Porterfield for her early enough, she could have dinner with us also."

That's *Doctor* Griffin to you, JoAnn thought, but managed to keep the scathing retort to herself. She did not want the others to think her that petty.

JoAnn made every effort not to look annoyed. Aware the only reason Constance had invited her was to keep her away from Adam, she tried to think of a quick, logical excuse to refuse. The thought of spending even one of the few evenings she would have in the nineteenth century in the company of this spoiled, well-endowed brat was downright repulsive; but before she could think of a logical reason to decline, Adam answered for her.

"I'm afraid JoAnn has also been asked to stay close to Father in case he has another bad spell during the next few days. According to John, these next few days will be the most telling."

Park was quick to add, "That's true. John explained how if my heart has any intention of acting up again, it will probably do so during the next few days. That's why I've been told not to exert myself for a while." His eyes brightened as if he'd suddenly hit upon a good idea. "Perhaps you might talk her into joining you next weekend. I should be much better by then."

"Next weekend? She will be here that long?" Constance asked, clearly alarmed. Pouting again instantly, she pulled away from Adam and crossed her arms over her ample bosom, causing them to bulge unnecessarily. Her green eyes narrowed to reveal a strong disapproval. "Don't you think that's a little much?"

"Yes, of course it is," JoAnn put in, aware all eyes had turned toward her. "I have already told them I plan to leave long before then." She then shot Park a determined glare, letting him know she meant what she said. "I've promised to stay only until the first of next week. By midweek, I'll be headed back to Pittsburgh." Mainly because she could hardly wait to tell Jean about this incredible adventure. She knew now that this was not something she would ever be able to keep to herself. It was too fascinating. "That means I will have left long before Saturday."

Constance's expression lifted as she breathed a terse "Good!" at the same time Park chuckled and said, "We'll see."

For several seconds afterward no one spoke then suddenly everyone spoke, as if they had all searched for something pertinent to break the silence and had found it at the precise same moment.

JoAnn, having heard a question directed to her, moved closer to Richard Goodman to answer but kept her gaze on Adam. "I attended medical school in New York, but I've been in Pittsburgh for several years now. That's where I completed my residency and I liked the place well enough that I stayed on."

For the next several minutes Richard continued to ask questions related to her career and despite her varied attempts to change the subject, he continued to focus their conversation on the fact he found it so hard to believe she was a medical doctor.

"It's just not possible," he said for the third time. "Not a beautiful woman like you."

"Hard to believe isn't it?" Park put in loudly, centralizing everyone's attention for the moment. "Beautiful *and* smart. Not a likely combination for a woman these days." Then aware he had the same as insulted the other ladies in the room, he cleared his throat and quickly added, "Present company excluded of course."

Carissa Davis narrowed her gaze when she looked first at Sarah Goodman to see if she had caught the unintended insult then at him.

"Yes, its almost as unlikely as finding a man these days who can keep his foot out of his mouth," she said with a meaningful lift of her brow then chuckled when she noticed how quickly Park pulled in his head and looked away.

"So tell me, is everyone staying for supper?" Adam interrupted, rescuing his father from further barbed comments. "If I'm not mistaken, Doris said something about a roast this evening and you all know what a fine roast she prepares."

"No, no," Shawn responded with a quick wave of his hands. "We just came by to leave those reports with you and to see how Park was coming along. When Cyrus stopped by the bank this morning to pick up the files you wanted, he told us about Park's accident — but he didn't mention how serious the accident really was. He said nothing about Park's heart having been involved."

"That's because we told him not to," Park explained with a quick lift of his shoulders. "We didn't want to worry anyone unnecessarily."

"Especially not your own patients," Richard said with a knowing wink. "Wouldn't do for them to find out just how very close to death their own doctor came. Might cause some of them to look around for a new, healthier doctor to take care of them."

"And will you be changing to a new doctor now that you know?" Park asked with a good-natured laugh, then cocked his head to a jaunty angle while awaiting a response.

"Only if we can get one in the borough who looks like her," he answered and gestured toward JoAnn. "Then not only would I change doctors, I would immediately

145

come down with some dreaded disease that would take years of constant care to cure."

"Richard!" Sarah scolded, then thrust her chin forward as if to warn him just how close to danger he had come.

"That is if Sarah, here, would let me," he quickly added, then grinned sheepishly while pretending to be greatly intimidated by his wife. "What do you think, Sarah? Would it be all right with you if a beautiful, young woman like JoAnn saved my life?"

"I'll tell you what I think," she said, rising quickly. "I think it is time for us to go." When she looked at him it was with a cocked eyebrow and tightly pursed lips but when she turned to tell JoAnn goodbye, her eyes sparkled with amusement. "It was nice to meet you. Perhaps we'll see each other again before you leave." She then turned to Richard and spoke in a very staunch voice. "Richard. Let's go."

"Yes, dear," he responded, folding his hands in front of him as he headed dutifully toward her. Seeing that her back was to him, he winked at Park when he added, "Whatever you say, dear."

"I say you wipe that silly grin off your face and come on," she responded without ever turning back, causing his eyebrows to arch questioningly while he quickly flattened his mouth.

By the time the two stood in the hallway door, others in the room had risen to leave. Following Dr. Lowman's orders not to exert himself, Park said his farewells from his chair and watched while everyone but JoAnn left the room. When she did not follow, he glanced at her to see why she had stayed.

"What's wrong? Why are you looking at me like that?" he asked, aware that unlike him, she had not watched everyone else leave. Her attention was on him.

"Why didn't you tell me about your headaches?" she

146

asked, already walking toward him. "You know very well, a persistent headache can indicate very serious problems. Has that swelling on the back of your head gone down any at all?"

Knowing he would never be able to stop her, Park leaned his head forward so she could examine the bump. "It's gone down a little, but still has a way to go." He winced when she applied pressure to the center of the swell.

"Why didn't you put ice on it?" she asked, frowning when she found the mass to be every bit as large as the day before. A bump that close to the brain could become serious if the swelling turned inward.

"Why would I do that?" he asked, looking at her oddly.

"To help reduce the swelling," she said, realizing she had done it again, mentioned something she shouldn't. But aware it was not the sort of information that could make radical changes in the past, she added, "If you have any ice, I'll show you how it works, though this really should have been done yesterday."

"We have some ice in the cellar helping to keep the food from spoiling. But it's covered with salt."

"That's fine. I don't plan for you to eat it, just put it against that injured area for a while. I'll go find Doris and ask her to bring us some," she said and left a very bewildered-looking doctor behind.

Chapter Seven

Cyrus Hess glanced at his younger brother with his usual look of annoyance while he quietly closed the stall gate.

"George, just when you ever going to get it through your thick head that that woman ain't no real doctor. If you'd just stop long enough to do some serious thinking on it, you'd realize the truth about her. If she was a real doctor like she says she is, why under God's blue sky would she be roaming around on Cambrian Iron land with no money, no clothes other than those she had on, and no horse. Can't you see that woman ain't nothing but a vagabond?"

"Ain't so," George responded. He thrust his chin forward and curled his hands into tights fists at his sides, ready to battle his older brother despite their obvious difference in size. At age sixteen, Cyrus had already taken on the look and bulk of a grown man. Even with several growing years still ahead of him, he stood well over six feet. George, too, was tall for his eleven years. He was already over five and a half feet, but he was no match yet for Cyrus—though their mamma claimed that day was coming. Their mamma was also the one who explained that the brothers had gotten their height from their father, who had been a large, strapping man who had towered five full inches over six feet.

Like their father, Cyrus had also grown thick through the back and shoulders while George still clung to the slenderness of youth. *Bone skinny,* Cyrus liked to call him even though it invariably set George's wiry arms to swinging like a windmill in a windstorm.

"You take that back about Miss JoAnn," George said, his arms very close to swinging right then. "I like her. She talks nice to me. Answers most any question I ask her."

"What has that got to do with her being a doctor?" Cyrus wanted to know, clearly unimpressed with anything his young brother had to say.

"Nothing. I just like her is all."

"Then you like vagabonds and road tramps 'cause that's what she is. She ain't no more a doctor than that loafer who came tromping through here last week looking for a handout."

"I don't care what she is," George said, swelling his chest out. "I like her."

"Go ahead and like her. Just don't keep trying to convince me she's a real doctor. Remember, rattlebrain, I'm almost out of high school now. I know enough to recognize a real doctor when I see one."

"If you think you're so smart then how come you ain't going on to night school next year like Mamma wants?" He jabbed his skinny chest with his thumb. "I'll tell you why. Because you know you would never make it through, that's why."

"No, because I don't see no need for it," Cyrus corrected with a haughty lift of his chin. "I plan to work in the iron mill when I get finished with my schooling. You don't need no fancy education for working in no iron mill. All you need is enough common sense to follow your boss's orders once they's been give to you. Something I'm sure *you* wouldn't understand."

"I understand one thing. You ain't as smart as you think you are because Miss JoAnn is, too, a doctor from

Pittsburgh. Twice now I've watched her take care of Traveler's leg. She cleaned him up and bandaged him right proper both times. Didn't flinch or nothing when the carbolic acid started the wound to bleeding all over again. She just set about to making it stop."

"So she can tend to an injured horse," Cyrus said and curled his nose to indicate his disdain. "That still don't make her no doctor." After checking to see that the stalls George had just closed were securely latched, Cyrus reached for the lantern hanging on a nearby nail. "Could be she growed up on a farm somewhere. Most folks who growed up on farms know how to tend to injured animals."

George drew himself to his fullest height, his skinny chest rising and falling rapidly with the anger still building inside him. "She saved Doctor Johnson's life."

"Says who?"

"Says Mister Adam."

"If you ask me, I don't think Mister Adam really thinks she's no doctor neither or he wouldn't keep referring to her as *Miss* Griffin. He'd be calling her *Doctor* Griffin. You want to know what I think?"

"No, and I don't care what you think," George muttered, aware his brother had already made up his mind about his new friend and there would be no changing it. "It's time for us to go in to supper." He turned and stomped angrily toward the front of the stable.

"Well, I'm going to tell you what I think anyway," Cyrus called after him, then hurried to catch up. "I think Doctor Johnson just got the breath knocked out of him when he was throwed from that carriage and he would have got his breath again even without her help. Remember the time you fell out of the barn loft and landed flat on your stomach? You couldn't breathe for nearly two full minutes. Then just about the time you started to get dizzy and panic, you suddenly gasped and started to breathe again.

150

That's what I think happened yesterday to Doctor Johnson. Your pretty Miss JoAnn just happened to be there when that happened so she decided to take credit for it. That means she took credit for something she didn't even do."

George's lips compressed into a tight pucker while he continued his march. He didn't care what his brother said. He still liked Miss JoAnn. He liked the way she asked just as many questions of him as he did of her. It made him feel important.

"And another thing," Cyrus went on, not ready to give up until he had George convinced. "A real doctor would be more concerned about his other patients. Sure wouldn't be staying around here living off other folks the way *she* is. Why she even has them buying her clothes. Next thing you know she'll be moving in here to live."

"You haven't even met her," George shrieked and came to such an abrupt halt he kicked up tiny puffs of dust in the doorway. He was tired of listening to his brother say terrible things about someone he liked that much. "How can you know so much about someone you ain't never even met?"

"I may not have met her, but I got a good long look at her early this afternoon right after I got back with those bank files Mister Adam sent me for. She was standing right there when he handed me that second set of messages he wanted me to take into town," he replied, clearly unimpressed with what he had seen. "And I tell you right now that woman's way too soft and way too pretty to be no doctor."

"Pretty ain't got nothing to do with it," George stated angrily, then turned and hurried out into the yard. By the time Cyrus had caught up with him, he noticed their mother already headed in their direction. When she saw they were coming toward her, she placed her hands on her ample hips and waited just outside the flower garden.

151

George knew even before the lantern light fell across her face, she was angry.

"Vhat has been keeping the two of you?" she asked, looking from one son to the other. "Your supper has been on the table for half an hour. I cannot finish with the day's dishes until you two have come in and done your eating. You know that."

George narrowed his green eyes then gestured toward Cyrus with a fierce jerk of his blond head, his tiny chin trembling with anger. "Momma, Cyrus says Miss JoAnn ain't no doctor. Says she's a road tramp just looking for a handout. Tell him that ain't so."

"See?" Cyrus retorted, then wrinkled his nose. "You just called her *Miss* JoAnn. *You* can't even call her doctor."

Doris shook her head with exasperation. "Is that all you two boys have to be doing? Argue? Can't you get along for even one day vithout finding something foolish to quarrel about?"

"It ain't my fault," George wailed as if she had accused him of having personally set off this latest confrontation. "He started it by saying that Miss JoAnn ain't no real doctor when I know she is. Tell him. Tell him that she's a real doctor."

"She *says* she is," was all Doris was willing to inject. "And Doctor Johnson seems to think she might be."

"See there?" Cyrus said with a triumphant wag of his blond head. *"Might be.* Even Mamma has her doubts. And I think the only reason Doc Johnson is pretending to go along with the hoax of her being a doctor is because she's a guest in Mister Adam's house."

"Vill you two quit all this bickering?" Doris asked, then grabbed her sons by the arms and pulled them toward the house. "It is not that important vhat I think or vhat Doctor Johnson thinks because it doesn't really matter too much if she is a doctor or not. Vhat does matter is the fact that your supper is sitting in there on the table turning cold. Get yourselves in that house and vash those hands. Now."

"All I can say is that there is something not quite right about that woman," Cyrus mumbled, not ready to give in that easily. "And I for one plan to keep a very close watch on her while she's here. She's after something and I intend to find out just what that something is."

Truth was, until a few minutes ago, Cyrus had just thought Mr. Adam's new house guest a bit strange, but after hearing some of his own brash arguments, he had convinced himself there was something downright sinister about her.

"You just tend to your chores, young man," Doris warned with a firm wag of her finger. "That young voman seems harmless enough to me. True she has strange habits and a peculiar vay of saying things, but she's only to be here a few more days. Meanvhile, you two need to keep in mind that it is Thursday night and that both of you stayed home from school today. You need to eat your supper and get to the school vork you missed. It'll be bedtime soon; and vhether or not you have your lessons completed, you are *not* missing another day of school. Tomorrow is Friday. Too many tests are given on Fridays. Now inside vith both of you."

JoAnn watched Park curiously while he sat in the elegantly designed rococo chair carefully studying the black and white hand-carved pieces scattered across the chess board. Although he had removed his dinner coat and had loosened the narrow ribbon he wore for a tie within minutes after having left the dining room, he still wore a loose-fitting dinner shirt buttoned to the collar and a pair of dark gray slacks held in place by a black leather belt.

Why the man had insisted on dressing for supper when he was supposed to be convalescing was a mystery to her, but Park had demanded to return to his room shortly be-

153

fore five o'clock and by seven o'clock when it came time to eat, he was dressed in a dark gray three-piece suit very similar to the one he had worn the day before.

Adam also had slipped into a stylish coat and vest before dinner, making JoAnn wonder if it was a tradition in this house to dress for the evening meal.

After a delicious meal of steak, carrots, beans, and stove-browned potatoes, the men had decided they should retire to Adam's study where Adam, like his father, immediately loosened his tie, but unlike his father, had remained in his coat.

Now the two men were engrossed in a chess game. The board was quite elegant for that time period. It looked like it had been made from small squares of white and blue marble and it sat on a small table in Adam's study just the right size to be left on display. The pieces were already disarranged when they entered the room, letting her know this was an ongoing game. And although they had continued to play for over an hour now, there were still several major pieces to be had.

"Not much you can do now that I have both your castles *and* both your bishops," Park said, glancing at JoAnn with a cocky grin, obviously believing his last move quite clever. He leaned back in his chair and stretched his right leg so he could rub Shadow behind the left ear with the toe of his boot while he waited for Adam to make the next move. To show appreciation, Shadow opened his mouth and dangled his long pink tongue.

"I still have my queen and both my knights," Adam commented, then frowned while he studied his new choices. His blue eyes caught the lamplight as he gazed from piece to piece. "This could take a while. Why don't you pour us a couple of brandies?"

"Can't," Park remarked all the while studying him while he studied the board. "Remember I'm not supposed to exert myself and the brandy is all the way across the room. Besides, you'll need to keep all your faculties about you if you plan to get out of that predicament." He indicated the board with a forward thrust of his chin then glanced at JoAnn and offered her a friendly wink as if wanting her to feel a part of the game.

To JoAnn, it seemed extremely odd to be sitting in a lamp-lighted room filled with nineteenth-century furniture watching these two men engrossed in a game of chess, especially dressed like they were. Even after having been there a day, she still had a hard time establishing in her mind just what to think about the very strange situation in which she so suddenly found herself.

It was easy enough to understand that the events that happened around her were as real as they could be to these people, yet to her those same events were not all that real. They were not a part of *her* world — not a part of *her* time. It was like being in an accurately portrayed movie and yet trying not to participate with the other actors for fear of causing a dramatic change in the ending.

She had done what to her seemed the impossible. She had traveled back in time, yet she could be there only as an observer. She had no right to be anything but, no right to intrude in any way. Even so, just knowing she was there, experiencing life as it was in 1889, caused a bewildering yet extremely heady sensation to settle over her. It felt almost like having lost all rationality but at the same time being completely conscious of the fact.

"Ah-ha!" Adam said, startling her from her musings. His smile widened to display a fine set of curved dimples when he reached forward to move his knight in the place of one of Park's pawns. "Check!"

JoAnn and Park both looked at the board, surprised.

"Go ahead, Father. All you can really do is move your king forward a space," he announced, his blue eyes sparkling with triumph. "But even if you do that, he's a dead man."

Park crossed his arms and studied the board a minute more before grunting his defeat. "The only reason you won is because it's been very hard for me to concentrate. I'm still not feeling well, you know."

"Not feeling well?" Adam scoffed. "I thought you told me the swelling at the back of your head had finally gone down and that your headache was nearly gone."

"Oh, but I'm still feeling awfully weak," he countered, then offered a few shallow coughs for proof.

"If you're still feeling so weak, then why did you stay downstairs most of the afternoon visiting with your friends and why did you insist on coming in here to play chess with me instead of heading on back to bed after you finished eating?"

"Because I knew if I didn't come with you, you would end up burying your head in those blasted bank reports again. It isn't healthy for a young man to spend so much time bent over a desk reading and updating reports. I wish now I'd told Richard to take those fool reports right back to Stephen Saine's desk where they belong. He and your namesake cousin are the ones who have to make all the final decisions. Besides, you can't possibly keep a close watch over me like you promised Lowman *and* spend so much of your time nosing through all that paperwork."

"Are you feeling neglected?" Adam looked at his father with obvious skepticism. "But then how could you possibly feel in any way neglected when you have a beautiful young woman like JoAnn to keep you company."

"It's not that *I'm* feeling all that neglected," he admitted, then gestured toward JoAnn. "It's just that I didn't want you continue being rude by neglecting our guest, and I knew that if I didn't suggest we all retire together, you'd close yourself off in here and spend the next several hours reading through more of those confounded reports."

"That's because I promised Richard I'd have Cyrus drop my findings by his house on the way to school so he can then take them with him to the bank tomorrow morning."

"And will the world come to an end if you don't do that?" Park wanted to know, wishing his son would finally place his priorities in a more logical order. Hard work was admirable to a point, but when a man fashioned his whole life around his work, it went well beyond being admirable. It became obsessive.

"Well, no, I'm sure the world wouldn't come to an end, but—"

"Then hush up and set the board again," Park said, as if lecturing a small child. "I think JoAnn deserves the chance to show us what she knows about chess."

JoAnn's eyes widened with alarm. Having seen the determined way these two played, she wanted no part of it. She immediately sat forward in the brocaded chair and held her hands out to indicate an early surrender. "I told you. I haven't played chess in years."

The fact that she'd played chess at all had surprised Adam. Most women avoided any game that required that much concentration. "Then perhaps you'd rather take on the loser," he suggested, giving his father a quick, knowing glance, already aware what he planned to do next. Just as soon as his game with JoAnn had gotten underway, his father would have suddenly decided he was tired and would have left them to finish the game alone. "My father may be cagey, but he *can* be outsmarted."

"I'd rather sit here and watch you two play another game," she said, which was true. She loved to watch Adam's facial expressions while he contemplated his moves and she loved to hear Park gloat and cackle whenever he made a particularly clever kill.

"And I'd like to oblige you," Park said, already leaning forward in his chair. "But Adam's right. I do need my rest."

Adam blinked, trying to remember when he had said

157

such a thing. "Then perhaps it is better that we all retire for the evening. It is getting late."

JoAnn glanced at the clock. It was only eight-thirty. What time did these people go to bed?

"No, no, don't feel you two have to go to bed just because I plan to," Park insisted. He waved off Adam's assistance then pushed himself to his feet. "I'd hate to think that just because I started feeling a little tired I'd spoiled the evening for you two." He then met Adam's gaze. "Besides, you promised to go out to the stable and have another look at Traveler's leg before bed and since JoAnn knows so much more about the animal's injuries than you do, I think she should go along with you."

Alone? JoAnn wondered and shifted nervously in her chair only to be reminded of the cumbersome bustle that had prevented her from sitting comfortably all evening. For some reason, the thought of being alone with Adam in a stable at night made her stomach muscles tighten and her pulse rate accelerate considerably. It did not take much in the way of perception to realize that these sudden bodily reactions of hers were very much the result of the strong physical attraction she felt toward Adam.

Although she knew she shouldn't be attracted to him at all, she was. She was from another time — another world. She should not allow the sort of feelings to develop that might tempt her to try to come between him and Constance Seguin. It was not her right, especially after Constance had made her place in his life so perfectly clear. "Oh, but George and I examined the leg again this morning just before lunch. That cut is coming along quite nicely."

"Still, I'd feel better about it if you'd take one more look at it before bed tonight. That horse is special to me."

Aware there was no graceful way to get out of cooperating, and feeling it was the least she could do to repay his kindnesses, she finally relented. "I guess it wouldn't hurt

158

to have another look. Besides, the more often that bandage is changed and that wound cleansed the better."

Having agreed to go, she waited in the study while Adam walked with his father upstairs and helped him into bed. Too restless to sit any longer, she stood and paced about Adam's study. Eager to distract herself from what was about to happen and how it had clearly affected her pulse rate, she glanced at the titles of some of the books in the room. Not having thought of Adam as being a man who might enjoy poetry, she was surprised to see so many slender volumes of verse scattered among the other books, most of which dealt with more serious topics such as chemistry, finance, animal husbandry, geology, and cooking.

Curiously, she slipped a volume of Keats's work from the shelf and opened it. There on the flyleaf was Adam's name and the date the book was purchased.

"Are you an avid reader?" Adam asked, having returned while she stood near the shelf slowly thumbing through the pages.

"Not as avid as I should be," she admitted and turned to face him. Another wave of awareness washed over her when she saw how handsome he looked in the muted light. There was something to be said for the lack of electricity. "With all the different medical journals I have to keep tabs with, I rarely find time to read for pleasure anymore." And that was a shame.

"Do you like Keats?" he asked after he had stepped forward to see which book she'd selected.

"I did in college, but to tell you the truth, I haven't read much of his work since." She glanced at the open book then up into Adam's strong face and felt another strong, fluttering sensation when she noticed how close he stood. "May I take this book upstairs and read it tonight?" Having slept fifteen hours the night before, she knew it would be awhile before she fell asleep.

"You may have the book," Adam responded, hoping that might bring forth a smile. He loved it when she smiled.

"Oh, but I can't take your book," she insisted and fought an odd desire to blush when she tried to pull her gaze away from his but found it impossible to do. There was just something about the way he looked at her that prevented her from glancing away, something about him that made her want to search his eyes more deeply. If only she could be fortunate enough to meet someone like him in her own time. She had not felt this physically drawn to any man since that day she first met Thomas Rourke.

"I insist," he said, unaware her thoughts had drifted. "Take the book with you when you leave next week. It will give you something special to remember us by." Suddenly it was very important to him that she remember them, and that she remember them fondly. He dropped his gaze from her huge, almond-shaped eyes to her gently curved mouth and fought a very real, very sudden desire to take her in his arms and kiss her soundly.

Aware how very close he was to doing just that and remembering his vow not to become seriously involved with any woman ever again, he quickly turned away. When he spoke again, his tone was suddenly abrupt. "But for now, you can set that book on the table just outside the door. That way you won't forget to take it upstairs with you when we return from the stable."

Feeling unaccountably shaken by the sudden abruptness in his voice, JoAnn hurried to obey. She wondered what she had done to upset him as she set the book on a small table in the hallway then followed him out onto the back porch. There he paused just long enough to light a small lantern.

While she followed in the dim island of light the lantern provided, she tried to think of something to say that might break the uncomfortable silence. When nothing

160

else occurred, she decided to fall back on that old staple, the weather.

"It certainly did turn cool tonight," she said, and since she had finally become accustomed to walking in the dress without having to lift her skirts, she crossed her arms over her chest to emphasize the point she'd just made. "I guess it's because of that rain shower we had just after sunset."

"I'm sorry. I didn't realize. Would you like my coat?" he asked, already reaching for his sleeves.

"Oh, no. I'm not uncomfortable. Truth is I find the cooler temperature a little invigorating. It was so hot earlier when I took my walk, I found it hard to believe it's only March."

"And how was your walk?" he asked, wondering why she had insisted on taking off like that in the heat of the afternoon.

"Very pleasant. I enjoy being out in the country, listening to the different birds call to one another and the wind rustle through the trees. It is so peaceful here."

He looked at her questioningly, never breaking stride while they continued toward the stable. "But I thought you hated the quiet. I thought all this peacefulness made you feel out of place."

"In a way it does," she said, recalling the forgotten conversation with a sudden leap of her senses. "But you were right. A person gets used to it after a while and eventually even starts to enjoy it."

"Then you are glad you decided to stay?"

"Yes, I am," she answered honestly. "To be truthful, I needed this." She glanced again at her peaceful surroundings, at the stars and half moon peeking through the night clouds overhead, then at the soft shadows beneath the towering trees that lined the far side of the sloping fields, and finally off to the south at the faint amber glow of Cambria Iron several miles away. "I needed the distraction. My friend, Jean, was right. I had allowed myself to become too wrapped up in my grief. I was practically wallowing in my own misery."

Adam glanced at her, having noticed the pained catch in her voice. "When did your parents die?"

"Two weeks ago." She could have told him the exact date and hour for both of them, but knew that would only confuse him. How could someone have just died yet the death date be over a hundred years into the future? She would then have to tell him everything that had happened, and he was having a hard enough time accepting the simple fact she was a licensed doctor. If she tried to convince him that she had come from another time, he would think her completely addled and in turn would discount everything else she ever told him. *Or* he would decide she was an impossible liar which would cause her to lose whatever trust he might have in her. After all, what could be more absurd?

She tried not to think about his reaction. "But at times it feels like it all happened just yesterday."

Adam nodded. That explained why she had cried herself to sleep the night before. She had had just enough time to get over the initial shock of their deaths and was starting to feel the real loss. "If you don't mind me asking, how did they die?"

Remembering what she had told Doris, she shook her head to indicate she didn't mind but did not return his gaze after that. Instead, she stared again into the darkness beyond.

"They died together within hours after a terrible carriage accident," she said in an amazingly calm voice. For the first time since their deaths, she was able to talk about them without an overwhelming pain gripping her throat. She decided the unemotional response was because she had verbally changed their mode of travel from an automobile to a carriage. That one change had made it seem

162

like she was talking about someone else and because of that, the usual tears did not form.

It felt oddly soothing to be able to talk about them without all that misery cutting her short. "I was so upset by their deaths, I suddenly found myself unable to do my work. I could no longer make simple decisions. That's why I finally asked for some time off. I was so distraught, I could not concentrate on what I was doing. I had started to make a lot of senseless mistakes, which is definitely not good when you are a doctor trying to save lives."

Again Adam found himself actually believing her, at least the part about being a doctor—though it was still hard for him to think of a woman that beautiful and that lacking for details as being a licensed anything. The woman had a hard enough time remembering what year it was. Then it dawned on him that perhaps her inability to retain common details had to do with the fact she was still mourning her parents' deaths, which meant her memory problems were temporary. Knowing how hard it had been for him to concentrate on anything shortly after Dorothy died, he nodded with this new understanding. "The death of a loved one can affect you that way."

Adam's tone had been so tender and so sincere it brought JoAnn's gaze to his. "That's right. You lost a wife and a child. Doris told me about it."

Now it was Adam's turn to stare off into the distance while he slowed his pace but continued to walk. "That was a long time ago."

Clearly, he did not want to talk about their deaths.

"And yet you've managed to get on with your life remarkably well. I just hope I can do the same." But then *he* was in no way responsible for his loved ones' deaths and therefore did not have to struggle with the guilt she felt.

"We all cope in our own way." He continued to stare off toward the stable. "I coped by burying myself in my work."

163

"Which I understand you still do," she said, unaware that made it sound like she and Doris had discussed him at some length.

"I find time for some pleasures," he admitted, then looked at her again. "Though maybe not as often as I should."

The vulnerable look on his face caused a deep, dull ache to spill from her heart. Suddenly, Adam seemed more human and less like someone who existed only in the past. It was as if he had just become more real to her, making this whole strange situation all the more genuine. "At least you have Constance to help take your mind off matters. At the moment, I don't happen to have anyone special in my life." And hadn't in quite some time.

For some reason Adam wanted JoAnn to understand his relationship with Constance. By design, theirs was not a serious relationship. There were no commitments. "Yes, I do have Constance to help take my mind off my problems. I also have George, who proves to be a constant and welcomed distraction whenever I'm here. But keep in mind, they are both just friends. Nothing more."

"Constance is a friend who obviously thinks very highly of you," JoAnn put in, knowing that if Constance had been there to hear him proclaim that she was just a friend and that he had just put her on the same level as an eleven-year-old boy, she would be furious. Clearly, the woman thought of herself as being more than a common friend—*much* more.

While wondering what Constance's response would have been had she been there to hear it all, JoAnn paused to one side and allowed Adam to open the stable door. "She really is quite taken with you and you must admit, she is very lovely." For some reason those words left a bitter taste in JoAnn's mouth.

"That's true, but she's so young. At times it is hard for us to find topics of mutual interest worth discussing. As

164

you have seen, she can behave very childishly at times."

JoAnn blinked, aware Constance appeared to be about her same age. "And how old are you?"

"Thirty-five."

"Which should make her only a few years younger than you," she commented and wondered if he thought her young and childish, too.

"Hardly. She's only twenty-five."

Twenty-five? Why that woman looked all of thirty-four. "Are you sure?" Either Constance had lied about her age to impress Adam or the women aged very rapidly in the nineteenth century, which might explain why Park had been so surprised to hear her age.

"Pretty sure. Our family has known her since she was in her teens, back when she used to come here to visit in the summer." Rather than continue discussing Constance when he would rather learn more about JoAnn, Adam redirected the conversation. "What do you do for relaxation?"

Blinking at such an abrupt change of topic, JoAnn paused to think. There really hadn't been much time in her life for relaxation during the past few years. "Sleep I guess."

That and watch inane comedy shows on television or go to the movies with Jean and pig out on popcorn and peanut-butter M&Ms; but she couldn't very well mention either of those. Not and come across sounding like anything but a first-class nut.

"Don't you ever attend a ball or go to the theater?"

"I've been to the theater," she admitted, remembering the Broadway plays she and Tom had seen together the summer before she had found out the sordid truth about him. "But I can't say that I've ever been to a ball." Not even to one of the many charity balls the hospital had held through the years.

Adam studied her curiously while she stepped quietly

into the darkness. Why would such a beautiful woman have never been to a ball? "Don't you like to dance?"

"Oh, I love to dance," she admitted, then knowing they were about to enter into a very confusing conversation because what she liked to dance to was classic rock, she quickly returned the focus of their conversation to him — an art at which she had become *very* adept. "What about you? Do you attend many balls?"

"Some," he admitted, then lifted the lantern higher and nodded toward Traveler's stall to indicate she should go first. "But not all that many."

He watched her sleek, graceful movements while she walked just ahead of him and wondered what it would be like to take her into his arms and hold her close while he guided her gently across the dance floor. He remembered the spring cotillion was only a few weeks away, but then in the same instance reminded himself that she would have returned to Pittsburgh by then. It would do no good for him to fantasize like that about a woman who planned to be there for only a few days — unless of course he could convince her to stay longer. The thought of doing just that caused a floodtide of hope to wash over him.

JoAnn waited until Adam had opened the stall before stepping inside and urging the horse to move to one side. As soon as she had enough room, she knelt beside the injured leg and started to unwrap the bandage she had applied that morning. She frowned when she noticed how much blood had soaked through.

"Looks like he reinjured his leg somehow," she said, employing her usual doctor's tone. "Bring me fresh bandages. And bring the carbolic acid. I'll want to rinse that wound again." When he turned away to do just that, she quickly added, "But leave the lantern here. I have to be able to see."

"You certainly seem accustomed to giving lots of orders," he commented while he set the lantern on a nearby

166

stool then hurried to comply. "I noticed that yesterday."

"I guess that comes from working in the emergency room," she admitted, aware now of how abrupt she had sounded. "I'm used to having a nurse beside me to supply everything I need and whenever we have a seriously injured patient to care for I generally don't take the time to say please. Sorry if I offended you."

"It's not that you offended me. It's just that I'm not used to having a woman order me around like that," he admitted, having hurried back with the supplies she had requested. Being a man of prestige and considerable wealth, he was far more used to having beautiful women bend in whatever way suited him.

JoAnn reminded herself that Adam was from another time and did nothing to come to her own defense, although she would truly love to give someone like Jane Fonda a clear shot at this guy.

"I'll see if I can curb my tendencies to be so demanding," she promised, aware she would gain nothing by trying to make a power play out of this. "At least while I'm still here."

That seemed to satisfy him and for the next several minutes their conversation focused on the horse's injury then on the accident itself. It was not until she had finished the new dressing and had disposed of the old one that Adam again brought the subject of their conversation back to her.

"There's something about you I don't quite understand." He tried to sound casual in his approach though it was a question that had bothered him most of the afternoon.

"And what is that?" she asked, thinking there should be plenty about her he did not understand considering the fact they were from two diversely different centuries. She stood, then brushed the loose stalks of hay and remnants of dirt from her skirts while she waited to hear what puzzled him.

"Why it is that a woman as beautiful as you are has never married," he said, also rising.

JoAnn stared at him, too startled by the fact he had again the same as declared her to be beautiful to realize he had moved closer. "I guess because I'm too used to giving orders," she replied offhandedly. "Most men can't handle it."

"Handle it? What do you mean by they can't handle it?" He was not sure why, but he felt she purposely avoided telling him the truth. He had sensed a certain ambiguity all evening. He felt like she might be trying to hide something from her past, something she did not want *any* of them to know. And it bothered him that she did not trust him with her secrets.

"Truth is, the right man never asked *me,*" she finally answered, aware he was not one to be sidetracked by any weak attempts at humor.

Adam thought about that. "The right man never asked, or there never *was* a right man *to* ask?"

"The right man never asked," she answered, wondering how they had ever gotten onto such a touchy topic. "Or at least he never asked me. Seems there was someone else in his life he liked better. Someone with a lot more money and a lot more to offer him careerwise. Her father had a flourishing medical practice in need of a bright, young doctor, which he was soon to be."

"I see," he responded, amazed at her sudden openness. "And did he eventually marry this other woman?"

"They're now married with two kids," she declared with a slight shrug as if to indicate she no longer cared.

Adam frowned, wondering what young goats had to do with this. "The man is clearly a fool."

JoAnn felt a slow warmth penetrate her cheeks. Aware

168

their conversation had become far too serious and in such a short time, she tried to lighten the mood.

"I agree."

Adam reached out as if planning to touch her cheek as he had earlier but then thought better of it. Instead, he let his hand drop to his side and continued to study her face in the muted light. "I guess we'd better go on back to the house."

"I guess so," she agreed, wondering why the sudden suggestion to return to the house should disappoint her. After all, they had finished what they had come to do. Traveler had a fresh bandage. "It's been a long day."

And one she would not soon forget.

While she wiped her hands on a clean, damp towel, they headed toward the front of the stable where a brisk evening wind had pulled the door closed. Without thinking, she ordered, "Get the door." Then remembering her promise to try not to be so demanding, she smiled sweetly and added the word that would make it more of a request than a demand. "Please."

His wide, dimpled smile made that one word well worth the effort as he stepped forward to push against the door. When she again preceded him into the darkness, her heart pummeled wildly at the exciting thought of what it would be like to find a man like Adam back in her own time.

Chapter Eight

By Monday morning, JoAnn was quite enthralled with the people she had met and intrigued with the hardworking yet largely unpressured life-style in the year 1889. When compared to all the heartache and strife she had left behind, she was no longer as eager to return to her own time period as she had been. Truth was she now dreaded it. Dreaded returning to her parents' empty house where the worst kind of misery and loneliness awaited her. Dreaded having to audit her mother's records to see what had and hadn't been paid. But most of all she dreaded having to sift through their personal belongings so she could decide what to do with them.

For now, she would rather stay right where she was, hidden away in a largely uncomplicated world filled with kind, interesting people — far removed from the pain and turbulence she'd left behind.

It had been surprisingly pleasant to spend the past five days in such surrealistic surroundings while getting to know the friendly, uncomplicated people who lived there. Everyone, with the exception of one Constance Seguin, had willingly welcomed her as one of them, though some still doubted her claim to be a doctor.

Still she knew the time to return home was quickly approaching. The telegram from the bank in Pittsburgh that would prove her to be a fraud could arrive as early as that very afternoon. Cyrus had been told he would ride down into Johnstown to check for any return messages just as soon as he had returned from school. But until that telegram did arrive and finally reveal that she had openly lied to them, JoAnn would continue to enjoy what time she had left in this fascinating year 1889. As a guest or an observer. Nothing more.

Having conceded that she and Adam were destined by fate never to be anything more than casual friends — knowing any relationship that might develop between them would by necessity be short lived — JoAnn had thus far managed to keep any and all evidence of her rising attraction toward him closely guarded. Though she had found no way to stop her traitorous heart from revving or her palms from sweating whenever he came near, she had until now been able to keep such extreme physical reactions carefully hidden from him and vowed to continue to do so.

It would be far easier to live with the unrequited desire she felt toward Adam than chance actually falling for him, then having to leave him behind when she had to go. If she allowed herself to fall in love with him, she would end up deeply heartbroken again and feeling more alone than ever. She had already suffered enough heartache in her life.

Everyone whom JoAnn had ever allowed herself to love had been taken from her and the dark, aching voids caused by those losses were at times too painful to bear. She had already lost her first love, Thomas Rourke, all four grandparents, and both parents; she did not need another such tragedy emptying her life. She had strongly resolved to come away from her adventure unscathed, and had thus far managed to remain little more than an interested bystander, a mere guest in Adam's home.

But Adam's resolve, which could be every bit as strong as JoAnn's, had taken off in an entirely different direction. After coming to terms with the startling realization that JoAnn Griffin had rekindled emotions within him that he

171

had thought long since dead, he had decided to do whatever was necessary to keep her there.

Despite the fact she continued to keep secrets from him, he still desired her. Her peculiar reactions to some of his questions, or perhaps it was the artful way she managed to change the subject whenever he tried to find out something new about her, let him know something was wrong. But he could not decide if her evasive behavior meant she was running from something or perhaps hiding from someone — or if it was simply because she was an extremely private person.

But whatever caused her to behave so secretively, it was not enough to diminish his desire for her. Even her obvious confusion about certain facts and her bossy nature — which still emerged periodically — did nothing to deter his craving for her, though the bossiness did tend to make him want to grab her by the throat and throttle her from time to time.

Truth was, Adam wanted the beautiful, intriguing JoAnn Griffin as much if not more than he had ever wanted any woman he had ever met; but knew he would need more than the few days she had promised him to put that point across to her. He had to find some way to keep her there. He refused to let her slip out of his life as easily as she had slipped into it — not without first having gotten to know her better.

"Looks like another bad storm brewing off to the northwest," he commented, pointing off toward a distant patch of dark gray clouds just a few seconds after he and JoAnn had stepped out onto the back porch. Although it was only three o'clock and normally he would still be in his study taking care of the paperwork Cambria Iron had sent earlier, he had found himself unable to concentrate and had decided a short break was in order. "I know I promised to send Cyrus into Johnstown this afternoon right after he returned from school to see if there was a response yet to your telegram; but it looks like I won't be able to do that until

172

tomorrow. I'll need his help herding the horses into the stable and keeping them there until this storm blows over. Judging by the shape and density of those clouds, we could be in for some hail."

"Of course," JoAnn said, delighted that the approaching storm was about to provide her an extra day to enjoy her special paradise. "Your horses must come first."

Adam stepped off the porch and headed toward the stable. A brisk wind tugged at his hair, billowing it away from his face, when he glanced back over his shoulder. "I'll probably find Cyrus either in the barn or the stable, but I think George is still in the house. Would you go back in and tell him I'll need his help, too?"

Aware the boys had been home only a few minutes, barely long enough to have put their books away and change out of their school shirts, JoAnn hurried back inside to locate George. As expected, she found him in the kitchen trying to coerce his mother into letting him have a third cookie with his afternoon glass of milk. If one thing could be said about George: he loved to eat.

"George, Mister Adam needs you outside. There's a storm coming and he wants to get the horses into the stable as quickly as possible." She wondered then why the concern was just for the horses. There were cattle out there, too.

"But the sun's shining," George responded, more of a statement than a complaint when he glanced up from his cookies. He then looked out the window to make sure.

"The clouds are still a few miles off; but you know how quickly these March storms can move in," she said, remembering the sudden storm that had brought her there. One minute, there had been a few light clouds drifting lightly overhead and the next, a roiling mass of black thunderclouds. "These March storms can be on top of you before you know it."

"That's a fact," he admitted. "And those horses do spook awful easy. " He grabbed what was left of his two cookies

173

and headed toward the door. "Better get them inside before they break out of the fence again and end up scattered all over the mountain," he stated, walking with far more importance than the task really warranted. "Horses can be so dumb about storms. At least cows have enough sense to stand under the trees where they're less likely to be rained on."

Wanting to help, JoAnn hurried out of the house behind him and was surprised to see how much force the wind had gathered in the few minutes she had been inside. Holding her skirts down as best she could, she caught up with George. The two were halfway across the yard when Adam emerged from the stable and ordered her back into the house.

"But I want to help." She had to shout at top volume to be heard above the roar created by the wind.

"You'll just be in the way," he yelled, then frowned to show his annoyance. At that moment, the clouds blocked out the sun and suddenly it felt as if dusk had fallen. "Go back in the house and help Doris. You'll be of better help there."

JoAnn's first inclination was to argue. She wanted him to know that she could, too, be of some help; but as difficult as it had become to keep her skirts from catching the wind and billowing up into her face, she eventually agreed to return to the house. She wouldn't be of much help to anyone if she spent the entire time struggling to keep her dress down and her dignity intact.

Instead of helping Adam with the livestock as she had wanted, she returned to the house and aided Doris by closing and latching all the windows. While she hurried from room to room doing just that, Doris ran outside to shoo the chickens into the henhouse and latch the two dozen little doors along either side then brought in the linen she had left on the clothesline.

"Why God refused to give those chickens any brains is

beyond me," Doris muttered as she burst into the house, her red hair askew from the brisk force of the wind and her arms filled with wadded bed sheets.

Seconds after she had shouldered the back door closed and headed for the table where she planned to deposit the sheets, a flash of blue light flared through the windows followed by a loud clap of thunder that literally shook the house. Then, as if the racket had been what summoned the storm's wrath, the sky opened up and drenched the countryside with a heavy torrent.

Unable to see the barn or the stable from the kitchen windows, JoAnn went into George's bedroom at the very back of the house and stared at the slanted downpour through the windows. But the sky had become so dark and the rain fell in such thick, steady sheets, she couldn't see anything very clearly. Even when the sporadic flashes of lightning illuminated the yard, she could barely make out the shapes of the buildings and had no hope of identifying anything smaller. There was no way to know if Adam and the boys had been able to get the horses into the stable or whether they had fallen to some unseen danger of the storm.

Still she continued her vigil and after about fifteen minutes of steady rain and intermittent bouts of lightning and thunder, she noticed someone headed toward the house. Her heart jumped with immediate fear when another flash of lightning pierced the darkness and she saw that it was Adam. And he was carrying George. With a hunched Cyrus only a few steps behind.

Fearing the worst, she hurried back through the kitchen, toward the hallway that led to the back door. She heard two sets of heavy footsteps on the planked floor outside just seconds before the porch door banged open, filling the back hallway with a sudden blast of cold air. When she swung through the hall door and saw Adam's worried expression then noticed the patches of blood spreading across his rain-

175

soaked shirt, she went into immediate action.

"What happened?" she asked as she rushed forward to help. Because of the pained expression on George's face and the way he was hunched forward with his arm pressed to his waist, she felt certain the boy had injured either a hand, an arm, or his stomach. She glanced at the floor to see if there was blood there, relieved to see only puddles of water thus far. She felt it safe to assume no artery was involved.

"George tore the back of his hand on a piece of metal," Adam said, his face twisted with concern. When he spotted Doris standing in a nearby doorway with her hand over her mouth and her face as white as a sheet, his expression became apologetic as if he somehow blamed himself. "I couldn't make it stop bleeding," he said, then turned to glance at Cyrus. "Go upstairs and get my father."

"That's not necessary," JoAnn insisted, already reaching for George's hand which he still held protected against his body. She might not be the most competent doctor ever to grace this earth, but she could handle a simple emergency like this.

Cyrus looked to Adam questioningly while JoAnn quickly examined the wound.

Unaware of the uncertain glances, JoAnn moved the hand into better light. Beneath the blood, there was a two-inch gash across the back of his wet hand, just above his knuckles.

"Put him on the dining-room table," she commanded, wanting George high enough so she could work without stooping, then stepped back to allow Adam room to do as she had ordered.

Shaken from the sight of that much blood coming from such a small area, Adam hurried down the hall with Doris and Cyrus both right behind him. He waited for JoAnn to clear the table then placed the boy directly beneath the chandelier.

Because Cyrus was dripping water onto the small carpet centered beneath the table, he stood off to one side while Adam and Doris moved closer, eager to keep a reassuring hand on George's small shoulders.

"Doris, I'll need plenty of bandages, carbolic acid, and half a dozen or more clean cloths. I have to stop the bleeding," she said in a sharp, demanding tone, knowing Doris was the most logical choice to take on the duties of her nurse. While waiting for her to return with the items she needed, JoAnn noticed George's frightened expression and lowered her voice to a much softer tone, all the while holding the hand above the level of his heart. "You sure are a brave young man. I'd be half out of my mind if I cut myself like that."

George offered a tentative smile and gestured toward the injured hand without actually taking his gaze off of JoAnn. "I've been hurt a lot worse than that."

"That's true," Adam said, pushing the boy's wet hair away from his face while trying not to look too concerned. "This is the most accident-prone young man I've ever known. Always injuring himself somehow. Isn't that right, Cyrus?"

Cyrus shifted his weight from one leg to the other. "Shouldn't I go get your father?"

"Don't need his father," George snapped with an angry glare. "Got a good enough doctor right here."

JoAnn looked at the boy with surprise and as soon as Doris had returned with the needed items, she did what she could to merit his confidence. While he lay flat on the table with his eyes pressed closed and his face turned toward Adam, she flooded the wound with the carbolic acid then slowed the bleeding by applying pressure with a folded cloth.

When certain the bleeding had stopped, she set the stained cloth aside and bent forward again to have a closer look. While examining the jagged tear, she wondered if there was such a thing as a tetanus shot yet then realized that if the boy was truly accident prone and if there was such a thing, he would have already had such a shot several times over.

"You have a pretty bad gash there, but I don't think it is quite deep enough to warrant stitches. All it really needs are a few little butterflies and a patch of gauze over it." She glanced first at Adam then at Doris. "Do you have any butterflies?"

Suddenly even George looked doubtful. "What do you need butterflies for?"

"Next she'll be asking for snake oil and bat wings," Cyrus muttered with narrowed eyes as if she had just proved something to him.

"Not butterflies like those that fly around in the garden," she explained, aware of the children's misconception. "The butterflies I'm talking about are tiny adhesive strips used to close small wounds. Some people call them Steri-strips." Again she glanced at Adam. "Do you have anything like that?"

When Adam then looked at her as if a few of her circuits might have shorted, she realized the mistake. Obviously, there was no such thing in 1889. Frowning, she thought of the emergency medical kit in the trunk of her car where there was a whole box of butterfly closures, but realized they would be of little help to her now. She wasn't about to go running off with no explanations in the middle of a thunderstorm just to get her medical kit. Not when the cut had turned out to be so minor.

Quickly, she amended her request. "I'll settle for a few clean bandages and a sewing basket." With no Steri-strips to pull the skin together, she would have to take a couple of stitches after all. Then she would need to bind the hand well enough so he wouldn't be tempted to flex it for the next few days.

Adam turned to Cyrus, who looked as if he still held major doubts concerning JoAnn's sanity. "Go upstairs and ask Father what he did with his medical bag. She'll probably find what she needs in there."

When Cyrus returned minutes later, not only did he have Park's medical bag, he had Park as well.

"I understand we've had a little accident," Park commented while he came across the room to see what had been done thus far. It was evident by his dazed expression, he had slept through the worst part of the storm. He blinked hard while bending over JoAnn's shoulder. "That's a nasty cut you got there, young man."

George nodded that he agreed.

"Good thing Doctor Griffin was here to take such quick care of you," he said, already setting the leather bag on the table beside the boy. He promptly unbuckled the top and reached inside.

Thinking Park was about to take over, JoAnn stepped to one side and was surprised when he instead handed her a small folded cloth that held a large, curved needle. "I also have some surgical thread in here somewhere." He then produced another cloth that held a tiny card with heavy black thread wrapped around it.

While JoAnn worked to hook the coarse thread into the needle, Park continued rummaging through his valise. Seconds later, he came out with a small dark-green vial. Producing a tiny piece of folded muslin from a side pocket, he dampened it with the contents of the vial then handed the wet cloth to JoAnn.

When she glanced at the vial and noticed the words *Erythroxylon Coca,* she realized what she was supposed to do and quickly dabbed the liquid cocaine onto the wound to deaden the damaged area. She then drenched the needle with turpentine Park had handed her and reached for the injured hand.

When George's body stiffened at the sight of the needle, Adam knelt beside the table so he could be closer to eye

179

level with the frightened boy. His heart went out to his young friend, who was just one year older than what his own son would have been had he lived, which was one reason why Adam was so fond of him. It was also why he was so proud that George was the bright, inquisitive young man that he was, so quick to ask questions and just as quick to grasp ideas. "Don't look so frightened. This will all be over in a couple of minutes."

"That's true," JoAnn put in, admiring Adam's easy show of compassion. "And keep in mind that this is something I've done thousands of times." Though not with a needle quite so large or with thread quite that coarse. "I'll be through in no time."

In an effort to help take her son's mind off his hand, Doris stepped forward and dabbed at his damp face and neck with a small, dry towel.

"Can you believe the veather ve have had lately?" she asked of no one in particular. "I can't remember ever having had such a vet spring."

"Isn't that the gospel truth," Park injected, as eager as everyone else to distract the boy. "I'll bet we've already had twice the rain we normally have this time of year. Have you seen the rivers lately?"

"Spied the Little Conemaugh just last veek. Like an angry monster it vas. And if it keeps raining much longer, Johnstown is in for the devil's own. That dam is sure to break this time," Doris said with a grim shake of her head. "You mark my vords."

JoAnn had just taken her second stitch, but had yet to make a knot when the significance of Doris's words sank in. Unable to focus on anything else, she turned to stare at her with speechless horror, only vaguely aware Cyrus had anything to say.

"Momma, you've been telling that tale for as long as I can remember," Cyrus complained, clearly not impressed by his mother's forewarnings. "You say that same thing

180

every year about this time."

"I'm not the only one who thinks that vay," she said, in ready defense of herself. "There are others just like me. Vhy just last veek vhile I vas in town to do the marketing, I heard there is a petition started that vill force those rich men at the hunting and fishing club to have that dam repaired. And I heard hundreds of names have already been put to it. So I am not the only one who vorries about that lake."

JoAnn felt her insides coil into a painful knot, so stunned by the impact of what she had just heard, she had yet to move.

"JoAnn?" Adam asked, wondering why she had not completed the last stitch. "You look pale. What's wrong?"

"It's Eighteen eighty-nine," she said in a frightened voice, as if that alone should explain it.

Adam looked at her strangely, his eyebrows drawn with careful regard. "I thought we had already established that fact. Remember?"

"No, I mean it is *Eighteen eighty-nine!*" She wondered why she had not made the connection before then. She had known about the terrible flood of 1889 most of her life.

Truly perplexed by her odd behavior, Adam ran his fingers through his wet hair. "Why is it you can never seem to remember what year it is?"

JoAnn looked at him for a long moment, trying to figure out why he wasn't more concerned about the year, then it dawned on her. He couldn't possibly know. What was history to her was still a part of the future for him.

"Here let me finish that for you," Park said, stepping forward and taking the needle from her hand. He glanced at Adam with obvious concern. "Maybe she should sit down."

Adam agreed and moved to help her into a nearby chair but JoAnn waved him away when she realized what a spectacle she had just made of herself. She needed to get a grip before they all decided she'd lost what was left of her mind.

181

Even George now looked at her as if she had suddenl̶y̶
grown a third arm.

"No, I'm fine," she said, but without the conviction sh̶e̶
had hoped. Now that her memory had been jogged, sh̶e̶
could not put the horrifying thought out of her mind.

Doris was right. Eighteen eighty-nine was indeed th̶e̶
year that three miles of water finally pushed through th̶e̶
large earthen dam that had held the large pleasure lake i̶n̶
place for so many years. The sudden break would sen̶d̶
twenty million tons of water crashing down the Littl̶e̶
Conemaugh Valley in one, huge murderous mass. O̶n̶
May 31, 1889, over two thousand people were drowned be̶-̶
neath the crushing weight of that forty and sometimes sev-
enty-foot mountain of rolling water, or else were burned t̶o̶
death while trapped in the huge fire that followed. How̶
could she have forgotten the date? Only a few years ago sh̶e̶
and her parents had attended a special centennial remembrance honoring all those who had died. How could sh̶e̶
ever have forgotten something as horrible as that?

"Are you sure you don't want to sit down?" Adam aske̶d̶
and gripped her by her shoulders as if afraid she was abou̶t̶
to faint.

Aware Park had taken over the repair of George's hand̶
and needing a moment to collect her suddenly jumble̶d̶
thoughts, she looked to Adam gratefully. "Perhaps I shoul̶d̶
go up to my room and lie down. I do feel a little light-
headed."

"I'll help you," Adam said and with a worried expression,
continued to hold her by her shoulders while he walked beside her out into the hall.

"I didn't think doctors got light-headed over the sight of
blood," Cyrus said. His eyes narrowed accusingly. "I
thought doctors were stronger than that."

"Might not be the blood that caused her trouble," Park
explained while he reached for the bandages he would
need. "Could be any number of things that made her

182

suddenly feel so faint."

"Like what?"

"Well, it's quite possible that something she ate earlier did not settle right in her stomach. Or could be she's coming down with something like the tremors. Or her problem might even be something as simple as not having had enough sleep, which is probably the case. I think that little lady has a lot more on her mind than any of us realize." He glanced at the older boy and saw that he was still dripping wet. "And if you don't go to your room and change into some dry clothes right away, you might find yourself feeling a little light-headed, too."

"Better do what he says and stop all your worrying about everyone else," George put in with a wrinkled nose. "It would be about your luck to catch pneumonia again when you almost died from it last time."

Reluctantly Cyrus left the room to do as told, but not before turning to toss George one last angry glower.

"You gave me quite a fright," Adam said as he placed the glass back on the lamp he had just lit then turned to where JoAnn had settled on the edge of the bed, her hands folded primly in her lap. Although she still looked a little pale, she had gotten most of her coloring back. "What happened to you down there?"

JoAnn fought the overpowering urge to tell him the truth. "I don't know." Although part of her desperately wanted to warn Adam about the coming disaster, she didn't dare. She had promised herself not to interfere with the events from the past. To be anything beyond an interested observer while visiting this era would be the same as purposely tampering with fate. She had no right to do anything that might alter the future. *Her* future. Her very life. By warning them about the flood, she could jeopardize her own existence. Her own great-great grandparents would

183

never have met and married had the flood not killed her great-great grandfather's first wife. And if that were the case, the following generations of her family would never have been born.

Besides, she knew Adam lived high above Prospect Hill, miles from the water's angry path. And now that his father had suffered such a frightening illness and had been confined to his son's house, Adam would continue to spend most of his time there at home as he would during the coming summer.

Although she knew Adam would be affected by the flood in some way, because everyone in that area was, he was probably in no personal danger. The only one who might be in any real danger from the impending disaster was Park and only if he returned to his own house before then. According to what he had told her during the course of their different conversations, his house was somewhere on Main Street, which she knew lay in the very center of Johnstown.

If her memory served her correctly, that area was to be one of the hardest hit, especially there near the city park. Would he possibly be one of the ones to drown? She shuddered at the thought.

"You're shivering," Adam said and knelt beside the bed to have a better look at her. Her coloring was suddenly gone again. "You're coming down with something, aren't you?"

"No. I told you, I'm fine. It's just that while leaning against you on the stairs, part of my clothing got wet and that's left me a little chilled." She gestured toward the wet patches on the left side of the turquoise dress.

"I'm sorry." He had been so involved in what was happening, he had forgotten he was soaking wet. "I didn't realize."

"That's perfectly all right. A little water never hurt anyone," she said, then her eyes widened when again she was

184

reminded of the flood. A little water might not hurt anyone, but a *lot* of water could and would kill thousands.

"There's something you're not telling me," he said while he studied the odd expression on her face. "Something you don't want me to know about."

"It's not that I don't want you to know," she began, her mind already searching frantically for a way out of this conversation. "It's just that I thought you'd eventually figure it out on your own."

"Figure out what?" His forehead notched while he tried to guess the answer.

"That you're kneeling on my skirt hem," she said. "And have thus far soaked it to the knee."

Having thought he was finally about to be told the truth, Adam rolled his eyes toward the ceiling as if to ask for a wave of divine strength then took her hands and gazed longingly into her eyes. He knew he could not force her to tell him her secrets, though he dearly wished she would. He had such a strong desire to help her. "If there's ever anything you want to talk about, feel free to do so with me. There's nothing we can't discuss."

Though his hands were cool to the touch, a gentle warmth curled up JoAnn's arm, causing her whole body to tingle with awareness. Suddenly every nerve ending felt as if it had gone on alert. Having such a profound response to something as simple as holding hands both amazed and alarmed her. It made her feel like she was back in high school. "Thank you. You are very kind."

"Kind?" Adam stared at her for a long moment, knowing it was more than kindness that made him want her to open up to him. His desire to know more about her was overwhelming. So much so, he couldn't stop himself from speaking aloud his next thought. "You wouldn't think that if you knew the truth."

JoAnn's eyes widened at such an intriguing remark. "And what is the truth?"

Adam leaned closer, all the while studying every detail of her beautiful face. Even with wind-tossed hair and a tiny streak of dried blood near her ear, she was truly exquisite.

With Adam leaning so close and studying her so intently, JoAnn was suddenly aware of how dangerously masculine he looked in the soft glow of the lamplight, his wet clothing molded to his rugged body, and his dark hair curled softly at the nape of his neck, having dried without the aid of a brush. Her heart raced with further anticipation when she realized his gaze had strayed from her rounded eyes to her mouth.

"The truth is I desperately want to kiss you," he answered, then sank onto the bed beside her, putting him closer still.

JoAnn's pulses jumped, oddly aware when the mattress gave beneath his weight. "But why?"

Rather than answer when he knew that answer would only lead to another question, he dipped his head in preparation to take that first kiss.

"Adam, don't," she said in a voice that came out little more than a strangled whisper.

He paused with his mouth so close to hers she felt his breath against her cheek, which caused all manner of havoc to well up inside her.

"Why not?" He studied her earnestly.

"Because i-it's not right," she answered, then took a sharp, deep breath.

"And what's not right about it?" His voice was rich with emotion.

What was not right about it? her mind screamed, repeating the ludicrous question while her blood raced frantic trails through her body. Every inch of her had sparked to life, tingling with anticipation. She wanted to answer *everything* but found she could say nothing while her lips slowly parted to accept his kiss, as if they were the only other part of her body still able to function. The rest of her was somehow paralyzed by the intense pounding of her heart.

The slight parting of her mouth was all the encouragement Adam needed. Had she shown the slightest resistance, he would have respected her wishes and pulled away. He had to know what it was like to kiss her, what it felt like to have her mouth pressed hungrily against his.

The ensuing kiss started out little more than a tender sampling, a gentle exploring of a woman who had slowly but surely been driving him insane with her extraordinary beauty and her uncommon enthusiasm for life, as if everything fascinated her; but without forewarning the kiss suddenly exploded into something a lot more powerful, a lot more demanding. The moment his lips had descended upon that magnificent mouth and he had tasted her sweetness and felt her warmth, he was lost to his desires.

With a passion he had forgotten he could possess, he cupped his hand beneath her chin and tilted her head so he could press his mouth more firmly against hers. Each kiss became more deeply demanding than the last. Aware now that he had yearned to possess her since that first meeting, he pulled her into an empowering embrace and pressed her body hard against his.

At first JoAnn stiffened against the overpowering onslaught of emotions, aware this encounter was something she should never have allowed to happen. Even so, she could not find the strength nor the presence of mind needed to pull away. Despite the wetness that soaked into her clothing from his and now touched her skin, she felt the languid warmth she knew only he could create while it spread slowly through her being, temporarily coercing her to forget any earlier misgivings.

The floodtide of sensations that coursed through her body was so strong, it had filled her to her soul and left her with a weak and wondrous feeling of contentment. It was then, while she basked in the warm current he had created inside her that she realized she had wanted him to kiss her.

Wanted it very much. Despite the very real danger, knowing she could quite easily fall in love with a man as attractive and as alluring as Adam, she could not pull away. For some reason unknown even to her, though she left herself open to yet another emotional failure, she wanted the kiss to continue. She wanted to know just where it might lead.

It had been so long since her body had responded like that to a mere kiss, she had forgotten just how powerful such inner emotions could be. At the moment, they ruled every part of her, causing her to become so caught up in the spinning vortex of these reawakened desires she could no longer appraise the resulting danger.

In the far recesses of her mind she knew there would be consequences to face if she allowed this kiss to progress much further. Even while one of his hands was roaming the curves along her back and shoulders, she refused to speculate on just how serious or how utterly debilitating those consequences might be. She was very, very close to falling for this guy and if she dared allow herself to become any more involved with him, she was most certainly headed for yet another devastating heartbreak. Still, she could not find the strength needed to pull away.

Instead, she trembled from the astonishing effect of his touch while his hand continued to drift over her shoulder then down her spine where it joined the other in a very real effort to draw her closer still. It had been years since she had let a man's kiss affect her like that. Years since she'd let a man's hands roam her body like that.

If only there was some way she could made Adam a permanent part of her life, but she knew that was impossible. As soon as that telegram arrived, she would have to leave. And after he'd discovered how she had lied to them, he would never let her come back, even if she wanted.

It was the painful realization that one day Adam would despise her with the same intensity he now desired her that finally gave her the fortitude needed to pull away and place a restraining hand between them. With her whole body still trembling, she turned and stared vacantly at a distant wall.

"That should never have happened," she said when she finally recovered her emotions enough to speak.

Rather than argue that he thoroughly disagreed, Adam quickly rose from the bed and stepped away. He knew if he stayed close, he would be too tempted to try to kiss her again and he certainly did not want to force her into something she was not ready to face.

Hiding his disappointment behind a false calm, he turned to her again and noticed the dark areas staining her dress.

"I've gotten you very wet," he commented for lack of anything else to say. "Here you are, obviously coming down with something, and I am inconsiderate enough to let you get this wet. I'd better leave so you can change into dry clothes."

As he headed for the door, JoAnn felt a strange desire to call him back, but knew that could only cause further complications between them. Complications that would make her leaving just that much harder for them both.

Instead, she let her ever-present need for self-preservation take hold and continued to sit numbly on the bed while she watched him close the adjoining door into his own bedroom. When she heard his muffled footsteps fall across the carpet, then fade into nothing, she tossed back onto the bed. She had not expected to react quite so strongly to his kiss; and now that she had, she was not sure how to judge the situation.

What had caused her to react like that? Although she knew she had found him attractive right from the start, there was no way she could be falling in love with him. They were from two entirely different time periods, and in a sense from two entirely different worlds. They didn't have enough in common with each other to fall in love.

So why were her toes still curled into tiny little balls and why was her heart still racing at a ridiculous speed? And why did she now wonder what it might have been like to let him make love to her? Would he be a gentle lover or a commanding lover? She suspected he could be both.

Pressing her eyes closed, she tried to shake the breathless feeling that still held her. She must not allow herself to think about him in such a way. She had to remember that she and Adam could never be more than mere friends. *Ever.*

Chapter Nine

Although Adam was disappointed by how readily JoAnn had pulled away from the kiss the afternoon before, it in no way dampened his desire for her. He still found her incredibly attractive, and was intrigued by her unique enthusiasm for everything around her.

No matter how much George teased her for being so "citified," she still wanted to know how things worked and even risked making herself look foolish by seeing if she could get them to work for her. She seemed especially delighted with playing with the autoharp or winding up and listening to the graphophone.

Although she had admitted to having led a very sheltered life, it amazed him at times the things she did not know. Why would a woman from the city not know what a jelly press was or what a meat grinder looked like? Surely they had such things. But then again she might be from a wealthy family where the housekeeper had refused to let her enter the kitchen. Or perhaps the problem she had with remembering what things were and how they worked had to do with the continued preoccupation over her parents' deaths.

But even with such a limited memory span, her attention to detail was enormous and she continued to fascinate him with how engrossed she was with life.

In addition to being so fascinated by her, he also admired how she had set all other concerns aside and taken charge when he'd brought George in from the storm. She was the type of person who stepped in to help when she saw a need. Still, he worried about the dizzy spell she'd had just when she was finishing tending to George's wound. For a moment she had become so dazed and disoriented, she had not responded to his voice. Apparently, she was not yet getting the rest she needed to stay healthy, probably still crying herself to sleep at night. And it was undoubtedly that same lack of sleep that had made it so hard for her to concentrate, hard to remember such common facts as dates or places, or even how to use a garlic mill. She was still too deeply engrossed in her loss.

Sadly, he wished there was something he could do to ease her pain but knew from experience that only time could take care of such matters. Even the best doctors had no cure for grief.

Which led him to his next consideration.

After having watched JoAnn take such decisive action on two separate occasions, he had finally conceded that she might be a real doctor after all. Judging by the efficient and natural manner in which she had handled both situations, she had to be.

Even so, most of those who had met her thus far continued to be leery of the claim, yet were confident enough in what he and his father had said about her to eventually admit she had some sort of detailed medical training. How else could she have known what to do for Park and for George?

But then again, Constance could be right. It was possible JoAnn was a nurse or a doctor's aide just pretending to be something more. But he doubted it. She had shown skills far beyond those of a nurse or an aide. Still, it bewildered him to think of her as a practicing doctor. But then

192

everything about that woman bewildered him. And fascinated him. And made him yearn to know her better.

If only she would let go of whatever barriers she had thrown around herself and open up to him. But at the moment, he had a hard enough time even keeping her in the room.

"I'm sorry," he said, aware Constance had said something else, probably about JoAnn, who moments before had left the room. Though he tried, he could not concentrate on what she had to say. His mind was too filled with other thoughts, thoughts of a fiery kiss that had left him weak and wanting, thoughts of what it would have been like to take that kiss to completion. "What did you say?"

Constance crossed her arms, clearly annoyed by his lack of attention. "I wanted to know why — if your father thinks so grandly of this Miss Griffin — why he doesn't simply go ahead and pay her train fare back to Pittsburgh then let her wire him a reimbursement after she gets there?"

She gave her long blond curls a resolute toss then turned to face him squarely, her green eyes glinting with determination while she continued in her deep, Southern drawl. "After all, she has been here for nearly a week now and has not heard one little word from that bank of hers. I'm startin' to wonder if she really has any money in that bank after all."

Adam sighed, annoyed by Constance's persistence in the matter, and by her unwillingness to listen to reason. "I thought I explained that to you. The reason she has not heard from the bank yet is because I have not had a chance to send Cyrus into town to check for a return telegram since late Saturday. I had intended to send him yesterday afternoon just as soon as he had put his things away after school, but that storm blew in about that time and I needed his help with the livestock."

"I wish I'd known," she muttered, tapping her booted foot beneath her satin skirts with an irritating staccato. "I could have stopped by the telegraph office on my way out here to see if there were any messages for her. Or I could have stopped by the bank to see if perhaps they had received their notice." Her emerald eyes narrowed perceptibly when she touched a delicate finger to her lower lip. "Maybe I should do that now. I could be back here with the telegram before nightfall."

Although it was tempting to use any excuse to be rid of her ceaseless chatter for the next couple hours, having grown tired of her constant condemnations, Adam knew it offered only a temporary respite. Besides, he was in no hurry to hear from JoAnn's bank, knowing that as soon as the verification arrived, she would have the money needed to leave.

He would rather Constance finish her visit now and have no excuse to come back that night.

"That won't be necessary," he assured her. "Cyrus has agreed to go this afternoon right after he returns from school." He glanced at the clock and wondered what kept the boys. Normally they were home between two-thirty and three o'clock. It was nearly four. If they were much later coming in, he would have to delay the trip yet another day. Darkness came early on this side of the mountain and he did not like the thought of Cyrus riding along the wooded roads after dark. He fought a smile when he realized he would soon have the perfect excuse to keep JoAnn there yet one more day.

"Just as long as someone goes," she muttered with an obstinate tilt of her head then glanced toward the door where JoAnn had last been seen. "If she stays here much longer, people will start to talk."

Let them, he thought, but had good enough sense not to state that aloud. "I don't see why anyone would talk. She's been of great help to Father."

"No doubt," Constance muttered, then glanced at Adam, her delicate eyebrows arched questioningly. "And when is your father planning to return home so that you can go back to work?"

Adam shrugged, knowing full well she wanted to know because he was far more accessible to her when he was in Johnstown than when he was five miles into the mountains. "When Doctor Lowman says it is okay for him to."

"But why is the doctor waiting so long? It's not as if your father would be alone. You would be there almost every night, like always, and he does have those two housekeepers."

"Neither of whom is a live-in and neither of whom has what it takes to make him stay in bed and rest. If Father went home now, he'd be back at work by midmorning tomorrow." Adam also glanced at the door, wondering what was taking JoAnn so long. All Constance had asked for was a drink of water and it really had not been JoAnn's place to go after it. She was just as much his guest as Constance. So why had she been so quick to volunteer? He suspected the reason had to do with having a few minutes of distance from Constance who was in a particularly vexatious mood that day, though she had not been in a truly pleasant mood since her first trip out five days ago.

"Oh, I think you'd be surprised at how much control those twin housekeepers have over your father," Constance said with a knowing wag of her head. "Especially Shelly. She may be half your father's age and half his size, but she's like an old mother hen when it comes to takin' care of him."

At that moment, JoAnn reappeared carrying a large-handled silver tray with a frosted pitcher of ice water and three drinking glasses. As hot as it was, especially in the stifling amount of clothes they had to wear, she decided they might all enjoy a tall, cool glass of water.

"Who's like an old mother hen when it comes to taking care of Park?" she asked, more as a way of letting them know she had returned than anything else.

"Shelly Drum. One of father's housekeepers," Adam answered noticing how quickly Constance's back had

195

stiffened upon JoAnn's return. "Constance thinks she would make a good nursemaid."

"And she would," Constance said, whirling to face JoAnn in ready defense. "Between the caring ministrations she and her twin sister, Sheila, could provide, he would want for nothing."

"He wants for nothing here," Adam reminded her, then abruptly changed subjects because it did not matter to him one whit whether his father's housekeepers were capable enough or not. He was not ready to send his father home. "This happens to have been the first vacation from work he or I have taken in years. It's been nice to have this chance to spend extra time together."

"Oh?" Constance asked and placed her hands on her tightly corseted waist while she eyed him suspiciously. "I was under the impression you were havin' a lot of your work brought out here to you so you wouldn't fall behind. How much time can that leave you to be with your father?"

"It's true, I have had to spend most of my afternoons trying to keep up with all the paperwork the bank and steel plant keep sending over," he explained, wondering why he suddenly felt on the defensive. As long as he finished the important work when it was due, what he did with his time was no one's concern but his own. "But I've devoted many of my mornings and most of my evenings to visiting with Father. After having found out just how fragile his life can be, I am eager to have this time to share with him."

"And is *she* there when you share your time with him?" she asked, obviously having decided to take a more direct approach. She then looked toward JoAnn with a menacing glare.

JoAnn pretended not to notice, determined not to give her the satisfaction of seeing how annoyed she had become. She did not like Constance Seguin. The woman was too possessive and demanding, and thought far too much of herself. Because of the way she constantly hovered around

Adam, she reminded JoAnn of a hungry cat guarding its kill.

"Usually, she is with us," he answered truthfully, aware of the tension between the two women, but at a loss over what to do about it. "She's fine company."

"As fine as me?" Constance asked, suddenly taking on that seductive little girl look she used so often. Glancing briefly at JoAnn, as if wanting to make certain she was watching, she then reached out and curled her arms possessively around Adam's.

"Far different from you," he admitted, then smiled when he realized just how different. The two were as different as night and day. As different as a she-wolf and a curious pup. As different as a gaudy diamond and a elegant pearl.

Misinterpreting his smile, Constance pressed her cheek against the solid muscle of his upper arm and flattened her ample breasts into his side. "As long as you understand that you belong to me," she said with a sultry smile and a playful wink, making JoAnn wonder just what sort of relationship the two shared. It sickened her to think of Adam making love to Little Miss Dolly Parton there.

Rather than allow an argument that might embarrass them all, Adam decided it was time to change the subject again. Hearing the back door slam shut, he took immediate advantage of that. "I think the boys are finally in from school." He quickly pulled away from Constance's possessive grasp. "I'd better go remind Cyrus that he needs to ride into town and check on that telegram. He'll have to leave right away if he's to be back before dark."

"I'll go with you," Constance said and cut JoAnn a taunting gaze while she hurried to follow.

"That won't be necessary," he answered, then realized he would be leaving the two women alone with no intermediary; and knowing Constance's sharp tongue and her intense dislike for JoAnn, he decided that would not be very wise. "On second thought, perhaps you should come." He then turned to JoAnn and wished for all the world it was her coming with him instead of Constance. "We'll be right back."

Feeling more apprehensive to know her time of reckoning was now only hours away than annoyed over the way Constance continued to show such an overt possessiveness toward Adam, JoAnn sank into the nearest chair with the serving tray balanced precariously across her lap, not caring that she was crumpling the bustle sewn into the back of her pink skirt. She could not decide whether to stay and face Adam and Park with the truth, or slip quietly out of their lives before Cyrus had had time to return.

It was a hard decision to make, especially when the truth was so utterly unbelievable. Still, she knew she could not simply walk out without having given some sort of an explanation — leaving them to discover her deceit after she had gone. They deserved better than that. Even if she decided not to tell them the actual truth, she should stay and find some way to explain why that bank had never heard of her. It would be better than letting them hate her.

While lost in such troubling thought, she heard footsteps just outside the hall door. She turned her head in time to watch Adam and Constance reenter like a couple still joined at the hip. When she noticed the sour look on Adam's face, she wondered if it was because of the shameless way Constance continued to cling to him or because of the folded piece of paper he held in his hand.

"Cyrus has already been to the telegraph office," he said as a way of explanation then pulled away from Constance so he could hand the paper to her. "When the teacher let them out early, he decided to go straight there. Here is your telegram."

JoAnn felt her insides crumble into nothingness. "My telegram?"

Swallowing hard, she set the serving tray aside and accepted the folded paper. When she did, she noticed it was addressed either to her *or* to the Morrell State Bank. Obviously they did not plan to send duplicate telegrams. She also noticed the telegram had a small wax seal where the edges overlapped in the center which meant no one but the telegraph operator had read it yet. Her lie was still safe — at least for now. She might be able to get out of there without anyone ever having to know of her deceit.

Forcing an expectant smile, she broke the seal then turned so only she could read the short message:

No such person known to this bank. Request denied.

Without offering to let anyone else see it, she refolded the telegram then tucked it into her skirt pocket, hoping that old adage "out of sight, out of mind" would prove true.

"Well? What did it say?" Constance asked, studying her with an intent gaze.

"The transfer has been approved," she said simply, knowing that was what Constance wanted to hear. "I can leave anytime."

Constance offered such a genuine smile of triumph that JoAnn felt a strange urge to punch her though she knew the young woman had a legitimate reason for wanting her to go. Until last week, when she had suddenly appeared to them out of nowhere, Adam had spent much of his free time with Constance, which was really as it should be. And although the thought might not set all that well with her, within a very few hours, when she was again gone from their lives, these two would go right on with their lives, their relationship virtually unchanged.

"Would you like to ride into Johnstown with me?" Constance suggested in her sugary Southern voice. "If we leave now, my driver could have us there before the bank closes. Porterfield is very good when asked to hurry."

Knowing Constance would never agree to let her off anywhere except at the front door of that bank, which

199

meant she would have to try to find her way back to that hole alone and in the dark, JoAnn quickly declined. "No, I'd rather wait and walk into town early tomorrow."

"Walk?" Adam responded, clearly dismayed. "Don't be absurd. Woodvale has no bank and Johnstown is nearly five miles from here. I'll rig the carriage and take you down first thing in the morning, in time to be there when the bank opens if you like."

"But if she went with me now, she could be on a train back to Pittsburgh by nightfall," Constance put in, her oh-so-sweet smile faltering.

"But if she waits until morning, it will give her more time to tell Father goodbye and the chance to check on Traveler's leg one last time. Tomorrow is soon enough for her to head back home."

Without hesitating, JoAnn agreed to Adam's offer—though she knew she would not be there come daybreak. She would slip away sometime in the night.

It was just after four A.M. when JoAnn prepared to step quietly from the room adjoining Adam's, dressed again in her dark blue linen skirt and delicate silk blouse. Because she had no further use for the two dresses Park had given her—the dresses she had alternately worn for the past six days—she felt compelled to leave them behind. Sadly, she folded them neatly and placed them on top of the bed, though the pink one needed laundering. She also left the boots she had worn only once, the hat she'd never worn, and a brief note thanking Adam and Park for their hospitality. She offered no other reason for such an untimely departure than the claim she did not want to bother Adam with driving her and that she really did prefer to walk.

The only item JoAnn carried with her to remind her of her week's stay was the book of poetry Adam had given her that second day there. With tears stinging her eyes, aware

200

she would never again see Adam's smiling face nor hear Park's teasing remarks, JoAnn crept soundlessly through the house and out into the night.

She paused long enough to give her surroundings one last, yearning look, wanting to commit as much of it to memory as possible. Then with nothing but a partial moon to guide her, she turned and headed down the narrow carriage drive toward the main road. She stayed on that road until she eventually arrived at the bend where a small pile of rocks still marked the opening through time.

While bearing an unexplainable feeling of loss, she prodded the air with her hand until she found the opening then stepped quietly back into her own time, surprised to feel her head bump against something when she was halfway. Turning to face the hole from the other side, she carefully felt for the inner rim and discovered the passageway had shrunk considerably, as if slowly healing itself. The top curve, which before had been at least seven feet off the ground was now only about five and a half feet.

Startled by such a discovery, she wondered how long it would be before the opening had closed enough to prevent her from wriggling through. It had never occurred to her that the hole might not be something permanent. Without realizing the risk, she had come very close to being trapped in the nineteenth century forever. Another few weeks and her fate might have been sealed. By that time, the hole could have become too small to use. Another couple of months and there might be no hole at all.

Shaken to know how close she'd come, she turned away from the opening and was relieved to see her car still there. She had worried that Jean might have driven over to Woodvale Heights and eventually found the car then used the spare set of keys she'd lent her a few months ago to move the vehicle to her parents' house. Jean was the type who would worry about a car left out in the woods like that and would have been just angry enough with her for having disappeared to want her to have to walk home.

After feeling around in the weeds until she finally located the keys she had hidden there, she hurriedly opened the door and slipped gratefully into the padded leather seat. Wriggling until she felt comfortable, she glanced at the clock. It was four-forty. She then pressed the button that temporarily showed the date in place of the time. April third.

The same week that had passed while she was in the year 1889 had passed in the year 1992. But instead of the day being Wednesday, it was Friday again. She wondered about the two-day difference and decided to check out a few books involving time travel and time displacement to learn more about what had happened.

Spotting the prescription pad on the dash where she'd left it, she reached for the tablet at the same time she turned on the overhead light. She was relieved to see that her quickly scrawled note was still there. It meant Jean had yet to find either the car or the note and would not be asking a lot of questions about this "adventure" of hers. For some reason, though she was not quite sure why, she was not ready to share what had happened with anyone. Not even her best friend. In time she felt certain she would tell Jean everything, but not yet.

After setting the pad aside, JoAnn dried her still damp car keys on her sleeve then shoved them into the ignition switch, fired the engine, and turned the small sports car toward the narrow, winding road that would take her back to her parents' house. While fiddling with the radio, she felt an odd combination of relief and sadness: relieved to be safely back home in her own time, yet sad to know she would never see Adam again. In the one short week she had been away, he and his father had become an intricate part of her life and she would miss them both. But her return had been inevitable.

Five minutes later, she turned into the driveway. Her

headlights swept across her parents' yard revealing the many handcrafted items scattered across the lawn in front of the two-story half-brick, half-frame house. The sidewalk, the birdbath, and all the many plaster and wood adornments were exactly where she had left them. She was back among the familiar. Yet somehow it all had the feeling of being oddly unfamiliar. There was such a sense of unreality accompanying her return, it was as if she no longer belonged.

An eerie feeling washed over her when she pulled her car into the garage and killed first the engine then the lights. Grabbing her keys, she reached into the back for her sweater then headed immediately for the house.

Once inside, she fought the urge to head straight to the refrigerator for an ice cold diet Coke and went instead into the living room. She flipped on the lights, temporarily amazed at how instantly they had responded, then headed for the answering machine. As expected, she had so many messages, the light no longer blinked but stayed on continually.

After rewinding for several seconds, she moved the lever to play and grinned when she heard the irritation in Jean's voice. Aware she had not found the front of her more current messages, she rewound some more. This time when she moved the lever to play, she was in the middle of a message Jean had left the day before she had driven to the pond to think. Rather than fast forward to the next message, she listened to the old one again while settling into a comfortable chair.

Pushing her shoes off with the tips of her toes, she tucked her feet up under her and listened to message after message, most of which were from Jean, each sounding a little more annoyed than the last.

"If you don't pick up that phone right now and talk to me, I'm going to have the police sent out," was one such message. JoAnn lifted her eyebrows and wondered if she had followed through with that threat while she listened for the beep that would indicate the next message.

"You don't answer your parents' phone. You don't answer your car phone. How am I to know if you are all right if you don't answer your phones? Give me a call!" She made no mention of having sent the police.

"Look, JoAnn, it's now Tuesday afternoon. You've refused to return my calls for nearly a week and I'm starting to take this personally. Either get up off that lazy butt of yours and answer this phone right now or scratch me off your Christmas list." There was a very loud click after that particular message because Jean had obviously slammed the receiver down, which meant her friend was sincerely angry with her. The last message let her know just *how* angry.

"Okay. I give up. If you don't want to talk to me then so be it. Just remember that you used to have a good friend here in Pittsburgh who truly cared." There was a long pause, then, "And remember that I'm still here for you when you finally decide you want to talk."

JoAnn smiled. She considered calling Jean right then to explain that the reason she had not responded to her calls was because she had been away; but decided that five o'clock on a Friday morning was not the appropriate time to do that. Thinking she would wait until nine or nine-thirty and catch her at the hospital about the time she finished her morning rounds, JoAnn headed off for the guest room — which had at one time been her room. Without bothering to take a needed bath or slip into a fresh, clean gown, she fell face forward into the unmade bed and within minutes was sound asleep.

Thinking JoAnn must have overslept, Adam tapped lightly on the door with his knuckle. Although in no hurry to see her leave, he did want to have a talk with her before

204

they left. He wanted to tell her how he felt about her and ask for her permission to come to Pittsburgh and call on her.

"JoAnn? Are you awake?" He rapped harder, growing impatient. Now that Doris had asked to ride into Johnstown with them, this could be their only opportunity to talk privately. "I need to ask you something." He frowned when there still came no response from within then rattled the doorknob, thinking that might help wake her. "JoAnn?"

When she still did not answer, he turned the knob and opened the door just wide enough to peer inside. His heart sank like a lead weight when he noticed the neatly folded clothing on a perfectly made bed. His apprehension mounted when he next noticed a folded piece of paper perched on top of the clothing.

Seeing his name neatly scrawled across the outside, he hurried forward and snatched it open. His face paled when he realized he had come too late. She was already gone.

Frustrated, he rumpled the note and tossed it aside while he stared at the clothing, sadly remembering how beautiful the dresses had looked on her. Feeling suddenly lost, he sank down beside the garments and lifted a sleeve to his cheek, and was made all the more miserable when he detected her sweet scent. Curling his hand into a tight fist, he decided he could not let her leave like that. He had to find her. He had to tell her how he felt.

After clamoring out of the house like a madman, he hurried first to the stable then to the barn where he readied a horse and carriage with amazing speed. Within minutes, he was on his way, thinking because JoAnn was unfamiliar with the area, she would stay with the main road.

When he did not pass her along the way, he headed immediately for the Morrell bank. The lobby had been open for almost an hour, but none of the tellers remembered having waited on her. Aware the telegram might have been worded so that any bank would cash her draft and, not having time to check them all, he headed next for the train depot.

Convinced she would choose the Pennsylvania Railroad over the B & O since the Penn had the shorter route and a better means to carry more passengers, he went there first. But when the ticket master could not remember having sold a westbound ticket to anyone like he described, Adam headed next to the B & O station several blocks away. Again, he was told no such woman had been in.

He decided she was probably out shopping for new clothes, since she had left the dresses his father had bought and had never recovered those stolen from her. But because he had no idea where she might shop for those clothes, he realized his only real alternative was to chose a train station and wait for her.

Angry with her for putting him through such turmoil, he raked his hand through his hair and decided on the Pennsylvania Railroad. But first he hurried to leave a note with the ticket master there, just in case she chose the B & O. Either way, he intended for her to know how he felt before she left.

"If she doesn't answer one of her phones this time, I'm cutting my afternoon rounds short and heading for Woodvale," Jean Gallagher told Nurse Walls as she punched the last four digits of her calling card number into the keypad then sat back in one of the three padded swivel chairs in the nurses' station. "And if after I get there, I find out the only reason she hasn't been answering her telephone or returning any messages is because she's still wallowing in all that foolish guilt and self-pity, without any regard for anyone else, I'm going to wring her scrawny neck. How dare she put me through all this worry."

"Maybe she's not answering the telephone or returning your calls because she's not there," Nurse Walls suggested, annoyingly pragmatic in her reasoning.

"She's there all right," Jean muttered already counting the rings, knowing all too well the machine picked up on the sixth. "Where else would she — ?" Her eyes widened with surprise when instead of the short, ten-second message she now had committed to memory, she heard a simple but groggy hello.

"JoAnn?"

"Yes?"

"You're there?"

"Yes."

"Then why haven't you been answering your telephone?" she demanded, sounding very much like an irate mother. "I've called at least twenty times in the past week."

"Because until a few hours ago I wasn't here to answer any calls," JoAnn admitted, then rolled over to look at the clock on the nightstand. She blinked with confusion when she saw it was after ten o'clock. She had gotten accustomed to getting up with the chickens like everyone else at Adam's. Her heart constricted when his image immediately came to mind.

"And just where have you been?" Jean wanted to know, turning the chair so she would not have to look at Nurse Wall's staunch I-told-you-so expression.

"I decided to take a little vacation from my vacation. I had to get away from here. I needed time to think," she said, keeping her answer simple. She was still not ready to let anyone in on her secret, still apprehensive about what might take place should the information fall into the wrong hands before that opening had time to close. It still frightened her to think what might happen should a person from the present decide to take advantage of such a unique situation by going back in time and tampering with events from the past just to see how it might affect the future.

She was now as concerned for her new friends from the past as she was worried about the effect that tampering

207

might have on the present. It would not take much to change the whole course of history, especially with the flood only a couple of months away. If the people in the valley were warned of the impending disaster in such a way they finally believed it possible, precautions would be taken that could change the lives of thousands of people; which would in turn change the lives of anyone whose lives were connected to those people.

In her family alone, had her great-great grandmother, Mary Griffin, have lived, then her great-great grandfather, Reginald, would never have remarried and had her great-grandfather, Anthony. In turn, Anthony would never have married Sarah Bruns and given birth to JoAnn's grandfather, Harrison. That meant Grandfather Harrison would never had married Zilphia Hitt and had her father, Lowell, who would never have married her mother, which meant she would never have been born. Undoubtedly, by changing fate, thousand of others would be affected in just such a way. She could not allow that to happen. She had to be extremely careful and conscientious in how she handled the present situation.

"And just where did you go?"

"Up farther on the mountain," she answered vaguely, still undecided how much she should acknowledge.

"Camping?" Clearly, Jean found that hard to believe.

"Sort of."

"You?"

"Yes, me," she said, taking a defensive tone. "Why not me?"

"Because you, my dear, are *not* the type."

"Oh, and what type am I?"

"The stay at home, never stray far from your microwave or cozy little bed type."

JoAnn sighed, aware Jean was right. "Well, maybe I took my microwave with me."

"Yeah, right," Jean muttered flatly, then suddenly her

voice took a more serious tone. "You sound tired. Are you getting enough sleep?"

"Yes," she answered honestly because until last night, when she had been afraid to fall asleep at the usual hour for fear she might not awaken until morning, she had slept through four nights like a baby. "Fact is I was asleep when you called. It just so happens you woke me."

"Then maybe you're getting too much sleep," Jean countered. "That can be almost as detrimental as not getting enough."

"You worry too much," JoAnn insisted, frowning when she glanced down and noticed she was still in her clothes. Without wanting to, she thought back to another morning when she had awakened to find herself in those very same clothes. She pressed her eyes closed. It hurt to think about that morning. It hurt knowing she would never again awaken in that room and would never again be able to rush downstairs and see Adam's smiling face.

"You *make* me worry too much," Jean quipped.

"But why do you insist on worrying like that even when there's *nothing* for you to worry about?"

"Are you sure about that?"

"Jean?" JoAnn spoke the name with mock annoyance. "Get off the phone and back to work. You have patients to see and I have things to do."

Jean hesitated. "Will you be there should I decide to call you again this afternoon?"

"Yes, I'll be here," JoAnn assured her, then felt another deep feeling of loss when she added, "I'm back for good. Goodbye, Jean."

Later, after JoAnn had showered, changed, and returned to her mother's desk, she started back where she had left off a week earlier. Sadly yet methodically, she flipped through the two large ledger books, studying each page one line at a time, trying to decide which bills had been paid and which had not. But the more time she spent at her mother's desk, the more she thought about how much she missed them, and the more melancholy her mood became. By the time Jean telephoned at four-thirty, she was so depressed and lethargic, evidence of it came through in her voice.

"What's wrong?" Jean demanded, aware her friend sounded even more unhappy than she had that morning.

"Nothing."

"Don't give me that, Jo. Something's wrong. Very wrong. What's happened?"

"Nothing has happened. It's just that I've been going over my mother's books again this afternoon and I guess it's made me feel a little blue."

"And lonely?"

JoAnn closed her eyes. As usual Jean was right on target. "A little."

"Then get a blanket and pillow out. I'm on my way."

"But you have to work tomorrow."

"No I don't. It's my weekend off."

JoAnn thought about that. It was *last* weekend Jean had to work. "But don't you have a date with what's-his-name?"

"Not until tomorrow night and I'll be back in plenty of time to go out to dinner with what's-his-name. Do you need for me to stop off somewhere and get anything while I'm out?"

"I could use some milk and some bread," JoAnn said, knowing hers had to be tossed out earlier that day. "But I can go get that myself."

"And you're probably out of popcorn and those little peanut butter things you're addicted to," Jean said. "I'll stop off and get plenty of everything. I'll bring a couple of good movies, too. They're ones I taped earlier this week but haven't had a chance to watch. See you in a couple of hours — oh, and, Jo, stay away from your mother's desk for now."

Before JoAnn could protest again, Jean had hung up

and was headed to her bedroom to pack an overnight bag.

Following Jean's orders, mainly because she was too emotionally drained to do otherwise, JoAnn did not return to her mother's desk. Instead she went into the kitchen, grabbed a bag of Pecan Sandies, and popped open a diet Coke. She then headed for the living room to watch a few late afternoon sitcoms, thinking a little comedy might be just the thing to lighten her mood.

But nothing about the shows seemed funny anymore. Even the reruns of her favorite comedy bored her. Finally, she flipped the television off and went outside to wait for Jean. Plopping into the nearest lounge chair, she turned her face toward the last vestiges of light pinkening the sky high above the treetops and wondered if Adam might be watching a similar sunset.

It was then she realized she still thought of him as existing during the same time she existed, as though he were just a few miles away rather than an entire century.

She knew she had to do something about that because now that she was safely back in the year 1992, Adam was inarguably a part of the past. For him to exist now, he would have to be over one hundred and thirty years old, and Park would be nearly one hundred and sixty. Even little George would have to be about one hundred and sixteen. Such a realization saddened her even more because she already missed her friends from the past, missed them dreadfully. *Especially* Adam.

Although she had not yet been gone from there even twenty-four hours, it felt as if days had passed. Weeks. An entire lifetime. And in a way a lifetime *had* passed. Adam's lifetime. Fighting the anguish, she closed her eyes and she tried to make sense of what had happened. But the more she thought about her little adventure the more confused and unrealistic it all seemed; but not unrealistic enough to

211

let her stop missing the people she had left behind, missing them almost as much as she missed her parents. Perhaps that was because they were just as dead to her now. She would never see them again. Clearly, nothing was ever permanent, especially not in her life.

By the time Jean's dark red BMW pulled into the drive, JoAnn had worked herself into a full-fledged depression and nothing Jean said or did seemed to pull her friend out of the darkness.

"You frighten me," Jean finally admitted that following afternoon, aware it was almost time for her to go but afraid to leave JoAnn alone. For the past twenty hours, she had done everything she could to lift JoAnn's spirits but nothing had worked.

"Why do I frighten you?" she asked, slipping into the chair across the table from Jean's and pouring herself a glass of the bright yellow fruit punch Jean had just mixed before slumping forward on her elbows.

"Because nothing makes you laugh anymore. Nothing causes you to react. You are walking around here like some sort of zombie, responding to whatever I say with words but not really reacting to any of it. *That* frightens me."

"Sorry," JoAnn said with a shrug, wondering what Jean expected her to do about it.

"What's the matter?" Jean asked, trying a whole different approach. She pouted that playful little pout of hers that had worked so well during their teen years. "It's as if you don't find our conversations fulfilling enough anymore."

JoAnn looked at her strangely as if to ask, *should I?*

"That's it," Jean said with a wild wave of her hands, scraping her chair back as she came to her feet. "That's the final straw. I can't take this dark, reflective mood of yours any longer. You have obviously cut yourself off from the rest of the world for too long. You are coming back to Pittsburgh and spending the weekend with me."

"Thank you for the offer, but I can't. I have too much to

do here."

"It can wait. In fact, it should wait. You have spent far too much time dwelling on what happened with your parents. The whole idea behind taking eight weeks off was so you could find some way to work through your problems, and do so with no interruptions, no outside interferences; but you aren't even trying to find any solutions. All you are doing is wallowing in your misery." She then stepped toward JoAnn and shook her gently by the shoulders. "Jo, you have to look to the future. You can't keep living in the past."

JoAnn's mouth fell open. Leaning back in the chair, she stared at her friend, dumbfounded. "How do you know about that? How did you find out?"

Jean blinked, baffled by this sudden turn in conversation. "Find out about what?" She knelt so she would no longer be looking down at JoAnn.

"About my trip back into the past. About the six and a half days I spent in the year Eighteen eighty-nine? How did you ever find out about that?"

Jean closed her eyes briefly. When she reopened them, her eyes were filled again with concern. "Jo. You have got to check yourself into the hospital and the sooner the better. You're starting to hallucinate."

Chapter Ten

"But it wasn't an hallucination," JoAnn said, pushing herself out of the chair. "I really did go back in time."

Aware JoAnn believed what she said, Jean motioned for her to sit down again. Thinking the best way to help her friend see the unreality of what she had just claimed was for her to talk about it, she pretended to go along with her. "Then maybe you'd better tell me all about it."

Jean took the chair next to JoAnn's and offered no comments while JoAnn told her about the freak storm and how lightning had supposedly opened some sort of invisible hole in time. Not wanting to distract her from her curious tale, she continued to listen quietly while JoAnn went on to tell her about some of the people she had met and some of the things she had seen and done after having stepped through this strange hole in time.

"I probably would have stayed longer if it hadn't been for that telegram arriving when it did," JoAnn said sadly. "Although there was so much to which I was not at all accustomed, I really did enjoy myself there. It was so different from anything you could ever imagine."

"So the only reason you finally left was because you were afraid of being exposed as an imposter?" Jean asked, trying to understand how the delusion might relate to her parents' deaths. "You were afraid they would find out you weren't exactly what you had pretended to be." She frowned when she realized JoAnn might be suffering an identity crisis. Perhaps the self-doubts brought about by the deaths of her parents and her inability to save their lives had made JoAnn feel like an imposter even to herself and therefore worried it was only a matter of time until everyone else found out.

"That may not have been the only reason I left when I did, but it was certainly one of the main ones," JoAnn answered, verifying the answer with a brief nod. "But it really is a good thing I had to leave when I did because I had started to feel a lot more than mere friendliness toward Adam. It had become increasingly harder for me to keep my growing desire for him hidden."

Her eyes glittered with something Jean could not yet categorize.

"Jean, you should have seen him. Not only was he tall and gorgeous, he had a killer of a smile. The kind that formed those long, curved indentations in his cheeks and tiny crinkles around his eyes. He also had a thick head of wavy dark-brown hair that he kept brushed away from his face with a slight sweep, *blue*-blue eyes, and the longest eyelashes you've ever seen on a man. Like I said, he was absolutely *gorgeous*. The kind of man most women would knowingly *die* for. And in addition to being incredibly handsome, he was also very educated, especially for a man of that era. Perhaps he was a bit too chauvinistic at times, but then I guess that was to be expected. All men were pretty chauvinistic back then. Some so much so it was ridiculous. But what really bugged me is that hardly anyone, not even the women, wanted to accept the fact that I was a doctor. In fact, I think Park was the only one who ever truly believed me."

Jean was glad to hear JoAnn using the past tense instead of present, it meant she was at least trying to put her illusions behind her; but the casual mentions of being doubted as a doctor and being willing to die for an imaginary man worried her. "And do you think Adam desired you, too? As much as you desired him?"

"I don't know if he desired me as much as I desired him, but he was interested enough to kiss me," she admitted with a tiny smile, thinking back to that rainy afternoon. Her heart soared at the memory of his lips pressing so intimately against hers. "And if I hadn't pulled away when I did, I think we might have ended up making love right then and there — with all those people still in the house. In fact, I know we would have."

"And are you in love with this Adam Johnson?" Jean wanted to know, aware by JoAnn's expression that she truly believed every word she had said. She believed her hallucinations were real, as real as any other aspect of her life. JoAnn truly believed she had gone back in time and fallen in love with someone named Adam. But why? Was she in such desperate need of someone to love that she was willing to create the perfect man? And why a man from the past? What significance was there in the perfect man being from the nineteenth century?

"Don't be silly," JoAnn admonished. "I didn't know him long enough to be in *love* with him," she said, as if trying to convince herself as much as she hoped to convince Jean. "Love is something that takes time to develop. You know that as well as I do. It's something shared by two people who have a lot more in common than raging hormones. What could Adam and I possibly have in common? We aren't even from the same time period."

She paused for a moment to think more about what she did feel for him and again a tiny smile lifted the outer corners of her mouth. "But he is the sort of man I could eventually have fallen for, and hard. Which is why it is good I got out of there when I did — before I became too emotionally involved. I'll miss him enough as it is."

"I gather this Adam of yours was not at all like Thomas," Jean surmised while watching JoAnn's face carefully, wondering just what sort of man she had conjured. "I guess there's not much chance he had someone else more important in his life."

"You're right, Adam is absolutely nothing like Thomas," JoAnn said with certainty. "But he does have someone else who I'm sure is more important to him than I was. After all, he's known her for years. He knew me only that one week."

"He does have someone else?" Jean asked, surprised. Her frown deepened. JoAnn had just claimed he was very different from Thomas yet allowed him to have many of the same faults. She also did not like the way JoAnn kept changing from past to present tense, as if she was not sure where his image belonged. "You mean to tell me you believed Adam was the perfect man for you, yet he had another woman in his life, one he felt was more important than you?" Was she still hurting over the loss of Thomas? Enough so to have created his imaginary counterpart? Surely not. Surely by now she had come to see what life would have been like with that egocentric. He never would have loved her enough to stay true to her and because of that she never could have trusted him. What kind of life would that have been?

"I didn't say he was the perfect man," JoAnn reiterated, frowning at Jean's attempt to put words in her mouth. Why did Jean always have to overanalyze every situation? "He was just someone I found very attractive. And, yes, he did have another woman in his life who was a lot more important than I was. Which is really as it should be." She said that with far less conviction than she had hoped. Truth was, the thought of Adam carrying on his life with *Miss Constance* at his side made her stomach crawl. "It's not as if I could have ever laid a personal claim on him. After all, I'll never even see him again." She tried to ig-

217

nore the sharp stab of regret that followed such a remark.

"Then you have no immediate plans to go back into this other world of yours?" *That* was certainly encouraging.

JoAnn studied her friend for a long moment, then looked down at the hands folded in her lap and spoke in a quiet voice. "You don't believe me." As if she hadn't suffered enough during the past few weeks. Now she had a best friend who did not believe a word she had said. But then, in all fairness, it was an incredible story. Still, she had hoped Jean would at least give her the benefit of the doubt, especially after all these years. It had not been easy to open up to her and tell her everything.

"It's not that I don't believe *you*," Jean replied, choosing her words carefully. She raked her red-tipped fingers through her short brown hair. She did not want to say anything that might hurt her friend, especially while in such a fragile state. "It's just that I don't believe in time displacement. I never have. Oh, I know all the theories and some of them seem almost credible; but that's all they are: theories. As far as I know, no one has actually proven that man can traverse the barriers of time."

"So you think I'm making all this up. That I'm lying to you for some reason."

"No. I don't. I think you truly believe every word of what you've told me. And that worries me." She reached forward to rest her hands over JoAnn's, hoping that might help reach her. "I don't know why and I'm yet not sure how, but I'm very afraid you will try to use this strange fantasy of yours as another excuse not to get on with your life. It is possible you'll decide you'd rather continue to withdraw into this contrived world of yours than do what you can to face the reality of your parents' deaths."

"But I *did* go back in time."

"That's impossible."

JoAnn thought about showing Jean Adam's book, but realized that would prove nothing beyond the fact an Adam Johnson had indeed existed in the year 1889. Jean would think she found an old book in among her parents' belongings then chose to include the name and date she'd found inside as part of her fantasy.

Aware she was not about to change Jean's mind, not without taking her out to the pond and actually shoving her through the hole—and not all that certain she *wanted* Jean to believe her—JoAnn decided it would be better to pretend to agree with her. At least for now. "Perhaps you are right."

"You know I am," Jean stated, relief evident in her voice. "Jo, you really should come back to Pittsburgh with me."

"And check myself into the hospital so you can keep a closer eye on me?"

"Jo, if you stay here, you'll just continue to dwell on your problems. And not because you are trying to find any solutions; but because you have some strange need to punish yourself. I can't let you do that."

"You have it all wrong." JoAnn looked directly into Jean's hazel eyes, trying to make her believe. "It's true, I am still hurting from the loss of my parents and will for quite some time, but I'm not *dwelling* on their deaths like I was at first. Truth is, there have been times during these past few days that I've managed to put them completely from my mind." Which was true. She had become so fascinated by everything going on around her while at Adam's, she'd had neither the time nor the inclination to dwell on things from the past. Or would that be things from the future? She'd never been sure how to categorize such thoughts.

"JoAnn, you are deluding yourself or else you are trying to delude me. How can you possibly put all thought of them aside while you are living right here in their house, sitting on their furniture, eating from their refrigerator?"

"I'm not going back to Pittsburgh with you," JoAnn said with finality. "All I'd end up doing is moping about the apartment complex while you go out with what's-his-name. What kind of weekend would that be for me?"

"We could make it a threesome," Jean suggested brightly, knowing there was not enough time to find someone for her.

"I hate threesomes."

"Then I'll cancel my dates for tonight and tomorrow so I can spend my time with you. John will understand."

"There's no need for that," JoAnn said, waving her arms emphatically. "I have too much to do here. I'm *not* going."

"Then I'm staying." Jean thrust out her chin and shook her head to show she could be just as stubborn.

"No, you're not. *You're* going. *I'm* staying," JoAnn stated, then forced a smile. "I don't need a nursemaid."

"But we don't spend enough time together anymore," Jean argued, trying a whole new approach.

"That's because you have someone else sharing your time these days. You have what's-his-name."

Jean sighed, wondering why JoAnn couldn't just say the name, John. "Still, I should find more time for you. You're my best friend for heaven's sake. We've been together since grade school."

"Which is why I understand. Hey, I was no better when I thought I was in love with Old Tom. I enjoyed his company to the point I spent nearly every spare minute I had with him."

"But that was different. I was attending a different med school at the time. You couldn't have spent your time with me even if you'd wanted."

"The fact that you were a few hundred miles away doesn't account for the fact I didn't share my time with you. I could've written you more often than I did or I could've driven over and visited you more than twice. But I didn't. Still, that doesn't make me any less your friend. Just like you being with John so much doesn't make you any less my friend."

"Still, I should stay."

"No you shouldn't," JoAnn stated emphatically. "Look, it's not that I don't enjoy your company; but when you're here, I don't get anything done and the sooner I finish all this, the sooner I can put it all behind me and get on with my life."

Jean pursed her mouth into a wary frown. It certainly sounded reasonable enough — and encouraging. "Can I at least drive out from time to time to check on you?"

"As long as you continue to bring food," JoAnn teased, eager to put an end to the confrontation. She did not want to return to Pittsburgh — not just yet. And she didn't want Jean staying there with her. There were still too many things she needed to work out in her mind and she needed to be alone to do that.

"And you'll be here to answer your telephone when I call?" Jean asked. Her expression relaxed a degree, relieved JoAnn's sense of humor had returned.

JoAnn sighed. "If I don't answer the telephone the next time you call, may I sprout tiny red horns and a black pointed tail."

Jean grinned, already weakening. "Well, that would certainly fit your personality."

JoAnn lowered one eyebrow. "At least I *have* a personality."

Jean laughed and hugged her friend. "It's just that I worry about you."

"Which is fine," JoAnn said, stifling a return grin when she then tossed a few of Jean's own words back at her. "As long as you don't continue to dwell on my problems the way you have. It's as if you have some strange need to punish yourself. I can't let you do that."

221

Aware what JoAnn was attempting to do and glad she felt in a playful enough mood to try, Jean finally relented. "I'll go. But I plan to call every chance I can."

"If it will make you feel better," JoAnn said, "then by all means call. Just don't call every single day like you did last week. It makes me feel like a small child. Like you don't really trust me."

"I don't," Jean replied flippantly. "Never have. But I'll try to limit my calls somewhat if you'll try to hurry and finish everything you have to do here so you can come back home. I want to be able to stop in and check on you from time to time and make sure you are not slipping into another of your moods. I can't stand it when you get all moody."

When Jean left less than an hour later, JoAnn had to admit she was in much lighter spirits. So much so, she decided not to return to her mother's ledger books right away. Instead, she slipped on a pair of work gloves, an old worn sweater, and went outside to pull weeds out of her mother's flower gardens.

Even though she had no intention of keeping the house, because it was too far from where she worked and held too many heart-wrenching memories, she knew any yard work would help the resale value when the time finally came to let go of it. Besides, she had an odd desire to be outside enjoying the late afternoon sunshine. She had seen so little of the sun while back in the year 1889. She knew that was because it had been such a terribly wet year. She shuddered when she again remembered the result of all that rain and tried harder to focus her attention on the work at hand.

It was nearly dark before she finally put aside her trowel and returned to the house to shower and slip into a cuddly summer-weight jogging suit. Famished, she tossed one of the barbecue sandwiches Jean had brought into the microwave for a minute then retired to the living room to watch those movies she and Jean had never found the chance to watch.

She was tired, but still in a contented frame of mind when she went off to bed shortly after midnight.

But by Sunday morning her melancholy mood had returned. During the night she'd had a very vivid dream. In that dream Adam had been angry with her. He had demanded to know why she had slipped away in the night like that, and right in the middle of her attempt to explain, her mother appeared from nowhere to tell her how unfairly she had treated Adam and his father.

"You were not taught to treat people like that," she had scolded, her voice distant though her face had hovered very close. "Just because I am no longer there to remind you of what is right and what is wrong does not mean you can simply forget everything that is decent and just."

Her mother's image had then drifted over to where Adam still stood glowering at her and gently took his arm; then the two moved away from her, ignoring her desperate pleas for them to come back and let her explain.

Even after she had come awake and assured herself the whole thing had been a dream, probably brought on by all the spicy food she had eaten the night before while watching television, she could not shake the feeling that she had disappointed her mother yet again. First, by letting her and her father die, and now by having treated Adam and Park so unfairly.

For the rest of that Sunday, JoAnn tried to push the painful feelings aside, but couldn't. She also could not push aside the troubled thought that she may have hurt Adam more than she realized by having left in the night the way she did.

At the time, it had seemed the logical way to handle a very complicated and uncomfortable situation. It meant being able to slip away without any of them ever having to know she had lied to them. Had she stayed, and had Adam gone with her to the bank, she would have been forced to admit the truth to him, or at least a large part of it. She would have had to admit there was no money waiting for her and that there never would be. She had been refused the transfer because the bank in Pittsburgh had never heard of her. And with good reason. *No one* from 1889 Pittsburgh had ever heard of her. She did not exist yet.

She stared miserably at the creamy surface of her now cold cup of hot chocolate while she thought more about what she had done to Adam.

She felt she had a good reason for sneaking away like she did. How could she ever have explained that she was actually from another time period, visiting on a whim, when she did not fully understand how the time transference had happened herself? Like Jean, she had never believed such a thing possible. But obviously they had both been wrong.

It was while she tried to find a logical reason behind what had happened that she decided to make a trip into Johnstown the next day and check out as many books as she could find on the subject. Suddenly she was very interested in knowing how such a thing had happened.

By Monday night, JoAnn had so immersed herself in books about time travel and time displacement she was unaware of anything else happening around her.

By the time she had started the fourth of the five books she had found, she realized they all had one feature in common, they all started out by explaining how every tangible object in existence possessed not only length, breadth, and depth but also a fourth dimension called time and a fifth called space. Clearly, if time or space were not present the object could not possibly exist because all objects required a time and a space in which to exist.

It also became obvious to her that all humans were in

effect involuntary travelers in time. Their trip started at birth, ended at death, and moved only into the future at a rate over which no one had any control.

According to most of the theories she read, time was not merely the aging process or something to be associated with clocks and watches. It was, in its own strange right, a dimension. But was it a dimension through which man would ever be able to travel?

Most of the authors agreed it was possible. Many leaned toward the theory that because time and space were so directly related that the unexplored black holes in far outer space were possible entry points through time. Other authors and scientists theorized there could be other such space tunnels, each linking different time periods. But one analogy was vastly different from the others and it was that theory that interested JoAnn the most.

In that particular analogy, time was compared to a phonograph record, which as everyone knew was a disc not of concentric grooves fanning out in all directions, but instead a disc that held one long, continuous spiral. The spiral began near the outside and ended close to the center. Like the progressive channel of time, the groove on the record ran an ongoing route. The stylus of the record player started at the edge of the disc and eventually arrived at the center — unless some jerk or fault caused it to jump back into an earlier part of the spiral or skip to a later part.

JoAnn's eyes widened at how much sense that made and she read the next paragraphs aloud so she could absorb their full meaning.

"If that theory is true, then it makes perfect sense to believe that the 'spiral' of time that man occupies today runs very close if not right up against the 'spiral' of time that represents some era in the past, and equally as close to another 'spiral' that represents tomorrow. But what

225

conceivable kind of 'jerk' or 'fault' could cause our particular 'life needle' to jump a groove either way? Certainly none that can be easily visualized."

JoAnn swallowed, aware she had the very answer to that author's question. She knew exactly the sort of fault that could allow a person to "jump" into another time period; and it caused an eerie feeling to realize she had personal knowledge that went far beyond what was in these books. She had actually experienced what this last man had merely theorized.

Setting the books aside after she'd finally finished, JoAnn thought about what all she had learned in so short a time. Suddenly it all seemed more real to her. Reading what others had to say about the possibilities and probabilities of time travel had made her better understand what had happened and how.

It also made her miss Adam even more, reminding her that he was not just some figment of her imagination like Jean had hoped to convince her. He was every bit as real and wonderful as she remembered — just living his life in a different time groove than her.

Later that night, while trying to distract herself with yet more television, she found she could not stop thinking about Adam. Could not help but wonder what it would be like to see him again, to hear his deep laughter and gaze into his glimmering blue eyes one last time. It was then she realized that the only time she had been able to cast aside her melancholy mood and actually enjoy herself had been while she was in the past. While visiting Adam she had laughed, learned about a whole different way of life, and had felt unusually alive. It would be nice to enjoy just one or two more days of that, but she knew if she dared return, she would be tempted to stay longer and realized the very real danger in that.

If the time passage continued to close as rapidly as before, she could quite conceivably become trapped in the year 1889. She knew she could never cope. She was too used to speaking her mind and too used to the sort of comforts electricity provided, too used to plumbing that actually went into the house instead of being confined to a few rooms near the back. She shuddered at the memory of sitting on that cold chamber pot in the middle of the night when nature's call had eventually become too insistent to be ignored. She now had a whole new respect for bedpans and a real feeling of sympathy toward those patients forced to use them.

Furthermore, not only would she lose a lucrative career, one that was important to her even though she still doubted her competence, she would also lose everything else she had worked so hard to have. She would lose her beautiful bilevel apartment overlooking the river, her brand new Corvette with most of the extras, and all the different conveniences that filled the kitchen she so rarely used. Going back would not be worth the risk of being trapped. Not even to see Adam again.

Having made her decision to stay right where she was, she tried to busy herself for the next few days with her mother's ledgers and an ever growing pile of receipts. The more she worked, the more receipts she found, until she had a shoe box full. It was almost as if the desk was producing the tiny pieces of paper somewhere just out of her sight.

But the whole time she worked, her mind kept drifting back to Adam. She missed him dreadfully. Missed more than his laughter and the great way he looked in a pair of tight-fitting work trousers, she missed his touch. Missed feeling his hand at the small of her back whenever he escorted her from one room to another. Missed the way he reached out to touch her cheek at the oddest times. Missed his hand brushing lightly against hers whenever they both reached for the salt well at the same time. Missed him so much in fact, she considered a whole new

227

plan, one in which there would be little risk in her being trapped in a bygone era because she would only have to return for one day. There would be no need to stay any longer than that.

The plan was simple. Go back and tell Adam the truth about what happened and convince him to leave his life in the 1880s and come into the future with her. She would tempt him with promises of the unknown then teach him all about this modern world, and would have a wonderful time doing so. She would love to see his expression the day he had his first ride in an automobile or an airplane, or the first time he watched her put her clothes into the washing machine then turn it on. There were so many things about her world that would fascinate him, and as bright as he was, he would catch on quickly.

Then she realized the one real flaw in that plan. Although he might be fascinated, Adam would never be happy in her world. In the time where he lived now, he was not only well respected by his family and peers, he was also a man considered to be well educated and resourceful. A man to be reckoned with. But in her world, he would be little more than a curiosity. He would seem foolish and awkward, always having to turn to someone else for help or an explanation. Knowing how that would hurt his male pride and frustrate him in much the same way she had felt frustrated while visiting in his time, she pushed the idea aside. She could never ask Adam to set his identity aside for her. Not that he would. Even if she were able to convince him of the truth.

Still, knowing how unhappy Adam would be were he to be lured into her time period did not stop her from thinking about him. It did not stop her from remembering the many innocent touches that had set her heart to racing nor the passionate kiss they had shared in that heated moment after the storm.

By the following week, JoAnn could think of little else

and it frustrated her to know he could never become a permanent part of her life. It seemed unfair to her. After having spent the past twelve years struggling to become a doctor, then struggling to be accepted at the hospital where she now worked, she felt as if her world had always been in some form of upheaval. Then just when her life had finally settled into a set routine with no significant personal problems, suddenly she was beset with one major upheaval after another.

Still, she tried to put the handsome image of Adam Johnson out of her mind, just as she tried to put aside the knowledge that there was soon to be a devastating flood in his time—one that would destroy thousands of lives, possibly killing some of the very people she had met during her short stay. It was not something she wanted to think about.

When she returned the books on time travel to the library, she refused to check out any of the many books written about the flood of 1889. And even though she was within a few blocks of the Johnstown Flood Museum and had to pass by there on her way back around to Woodvale Heights, she refused to stop and have a look at the many exhibits inside.

She did not want to be reminded of the morbid details—especially not now that the names of those involved represented flesh and blood people. People who were every bit as important and every bit as full of life and vitality as those in her own time.

She had no desire to know who had died and who had been spared. It was enough to be plagued with what little she remembered about the flood from high school history and local yore, that there were 2,209 victims to die in the flood or the resulting fires and that hundreds more died soon thereafter from other injuries sustained during the flood, or from exposure following the flood. Or from the outbreak of typhoid that eventually took hold.

That Thursday afternoon, while packing many of her parents' belongings into boxes to either take back with her, or send to her aunts in Texas, or give to Goodwill, she continued trying to keep her thoughts off Adam, but with little success. He had become a constant ache in her heart.

While she wondered why he had become almost an obsession with her, she came across the Johnstown area telephone book.

Sitting cross-legged on the floor, she flipped through the white pages, looking for important telephone numbers her mother or father may have scrawled in the margins that might be important enough to note elsewhere. When she turned to the section with people whose last name began with a J, her gaze fell to the name Johnson like metal to a magnet.

With no apparent objective, she counted how many Johnsons there were and, with business listings included, she was surprised to find there were one hundred and eighty-nine. Morbidly aware Adam would be about fifty years in his grave by now, she wondered if he had left any direct descendants. If Constance ever did manage to drag Adam to the altar, there was a possibility the two would have had children who in turn would have had children of their own.

With that thought plaguing her, she scanned the first names of the many Johnsons. Her mouth gaped when a little over halfway down the list she noticed a Park Adam Johnson. It took all the restraint she had not to call the number.

While she sat there, staring at the name, she wondered how old this Park Adam was and if he might have the same deep, mellow voice as Adam. Or if he in some way looked like Adam. Was it possible this Park Adam had the same endearing smile, that same impossible sense of humor? Would he know what had become of Adam?

Whether or not he had ever married Constance Seguin? Whether or not he had lived a full and happy life?

A bittersweet sadness washed over her while she thought first about this man named Park Adam then about Adam himself. With the telephone book still open to the Johnsons and pressed intimately against her heart, she ached with the selfish need to touch him again, to feel the wondrous sensation of his lips pressed against hers one last time. Eventually, she became so heartsick, she decided to do it, to go back for one last visit — *but just for a few days and only if the hole was still large enough to assure a safe return.* She would not risk being trapped in the year 1889.

Since there were still several more weeks before her scheduled return to work, it was an easy matter to put off packing her parents' belongings a few days longer. Having already packed the entire top floor, there were only a few rooms left anyway.

A slow smile stretched across her face when she thought more about her decision, and of how annoyed Constance would be when suddenly she returned for another short visit. Knowing how aggravated the voluptuous little blonde would be was just the added incentive JoAnn needed to convince herself to go through with it.

Only this time, she intended to enter the past better prepared. It was likely Adam had kept those clothes she had left behind, since they were in very good condition, but she did not want to wear just those two outfits, which were so horribly uncomfortable.

The following morning, JoAnn first drove over to her parents' lawyer's office to sign a few papers, then went on to the Richland Mall and found several comfortable floor-length cotton percale or crepe dresses that might be worn to an evening poolside party. She was careful to select garments that had no zippers or Velcro fastenings that would be hard to explain to someone from another time. She then purchased luggage made of tweed and leather that looked more like the valises of yesteryear than actual suitcases.

The moment she returned to her parents' house, she packed the new items along with plenty of lightweight gowns and comfortable lingerie to wear beneath. Although she had grown rather used to wearing very little makeup, a direct result of the week she had spent without any, she nevertheless slipped a small compact of face powder and another of pink blusher into the side pocket of one of the bags.

She also thought to convert a couple of thousand from cash to gold so she would not have to feel so beholden to everyone else. She was too used to paying her own way and did not want to continue living off the others like before; and too, after having that dream, she wasn't all that sure Adam would welcome her back into his home. He might be angry with her for the sneaky way she had slipped off in the middle of the night. It was something to consider while packing to return to the year 1889.

While preparing to leave that Friday morning, she put on the dress she had bought that she felt looked most appropriate. It was a comfortable empire-cut, floor-length blue and white percale with a flounced skirt and a modestly scooped neckline. The sleeves were puffed and had fitted cuffs that buttoned just below the elbows. Although the dress was vastly different from what she had worn for Adam before, she felt it was far more correct than what she had worn that first day she met him. At least it covered the appropriate areas, more so than many of Constance's dresses had done.

Before closing her bags, she thought to pack a bottle of roll-on deodorant, a bottle of her favorite cologne, her sunglasses, a six pack of diet Coke, and her camera, which she hoped was small enough to be used discreetly. This time she wanted permanent memories of her adventure so she would be far less likely to forget what everyone had looked like, especially Adam. She wanted to be able to hold him in her heart forever.

By ten o'clock that Friday morning, just after calling to leave a vague message on Jean's answering machine explaining she would be gone for a few days, JoAnn left the house headed back to the pond.

Because she did not want leaves stuck all over her car like last time, knowing a few of them produced an acid that could damage the finish, she parked in the middle of a small clearing a few hundred yards from the pond. After setting the two valises aside, she locked the car and put the keys into a plastic sandwich bag then again hid them in a clump of grass.

When she slid the small valises through the invisible hole near the bed of stones, she again noticed the opening was smaller but had not shrunk nearly as much as she had expected. Obviously, the hole was not healing itself at quite the same rate as before. And because the shrinkage had slowed considerably, she realized it could be weeks yet before it grew too small for her to fit through. That significantly reduced the chance of her becoming trapped while visiting the past again.

Still, it saddened her to realize that one day, probably within the next few months, that small opening in time would close completely. She had to face the eventuality that one day very soon she would again have to put Adam out of her life, this time forever. Even though it was no longer quite as imperative she limit her stay to only a few days, the visit was still to be only temporary.

Pushing those morose thoughts aside, she lifted her skirt several inches and stepped delicately through to the other side then quickly picked up her bags again. With one in each hand, she headed toward the road and noticed the scarred tree where Park's carriage had struck. She glanced around to see if there were any remnants of wreckage left and was surprised to notice the pink blanket

233

of crown vetch that had covered the area just a few minutes ago, while still in the year 1992, was suddenly gone. Obviously crown vetch was not an herb native to that area.

Aware that during the two weeks she had been gone Park could have easily regained enough of his health to move back home, and knowing how unlikely it would be for Adam to be home that late in the morning, and not about to arrive at his house unannounced after having left there so abruptly, JoAnn turned toward the river and headed down a road she hoped would eventually lead her to Johnstown. Because the road was steep, muddy, and winding, and first went through Woodvale before traveling on to Johnstown, it was nearly two hours before JoAnn finally arrived at the edge of the thriving borough.

Noise and movement were all around her when she crossed the bridge that spanned the raging Little Conemaugh River, allowing her to travel safely from a largely residential borough of Woodvale into what a small decorative sign claimed to be Johnstown Proper. Rickety trains clattered along two different sets of tracks while people of all types bustled along the paved streets in carriages, on wagons, and on horseback.

Dogs barked at the drivers and gave chase while cows and goats ambled slowly through the alleyways, stopping to nibble on whatever vegetation they found. Large pillars of smoke billowed from the two clanking mills forming a thick gray haze high over her head. The larger of the two mills was still a few miles down the river but clearly visible from the bridge and the smaller mill stood less than a mile behind her. The boarded sidewalks that lined the cobblestone streets were thronged with midweek shoppers, food peddlers, and roving vendors — even this far away from the main business district, which she knew lay much closer to the area where the Little Conemaugh and Stony Creek rivers came together, near the huge

234

stone bridge at the opposite end of town.

Staying with her original plan, JoAnn first went in search of a local bank where she had her gold exchanged into the currency of the time. She left there with a pocketful of heavy coins including plenty of three-cent pieces, halfdimes, full dimes, a few two-and-a-half-dollar gold pieces, and several five-dollar gold pieces.

With enough money to be self-sufficient for quite some time, she started searching for a decent hotel so she could finally be rid of her baggage. She passed up the Hulbert House, only a block away. Although there was no present danger in staying there, she felt eerie just knowing from what little she remembered of her high school history that the beautiful new hotel had collapsed during the flood "like a house of cards."

Instead, she walked a few blocks farther to the Emerald Hotel. As soon as she had signed the register and paid her dollar, she headed upstairs to the corner room she had been given, eager to put her things away and return downstairs. It was already midafternoon and she wanted to find out where Park lived before dark, thinking he might be more receptive to her sudden return than Adam.

Chapter Eleven

Like last time, JoAnn was easily swept into the unique ambience of the time period. Upon leaving the Emerald Hotel, she became instantly enthralled by the sights, smells, and sounds of a Johnstown gone by. Most of the people strolling the boardwalks were friendly, offering a slight nod as she passed, though a few of the older women turned to give her clothing a questionable second look after she passed.

Or perhaps it was not her clothing they noticed but that she did not wear a small hat when outside like most women of the time, nor did she wear her hair up in fat curls or a prim little twist near the nape of her neck. She was too used to wearing her hair unbound, draped over her shoulders, protecting her neck from unwanted drafts. The only time she ever confined her long, thick mane was when she was forced to stuff it into a surgical cap while working in Emergency.

"Excuse me," she said to a particularly friendly looking man standing in front of a tobacco shop. She had roamed the unfamiliar streets for twenty minutes with very little success. Although some of the larger buildings looked somewhat familiar to her, others were a complete mystery, making the streets seem all the more foreign. "Could you direct me to Doctor Park Johnson's house? I need to speak with him."

"Certainly can," the tall man said with a polite nod as he tucked a small leather pouch into the pocket of his striped vest. "But I imagine you'd have better luck finding him at his office this time of day." He glanced at the Lutheran church a few blocks away where the clock in the tower revealed it was nearly three o'clock. "And you'd better hurry because if he has any house calls to make, he'll probably start them pretty soon."

"But I thought the doctor was recovering from an illness," she said with a questioning frown. She thought it odd to hear that Park might have returned to work this soon.

"He was, but I guess it wasn't all that bad an illness. I saw him earlier this week when he was on his way to see the widow Wray. Seems she's not taking the death of her sixth husband as well as she did the others. Either that or she hopes to lure old Doc Johnson into being number seven since he's been a widower for going on eleven years now."

"Six husbands?" JoAnn repeated, interested despite herself. "She's lost *six* husbands?"

The tall man nodded then as if suddenly realizing his manners swept his bowler hat off his head and held it to his chest. "That's why some people call her the Black Widow Wray, because she's always in mourning and having to wear black. Others call her that because her husbands all seem to die by very mysterious means. At any rate, that's where he was headed Monday afternoon. Said he'd been back at work for nearly a week. Looked pretty glad of it, too."

JoAnn's frown deepened. That was too soon for a heart patient to be back to work. "And where is his office?"

The man directed her to the new hospital, since it

was easier to find. "Doc Johnson's office is just down the street from the hospital, over on the east side. He should still be there about now, but if when you pass by that hospital you see a big black dog lying near the east entrance, the doctor is over there instead. That dog's how we know where we can find him. If you ever spot that animal lying outside a door somewhere, it's a sure sign the doc is inside. Seems those two are inseparable."

JoAnn smiled, remembering Shadow's loyalty. "Then if he's in his office, the dog will be lying outside there instead?"

"No, he gives that dog special privileges in his own office. Has him a special bed made up beside his desk. Good thing he gives that dog regular sulphur baths. Most folks would worry about having themselves looked at in the same place where a dog is allowed to stay, but as it is that dog stays cleaner than most his patients." The man chuckled as if finding what he'd just said very funny then nodded toward the center of town. "But if for some reason he has gone on home, you'll find his house is over on Main Street. About six houses down from the city park. Not all that far from the Methodist church. It's a fine, big three-story house made mostly out of red brick with lots of white and black trim. You can't miss it. It has a small stable and carriage house off to the left and a front garden filled with big yellow flowers. I pass right by it every evening on my way to work."

"Thank you," she said, wondering what this man did that allowed him to be off buying tobacco during the day. Turning to follow the directions she'd been given to the hospital, she decided he probably worked second shift at the iron mill, either that or he tended one of the many saloons scattered along Washington Street.

After having to cross several streets, all clattering from the many horses, carriages, and wagons that passed over them, she finally found the hospital. But when she did not see Shadow lying near the east entrance, she next headed in the direction of Park's office. She found the small stone building easily enough but when she reached for the latch to let herself in she noticed a note pinned to the curtain just inside the glass. The doctor had gone home for the day but could be called on at his residence should an emergency arise.

Worried that the reason he had gone home early was because he had suffered further problems with his heart, she headed toward the center of town where she found first the city park then located his house a block away.

Although she had recognized the house from the description she had been given, his residence was confirmed by a small wooden sign hanging near the front gate with his name and the street number. Still worried, she hurried through the tall iron gate that had been left open, up the cobblestone walk, to the front door where she had her choice of pulling the chain to a small brass bell or tapping an elaborate brass-plated door knocker. Choosing the knocker, she rapped lightly three times and waited for someone to answer.

"Can I help you?" A small woman with short wisps of brown hair curling out from beneath a starched white mobcap asked as she swung the door open and peered out at JoAnn expectantly. She looked to be in her early thirties.

"Yes, I'd like to see Doctor Johnson," she said, aware by the slender woman's plain black dress, her crisp white apron, and her work-worn hands, she had to be one of Park's twin housekeepers.

Taking a quick step back to let her in, the housekeeper asked, "And who should I say is calling?"

"Tell him that JoAnn Griffin is here to see him."

"And will he need his medical bag?" she asked, looking at JoAnn with a raised brow as if trying to guess her illness.

"No, this is a personal visit," she assured her. "All he'll need is his friendly smile." Which she was not all that certain she would see. At least not until she'd had a chance to apologize for her rude departure.

"I'll tell him you are here," she said and gestured toward a nearby doorway, indicating JoAnn should enter.

Accommodating her, JoAnn soon found herself in a tastefully decorated receiving parlor, done mostly in dark reds, whites, and blacks. The housekeeper stayed just long enough to switch on the overhead electric lights and light two small table lamps though it was not what JoAnn considered a dark room. She then hurried to the back of the house to find Park.

Too apprehensive to sit, not knowing what sort of reception to expect after having left so abruptly two weeks earlier, JoAnn paced about the room, staring at the massive landscapes and individual portraits that hung high on the twelve-foot walls without actually seeing them.

Several minutes later, Park entered and JoAnn was relieved to see that his coloring was good and his walk steady, but noticed he looked extremely tired.

"I understand you've already gone back to work," she said as a way of starting what she hoped would turn out to be a friendly conversation. "Don't you think it's a little too soon for that?"

"I'm not working as many hours as I did before," he explained with a wide smile and an outstretched hand, clearly not offended to see her again. "Although I don't want Adam to know, I'll admit I do still feel a little weak at times and my chest still hurts whenever I take a very deep breath, which I suspect is due to all that pounding he said you did on me. But other than that, I've been

240

feeling just fine. Even John is amazed at how quickly I recovered." He chuckled as he gestured toward a nearby sofa, indicating she should sit. "But I think he was hoping it would take me a lot longer so he could continue taking care of my patients for me. He might not be too fond of all the extra work, but he does have his eye on a brand new Stanhope and can use the extra income about now."

His grin then widened. "I think it upsets him that I bought one before he could." He shrugged and sank onto the sofa beside JoAnn. "But then I had to replace my broken carriage with something, didn't I? Might as well have the best. After all, Shadow and I spend many hours a day riding around in my carriage while I call on my housebound patients. And when Traveler's leg gets well enough to pull again, I think he deserves something a little fancier behind him."

JoAnn offered a knowing wink. "How kind you are to be so considerate of your animals."

"Yes, it is nice to know they have the best," Park admitted with an answering smile. "And it is also nice to be first in getting the newest conveyance to come out of New York. If you want, I'll take you for a ride in it later," he promised, then leaned back against the scrolled sofa to make himself more comfortable. "So tell me what brings you here this afternoon? You obviously are not sick and even if you were, I have a feeling you'd be the type of doctor to try to heal yourself."

"You want the truth?" she asked, willing to give him at least a partial dose of honesty.

"Why not?" he replied with a casual wave of his hand. "I'm game."

"The truth is I came here because I want to apologize for having left in the middle of the night the way I did two weeks ago."

"And would it be out of line for me to ask why, you

241

left suddenly like that?" Although his smile faded when he asked the question, it was not replaced by the angry scowl JoAnn had expected, nor was there anger in his voice. He seemed more concerned than anything else and that fact touched her in a way no words could.

"No, I guess not," she said, looking momentarily at the hands folded in her lap, then back into his pale blue eyes — eyes so very much like Adam's. "The reason I left without a word like I did is because I did not want to face having to tell either of you goodbye. Truth is, I don't think I was really ready to leave even though I felt it was clearly time to go; and because of that I was afraid I'd be easily convinced to stay." Which was partly true.

Park studied her brown eyes a long moment then crossed his arms and tilted his head to one side as if trying to gauge her. "I think you should know, there is only one way I'll accept your apology."

"And what way is that?" she asked with a cautiously raised eyebrow. She had not expected any conditions.

"That you prove to me how truly sorry you are by staying for dinner. Shelly is roasting a big, fat goose one of my patients gave me yesterday afternoon in lieu of a cash payment. There'll be plenty."

"Will Adam be here?" JoAnn asked eagerly, then winced when she realized how very much like an adoring teenager she had sounded.

"Of course, Adam will be here, but there's a problem. So will Constance Seguin."

Not wanting Park to realize how very attracted she was to Adam, JoAnn tried to cover her earlier outburst by calmly asking, "And why is that a problem?" It took all her restraint not to show any disappointment. She did not want to deal with Constance just yet.

"Because with her here you won't have a chance to apologize to Adam like you just did for me," he said and tapped his fingertips together as if trying to find a way around the predicament. "I won't have you apologizing to him in front of her and I would really like for him to hear that apology right away."

"Why? Was he angry with me for having left the way I did?"

"I don't know if angry is the right word, but he sure did become awfully moody right after that. He hardly said one word to me that morning after he came back from looking for you."

"He went looking for me?" she asked, feeling absurdly pleased yet at the same time a little guilty. She hadn't expected him to be that concerned.

"He surely did. And when he didn't find you, he came back here and locked himself in his study for the rest of the day. If he hadn't already canceled one of his classes the night after I was injured, I think he probably would have stayed in his study the rest of the week. But as it was, he was forced to come out late Thursday afternoon, get dressed, and go back into Johnstown to teach his class. When he returned here that night he wasn't quite as moody as he had been before, but he was just grouchy enough that next day I decided to come on back here. Besides, with him hiding away in his study all day burying himself in his work, there wasn't much for me to do. I was bored silly."

"I gather he found my leaving like I did pretty insulting. I really did not intend for it to be an insult. I just wanted to get away without having to face him again."

"Yet here you are ready to face him now," Park said and his smile returned. "I'd say that's a pretty good sign. But because Adam was so very moody right after you left, I think it would be a pretty good idea for him to hear your apology right away." Tilting his head back against the sofa, he stroked his chin and narrowed his eyes, lost in thought. "If only there was some way to

243

uninvite Constance to dinner tonight."

"You can't do that. It would be too impolite," JoAnn said, though in truth she rather liked the idea.

"Then I have to figure out a way to get Adam away from her so you can talk to him early on," he said, still deep in thought. "But what can I possibly do to get that woman out of the room?"

Shove her through a window perhaps? JoAnn thought with a perverse smile, but managed not to speak the notion aloud. "Maybe I could go to him and apologize right now. Where is he?"

Park scowled. "Probably already with Constance. There was some sort of reception they planned to go to this afternoon. Had something to do with that dam up at Lake Conemaugh."

JoAnn's stomach knotted. She wasn't sure if the painful contraction was from knowing Adam was off somewhere with Constance, or from the mention of the very lake that would eventually devastate that entire city. "When are they due here?"

"I told them that unless an emergency came up, we'd eat about seven," he said, then his face lit with an idea. "I know how to handle this. When they first arrive, they'll go into the parlor. I'll feign a little emergency of my own that is sure to lure him out of the room. Once we have him alone in some other part of the house, I'll leave so you two can make amends without an audience."

"And how will we then explain my sudden appearance to Constance when the time comes for us to return to the parlor?"

Park looked at her, clearly unconcerned. "Won't explain a thing. It's none of her business who I invite to dinner or why."

With nearly two hours before Adam and Constance would arrive, and because JoAnn had muddied her

244

hem and shoes during her five-mile trek into Johnstown, she left Park's house long enough to return to the hotel and change into a fresh outfit. She chose a floor-length, off-the-shoulder mint crepe with a sashed waist. Then she selected a pair of dress shoes with only a slight heel that would barely be seen beneath the ruffled hem. She did not want to feel tall and dowdy while standing next to Little Miss Southern Comfort.

Knowing Constance's hair would be done up in a dazzling array of blond curls, JoAnn decided her hair needed something special and took out the bag of decorative combs she'd brought with her. After carefully pulling the front of her hair back and up in an artful sweep, she anchored it in place with two ornamental combs then allowed the length to flow in soft waves down her back and over her bare shoulders.

By six-thirty she was again at Park's house, anxiously awaiting the arrival of Adam and Constance. When she heard the clattering of a carriage through the open windows as it pulled into the drive beside the house, she hurried into the back bedroom exactly as Park had instructed. Although she was not certain the sort of emergency he intended to feign, she did not doubt its effectiveness and knew that within a very few minutes she would again be face-to-face with Adam. She also knew he would not be too terribly pleased to see her, at least not until she'd had a chance to apologize.

Standing near the open window that opened into an immaculately kept backyard, JoAnn took deep breaths to steady her frazzled nerves while she waited. Although she knew Park stood only a few feet down the hall for she had just seen him pass, she nearly jumped out of her skin when she heard a heavy, cluttering crash just outside her door that included the sound of glass breaking followed by rapid footsteps and Park's loud shouts.

"Adam, I've just knocked over that blamed hall clock. Can you come here and help me set it back right?"

Within seconds, she heard Adam's deep voice, but could not determine his words until he came closer.

"You're lucky you weren't hurt."

"I know. And I can't imagine what caused it to topple over like that. All I was did was adjust the time. Maybe it had something to do with the noise I heard in the bedroom just before it fell."

"Noise? What noise?"

JoAnn stood with her heart lodged firmly in her throat, waiting for the two men to appear in the doorway and when they did, she thought for certain her legs would cave beneath her. Adam's expression went from disbelief, to sudden caution, to sheer anger all in a moment's time.

"What are *you* doing here?" he asked and stepped forward to fill the doorway but without actually coming inside.

"She has something she wants to say to you," Park answered for her, then placed both hands on Adam's shoulders and shoved him on into the room. "Something I didn't think needed to be said in front of Constance." Then before Adam could protest his father's actions, Park reached inside the room and pulled the door closed, leaving them very much alone and JoAnn feeling very awkward.

"Well?" Adam asked, looking more perplexed than angry when he finally spun about to face her. "What is it you wanted to tell me?"

"It's not so much what I want to tell you," JoAnn began, pausing to wet the lips that had so suddenly gone dry with the tip of her tongue. "It's more what I want to ask of you. I am here to apologize for having left the way I did, without offering you or your father a proper goodbye. I realized later, after it was too late, just how inconsiderate I'd been. It was the wrong way to handle my leaving."

"And why did you handle it that way?" he asked, coming forward, clearly interested in her answer.

"I'll try to explain it to you the same way I explained it to your father. The truth is, I don't think I was really ready to leave even though I knew the time had come for me to go. I was afraid that if I stayed to tell you goodbye personally instead of in a note, you would do or say something that would convince me to stay like you did before and I really did need to go."

"And what makes you think I wasn't ready for you to leave?" he asked and crossed his arms as he moved closer still.

It was then JoAnn noticed how extremely handsome he looked in his three-piece suit. This one had a different cut than the ones before making her wonder if it was new.

"After all," he continued, "you had already been a visitor at my house for nearly a week. That was longer than most guests stay."

JoAnn felt a sharp stab of regret and looked away. She had not expected such a cold response. "Were you?"

"Ready for you to leave?," he asked, as if wanting to be sure of the question. He then uncrossed his arms and reached out to take her unexpectedly into his arms. "No. I wasn't. And you are right. I did hope to convince you to stay and if that didn't work, I intended to ask your permission to start calling on you."

JoAnn was too distracted by the excitement and warmth that had slowly invaded her senses to do the right thing and pull away. After all, Adam belonged to another woman. She had no right to come between them. Even so, rather than discourage him like she should, she leaned into the unexpected embrace and peered questioningly into his smiling face. "Isn't Pittsburgh a little far for you to be calling on a woman?"

"Not when the woman is as beautiful and compelling as you," he admitted, glad at last to have the chance to tell her how he felt. "If you want the truth, I was very upset when I discovered you'd left. You had taken away my only opportunity to tell you how I felt."

"And how is that?" she asked, wondering why she did not try to change the direction of the conversation. She was not there to make him want her. She was there simply because she'd missed him. Still, she was curious to know how he felt.

"Intrigued," he stated with a sudden smile while his glittering blue eyes scanned her upturned face. "To say the least."

Feeling warmed to her very toes, JoAnn returned his smile, as amused as she was pleased by his choice of words. "Am I to gather by that smile of yours that I am to be forgiven for my misdeed?"

"Madam, you were forgiven the second I saw you again. There is just something about you that will not allow me to stay angry with you."

"Good. I'd hate to think I'd jeopardized our *friendship* by having acted so foolishly."

"Looks to me like our friendship is still very much intact." He studied her upturned face for a moment more, then realized how carefully she had stressed that word friendship, as if to warn him that she was not yet ready for anything beyond that. Although he desperately yearned to take full advantage of their closeness and kiss her passionately, he took a deep breath and slowly pulled away. "Are you staying for dinner?"

"Yes. Your father invited me. I was just freshening up. I'll be in in a few minutes," she said, feeling her legs a bit too shaky to walk just then.

"You'll find it just down the hall and to the left," Adam said, then promptly headed toward the door.

JoAnn stared after him, puzzled, then remembered the last time she'd mentioned freshening up and wanted to laugh.

While Adam reached for the door handle, he turned to look at her again.

"I'm glad you're back," he said, then when he turned to walk out into the hall, he found his father standing there with the oddest grin perched on his wrinkled old face.

"I suppose you had something to do with her coming back," he said, looking at him suspiciously.

"Not me," he responded, then held out his hands in a show of innocence. "All I'm guilty of is sabotaging an old worn-out clock. Her coming back here to apologize to us was all her own idea." He then winked at JoAnn as he fought a definite urge to grin. "Although I have to admit, I'm glad she did it."

Adam stared at his father, as if trying to think of a proper response, then turned and headed down the hall, shaking his head.

Park watched after him, looking very pleased, then turned to JoAnn and whispered, "See you in a few minutes. We have more work to do." Then he hurried down the hall as spritely as a man of twenty.

JoAnn wondered what work he could possibly mean. She had already apologized to Adam and he had generously forgiven her. What more was there to be done? Knowing the answer would soon reveal itself, she waited only a few minutes before making her appearance and, as expected, Constance was not at all pleased to see her. Although she had been thoroughly relaxed while seated in the center of a plump red and white medallion-backed sofa when JoAnn first entered the room, she immediately tensed. The gleam in her eyes turned as red as the tightly fitted dress she wore and as red as the couch upon which she sat, making JoAnn wonder if dear Constance had selected her outfit to match with the decor.

"I thought you'd already returned to Pittsburgh," she said, looking suspiciously from JoAnn to Park to Adam. As if unwilling to face a woman she clearly considered her adversary while sitting, she stood and hurried across the room to Adam's side, where she hovered at his elbow in her usual catlike fashion.

"She did," Park said, quickly interceding, as if wanting control of the situation. "But she's come back for a short visit."

"How short?" Constance asked bluntly, then narrowed her green eyes to indicate that no matter how short the visit, it would be too lengthy for her taste.

"That depends," JoAnn replied, perfectly willing to answer for herself. "I'll stay only as long as I feel welcome."

"Which could be an eternity," Park said in a very cheerful tone. It was obvious he was enjoying himself when he turned to JoAnn and smiled. "If that's how long you plan to stay, you might as well get your things and move in with us today."

Constance spun about to glare at Adam, apparently expecting him to say something reassuring and when all he did was stare curiously at his father, she took a sharp breath and thrust her proud chin forward. "I don't think that would be very appropriate."

"Why is that?" Park asked, looking truly puzzled, clearly wanting to play this for all he could.

Constance's eyes widened then narrowed again. "Well, for one thing, she is not married and neither are you or Adam. Although everyone knows that Adam couldn't possibly be interested in someone like her because he's presently interested in me, they might decide *you* have an inappropriate desire to have her around. Keep in mind, she is probably half your age, nearly the same age as your own son. If she moved in *here* with the two of you, even for the littlest of whiles, tongues would wag. It was bad enough when she was stayin' with you out at Adam's."

"She's a little older than half my age," Park replied, then stiffened his chin as if insulted by her remark. "And I think I'd like to have a few tongues wagging about me." He then looked at JoAnn and held out his hand to her, bowing slightly when she extended her own. "What about it? Would you like to stay here for a few days? It would save having to spend all that money for a hotel and you would have a much larger room."

JoAnn's original inclination had been to decline, albeit politely, but when she heard another one of Constance's sharp gasps, she could not help joining in the torment. "Thank you. I'd like that."

When Constance turned her rounded gaze on Adam again, she was positively pale. "Adam, aren't you planning to say something? Surely you don't intend to let her stay here in the same house with the two of you."

"It's not my house," he replied with a shrug, then flattened his mouth into an annoyed frown when he noticed her start to sway.

"Oh, no, there she goes," Park muttered just as Constance's eyes rolled shut and she sank prettily into Adam's awaiting arms.

"She's fainted," JoAnn said, feeling a sudden pang of guilt for having had a part in causing the woman to actually pass out. The doctor in her took over. "Stretch her out on the floor," she said to Adam. Then to Park she said, "Put a pillow up under her feet."

She knelt at Constance's side and felt her neck for a pulse, relieved to feel a good steady rhythm. Then aware her breathing was restricted, she looked at Park, who was peering curiously over her bare shoulder then at Adam who was peering curiously *at* her bare shoulder. "Find some scissors. Hurry."

"Don't be so concerned," Park said as he stepped over to a small table, pulled open a drawer, and quickly scrambled through the contents. "She swoons all the time. She'll wake up again in just a minute and she'll be just as angry as ever."

"But she's not getting enough air," JoAnn warned, knowing that could only hamper her return to consciousness. Hurriedly, she worked the many hooks and buttons along the side of the red satin dress until she had the garment open. She then took the scissors Park handed her, reached inside the gap, pushed the white ruffled camisole out of her way, and cut the strings of Constance's corset, amazed at how the corset snapped, as if it had suddenly sprung to life.

When Constance's eyes fluttered open just seconds later, it was obvious she had expected to find Adam leaning over her instead of JoAnn. Her eyes narrowed with immediate annoyance. "What happened?"

"You fainted," JoAnn supplied, chewing on her lower lip while she studied the huge gap in Constance's dress. With the corset damaged, there was no way to force that dress closed. She blinked and tried to hold back an unwarranted grin when she then looked at Park, who obviously had realized the same.

Adam stood nearby looking as if he were at a total loss. "You did faint, but you are all right now. JoAnn cut your corset so you could breathe."

"She did *what?*" Constance's hands flew to her waist where she found a seven-inch gap in her gown. Her green eyes stretched to their limits.

"And it's a good thing she did," Park inserted with a confirming nod. "Because it sure has brought the color back to your cheeks. There for a while, you were as pale as a ghost."

Although JoAnn really did feel a little sorry for Constance's sudden predicament, she had to look away to keep from grinning at that last comment because there was now plenty of color in Constance's cheeks, most of it a bright crimson red.

"Adam. Take me home," she said, clutching the side of her gown while she quickly stood. Then without giving him enough time to respond, she headed for the door.

"Looks like we won't be staying for supper after all," Adam said with no real show of emotion when he started to follow. "I'll be back later."

Park waited until Constance and Adam had left before turning to JoAnn with a wide grin. "That reminds me. We still have that big plump goose waiting for us. Let's go eat the thing. I'm starved."

Chapter Twelve

"Now that we've finished eating, why don't we go on over to the hotel and get your things," Park said. "I can take you in my new Stanhope."

"That's not necessary," she assured him as she pushed her plate back, so full she wanted to let out the sash on her mint green dress. "I know you weren't serious when you suggested I stay here. You just wanted to torment Constance for some reason."

"Oh, but I was serious," he protested, then pulled his bushy white eyebrows together as if accusing her of something. "Are you trying to tell me you intend to go back on your word?"

"No. It's just that Constance was right. Some people would think my staying here overnight a little scandalous." Especially in that day and age, she mused.

"Don't you want to stay here with us?" he asked, looking suddenly hurt by her refusal to comply.

"Of course I do. I enjoy your company very much, but I don't want to start any unnecessary gossip."

"If there was to be any gossip, it would already have started. After all, you've already stayed with us an entire week."

"But that was at Adam's house where there were

several other people around. People you could claim were chaperons. It is my understanding that except for the nights when Adam stays here, you live in this house alone."

"That's true. My housekeepers do go home at night, mainly because I can't stand to have them underfoot. Still, I don't see why that should matter much."

"But it does," she said in earnest, at the moment more concerned with what might actually happen than she was with the proprieties of the time. Now that she had felt Adam's arms around her again, she wanted him more than ever. Wanted to be reminded of the incredible power of his kiss. Wanted to know what it might be like to have him make love to her. And that was a selfish thing to want. And a *dangerous* thing to want.

"Then I'll pay Sheila to stay the night. She's not married. Nor does she have a special fellow like her sister. She only has that dog waiting for her at home." He shrugged as if to indicate how simple he thought the solution. "As far as that dog of hers is concerned, she can bring him over here to stay the night, too. Shadow might enjoy the company." Though he doubted it. Shadow was too used to the attention that went with being the only animal in the house.

Park glanced under the table where the black lab lay patiently at his feet. "How about it, Shadow? Want some company? Someone to share a bone with?"

Before JoAnn could offer further protest, Park was up from the table and headed toward the kitchen. When he returned, he flashed a catlike smile. "It's all settled. Sheila will stay the night. Let's go get your things."

Having run out of plausible arguments, JoAnn finally relented and followed Park to the carriage house.

She stood to the side while he hitched a tall black horse to his new buggy. When he was finished she climbed reluctantly onto the shiny leather seat and watched him take up the reins.

Within minutes they had reached the hotel and had retrieved her bags. On the way back, they stopped at a small, wood-framed house near the north end of town for Sheila and coerced Mitchell, her large black and brown spotted dog into the carriage.

By nine o'clock Park had JoAnn settled into the same room she had used earlier when offering her apology to Adam. Mitchell and Sheila stayed in a small group of rooms behind the kitchen. And because Park, Shadow, and Adam had beds somewhere upstairs, that's where Park went shortly thereafter.

It was ten o'clock when Adam finally returned to a silent house. The only light flickered from an oil lamp. Moving quietly, he paused to bolt the front door then picked up the lamp and headed for the stairs. He was on the second step before it dawned on him that he should check to see if JoAnn was still there.

He crept down the hall to the room he felt certain she would use if she stayed, mainly because there was only one other spare bedroom and that one was upstairs filled with clutter. Elated to find the door closed, knowing that meant she was probably inside, he reached for the handle and turned it. When it resisted as if locked from the inside, he knew for certain she was there. Smiling, he hurried on off to bed.

He could hardly wait until morning.

Adam rushed to his father's house so he could spend some time with JoAnn before heading off to teach his night class. He had seen her only briefly at breakfast and knew that was not enough to sustain him for a full day. When he arrived he hurried through the lower floor but was disappointed to discover she was not there. Neither was his father, and for some reason that annoyed him. Wanting to find out where they were, feeling definitely left out and even a little betrayed, he headed straight for the kitchen.

"Did Father say where he and Miss Griffin were going?" he asked, looking from one twin housekeeper to the other. Except for the pitch in their voices and certain mannerisms, the two Drum sisters were impossibly alike. They were both short, dark complected, and immaculate in their dress. The only noticeable difference besides their voices and a few particular mannerisms was the fact Sheila was such a scatterbrain, and had an ugly scar on her right arm to prove it. The scar came from the day she forgot she had already stoked the kitchen stove then leaned against it.

Because Shelly was almost always the one to answer his questions, she glanced up from the onions she had just chopped with a questioning frown and she dabbed daintily at the perspiration on her forehead with the back of her sleeve. "Your father hasn't come in yet. His guest, though, did say something about taking a short walk. Said she wanted to see the park. Hates to stay inside."

Knowing the park was only a block away and still eager to spend some time with her before heading to the institute, Adam hurried to the front door but slowed his steps when he saw she was already coming up the walk.

"What are you doing back so early?" she asked as she entered the gate, remembering that Park had said it would be nearly six before he or Adam returned.

"Had an easy day," he lied, knowing it had been an

abnormally busy one. He had worked like a madman to finish the project Fulton had given him that morning. "I finished early so I thought I'd come on home."

"I'm glad you did. I could use the company," she said and continued forward toward the house. Just seeing him standing there on the small, shaded porch in front of Park's house set her pulses to racing at an incredible rate. The main reason she had come back was to spend a little time with Adam so she was glad of any such opportunity.

"Did you enjoy your walk?" he asked, his thoughts too jumbled by the sight of her to think of anything more interesting to discuss.

"Yes, it was fascinating." Her brown eyes sparkled while she continued to look up at him. She had watched a group of small boys playing stick ball in the park while their mothers chatted on park benches. In her own time such as that would have seemed rather mundane, but watching such activities in this time frame, with everyone dressed so oddly, it had been a delightful experience.

"You find everything fascinating, don't you?" he asked, knowing it was true. He stepped back when she passed then reached ahead of her for the door to let her inside.

"I guess I do," she admitted and paused in the doorway to glance back over her shoulder. "I like to see new things and meet new people. Don't you?"

"Never really thought much about it," he answered and stroked the strong lines of his chin while he thought about it. "I guess so." He had certainly enjoyed meeting *her*. "Do you take many such walks back home?"

"When at my parents' house, I do. But not when I'm in the city. Too much traffic."

"What do you do for entertainment while in the city?" he asked, still determined to find out more about her. In the three weeks since he had met her, she had rarely talked about herself "I remember you said you don't go to balls, rarely attend the theater, and hardly have time to read. What else is there to do?"

"I'm really too busy with my work to do much of anything else," she replied, knowing he would not understand her answers if she were to tell him the truth. How did one explain watching television, listening to the radio, or playing Nintendo to a man from the 1880s. "What do you do for entertainment?"

Aware she had diverted the conversation yet again, he narrowed his gaze while he followed her into the front parlor. "I usually go to the theater, or the opera, or to a ball when there is one, and I have been known to play a little ten pin. Or else I stay home and play chess with Father or I read. Do you ever go to the opera?"

JoAnn shook her head. She didn't even watch the opera on cable though she had come across it from time to time while switching channels. "I don't have time. I'm sure you'll understand when I explain that a woman has to work twice as hard and twice as long to have the same opportunities given a man."

"And just where is it you work?"

"I told you. I work at a large hospital in Pittsburgh," she answered. She did not want to give him a name, knowing he might ask around later and discover it did not exist yet. "I help take care of the injured people who come in or those who have sudden and very serious illnesses."

Adam twisted his mouth into a curious frown. "In what part of Pittsburgh is this hospital?"

"On the east side," she answered readily. "Not very far from where I live."

"And where do you live?"

"On the east side. Not very far from the hospital," she answered, then arched an eyebrow as she stifled a grin. "You certainly do ask a lot of questions. Have you been taking lessons in question asking from your little friend George Hess?"

Despite the annoyance of having had his question all but ignored, Adam laughed. "No, but if ever I wanted to perfect the art, he'd be the one to give lessons. He's a true master."

"Speaking of George, how are he and his family?" she asked, wanting to keep the topic of conversation away from herself. Too nervous to sit just yet, she walked across to an open window and gazed out at the front yard and to the busy street beyond. "And how's Traveler's leg? Park said the horse was still at your place and probably would be for a month or two yet."

"Now who's asking a lot of questions?" he teased, then followed her to the window. "Traveler's leg is better but as Father indicated, he's still not ready to pull a carriage and as for George and his family, you'll be able to see for yourself Saturday when we take a ride up there to check on them."

"You didn't mention anything about a trip to your house this Saturday." Part of her was thrilled by the thought while another part of her realized the danger. "Will your father be going with us?"

"I didn't mention the trip because I didn't think about it until you asked about Traveler and George, and I doubt Father will want to go since he'll probably need to rest," he explained, eager to have her alone. He knew that if they stayed at his father's through the weekend there would be a constant stream of visitors, some checking on Park's health while others were curious to see what their new house guest looked like. "I thought it would be a good idea for you to have a look at Traveler's leg and George's hand to make sure they are both healing properly. Of course, such a trip would mean staying the night at my house, but I don't see that as a problem. You didn't have any plans for this coming Saturday and Sunday, did you?"

"No," she answered honestly and realized that although it would mean being alone with Adam during the rides up there and back, the trip would give her the perfect opportunity to slip away and check the time passage for further shrinkage. If for some reason the hole had picked up speed in mending itself, she wanted to know. Although she was thoroughly enjoying herself, she did not want to take the chance of becoming trapped on the wrong side of that time barrier.

"Good, then it's settled. We'll leave before lunch." He then immediately changed the subject.

By late Saturday morning when the time came to leave, Adam had exhausted every means possible to encourage JoAnn into telling him where she worked or where she lived. Again he wondered why she seemed so determined to keep such secrets from him and was annoyed that she obviously did not trust him enough to tell him everything.

He had given her no reason to distrust him and speculated if there could be someone out there trying to find her, someone who had so terrified her that she wanted to leave no clues as to her whereabouts. Someone who wanted to harm her for some reason.

Just the thought that there might be someone like that out there made him feel very protective of her and he decided it was time to know more about her. If she did not open up to him soon, he would hire an investigator to look into her past. One way or another, he planned to get the information he needed to help her.

Originally JoAnn's plan had been to return to the present after only a few days, but after having discovered the hole was now shrinking at an almost nonexistent rate, she decided it would be safe to stay awhile longer. With weeks yet before she was scheduled to return to work, she saw no reason to hurry back to her parents' house. The problems there could wait, as could the problems at work.

JoAnn saw no reason to hurry back to the future. She wasn't nearly as frustrated by the lack of modern conveniences this trip, and almost everyone's attitude toward her had changed for the better, largely because Park and Adam had so willingly accepted her. She was happier than she had been in a long time and knew now that Jean had been right all along. The settling of the estate could wait awhile longer. It was more important she get away from her parents' house and find some time for herself. Time to forget her many problems and simply be happy.

Being in the past had proved to be the perfect distraction. It was a divine gift to be specially treasured, and even though she was still upset with God for having snatched her parents from her the way He did, she also felt grateful to Him for this wondrous experience of a lifetime — of *two* lifetimes. It had proved to be the perfect opportunity to get over her grief and inadequacies, and get back in touch with herself by rediscovering who she really was and what she truly wanted from life.

It seemed odd that just when she had decided there was nothing left to live for, nothing left that would ever make her life bearable again, she had been given the opportunity to know and care for these wonderful people. Being there with them had not only helped soothe her sorrow, it had made her realize there was still a reason to carry on with life. A reason to return to her work. A reason to continue being the doctor she'd always wanted to be.

She smiled when she slipped her small Instamatic camera into her skirt pocket. Since Adam was busy helping Cyrus repair a broken pulley in the barn, she knew she would have a little time to herself and decided to take a few pictures. She wanted to be sure she took back memories of this place by capturing them on film.

Glad it had finally stopped raining again, JoAnn moved from spot to spot, slyly pulling her camera out of her pocket and taking pictures of the area. While snapping a picture of the flower gardens along the back of the house from the shadows just outside the barn, she overheard George's and Cyrus's voices through a small window that had been propped open with a board.

"I wonder why they didn't go to that big fancy dance in Johnstown last night," George said, his voice forming more of a statement than a question. "I heard some of the women at church talking about it this morning. Seems to me Mister Adam would have wanted to take Miss JoAnn and show her off."

"To the cotillion? I imagine because he'd probably planned to take Miss Constance," Cyrus answered. Because his voice was deeper and harder to understand, JoAnn moved a few steps closer to the opening, her camera still poised as if planning to take a picture of the house while she listened. "And after having told Miss Constance some big whopper or another to get out of going with her, he didn't dare show up with someone else."

"Think so? Think he'd do that?"

"I think he'd do just about anything to be with your Miss JoAnn," Cyrus muttered, clearly not pleased with Adam's choice of companion. "That woman has got some sort of evil spell cast over him that makes him want to spend all his time with her."

"Stop that!" George protested. "You make her sound like a witch or something."

"Maybe she is," Cyrus shot back in ready defense. "Maybe that's what sort of doctor she is—a *witch* doctor."

"You take that back," George said. His voice rose several notches. "She ain't no witch doctor."

"Oh, shut up and hand me that rope. I didn't mean nothin' by it. It was just too good an opportunity to pass up. Mister Adam's going to be back any minute with that other pulley and we need to have this one out of the way before then."

Still clutching the camera in one hand, JoAnn leaned even closer to the small window, waiting to hear if something else might be said about her, curious to know why Cyrus thought she had Adam under some sort of magical spell. She was concentrating so hard on the sounds coming from inside the barn she did not hear Adam's approach until it was too late.

"What's that?" he asked, looking curiously at the small camera in her hand.

"What's what?" Her heart took a sudden jump when she realized she'd just been caught with something she would have one heck of a time explaining. Quickly she slipped the camera into her pocket.

"That," he said and nodded toward the narrow slit that was her pocket, frowning at such an odd reaction. "What was it?"

"That box?" she asked as if not sure what he meant.

"Is that what it was? A box?"

"Yes, it was just a box," she said, then glanced around for something to distract him. She noticed the pulley in his hands and decided that would have to do. "And what's that?"

"What's what?" he asked, confused by the unexpected change of topic, his thoughts still on the black box she had so quickly tried to hide.

"That thing in your hand. It looks complicated. What is it?"

"This? Just a pulley used to help lift the heavier bales of hay up into the loft."

"Is that the thing that was broken?"

"Not this one," he answered, aware she had successfully diverted the conversation yet again. "The pulley Cyrus broke earlier could not be repaired. This is a spare one I keep in the toolshed."

"How clever to keep a spare," she went on, her heart still hammering at a fierce rate, afraid at any minute he would change the conversation back to questioning her about her "box." She did not want to have to do or say anything that might make him think her peculiar, knowing he would never believe she was from another time period. Just because she had finally adjusted to the realities of time travel, she could not expect everyone else to accept it as willingly—*or at all*. "Is that because those pulleys break often?"

"Often enough," he admitted, deciding that if having been caught with that little black box made her that uncomfortable he would let the incident pass. "Nothing lasts forever."

265

"That's true," she said, already stepping away. "I guess I'd better let you get back to work." She gestured toward the barn with her chin. "I think Cyrus and George are inside waiting for you."

"How do you know that?" he asked, not having heard any voices but knowing that was where he expected to find them.

"I just know." She was not about to admit she had been eavesdropping and continued to walk away. "You'd better get on in there."

Adam watched her hurry across the muddied yard, up the back steps, and after wiping her feet on the tow sack left near the back door, into the house. He was still bothered by the obvious fact she had not wanted him to know what was inside that little box. Turning toward the side door of the barn, he shook his head, wondering why that woman had so many secrets and why she still did not trust him enough to share them.

"You bring that other pulley?" Cyrus asked when he looked down from the loft and saw Adam enter from the side.

"Right here," Adam answered and held it out as he headed for the ladder. He handed it up to Cyrus who took it and shimmied a support post then crawled out onto the main rafters near where the old pulley had been.

Using the tools he had left there, he quickly installed the new pulley then reached for the rope George had tossed up to him earlier. "Did you think to oil it?" he asked while he worked to thread the thick rope through the rung.

"Yes. She's ready to put to work," Adam said, standing on the floor beside several bales of hay that still needed to be lifted into the loft. "Toss down the hook when you're ready to test her."

Several minutes later, Cyrus did just that and as expected the new pulley held the weight.

"Good job, you two," Adam said, aware that even though they had wanted him there to supervise, they had done most of the work. "Now that the problem is solved, I'll go on back to the house."

"So you can be with Miss JoAnn?" Cyrus muttered in a resentful voice, barely loud enough to be heard below.

"And what's wrong with that?" Adam wanted to know, not having expected such a response from Cyrus. "Did you want me to stay and help you put these last few bales of hay into the loft?"

"No." His expression hardened while he shimmied back down the post to the floor of the loft. "I can do that."

George's face curled into a tight frown when he stepped closer to the edge of the loft and looked down at Adam. "Cyrus don't like her."

"Why not?" Adam couldn't imagine anyone not liking JoAnn. He watched Cyrus with a curious expression when the boy stopped to brush the dirt and cobwebs off his pants. "What has she done to make you not like her?"

"He don't like her because he thinks she's a witch," George answered for him.

"No I don't," Cyrus said to Adam in ready defense, scowling when he stood erect again. "I just said that to make George angry."

"But why?" Adam wanted to know, aware that Cyrus shot George a quick menacing glare as if warning him not to say another word.

But as usual George was not easily intimidated. When he noticed that Cyrus was headed for the ladder, he followed, not about to be left behind. "Tell him, Cyrus," he urged and stared at his angry brother, his skinny shoulders tossed back with clear defiance. "Tell him why you don't like her. Why you think she's a witch."

"Yes, Cyrus, tell me." Adam moved to where he could see the boys' faces better while they climbed down the ladder. "Why do you think she's a witch?"

Cyrus took a deep breath as he stepped onto the ground then shoved his hands into his pants pockets and stared at the hay-strewn dirt under his feet. "Well for one thing, she *knows things.*"

"Knows things?" Adam asked, thinking that a strange answer because if she didn't know things, they would declare her a fool. "What sort of things?"

Cyrus then lifted his unblinking gaze to meet Adam's and answered in a strangely ominous voice. "Things she don't bother to say aloud. Things she don't want other people to know she knows. Secret things. Mamma says she goes to a lot of trouble to keep the things she knows to herself."

Adam stared at him with a fixed expression, amazed that Doris thought such a thing about JoAnn. Knowing what a good judge of character Doris normally was, it gave him an eerie feeling to find out that she was so suspicious of JoAnn—especially when he knew at least part of what she'd said about her was true. JoAnn was holding back something. Something she didn't want any of them to know. He had sensed that from the beginning. He just hadn't realized anyone else had sensed it, too.

"Momma says she goes as far as to press her lips together in an attempt to keep from saying aloud whatever thoughts has crossed her mind. Momma saw her do that the day George hurt his hand. When we was talking about the dam. And I saw her do it again

268

yesterday when you was telling us about that petition those men in Johnstown are hoping to take to Washington sometime in July, the one demanding that the government do something to force the hunting and fishing club to make those repairs they say are needed." His hazel eyes rounded as a thought occurred to him. "I think maybe she's one of them."

"One of who? Of the club members?" Adam asked, thinking that absurd.

"Could be," he said with a foreboding nod. "Could be she comes from a family with lots of money. Maybe she's a'kin to the Carnegies or the Fricks or some other such wealthy family."

"But you told me she was a road tramp," George put in with a disgusted shake of his blond head as he dropped the last few feet off the ladder onto the ground near Cyrus, aware how dramatically his older brother's accusations had changed over the past few weeks. "You said she was a vagabond just out looking for a handout."

"Well, I changed my mind," Cyrus said with a forward thrust of his chin, again looking at George with a deliberately raised eyebrow, another clear warning to shut his mouth. "Now I've decided she's probably one of those people from the hunting and fishing club who goes up there every summer to laze around that fancy clubhouse and play silly games. I was obviously wrong about her not having any money. How else could she have afforded to put herself up at the Emerald Hotel the other night? That's one of the most expensive places in Johnstown."

"She can afford to stay there because she's a doctor and everyone knows doctors make plenty of money," George answered and moved toward Adam. "Look at Mister Adam's father. He makes enough to live in that big fine house on Main Street and drive the fanciest rig in all the county."

"I already told you, rattlebrain, she ain't no doctor. She's too pretty to be no doctor. Besides, if she really was a doctor, she wouldn't be able to travel around visiting people whenever she pleases. She'd have patients to take care of. You don't see Doc Johnson just taking off and visiting with people a hundred miles away."

"I ain't no rattlebrain. You take that back," George said, charging at his brother with both arms swinging.

"That's enough, you two," Adam said and lurched forward just in time to catch George by his webbed suspenders and just seconds before his little fists would have made contact with Cyrus's outstretched forearm. "Just because you two have a difference of opinion isn't any reason to come to blows." He then looked at Cyrus with clear warning glinting from his blue eyes. "And I don't want to hear any more name-calling from you. Your brother is not a rattlebrain. He may be a little hotheaded at times, but he's no rattlebrain."

"I'm sorry," Cyrus said, but with little feeling. "Should I apologize to Miss JoAnn, too?"

"No, that won't be necessary," Adam said, knowing it would not be right to make the boy apologize for having stated the truth as he saw it. It was only his interpretation of that truth that proved wrong. "She was not here to hear you say such things and I see no reason to mention them to her." He then looked at George, whom he still held by the suspenders. "Is it safe to let go of you yet? Or are you still determined to beat your own brother to a bloody pulp?"

"You can let go," George said with little enthusiasm. "I ain't going to hit him."

"Good. Now if the two of you would put the same

energy into getting the last of that hay stored away as you do into arguing with each other, you should be able to grab your poles and be fishing within the hour."

"Won't do us much good," Cyrus muttered, still in a dismal mood from what had just happened. "As high and fast as that water's been moving these past few weeks, the fish aren't going to be biting. When's it ever going to stop raining long enough for the creeks and rivers to go down to a more normal level?" Raking his hands through his sandy-colored hair, he then headed toward the hay hook. "Come on, George. Fish or no fish, we still have five more bales to move."

Chapter Thirteen

By the following Wednesday, Adam had grown weary of all the secretiveness and was determined to find out more about JoAnn Griffin. That evening, while Park was in East Conemaugh helping deliver the baby of a woman whose last two children had been stillborn, Adam decided to do what he could to encourage JoAnn to open up to him, knowing it was either persuade her to talk about herself or hire someone else to find out what made her behave so mysteriously.

"You never talk about yourself," he observed in a casual manner while he poured himself a second cup of hot chocolate. Because it was unseasonably cold that night, Sheila had prepared a large pot of the steaming drink and brought a tray to them in the parlor shortly after they had retired from dinner. She had also closed all the downstairs windows at some point during the afternoon and had lit several small fires in the downstairs fireplaces while he and JoAnn were eating. "Why is it you don't like to.talk about yourself?"

Although JoAnn had just settled into the cushiony sofa nearest the fire for a few relaxing hours of conversation with Adam, all of her systems jumped to immeliate alert, aware her cozy evening with Adam had just taken a sudden and unanticipated turn. "What do you mean? I talk about myself."

"No you don't. You talk *around* yourself but you never really talk *about* yourself. Whenever our conversation leans in your direction, you almost always turn it around to point at me." He sank back onto the sofa beside her, holding the delicate china cup in the curve of his muscular hand.

"That's because you lead such a fascinating life," she said, hoping to divert his attention with flattery. "You are a chemist, a geologist, a banker, a teacher, a landowner, and an environmentalist."

"A *what?*" Adam asked, letting himself become temporarily distracted.

"An environmentalist," she said already aware the term had probably not been used in the 1880s. "Someone who tries to conserve the land, keep it the way it should be. When you first bought this land, you told me how so much of it had been stripped of lumber and coal and how not only did you replant the trees on your own land, you asked permission to plant seedlings on the land owned by Cambria Iron that surrounds yours. That was the act of an environmentalist."

"That was an act to prevent dangerous landslides and slow the excessive watershed," he commented. He remembered having explained to her why his land was covered with grown trees when other areas of the mountain were virtually bare. "And I knew that if I didn't replant and in a big way, we'd eventually end up with no local source of wood."

"That is because you are a progressive thinker," she said with a confirming nod. Which was the same reason he had eventually accepted the fact she was a doctor even though he was from a time period in

273

which something like that was hard for any man to accept. It was even hard for women from that time period to accept the concept of a woman being a doctor because in 1889 very few women doctors existed, and what few there were either lived in the larger cities where there were enough liberal-minded people to accept them or else they headed out West where doctors were so few that even female doctors were usually welcome.

"See? You know an awful lot about me, but what do I know about you? You've been here another whole week and I don't know anything more about you today than I did when you appeared here last Wednesday. You won't even tell me how long you plan to stay with us this time or where it is you'll go if and when you do leave again. Why is that?" He tried to make his next question sound more casual than concerned. "You don't have any deep, dark secrets hidden away in your past do you?"

JoAnn blinked while she considered her answer to that. Technically, she did not have a past — at least not in 1889.

"No." She felt that was an honest enough answer. "I have no deep, dark secrets hidden in my past. Besides, I talk about myself all the time. How else would you know that I'm a doctor or that my parents died not quite six weeks ago? And how else would you know that I like a cup of hot chocolate before bedtime and have since I was a small child?"

"But you never mention anything very specific. I know you are a doctor who knows a lot about surgery, yet I have no idea the name of the hospital where you work nor do I know where you live. I do know you'll have to leave here soon yet I have no idea when you will go. For all I know, you could go running off in the night again at any time and I'd have a very hard time finding you."

"I won't do that," she promised. "That was a childish thing to do and I will never do anything like that again. I'll let you know when it is time for me to leave."

"That's reassuring, but I'd really like to be able to call on you after you do leave. Yet how can I do that when I don't know where you live? I don't even know *if* I should call on you. Every time I hint that I'd like the chance to know you a little better, to become a little more than simple friends, you change the subject," he said, clearly frustrated, then leaned toward her so he could study her facial expressions better. He fought the urge to touch her, knowing that might distract her from giving an answer. "Is there someone else in your life? Someone important enough to prevent you from opening up to me?" He took a deep breath then made the question more direct. "Does someone else already hold the rights to your heart?"

JoAnn thought about that, wondering how much she should tell him, then decided it would not hurt her situation any for Adam to know about Thomas. Setting her empty cup aside, she turned to face him. "At one time there was someone else in my life. Someone I thought was very important to me. But that was a long time ago and like you, I've managed to get over much of the resulting pain."

Aware she had referred to his own wife's death, he nodded that he understood. "Was this that same man who you said married someone else?"

She nodded, having momentarily forgotten that earlier conversation. "The very same."

"And did you love him?"

"I thought I did," she admitted. She never would have allowed him to take her virginity if she hadn't. If only she had known the truth, that he was simply

275

using her.

Adam saw the pain reflected in her dark brown eyes. "How long ago was that?" he wanted to know. Although he did not like knowing she had been hurt that badly by someone, he was glad she had finally opened up to him.

"Years ago. Back when I was still attending college."

"Then he doesn't live there in Pittsburgh," he surmised, remembering she had told his father how she had gone to some college in New York.

"No, he works for a private hospital in Illinois alongside his father-in-law, Dr. Wimberlain Stickrod. I haven't seen Thomas since he graduated the year before I did." Which she felt was fortunate. Had she seen him again, she might have been tempted to strangle him on the spot and murder would not look very promising on a medical résumé.

"His name was Thomas?" Adam repeated, memorizing the name, curious to know what the man who had once held JoAnn's heart was like. "And what did your friend, Jean, think of him?"

JoAnn looked at him, surprised. She did not remember having told Adam about Jean, but obviously she had mentioned her name and like everything else, he had committed the fact to memory.

"Jean only met him a few times but she did not like him at all. Jean has an uncanny way of seeing right through people. I guess that's why she ended up becoming a psychiatrist."

"So she's a doctor, too. Does she work for the same hospital you do?"

JoAnn shifted uncomfortably, wondering how to divert this conversation onto a safer topic without seeming obvious. He had already admitted noticing whenever she did that. "Yes. She does."

"What's the name of the hospital where you two

work?"

JoAnn tensed. She did not want him to have something tangible that could eventually be used against her credibility. Relief washed over her when at that moment someone knocked loudly on the front door.

Adam frowned, aware Park was still gone and remembering he had told Sheila to go on to bed. "I guess I'd better see who that is," he said, then reluctantly rose to his feet. He had finally maneuvered JoAnn into opening up to him and was in no mood for any outside interruptions. "I'll be right back."

Several minutes later, when he returned to the parlor, there were two men behind him. One looked to be about twenty-three and was rather handsome and debonair looking with dark curling hair and taut shoulders, and a smattering of freckles that had just begun to fade with age. He was slender but not what JoAnn would call bone-skinny and stood every bit as tall as Adam.

The other man was a full two inches shorter and looked to be about twenty-nine or thirty. He had sandy blond hair and light blue eyes with a slightly protruding chin that gave him a very determined, very authoritative look. Both men were dressed in business suits of the time, although the taller man looked like his suit was made from better material.

"Really, all we wanted was to leave your father an invitation to a big picnic we are holding in the city park this Saturday," the taller of the two men said as he followed Adam into the room with the shorter man right behind them.

"So you can try to talk him into signing that petition, too?" Adam asked with a knowing lift of his eyebrows then stopped halfway to glance at them while he waited for the answer.

"Well, that is what we were hoping," the shorter man

put in just before displaying a wide, pleasant grin. "At the moment, your father is one of the few doctors in town who has not yet signed our petition. But that's because he was still so ill when we were recruiting the doctors' signatures last month."

The other man nodded and took over the explanation from there, "And since we've invited quite a few of those people from this neighborhood who haven't yet signed to come and enjoy the free meal we're offering this Saturday, we decided it would be the perfect time to interest Doctor Johnson in our little crusade. You remember Cole Gifford, he's the man you and Constance met last week. The one who started this whole thing after having tried every other means to convince those people from Lake Conemaugh to repair that dam."

"I already knew Cole from work," Adam corrected. "I don't know him very well, but because he's now Cambria's head engineer, he's been at several of the same meetings I have to attend."

As if having been given a cue to take over the conversation from there, the shorter man stepped forward and resumed talking. "Cole is the one supplying the roast, enough for at least fifty people, even though he won't be able to attend. And Doctor Harrison Rutledge is supplying the pickles, potato salad, and plenty of fruit punch." He then shook his head and rolled his eyes skyward as if asking for divine intervention before quietly adding, "And, heaven help us, Doctor Rutledge's wife has volunteered to bake the cookies."

"But there is always the chance she'll have her housekeeper do the actual baking," the taller man offered, looking from his friend to Adam then back at his friend. "Maybe she won't try to bake them herself this time."

"I gather Jeanne Rutledge is not the best of cooks?" Adam asked, chuckling at the men's reactions. Then as if suddenly aware he had not introduced JoAnn to the two visitors, he gestured toward her with a slight wave of his hand. "Andrew. Anthony. I'd like for you to meet a new friend of mine."

Both men turned to look at her, neither revealing his thoughts while waiting for Adam to complete his introduction.

"I'd like for you two to meet Doctor JoAnn Griffin."

"Doctor?" the shorter one named Andrew said, clearly impressed as he glanced first at the other man then back at her. "You aren't by chance the one who saved Doctor Johnson's life, are you?"

"Then you've heard about me," she said as a way of letting him know she was, pleased she had not heard any skepticism in his voice. Realizing she was the only one seated, she quickly rose to her feet and offered a friendly smile. "News travels this town very quickly."

"That sort of news does. We don't get many women doctors around here," admitted the other, clearly as willing to accept the fact as his friend. He then smiled and extended his hand, "Hello. I'm Anthony Alani. I am also still pretty new to this town. I've been here less than a year."

"Pleased to meet you," JoAnn said cordially, then accepted his hand with a firm handshake that caused Anthony to look a little startled.

"And I'm Andrew Edwards," the other man said, also extending his hand. "I'm the minister at the Todd Street Methodist Church."

"Pleased to meet you, too," JoAnn said as again she shook the hand offered her. "I gather you are the men who are working so very hard at getting a petition together that might force the repair of the Lake Conemaugh dam." She wondered if they truly thought

279

they could succeed with such a thing.

"That's us," Anthony said, his expression suddenly grim. "Though we are running into far more obstacles than we'd first anticipated." He then turned to Adam. "Did Andrew tell you about the threat he's received?"

"No," Adam responded, clearly interested as he turned to look at the shorter man. "What sort of threat?"

"Seems someone wants to take my church away from me," Andrew said with a shrug as if he had not taken the threat quite as seriously as Anthony. "Plans to put me out on the street by the end of the month. All because I have refused to stop helping with this matter."

"Who would do such a thing?" Adam wanted to know. "Was it one of the deacons?"

"Don't know who did it," Andrew admitted. "The threat came in the form of an anonymous note. Fact is, in our group of eight, we have already received three such notes. All anonymous and all threatening."

"Mine told me I would never be able to get a legal practice established here if I continued to work against the good of the community the way I have," Anthony explained. "It warned me to pull my support from the group before it was too late, but at least it did not threaten me any physical harm like Cole Gifford's note did. In the message Cole received we were warned someone was going to get hurt—badly hurt."

Adam looked at them perplexed. "I figured there would be plenty of opposition against what you eight are doing because too few people believe there really is danger and too many of them treasure the revenue that hunting and fishing club brings to this area each summer. Still, I had no idea that your attempt to have that dam repaired would cause such problems. What have you done about the notes?"

"The notes aren't the worst of it," Andrew admitted. "Someone broke into my office in broad daylight and destroyed everything in sight. Whoever did that clearly wanted to convince me to quit helping with the petition."

"Did you report the incident to the police?"

"Yes, but there's not much they can do but keep a closer watch over the church and rectory. Until we know who is sending the notes, there isn't much more they can do to help us."

"Doesn't matter," Anthony put in. "We're taking whatever precautions necessary to protect ourselves. We never solicit signatures alone anymore. We now travel in pairs or groups of threes."

"Then I gather these notes have not slowed down your efforts," Adam said with a knowing nod.

"Slowed them?" Andrew asked, as if that were an incredulous statement. "By all means, no. If anything, we are all working harder than ever to get the thousand or more signatures Cole thinks we'll need to force federal intervention."

"We are not about to be intimidated by some local hothead who is such a coward he won't even identify himself in his notes," Anthony put in as he pulled a small white envelope from his coat pocket. "Here, give this to your father and assure him there won't be any trouble at the picnic. The police have agreed to keep a close watch over the proceedings." Then, as if in afterthought, he added. "And if the two of you would like to come, feel free. We are always happy to have a few extra supporters milling about."

Andrew nodded that he agreed. "Especially knowing that you have taken the time and trouble to go see the dam for yourself. That means you know as well as we do that the seepage coming out at the bottom is not from a natural spring like they want us to believe.

Anthony's right. You are just the sort of person we need there to help convince those people that dam does pose a very real danger to this town."

Adam looked at JoAnn as if to ask her if she would like to go. Her stomach coiled into a tight knot, a warning to stay out of the matter. But at the same time, she knew she would probably still be there come Saturday, since the time passage was no longer shrinking as rapidly as it had at first. Finally, she nodded. "I love picnics."

"Good," Andrew said, adjusting his coat unnecessarily in preparation to leave. "We'll start serving shortly after noon."

"Unless it's raining again," Anthony put in with a sigh of annoyance. "Which means we'll have to put it off a week."

Saturday morning, like so many other mornings that April, dawned bleak and gray, but when the dark, roiling sky did not produce any rain, Adam and JoAnn prepared to go to the picnic. Wanting to get there in time for Adam to help encourage a few signatures, they left the house shortly before eleven and were at the park by five after. Because Park was not quite ready when they left, he promised to arrive shortly afterward.

Since JoAnn knew she would be meeting so many of Adam's friends at the picnic, friends who would also know Constance and would have heard the rumor that Adam was not seeing very much of her at the moment, she had decided to do what she could to look her best for the event. She wore the elaborate pink dress and the tiny little pink and white hat Park had bought her several weeks earlier, during her original trip back in time.

Knowing the garments might come in handy during her visit, she had asked for their return while she and Adam were at his house the weekend before. She was just glad the day was cool so she would not have to worry about heat prostration while wearing so many layers of wool.

"You look beautiful," Adam said and gazed down at her with a mixture of pride and longing. He, too, knew many of his friends would be present and could hardly wait to introduce them to JoAnn.

"Thank you," she responded, blushing from the unexpected compliment and from his hand resting lightly at her waist as he helped her across the street. "I did my best."

Which was true. She had awakened before dawn so she could wash her hair and still have enough time for it to dry. Because she had no curling iron nor a blow dryer to help style her dark tresses into its usual feathery sweep, she had pulled the shorter hair back and anchored it in place with decorative combs while allowing the longer hair to drape softly past her shoulders.

Feeling awkward to have Adam staring at her so intently, she nodded toward the people who had already formed a small crowd at the far side of the park.

"Looks like a pretty good turnout," she said, having thought the threatening gray skies would have kept many of them away.

"I guess everyone is pretty tired of having to stay inside all the time," Adam surmised. "It's been three days now since the last actual rain. This is the driest the ground has been since just before we had that big snow three weeks ago."

"It snowed while I was gone?"

"Worst snow I've ever seen for so late in the year. Took nearly a week for the last of it to melt. Then the rains started back and the ground has been soaked ever since. That's why the business district nearest the point has already flooded twice this year."

Joann felt a foreboding chill, aware the saturated earth was one of the reasons the dam finally gave way. The ground had become too soaked to accept any more water which had made the runoff during the following rains all the more dangerous. "I just hope it doesn't rain again today."

"I don't know," Adam commented, glancing at the dark clouds that rolled dramatically across the gray sky. A sudden breeze stirred his chestnut hair. "According to Anthony, dark rainy days seem to encourage people to think in their direction. He claimed that whenever the sun was shining, it was usually much harder to get people to consider the possibility that dam could ever give way to a flood."

"Then I guess a quick shower wouldn't hurt matters any," she said as she too glanced overhead. Never having been a good judge of clouds, she had no idea if they might see rain that day or not.

"There's Andrew," Adam said, removing his hand from her waist to gesture to the crowd. "He looks very upset about something. I wonder what's wrong?"

"I guess he's having a harder time than usual convincing these people to sign that petition."

"Could be." Adam frowned as he stretched to see over the many people. "I wonder where Anthony is. You would think he would be here by now." He again put his hand at her waist but this time to hurry her along.

When they walked closer to the crowd, JoAnn turned her attention to what the others were saying. She heard something about a house having been burned down and a lawyer's office being ransacked. It was not until Andrew spotted them and waved them further into the crowd that she found out exactly what had happened.

"Yesterday, while Tony was moving a few things into his new office over on Franklin Street, someone broke in and demolished the place," Andrew began, his voice so strained in his attempt to be heard over the mutterings of the crowd, it sounded almost like the growl of a wounded animal. "The frightening thing is that he and Catherine Mackey were in another part of the building at the time and could have been hurt. Then last night, while the rest of us were all helping Tony clean up the mess, someone set fire to Cole Gifford's house."

Remembering that Cole Gifford was the name of the man who had conceived the idea of forcing government intervention through a well-worded petition, JoAnn felt a strong, sickening sensation curl through the pit of her stomach.

"You're not serious," Adam said, though he clearly believed every word. He shook his head at such an incredulous act while he ran a hand through his dark hair. "They actually burned his house?"

"At this point, we don't know if it was a they or just one person, but someone sure enough set fire to Cole's house. The fire department was able to get there in time to put out the blaze before the whole house burned. And later when we went into the rooms they had saved, we found kerosene poured across some of the furniture. The fire examiners also found an empty kerosene jug tossed haphazardly into the neighbor's bushes," he said, then met Adam's gaze with a glare so chilling it made Adam think he'd traded his lifetime allegiance to God for one with the very devil himself. "The fire was merely an attempt to cover a theft."

"Why? What was stolen?"

The muscles that ran down the sides of Andrew's

jaws pumped furiously while he struggled to control his rage. "Our petition was stolen. Cole had locked it away in the top drawer of his desk, but when he tried to open that same drawer shortly after the fire had been put out, he discovered it had been jimmied and the petition was gone. I guess whoever stole that petition didn't want us to realize he had it and had hoped the fire would cover the fact it had been taken. Didn't count on a neighbor boy smelling the smoke early on nor did he consider the fact that Mister Cohen right across the street had just installed one of those new telephones which meant the boy did not have to run three blocks to ring a fire bell. The fire department was on its way before any flames were ever seen from the outside. That's why they were able to put it out so quickly."

"So now you have to start over on the petition," Adam said gravely. "How many signatures did you have?"

"Over five hundred," Andrew responded. "And with less than three months before Cole is scheduled to travel to Washington for us, it does not give us much time to recover those signatures, much less recruit more. It took us over six months to get the names we had."

"Do you have a new petition ready to sign?" Adam asked, clearly wanting to take some sort of action.

"We now have two," Andrew assured him. "Which we plan to keep in separate locations."

As he reached into his pocket to extract the new petitions a slender man who looked to be a few years younger than Adam but with thinning black hair came rushing toward them. JoAnn stepped back to let him move closer to the other two.

"I just heard," the man said, his face hardened with anger. "I can't believe it happened."

"Well, it did. And now we have to start all over again," Andrew said, then glanced at Adam curiously. "You do know Doctor Harrison Rutledge, don't you?"

"Of course," Adam said. "We met at a charity auction last October." He extended his hand to the newcomer, then explained. "I was just about to sign the petition again. Or should I say the two *new* petitions. Care to join me?"

"You can bet I do," Harrison said with a resolute nod. "And Jeanne will want to sign again, too."

Handing each man a copy of the petition, the two signed then exchanged petitions and signed again. By that time, Park had arrived with Shadow only a few feet behind. The moment he heard what had happened, he signed them both, too. But it was not quite as easy for Andrew and Harrison to convince any of the others there to do the same. Having heard to what extent the opposition was willing to go, most of them were afraid to have their names appear on such a document and admitted as much aloud. No amount of swaying from Andrew, Harrison, or Adam made a difference.

Knowing these men were right, that the dam had fallen into an awful state of disrepair, the situation seemed all the more unfair and was all the more frustrating. So much so that even JoAnn caught herself trying to persuade the people to sign. Having convinced herself that she would not be changing the course of history by much, since the flood occurred at least six weeks before these men were scheduled to take the petitions to Washington, she felt justified in her efforts to help their cause.

She never went so far in her efforts to convince anyone she was from the future and therefore knew exactly what lay in store for them, but she did try to make a few of them understand the very real danger they could face should they continue to ignore such a serious issue. Yet the more she tried to make these people see that there was reason for so much concern, the more frustrated she became. No one listened to her.

She could not, however, be sure if her lack of influence over these people had to do with the fact that she was an outsider or if it was because she was a mere woman. Some even went so far as to turn their backs on her while she was talking. If only there was some way to make them listen, make them understand just how serious the danger had become. It was already April 27; that dam was due to collapse in just over a month.

"And what makes you such an expert?" asked a particularly testy little man with an undersized bowler perched at the back of his balding head after JoAnn had so readily agreed with Andrew's latest comment that the dam was substandard in both design and repair. With a cocky air, he looked from Andrew to the two men who stood flanking him. "What difference does it make if that dam does or doesn't have discharge pipes anymore? There's a spillway ain't there?"

"But it's too small and too shallow to handle the overflow should there come a flash flood at a time the lake was already full like it is now. Patrick, you have to remember that almost a dozen streams and creeks empty into that lake. And, too, I hear they've blocked that spillway with huge iron grates to keep their prize fish from spilling out into Stony Creek and more times than not those grates are clogged with so much dead leaves and debris that no water gets through at all."

The little man called Patrick sniffed then shifted his weight to one leg. "The way I see it, that dam up near South Fork has held up just fine until now. There was that one little incident in Eighteen sixty-two, but they repaired whatever caused the dam to break then and it has held fast ever since. What should make it want to come apart now? Why, it even held up during that bad flood in 'eighty-five when the water got all the way up to William Butler's house. If that dam was going to fail like you two say, it would have failed right then."

"Not necessarily," Andrew was quick to respond. "But that flood very well may have weakened the whole structure even more. If you'll remember, it was the summer after that particular flood that the seepage at the bottom became much more noticeable."

"That's not seepage," the old man snapped. "It's water from those natural springs. Everybody knows that."

When Andrew heaved a loud sigh and looked from the angry man to JoAnn for help, she nodded encouragement, wishing Adam had not stepped over to talk with another group. He would know what to say to help convince these three.

"There are no springs in that area," Andrew said in a carefully controlled voice, not about to give up. "That water is coming right through the dam."

"Say's who?" another of the men said, clearly as annoyed by what Andrew had to say as the others. "I'm tired of hearing about a disaster that is never going to happen. Every year it's the same old cry. 'The South Fork dam is going to break! Lake Conemaugh is about to come down upon us!' Wouldn't hurt Johnstown that much even that dam was to fail. Why, there's nearly fifteen miles of riverbed for that water to spread across before it gets here. Even if that dam did finally give way, about all it would do is swell the river's current a might, which is about all it did in 'sixty-two."

"That break was caused by a defective pipe and it

289

happened when the lake was down," Andrew reminded him. "Remember? There used to be pipes in that dam before some idiot pulled them out and sold them for scrap."

"Seems to me it was a smart idea if they can pop open like that anyway. Besides, it's not like we haven't had to deal with flooding around here before. Both those rivers jump their banks at least once every year. If that dam breaks, it'll just mean the borough having to deal with the Little Conemaugh jumping its banks one more time. What's the worst that can happen? Some of the businesses near the point might flood again."

"That's hardly realistic," Andrew said, waving his hands to show his growing frustration. "There has to be over twenty million tons of water up there. That lake is three miles long."

"Which is why I figure that dam must be a good one. It would have to be to hold back a lake like that. Besides, look at the men who own it."

Andrew stared at them with disbelief. "Surely you don't assume that the group of men who bought and repaired that old dam know what they are doing just because of all the power and wealth they have behind them. About all those men have done is pile a little extra mud and rocks onto an already faulty dam and plant new grass on the outer slope. They don't even care enough about what happens to us to see that their dam is kept properly repaired. Whenever there's a leak, about all those men do is plug it with a little more mud and hope the patch holds, which it usually doesn't. Those old wounds reopen almost immediately."

At that moment Park came up to the small group and frowned after seeing everyone's grim expressions. "I gather you aren't making much headway with these three."

"Doesn't look like it," Andrew admitted, still looking at the men beseechingly. "I've tried my level best to make them see the truth but they are determined to ignore every point I've made."

"Adam isn't doing much better with that other group," he said and indicated the four men who stood listening to him. Two were leaning forward with their arms crossed as if ready to fight and the other two stood with a leg cocked insolently. "I don't know why any of you even bothers. I gave up trying to convince the people in this town of anything years ago. They believe only what they want to believe."

"We believe only that which is believable," the angriest of the three men spouted. His back bristled as he turned and marched away, knowing the other two would quickly follow.

"It's a shame. They really can't see the danger," Park said, then put a supportive arm around Andrew. "But don't let it discourage you. You had over five hundred signatures before, I'm sure you'll still manage to get the thousand you need by the middle of July."

"I hope so, because if we don't have enough signatures to make Washington investigate, we will be fresh out of ideas that might be used to see that justice is finally done. We've already tried reasoning with the men who own the dam. Cambria Iron has even offered to help pay for the repairs. But those big-money bosses don't want to be inconvenienced with lowering the lake for any length of time."

He shook his head dismally then looked in the direction he knew the lake lay. "If and when that dam does finally go, as narrow as this valley is and as steep as that mountainside, the damage will be unbelievable. The force with which that water would come down that mountain is certain to cause enormous amounts of death and destruction all along the way—especially if the collapse were to happen while the lake is near its crest and the river below is already flooded, like it is now. I really hate to think how many could end up being killed."

Feeling a sudden need to be with Adam, JoAnn left Park and Andrew to their morbid discussion and walked over to where Adam still tried to convince the four men he faced.

"Other companies, especially the timber companies, have ravaged our mountainsides for years," he was explaining. "They have stripped the area of both coal and timber, leaving huge, gaping wounds in our countryside. That's what causes these dangerous flash runoffs after every mountain storm. Sad part is the companies don't bother to fill in the craters they've dug or replant the forests they've stripped. They expect Nature herself to take care of such menial labor. That's why I think we not only need to see that the dam is repaired, we also should see to it that our timber and grasslands are replaced. I myself have already replanted the land around my house. I've even gone as far as to put thousands of seedlings on land that doesn't even belong to me just to prevent dangerous mudslides in my area."

JoAnn bit the sensitive flesh of her lower lip. Though she wanted the men to understand that what Adam had said was the truth, she refused to inject her opinion, having already discovered how little these people thought of her opinions anyway. So instead of agreeing or disagreeing with whatever was said, she stood quietly to one side.

While listening to Adam expound his case, a morbid feeling washed over her. Because she was from the future, she knew for a fact that every word Andrew and Adam had spoken that day was true. And yet there was nothing any of them could do to prevent that dam from giving way. The flood was now barely over a month away. There was no longer enough time to make those repairs so desperately needed, not even should those wealthy industrialists who owned the dam suddenly agree to cooperate. With no drain pipes to help empty the lake, it would take half a year to pump the water level low enough to make the necessary repairs and then only if it were to stop raining long enough to prevent it from refilling.

Clutching her stomach, she glanced at those around her, aware how truly hopeless the cause. Sadly, she wondered which of these many men and women would be among the 2,209 who would not survive the crushing body of water and which of them would be left to try to pick up the pieces and get on with their shattered lives. Blinking away a sudden rush of tears, she studied Adam's intent expression while he continued to try to convince the men around him of the true danger.

Silently, she prayed that he and his father would be among those spared.

Chapter Fourteen

By the end of her fifth week in the year 1889 and the seventh week since she'd left work, JoAnn was so completely taken by her surroundings and by Adam Johnson in particular, she wondered how she would ever endure the day when it again became necessary to leave it all behind.

During the past several weeks spent getting to know Adam better, her attraction toward him had intensified immensely. And with good reason. Adam was everything she had always felt a man should be. He was strong and silent when he needed to be and yet he was open and warm when he wanted to be. He was confident, tolerant, dependable, responsible, respected, and above all else, as gorgeous and virile a man as she had ever known.

There was a certain masculine grace in the way he walked that reminded her of a sleek animal. He moved smoothly, with the agility provided by his male strength, and with strong self-assurance. He was a man of his time, dynamic, with the sort of convictions that should be admired and appreciated. He was also a man who deserved to be loved, which JoAnn found she could not help but do.

Despite a continued effort not to let her emotions

become involved, at some moment during this magical time JoAnn's barriers had slipped and she had fallen helplessly in love with the tall, handsome Adam Johnson. It was a fact, plain, simple, and painful.

Even if the size of the time passage continued to stay relatively stable, shrinking only a tiny degree at a time as it had over the past few weeks, within another week, her eight-week sabbatical would be over and she would have to return to work. She was scheduled to be at the hospital prepared for work at four o'clock on May twentieth and it was already the fourteenth.

Within five to six days JoAnn would have to forsake this unique world and return to her own. The only consolation was that she would again see Jean, the one person from the twentieth century whom she had truly missed. She cringed when she wondered just how angry Jean would be with her this time because although she'd called and left a message on her machine warning her she was planning to take a trip, the message had been purposely vague. By now Jean was probably beside herself with worry.

If only there was some way for Jean to know how truly happy she was at the moment and how very much in love she was with Adam. And how she dreaded returning to her own time and to the problems that still awaited her there.

The pitiful thing about her current situation was that she had known all along she could not stay in the year 1889 forever. She should never have allowed herself to be so taken with its occupants and she especially should never have allowed herself to fall in love with Adam. She had known from the outset she would end up hurting herself deeply if she did—but

295

having been aware of the painful consequences had not prevented it from happening.

And when she considered her feelings for Adam from a more rational standpoint, they were as illogical as they were painful. Considering the circumstances, what they felt for one another should never have developed into anything beyond friendship.

Adam was from a different world. An entirely different era. There was so very little they had in common, yet at times it felt as if he were her one true soul mate. Despite the vast differences in their backgrounds as well as the vast differences in their *fore*grounds, Adam believed many of the same things she believed and their individual happiness evolved from many of the same sources. Many of their ideals were similar and it turned out they both wanted much the same things from life. They both believed that family and true friends were the most important elements of any life and that they were to be cherished until death or beyond.

The only real flaw JoAnn detected in Adam's character was a continued chauvinistic attitude toward women. Like the others of his time, he thought them to have their set place in society and questioned any attempt they might make to take on a more masculine role. He truly believed women were to be cherished and protected and should never be forced into doing a man's work.

Even so, JoAnn had noticed that Adam was not quite as chauvinistic as some of the other men. He had no qualms about allowing her to have her say and on one occasion, when she had been told to butt out after having agreed with something Andrew had said at the picnic several weekends prior, Adam had come readily to her defense.

He had been her champion and she would be forever grateful for that. He had also defended her when people questioned her reasons for having stayed so long in Johnstown. He had quietly explained to people who really had no business knowing that she had taken time away from the hospital where she normally worked to recover from the tragic loss of both her parents. He had even gone so far as to acknowledge to an increasingly perturbed Constance Seguin that whenever JoAnn mentioned leaving, which she had on several occasions, he had purposely convinced her to stay. He wanted it clear to everyone that JoAnn had not yet stayed past her welcome, that it was as much his idea she continue to visit as it was hers.

Ever since JoAnn had realized her love for him, she had conceded that she was headed for a devastating heartbreak. She could no longer ignore the arousing brush of his arm against hers, nor the gentle warmth of his fingers when he pressed his hand protectively against the small of her back whenever they walked together, or when he used the tips of them to caress her cheek. She couldn't even ignore something as simple as the innocent brush of her long skirts against his pant leg, which meant he was standing far too close. She had also noticed that their gazes tended to linger a little longer each time their eyes met; and whenever they laughed together, it was with such true enjoyment, it caused tingles of joyful awareness to cascade over her body.

If only there was some way she and Adam could be together forever. But she knew that would be asking the impossible, and *that* was breaking her heart. Her career was as important to her as his careers were to him. Neither of them would be happy if either were ever transplanted from his or her present life-styles for very long. They were too much a part of their own time periods. Their destinies stood a century apart, and any opportunity for them to be together existed only as long as that precious time passage remained open.

JoAnn shivered at the sudden reminder of how she came to be there. *The time passage.* It had been nearly a week since she had last checked the dwindling size of that invisible opening. During the past few weeks, the shrinkage had slowed significantly, which had given her more time to spend in this special wonderland from the past than she had ever hoped. But that did not mean the passage might not suddenly start healing itself again at a much faster pace. She had to find another reason to be gone for an afternoon. She needed to reassure herself that her gateway remained open and offered no immediate threat of trapping her in the past. She also wanted a chance to look up her great-great grandfather while she was there and would need several hours for that. She needed the whole day to herself.

"Adam, I think tomorrow I'll walk over to Market Street and see if there are any new fashions," she said, looking down at the comfortable dress she wore with mock annoyance. It was a cool summer shift made from burgundy-colored cotton with white lace at the neck and a white cotton sash at the waist. "The clothes I wear may be fine for the city, but I've noticed the women around here dress very differently."

"And that has just now started to bother you?" Adam asked, amused that her clothing mattered at all because no matter what she wore she was far more beautiful than they.

"There, you see? Even you've noticed the difference," she said in ready defense. She struck the scrolled arm of the sofa with her fist for emphasis. "That settles it. Tomorrow I will try to find something a little more suitable to wear around here."

"Then it is safe to assume you plan to stay on a little while longer," he said, glad to know she was not leaving anytime soon. He then reached out to touch her cheek gently with his fingertips in a gesture that had become a habit with him. There was just something about her that beckoned his touch. "Tell you what. It looks like I will have most of the day free tomorrow. I'll go with you to help you carry your packages." He hesitated, then added, "That is if you will in turn promise to go with me this weekend."

"What's this weekend?" She wrinkled her forehead, trying to remember if anything special had been mentioned.

"I need to carry a load of lumber and posts to the house. Cyrus wants to repair the corral beside the stable this weekend. It was damaged during that bad storm we had last week."

"Which one was that?" JoAnn wondered aloud, remembering there had been two of a pretty serious nature the week before.

"The one we had last Thursday. Cyrus sent word that a large tree uprooted and crushed not only most of the fence, part of the tree also caught a corner of the stable and damaged the roof. And since you were kind enough to travel up there with me twice before, I thought perhaps I could persuade you into accompanying me yet again."

Aware the trip to his house would offer her the perfect opportunity to check the size of that hole, but feeling a little uneasy, knowing the weekend was still three days away, she finally agreed.

"Okay. If you'll accompany me tomorrow then I'll accompany you this weekend." She decided she could put off looking up her great-great grandfather until another day. By agreeing to Adam's suggestion, she would end up spending both the following day and the entire weekend with him and the thought of that thrilled her. Because even though Adam managed to find more and more time away from work with each week's passing, she could not seem to see enough of him.

"I think I should warn you though," Adam said, wanting her to understand his plans from the beginning. "We might have to stay up there a little longer this time. Although Cyrus and George can handle the repairs to the fence easily enough, I don't want them having to repair that roof alone. It's too dangerous a job for young boys," he said, though in truth he knew the boys could handle the roof repair as easily as the fence repair. He simply wanted an excuse to stay there a little longer. He liked having JoAnn as a visitor in his home. It was why he was finding reason to spend more and more time there. With JoAnn there, his house was no longer a place of sorrow. It was a place of laughter. "We might have to stay until Monday or Tuesday. It really all depends on how much damage I find when we get there."

JoAnn thought about that and realized it worked out perfectly for her if they did stay until Monday. Monday was the twentieth, the day she would have to leave. It would be much easier if all she had to do was walk the one mile rather than hike several, especially should it be raining again that day.

"Will we be leaving early Friday afternoon like last time?" she asked, remembering the trip two week-ends ago to take Doris the four cases of glass jars that had been ordered from Altoona.

"No, we probably won't leave until Saturday morning this time. I am planning to take you to a special dinner Friday night."

"What special dinner?" she wanted to know, thinking that odd. During her last few weeks there, Adam had proved to be more of a homebody, somewhat like herself. Except for short walks through the city park in the early evenings, before the night's chill set in, they rarely went out.

"Friday is Shawn Davis's fiftieth birthday and there is to be an elaborate celebration at one of his restaurants that evening for all his closest friends," he explained. "And since Father happens to be one of those closest friends, we've all been invited."

Remembering Shawn and his wife, Carissa, from their visits both to Adam's house during her first journey back and to Park's house during this second journey back, JoAnn nodded. She understood the closeness of their friendship and most certainly would go. "And why are you just now telling me? Surely you've known about it for some time." The Davises did not appear to be the type to put off planning of such an important event.

"Because I wasn't too sure you'd agree to go," he confessed. And he wasn't all that sure *he* wanted to go.

"But of course, I'll go. The Davises are very dear friends of your father's and I am presently a guest in his home. What should I wear?"

"Something terribly sophisticated," he admitted, his eyes glittering at the realization that no matter what she wore, she would undoubtedly be the most attractive woman there. "It's to be a formal dinner. Everyone will dress their best."

"But I don't have anything appropriate with me," she protested, suddenly feeling uneasy about the whole thing. If it was a formal affair, she would be expected to abide by all the latest social graces. What if the present social amenities were not the same as from her own time. By not demonstrating the proper etiquette, she could end up making a total fool of herself—and Adam.

"You'll find something tomorrow when we go shopping," he assured her, unaware of where her true fears lay. "There are several nice ladies' shops on both Market and Washington streets. One of them should have exactly what you need, especially this time of year what with all the cotillions and balls. But I think I should warn you. Constance will be at the dinner." When he saw a flicker of concern darken her eyes, he reached down to take her hand in his. She basked in the comforting warmth he brought her.

"But don't worry," he added. He kept his tone cheerful while his thumb gently stroked the back of her hand, continuing to calm her concern. "I'll see that Constance keeps that sharp tongue to herself." In a purely reflexive action, he then lifted her hand to his mouth, turned it over, and gently pressed her palm to his lips. "You should be safe enough with me at your side."

She did not jerk her hand away as she might have in the past. She closed her eyes. It was a lot more comforting to focus on her body's responses than concentrating on the cold shoulder Constance was sure to offer her on Friday night. Ever since Adam

302

had made his preference to be with JoAnn suitably clear, Constance Seguin had behaved very vindictively toward the both of them, starting rumors that in the end would hurt only herself because after JoAnn was gone, Constance would still be there and would be very eager to recapture Adam's heart. But she might have a hard time doing that if she continued to show her true colors the way she had during the past few weeks.

Which suited JoAnn fine. Adam deserved better than Constance. He deserved a woman who truly loved him.

Therefore, even though she would never use the garment again, JoAnn spent much of the money she still had at Akard's Dress Shop on an elaborately designed ball gown made of dark blue satin that glittered from the tiny gold brilliants woven into the bodice. The one-piece dress fit her curves snugly from the shoulders to the waist but, as was customary of the time, had several layers of gathered fabric sewn into the back to conceal a large derriere beneath the dark blue flounced overskirt.

She also purchased a small black cloak made of velvet and trimmed in satin and a set of black satin slippers. She knew the slippers would be more comfortable than ankle boots and far more appropriate for the time period than her pumps, which had started to show the wear of daily use. She couldn't use the gold chains she had with her, so she purchased a simple black velvet choker with a teardrop diamond anchored near the center, which could be taken back with her and the diamond set into gold at a later date.

When JoAnn emerged twenty minutes early from her bedroom at Park's house that Friday night, she went on to the parlor to wait for the others. She was surprised when she saw Adam was already there dressed in a handsome three-piece cutaway; but she was not at all surprised by her reaction to finding him there.

Her body filled with admiration and awareness when he turned to her and smiled. His blue eyes sparkled with more than just appreciation when he, too, took in her appearance. His dimples dipped at the corners of his curved mouth while his gaze wandered across her hair, which had been pulled high onto her head anchored with a gem-studded comb and allowed to cascade down her back in a swirl of soft brown curls. After memorizing every glimmering highlight, his gaze drifted to the delicate diamond at her throat then downward to the ample cleavage revealed by the daring cut of her beautiful new gown. "My but I will be the envy of every man there tonight."

"But only because you look so handsome in your new suit," she said, thinking the compliment deserved to be his. She turned toward the hall door and asked, "Where is your father?"

"He's still upstairs getting dressed," Adam explained, then seeing no reason to resist the sudden urge to touch her, he stepped forward and slipped a finger beneath her delicate chin. Longingly, he gazed into her dark, almond-shaped eyes, all the while wishing he could find the courage to kiss her again. If only he could know what thoughts lay behind those incredibly beautiful brown eyes. If only he could be certain she would not turn away from a second attempt to kiss her.

But JoAnn was not having as hard a time reading Adam's thoughts. When she saw his eyes darken with what had to be desire, she felt both exhilarated and frightened. Her heart pounded with a vibrance when she realized his mouth was only a few inches from hers, his lips parted as if contemplating a kiss.

"I think I hear your father," she said, so overwhelmed by the different emotions that now fought to control her, her voice came out barely above a whisper. Aware of her own budding desire, she knew that kissing him again would be her final undoing.

At that moment Park cleared his throat in the hallway outside, making Adam realize that the time wasn't right to kiss her, even had he been courageous enough to try. "I guess it must be time for us to go," he said and stepped aside just when JoAnn turned to greet the elder Johnson with a pleasant smile.

Adam studied her relieved expression with a raised brow and wondered what sort of thoughts tumbled through that pretty head of hers — annoyed that even though he had hired an investigator to find out more about her, she remained a complete mystery. The man had yet to find a single trace of this woman's previous existence. He had not found out where she worked nor where she lived, nor even where she had been born. Still, Adam remained as determined as ever to find out more about her, if for no other reason than to be able to understand the obvious differences between them.

"Ready?" Park asked, looking dapper in his dark blue coat with a blue and white striped vest.

"As ready as we'll ever be," Adam remarked and quickly pulled his roving thoughts back to the events happening around him. When he placed his hand at JoAnn's waist to escort her from the room, he realized that his time to take a second kiss had to come soon — before he lost the last of what little remained of his sanity. He wanted JoAnn desperately. And he was determined to have her.

Although the restaurant where the birthday dinner was to be held was only a few blocks from Park's house, Park chose to drive. JoAnn suspected he had decided on driving so he could show off his new Stanhope, but did not mention her suspicion when she climbed into the back seat with Adam. Instead, she commented on what a lovely night it was for a ride, though she gathered her cloak closer to her to evade the early evening chill.

"Yes, it is," Park agreed readily, waiting until Shadow was settled comfortably onto the seat beside him before lifting the gleaming black buggy whip out of its narrow holder. Snapping it lightly in the air, just behind the horse's left ear, sent the carriage forward at a brisk pace.

Within minutes they were in sight of the restaurant but because of an early turnout, buggies and carriages already lined the street on both sides and they ended up having to park three blocks beyond and walk back. Other than to give Shadow a distinctive place to stay while they ate, they had gained nothing by having driven.

After entering the restaurant, a tall man dressed in a trim black velvet coat took her cape and her handbag then gestured toward a large doorway to the right with an elaborate wave of his white-gloved hand. Rather than hold back the flow of guests coming in from the outside, she allowed Adam to place his hand at her waist again and direct her toward the opening. Park followed a few feet behind.

Inside the doorway, nearly a hundred people milled about the huge room, moving in small groups while engaged in casual conversation. More out of self-preservation than anything else, JoAnn ignored the elegance of the room and the fact that several men had stopped talking to turn and look at her while she quickly scanned the crowd. She was too busy searching for her nemesis, Constance Seguin. Her stomach tightened into a hard knot when she saw that Constance stood only a few dozen yards away, beautiful as ever while dressed in an elaborate gown of emerald green. Though she did not face the doorway, JoAnn could tell by the brisk bounce of her blond curls, she was busily talking to two men who looked to be about her own age, both seeming very interested in the conversation.

Aware of where JoAnn's gaze had gone, Adam nudged her playfully then leaned forward and whispered in her ear. "She's not going to appreciate the fact you look far more beautiful than she *ever* has. Expect the very worst."

"Well that is certainly reassuring," she muttered over her shoulder with a flat expression then slowly grinned when she realized the compliment. Flattered that he thought her beautiful, she felt a quick tremor through her heart but immediately dismissed the sudden fluttering as a bad case of nerves. She truly wanted to make a good impression on the people in this room — for Adam's sake more than her own — and therefore she did not want another ugly confrontation with Constance. "Uh-oh, she's noticed us."

"Just keep smiling," he said, then gently pushed her forward. "It irritates her to see you smile." He waited until they were closer before removing his hand from JoAnn's waist and extending it first to Constance to gently squeeze her gloved hand, then to the two gentlemen facing her to offer two hardy male handshakes.

While Adam introduced JoAnn to the two men, Constance's green gaze darted back and forth from JoAnn to Adam, as if she had expected to see something tangible. She waited until the men finally finished with the formalities then turned to Adam and flaunted that familiar sugary-sweet smile of hers while she wrapped her silky voice in a soft Southern accent.

"Adam, dearest, where are your manners? Don't you think you should be gettin' your guest a cool cup of punch to enjoy before dinner?" She gestured toward a large linen-draped table near the same door they had just entered. "I think I should like a cup myself. That is if you don't mind bringin' back two."

Adam glanced at the crowded table surrounded mostly by men, then at JoAnn, aware it would take him several minutes to work his way to the punch bowls. "How long until we eat?" he asked, then glanced at the huge porcelain-encased clock near the main door. Maybe there would not be time.

"Probably twenty minutes or more," she answered and continued to smile sweetly at him, though the pretty smile never quite reached the simmering depths of her jade green eyes. "I think my aunt said something about not servin' the food until at least eight o'clock. And as stiflin' as it is in here tonight with all these people strollin' about, we'll all be as parched as a desert by then." As if to prove her point, she then reached into the velvet folds of her emerald green ball gown and pulled out a folded silk fan. Popping it open, she fluttered the fan lightly in front of her face, all the while looking coyly up at an extremely annoyed Adam.

Knowing twenty minutes was plenty of time for

the two women to develop a hardy thirst, especially in an overheated room, he looked to JoAnn apologetically. "I'll be right back."

"Take your time. I'll be fine," she assured him, not nearly as upset by Constance's overt flirtations as she had thought she would be. She could tell by Adam's reaction, he had agreed to go for the punch out of simple politeness, and not because he was still under Constance's manipulative spell.

Constance waited until Adam was across the room before turning to JoAnn with what had turned into a clearly taunting smile. "Miss Griffin, I see you are still in Johnstown."

"Yes, I am," she answered, thinking the conversation a little inane, but if Constance wanted to pass the next few minutes stating the obvious that was fine with her.

"Why is that, I wonder?" she went on, then tapped the corner of her ample mouth with a gloved finger just before she stepped between JoAnn and the two men, presenting her back to them. The men took the hint and politely backed away, leaving Constance and JoAnn alone. "I thought you would have wanted to return to Pittsburgh by now. Don't your *patients* miss you?" Her voice dripped with such obvious sarcasm it sounded as if she had just accused JoAnn of something.

"I don't have a private practice so I have no set group of patients," JoAnn answered calmly though her heart rate had increased considerably. She could tell by the malevolent tone in Constance's voice, she was up to something spiteful. "I work in a hospital where I try to take care of whoever needs my help."

"Oh, come now, Miss Griffin. We both know that is not true," Constance said, then narrowed her gaze as if to indicate yet further misgivings. "I've had someone ask around about you. It seems no one at any of the hospitals in Pittsburgh has ever heard of you. Who are you really, Miss Griffin?"

"That's *Doctor* Griffin to you," JoAnn responded. A cold prickly feeling coiled up her spine when she realized she was about to be exposed as a fraud and in front of so many of Adam's friends. Not only would he be disappointed in her for having lied to him about certain matters, he would feel humiliated.

"I hardly think so," Constance countered, her smile still taunting. "If you were really the doctor you claim to be, someone with the Pittsburgh social registry would know of you."

JoAnn wondered just how important this social registry was and how to get around not being known by those on it. "Obviously that is not true, because I am a medical doctor and I do work in Pittsburgh." Perhaps not in this particular time period, but in her own time most certainly.

"I hope you can prove that," she chimed, cutting her green gaze to Adam, who had just worked his way to the punch bowl and was quickly filling two glass cups with the ruby red liquid. "For your own sake. I'd hate to think what Adam would do if he ever found out that you were not at all the person you claim to be. He does not react too kindly to those who try to deceive him."

A hard and throbbing ache filled JoAnn's chest when she turned to look at Adam, too, aware Constance was right. Adam valued honesty above all else.

"All I can do is have him check my credentials," she said, trying to sound aptly unconcerned when all the while she was hoping against hope it would not come to that. Her medical credentials did not exist in the year 1889 and she was in no way prepared to try to convince him that she was actually from the future. She was not ready to see the skepticism such an astounding revelation would bring to his otherwise handsome face — nor was she ready to be doubted by him.

"Then I take it you plan to continue with this farce?" Constance responded, arching her delicate blond eyebrows as if having just accepted a challenge.

"There is no farce to continue. I *am* a doctor and I *do* work in Pittsburgh," JoAnn said, hoping to bluff the blond witch with the partial truth. "And if you insist on pursuing this matter, then I feel I must warn you, you will end up looking like a fool."

"I'm not the one who'll look like a fool once the truth has come out," Constance said staunchly, then turned her shoulder to JoAnn to await Adam's return. When he came close enough to hand over the punches, she reached out her gloved hand and her taunting smile turned instantly sweet. "Adam, Miss Griffin and I were just discussing the fact that no one in Pittsburgh seems to have ever heard of her. Can you imagine that?"

"Pittsburgh is a large city," he countered, wondering how Constance had come across such information and realized she was also having JoAnn investigated. When he moved over to hand JoAnn her cup of punch, he noticed how pale she had become. He bristled at how Constance was purposely trying to humiliate JoAnn. "I'm sure the city has many people who know Doctor Griffin."

JoAnn found comfort in the fact he had referred to her as Dr. Griffin when Constance seemed adamant she should be tagged *Miss* Griffin. Enough comfort that she was able to calm her raging heart a degree. Adam would not be easily convinced b Constance's hateful accusations.

"But it does not." Constance turned to glare accus ingly at JoAnn. "I've asked several friends from there about her and none of them know a thing about her She's also not known at any of the hospitals. Not a one."

"You must have asked the wrong people," he argued, even though his own investigation had yet to turn up anyone who knew her either. "I'm sure if you were to ask the right people, you'd find out that she's a fine doctor. Just ask my father. He'll gladly tell you what a skilled physician she is." Angry that Constance had put JoAnn on the altar like that, he gently took JoAnn's elbow. "Speaking of Father, I see the black widow has him cornered again. I think JoAnn and I had better ease our way across the room and rescue him."

JoAnn glanced at Adam, grateful to him for not having listened to Constance's vicious accusations. "The black widow? Is that the woman who has already gone through six husbands?"

"The same. And I certainly do not want to see my father become number seven," Adam said, already nodding goodbye to Constance. "If you will excuse us."

"But Adam," Constance wailed, stepping forward to take his arm. "There's more I think you should know about her."

That last comment piqued Adam's curiosity. He wondered what Constance had managed to find out about JoAnn when his own man had been unable to turn up anything at all. Still, he pulled his arm free of her grasp. Whatever Constance had found out, his own man would eventually unearth. "My father's well-being must come first. I'm sure you understand."

Constance's green eyes bulged with such hatred and repressed anger when she then childishly stamped her foot at Adam that JoAnn wanted to laugh.

"Thank you for that," she said when they were far enough away not to be overheard.

"For what?" he asked, looking as if he truly did not understand what wonderful thing he had done. "We really do need to get over there and help free Father from the grasping talons of the Widow Wray. That woman can be deadly."

Chapter Fifteen

For the rest of the evening, Constance kept an eye on JoAnn and Adam, as if she fully intended to approach them again with whatever it was she had found out about JoAnn—if anything. But she obviously never found the opportunity to catch them alone again.

After Adam and JoAnn wrenched Park free from the evil clutches of the Widow Wray, the three remained together as a small group that was constantly surrounded by others. Despite the trouble that clearly loomed ahead for JoAnn, in the form of a very angry and very resentful Constance Seguin, she could not help but enjoy the fact that Adam's voluptuous little friend was fuming over the way he had refused to listen to her.

It was not until the following morning, after JoAnn and Adam had left Johnstown for his farm that JoAnn's lighthearted mood slowly darkened again. Knowing her time with Adam nearly gone, she had become increasingly sad until, by late that afternoon, she felt very much like crying. The twentieth was only two days away. Sometime Monday morning, she again would be forced to leave Adam and all her other newfound friends—this time forever.

That was why when she and Adam had said good-bye to Park early that morning, she had fought a very real urge to cry then. She knew that unless Adam decided to return early for some reason, that Saturday morning was the last time she and Park would ever see each other, and during the past several weeks she had come to care for him a great deal.

What was worse, she cared for Adam even more. That meant leaving him for the last time would be even more devastating than having left Park. Which was why she could not bring herself to smile again, not even when George later teased her about having a face so long it dragged the ground.

Her heart had grown too heavy in the past few days and her sadness too great to force even the slightest of smiles. It felt as if she had already lost an important part of herself, a part she would never recover; yet she still had nearly two days. Why couldn't she just enjoy what time she had left?

"What's wrong?" Adam asked, when he stepped out onto the back porch to see where she had gone. When he had come back downstairs from changing clothes, he had expected to find her waiting for him in the parlor. "Why are you standing out here?"

Not having heard the back door open, JoAnn threw her hand to her breastbone and gasped when she turned to look at him.

"Nothing's wrong," she lied, but kept her hand pressed over her rapidly pounding heart while she again looked off to the west where the sun had just dipped behind the tall trees that topped the next mountain. "It's just that I was tired of waiting inside. It is far too lovely an evening to waste it indoors."

"That's true," he agreed and followed the direction of her gaze with his own while he stretched his shoul-

315

der muscles then drew in a deep breath. From one of the flower gardens came the mixed scent of honeysuckle and roses. "But Doris just told me supper will be ready early. She should be placing the food on the table in just a few minutes, and you know how upset she can get if we are not there to eat it while it is still hot," he said, then again gazed off into the distance. "I have a thought. Since it is still nearly two hours until dark, perhaps you might like to take a short walk after we've eaten. There's a meadow near here that is usually covered with wildflowers this time of year, add to that a scarlet sunset and I think it would be quite a beautiful sight to behold."

JoAnn smiled, noticing how broad his shoulders looked encased in the pale blue cambric shirt he wore. Evidently he had opted for comfort over dress tonight, which suited her fine. She loved the way he looked in his shirtsleeves. It also made the fact she had chosen a long, light-pink summer dress with elbow-length puffed sleeves and a simple rounded neckline seem all the more appropriate.

"Sounds nice, but I imagine you are pretty tired after having worked on the foundation of that roof all afternoon." She wondered if it was the same meadow near where the time passage stood—*waiting*. "You would probably rather just sit out here and watch the sky turn colors from the garden."

Adam shook his head to deny her claim. He had never felt more exhilarated in his life. Just having her there put energy in everything he did. "Amazingly, I'm not really all that tired. But I'll do whatever you want." It did not matter to him what they did as long as they did it together.

Thinking it might be safer for them to stay within the sight of the house, especially as handsome as he

316

looked in that clinging shirt, JoAnn decided to forgo the walk and simply sit out in the garden together for a while.

After finishing a meal fit for royalty, that was exactly what they did. They cleared the leaves off the lawn swing and sank onto the wooden bench to enjoy the coming sunset. Only they soon found themselves not alone. George had spotted them out there almost immediately and quickly joined them.

Despite Adam's obvious efforts to convince the boy to go on to bed, the child stayed with them chasing the insects that flocked to the lanterns and pulling up lawn weeds with his toes, until finally it became too cool outside for any of them to remain.

Feeling defeated, for he had hoped to be alone with JoAnn while surrounded by flowers and a clear night sky, Adam followed George and JoAnn inside. When they entered the back door, he tried one last time to have JoAnn to himself. He sent George to ask his mother to put on a pot of hot chocolate, thinking the boy would stay and watch her make it. To his dismay, George returned within minutes claiming his mother would bring a tray when the chocolate was ready.

Disgruntled, Adam tried another approach.

"George, since I'm probably going to need you up on the roof with me tomorrow handing me the nails I'll need to put those shingles down, I really think you ought to go on to bed and get your rest."

"You planning to let me up on the roof with you?" George asked, clearly impressed. "But I thought you said it was too dangerous for me to be up there. I thought I was to help Cyrus with the fence."

"That was before I remembered just how old you are getting to be," Adam said, aware he would agree to anything if it meant he could finally have some time alone with JoAnn. He had not suggested this trip just so he could spend all his spare time with George and Cyrus. "You're nearly ten now, aren't you?"

"I'm *eleven*," George responded, arching his shoulders proudly. "Been eleven for nearly six months now."

"Then you are definitely old enough to help me repair the roof. But if that's what you really want to do, you'll need to get lots of rest. I can't have my best helper tiring out on me before I'm finished."

JoAnn studied George's reaction to Adam's open praises and knew exactly what Adam was trying to do. She fought the urge to grin when George's eyebrows pulled together into a truly earnest expression. "You're right. Maybe I ought to get on to bed." He turned to JoAnn and nodded politely. "See you in the morning," he said, then spun on his heel and headed toward the back of the house with a swagger that indicated the importance he felt.

"You did that deliberately," she accused as soon as the boy was gone from their sight.

"Did what deliberately?" he asked with a questioning expression, as if he had no idea what she had meant. He then indicated she should precede him into the parlor by giving a forward wave of his hand. "The boy is young. He needs his sleep."

When JoAnn entered the parlor, she noticed only two lamps were burning, one on either end of the long table that stood directly behind the same sofa where she knew the two of them would eventually sit. Her heart gave a tiny little jump when she realized how terribly romantic the soft lighting made the room look, but she quickly sought to bring the unanticipated reaction back under control.

"And don't you need your sleep, too?" she asked, then headed for the far side of the room to open one of the windows. Although the temperature had become uncomfortably cool outside, the windows in this room had not been opened all day and that made the air inside a little stuffy.

She felt a small wave of disappointment when she glanced at the clock just as she reached for the window base and saw that it was already after eight. She had only two nights left in that magical domain, and this one was passing all too quickly. "After all, you were up early this morning. You've had a long day."

Not long enough, Adam thought, while he watched her use both hands to tug the window open, but what he said aloud was, "I told you, I'm not tired." Certain she would head for the sofa after she finished, he quickly moved into position directly behind her, hoping to intercept her.

Unaware of what he had done and not wanting him to think she was hinting for him to leave, JoAnn responded, "I'm glad because I'm not ready to go to bed either."

She turned away from the window at the same time she took a small step and gasped in startled response when she nearly collided with his chest. She had not expected to find him that close. Nor had she expected to find his gaze quite that dark, nor quite *that* intent. Her heart responded to his unexpected nearness by setting off at a frantic rate. Every inch of her body came alive with anticipation.

"I-I just wanted to let some fresh air into the room," she said, suddenly compelled to explain why she was standing where she was, although she had no idea why.

"Glad you did." He swallowed hard while he let his gaze drift from her huge eyes downward to her slightly parted lips. Overwhelmed by a growing desire for her, a desire he knew he could not hold back much longer, he reached to touch her soft cheek with the tips of his fingers. He watched her eyes drift shut in response to his gentle touch. "Do you remember that afternoon several weeks ago when I kissed you?"

JoAnn's eyes fluttered open again at such a surprising question.

"Yes," she answered honestly yet hesitantly. It had been too powerful a kiss to be easily forgotten. "Of course I remember. It happened the day George cut his hand."

He continued to study her beauty with both amazement and appreciation, his gaze slowly drawn from where his fingers softly caressed her cheek to her long, silky black eyelashes, then to that regal, upturned nose of hers until it finally came to rest on the still-parted mouth that beckoned his. "Your response to that kiss was to pull away and tell me it should never have happened."

"I remember," she admitted in a silkier voice than normal. Aware of all the places his gaze had gone and that his normally pale blue eyes had again darkened with obvious desire, she found each breath she took more labored than the last.

"Well, would you mind telling me why?" he asked and continued to divide his attention between the seductive curve of her mouth and the sparkling roundness of her eyes.

"Why?" she asked, so overwhelmed by the wild rush of emotions building inside her, she was not able to follow his train of thought. "Why what?"

"Why that kiss should never have happened. Because unless you can give me a very good reason not to, I think I am about to fall prey to your incredible beauty and kiss you again."

"But why?" she asked, thinking the unexpected display of desire to be a little sudden.

"I've asked myself that same question many times. Why am I so drawn to you? What is it about you that haunts me and keeps me awake at nights?"

"I keep you awake?" She could hardly believe she was hearing any of this. "Are you trying to tell me that you are interested in me?"

"My dear JoAnn Griffin, you have *interested* me in a way few women can since that very first day I met you. That's why I was so determined not to let myself become involved with you there at first."

"I don't understand. Why wouldn't you want to become involved with me?"

"Because I was afraid of you, or rather I was afraid of what you could do to me." When she responded to that by looking beautifully perplexed, he explained further. "I was afraid because I knew I might eventually want to make you a permanent part of my life. And that is something I've avoided like the plague ever since my wife's death. Because it hurt so much when I lost her, I decided I never wanted to go through anything like that again."

JoAnn certainly understood that concept. It was the same reason she had not allowed another serious relationship into her life.

"Never again did I want to run the risk of developing another permanent relationship. That's why I've always chosen women like Constance Seguin and Patricia White to be my companions. They are pretty and flattering to be with, but they are in no way a threat to my ever after. Not like you."

"You think of me as a threat?" she asked, too amazed by his confession to yet realize where this conversation was headed.

"To my future, at least the way I'd once looked at it, yes," he admitted. "But now all that has changed. When I look at you tonight, I realize it's too late. I'm already involved. Deeply involved." He took a tiny step toward her, bringing their bodies to within scant inches of each other. "And I desperately want to kiss you again."

"But what about Doris?" she asked, forcing the words out between sudden gulps for air, aware the housekeeper could appear at any moment.

"I'm sorry, but I have no desire whatever to kiss Doris," he murmured, his head already bent to claim her lips in what turned out to be a long and violently sweet kiss. One that sent shock waves crashing through both their bodies.

When he pulled away minutes later, his breath came in short rapid bursts and his eyes glittered with a dark, unbridled passion while he studied her startled expression. A sinking dread crept over him. "Please don't tell me that should not have happened because this time I don't think I could take it, and I would definitely have to argue with you. Truth is, that should have happened weeks ago."

"Then why didn't it?" she asked, suddenly not caring that she would only be making matters worse by allowing the moment to continue. It no longer really mattered that she could be headed for a more devastating heartbreak than she had ever known. At that moment, all she wanted was to let him know how wonderfully affected she had been by his kiss and perhaps lure him into kissing her yet again.

Adam stared at her, perplexed. "Because I thought

you would be angry with me. I thought you would be so angry, in fact, that you would reject me yet again, and I wasn't quite sure I could stand having you pull away from me a second time."

"But I didn't pull away, did I?" she noted, smiling at his baffled expression, aware he had truly expected a far less tolerant response from her. "Does that make me a bad person?"

"Just a confusing one," he admitted, encouraged by her reaction. His dimples formed long crescents along the outside corners of his mouth when he realized she had no intention of admonishing him for what he had just done. "But then you've been confusing to me since the very first day I met you."

"Is that an insult?" she asked, knowing what it had to be was an *understatement*.

"No. Not an insult. Just a matter of fact." He studied her beautiful upturned face a moment longer. There was still so much he did not know about her, so very much he wanted to know. "You try very hard to remain a mystery to me, don't you? Is that so I will keep you constantly on my mind?"

Aware they were about to enter into an area of conversation she would rather avoid, JoAnn shook her head. "You make me sound more clever than I am. Actually, there's nothing all that mysterious about me. I'm just like any other woman."

"Hardly," he growled and dipped forward to take yet another kiss, this time slipping his arms around the small of her back, enabling him to pull her closer. With a yearning he had forgotten he could possess, he flattened his hands against her lower back, pressing her body tightly against his while he devoured her with hot, demanding kisses.

JoAnn's first thought was that she should do some-

323

thing to stop him, before their desire for one another became too great. But when it came right down to the very act of pushing him away and thus breaking the embrace, she could not. She had no real desire to end the wondrous floodtide of sensations he had so easily created inside her.

She knew she would soon be forced to leave Adam forever and would never again have a chance at such total happiness and for the life of her she could not understand why she had thus far deprived herself of the one thing she wanted most, which was to make love to and be made love to by Adam. Just once.

Although she was still very aware that by making love to him she risked an even greater heartache when the time came to leave, she decided it would be better than never having known the wonders of his love at all. Desperately, she wanted one wondrous memory to carry back with her — a memory of Adam she could hold in her heart long after she had returned to her own time. She would give herself that memory.

Having made that decision, JoAnn lifted her arms ready to slip them around Adam's neck but the faint sound of porcelain clattering against a metal tray somewhere in the distance brought her suddenly to her senses. The noise meant Doris was on her way down the hall with the hot chocolate, and she stepped back with a startled gasp. Her heart pounded at such a ferocious rate, having almost been caught in the act, she could hardly breathe quickly enough to keep up with her sudden need for more oxygen while she waited for Doris to appear.

"Here is the chocolate you vanted," Doris said in a cheerful voice when she swept into the room carrying a large tray. Her eyebrows notched when she lifted her gaze to the ceiling and glanced from one chandelier to another, as if wondering why anyone would want to be in a room with so little lighting. "Nice and piping hot, it is."

When she glanced down and saw the strange expressions on both Adam's and JoAnn's faces, she looked back at her tray, puzzled. "Is something vrong? It vas chocolate you ordered, vasn't it?"

"Yes, of course it was," Adam said and moved away from JoAnn. His whole body ached with an unfulfilled need while he struggled to regain his composure. "Miss Griffin likes a cup of hot chocolate before bedtime on nights when there's a chill. Set the tray on the table near the sofa where we can both reach it."

Doris did exactly as told then lifted the small porcelain pot and poured two cups of the creamy brown concoction. She handed one of the cups to JoAnn then held the other out to Adam. "Is there anything else you'll be needing before I set myself off to bed?"

"No," Adam answered a little too quickly, then grimaced at the urgency he noted in his own voice. In an effort to control that urgency, he took in a slow, deep breath and held it while he silently counted to four, then in a much calmer voice added, "This will be fine."

Doris nodded as she stepped away from the tray then looked at Adam curiously. "Since you asked to have such an early supper tonight, vill you be vanting an early breakfast, too?"

JoAnn's eyebrows arched. So that was why they had eaten so much earlier than usual. It had been a specific request from Adam. She wondered why he had not bothered to mention that fact to her.

"No," he answered. He tried not to look guilty

while he avoided looking at JoAnn directly. "Breakfast can be at the regular hour."

"Good. I do like my sleep," Doris admitted and paused to give them both one last curious look before leaving the room and heading toward the back of the house.

Feeling awkward to be alone with Adam again, especially after what had happened before, or rather what had *almost* happened, JoAnn set her cup back onto the tray then moved to the front of the sofa as though she planned to sit, but never actually did so.

"Why did you want an early supper?" she asked, curious to know his reasoning, especially when he was normally such a stickler for routine.

"Because I'd hoped that by eating early, we could have a little more time alone tonight," he admitted and frowned when he remembered how his evening had not quite gone according to plan. "I hadn't counted on George being so eager to join us."

"But you should have," she said, then glanced down at the sofa, thinking she should sit, if for no other reason than to take some weight off her unsteady legs. But something inside her warned her not to because if she did, he might take the act as a sign of disinterest; and if he did that, he might not try to kiss her again. And she definitely wanted to be kissed again. Her insides spun wildly at the mere thought of it. "You know how very much that boy adores you. He loves it when you are here."

"And I enjoy being here with him," Adam admitted, also setting his cup down after only one sip. Now that he had sampled JoAnn's erotic sweetness, the imported chocolate in his cup tasted almost bitter. With his hands now empty, he casually walked to the

326

door and grasped it by the edge. "At times George is almost like a son to me. I guess that's because, had my son lived, he'd be nearly that same age," he explained while he slowly closed the door and twisted the lock with a deafening click that filled the room with mounting expectation. Very eager to take up where they had just left off, he then headed toward her with slow, lithe movements until again they stood only inches apart. "But just because I enjoy being with the boy doesn't mean I want to spend my every waking minute with him when I'm here."

"Oh?" JoAnn asked in a tiny voice. Her legs felt more wobbly by the minute while her heart raced with rising anticipation. "And why not?"

"Because there are times when I prefer *adult* company," he responded. His gaze dipped to the sensuous curve of her mouth before slowly returning to her eyes.

"Adult? You mean, like Doris?" she asked, knowing that was not at all what he had intended to imply. Feeling giddy with exhilaration, much like an infatuated schoolgirl, she fought the urge to giggle when she saw his eyebrows flatten after that last question.

"Hardly!"

Again the word came in a low throaty growl and within seconds his mouth returned to claim hers in another deeply seductive kiss. His arms slipped immediately around her as again he drew her body into the tantalizing warmth of his embrace.

Knowing it was exactly what she wanted, JoAnn moaned an appreciative response and slid her arms up then around his neck, eager to treasure the wondrous moment to its fullest.

Again it did not matter to her that she was heading for a far worse heartbreak than before just by allowing herself to fall prey to this lunacy called passion. It felt too right to be in Adam's arms, to revel beneath his astonishingly tender touch. Allowing their passion more freedom seemed the natural thing to do. She would not fight the desire building inside her a moment longer.

JoAnn loved Adam deeply and even though they could never have the sort of permanent commitment she'd always longed for, she would not deprive herself of this one chance at genuine happiness. She had denied her feelings far too long. She would give of herself willingly and take from him eagerly, and suffer the consequences when the time came.

"I want you," Adam said huskily when he was able to pull his mouth free of hers. He had to let her know how important this was. "I've wanted you since that first day over seven weeks ago."

"And I want you," she confessed just before he dipped his mouth for yet another deep, devouring kiss. Trembling with a need that had not been fulfilled since her ill-fated love affair with Thomas Rourke, she leaned against Adam, pressing her body closer.

When she divided her lips to moan aloud her ecstasy, Adam took full advantage and quickly darted the tip of his tongue inside, causing her whole body to ache with growing anticipation. Her heart soared ever higher with every tiny thrust of his tongue, aware each time it darted deeper and deeper, as if craving more and more of her sweetness.

Overwhelmed by the intensity of need that had swept over her, she ran trembling hands over his powerful back and shoulders, timidly exploring the thick muscles through his shirt, muscles that had grown solid and strong from years of hard, honest labor instead of an occasional workout at the local gym. The rippling movement of those powerful muscles beneath her sensitive fingers heightened her awareness of him even more.

While burying her hands deeper into the soft material of his shirt, she became so overwhelmed by the feel of his agile body pressed so intimately against hers, and by the sheer wizardry his mouth performed upon hers, she was only vaguely aware that his hands had begun an eager exploration of their own. It was not until he had undone several of the buttons down the back of her dress and she felt the soft material slacken that she knew undoubtedly where his exploration was taking them. Her heart overflowed with the love she felt for this man while she continued to push all thought of ever having to leave him aside. She would not let anything come between her and this one moment of happiness.

While Adam continued to work the many buttons down her back with one hand, the other moved to the front of her dress to take in one aching breast. Even through the soft cottony fabric, she felt the raging fire of his touch, glad now she had chosen not to wear her bra. Having to stop and explain such an unusual garment to a man of the 1880s would have caused an unbearable delay to the wondrous event that was about to happen.

Within seconds Adam had the dress completely undone and the fabric pushed down to her waist, out of his way. He wondered at her lack of a chemise but not for long for his desire to hold her naked in his arms was too great. Eagerly he stepped back just enough to work the material down over her slender hips, until it finally dropped to the floor in a soft puddle of pink, carrying the ankle-length half-slip with it.

JoAnn gasped when the cool air brushed her heated skin, causing her nipples to tighten while tiny bumps of exhilaration scattered across her body. Before he could reach for what should be her bloomers and discover they were not bloomers at all, she arched her back to lure his attention elsewhere while she hurriedly worked herself out of the bikini-style underwear she had on then reached immediately for the tiny buttons that held his shirt.

Unable to ignore what had been so eloquently presented him, Adam eagerly explored the rounded softness of her breasts, caressing the fullness with the curves of his hands while his thumbs gently stroked the tips until they grew rigid with a woman's need. Despite his own ever-increasing need, he fought the urge to conquer quickly, determined to make this as enjoyable for her as he knew it would be for him. He would not allow her first time to be one of hurt and confusion, he would claim her as gently and as gratifyingly as he could.

Meanwhile, JoAnn continued to work with his clothing, until she had every opening undone. Slowly, she pushed the garments back and off his body, her gaze watching her own movements, mesmerized, while she exposed his hard muscles to the glistening lamplight.

With bodies now naked and pressed intimately together, the kiss deepened and what had started out as tentative explorations of each other became instantly more frantic, their needs more pressing. Willingly, JoAnn hurled herself into the swirling sea of sensations that had so quickly engulfed her, surrendering to a floodtide of need so turbulent, it was all she

330

could do not to cry out with the sheer rapture that had filled her.

Giving her heated emotions full rein, JoAnn closed her eyes, aware they were well past the point of turning back. Which she had no desire to. She loved Adam with far too much depth and intensity to consider anything at that moment but the very real pleasure they would soon share.

Lost now to the passions Adam had aroused in her, to the desires that flourished with each new place he touched and kissed, JoAnn ached with a need so volatile, so intense, it had to be fulfilled. The sweet taste of his mouth whenever he returned to devour hers and the familiar scent that enveloped him only served to excite her further.

While Adam continued such bewildering magic, JoAnn's blood raced hot trails beneath her skin, making her feel more vibrant, more alive than she had ever felt before. Never had she felt such a blazing need, such burning excitement — not even in the arms of Thomas Rourke, whom she had at one time hoped to marry. Never had her pulses pounded with such incredible force, throbbing and swelling in every part of her body while her senses whirled endlessly through a wondrous state of delirium — intoxicating her further, heightening her passion while she continued to yield instinctively to his touch.

Soon JoAnn's body felt as if it were on fire, writhing with burning need. Her hands dug into his back with all the strength she possessed, her way of letting him know she wanted, somehow, someway, to bring him closer. She wanted him to be a part of her, if only for the one night — so much a part of her that the heartbreaking fact they could never share a future together would be temporarily forgotten.

331

Adam was astounded by such passion. Aroused to the point of madness, he groaned while he pulled her with him onto the cushioned sofa. Lying partially atop her yet partially to one side, he continued to torment the woman he loved with careful ministrations until he had her writhing in his arms.

Then just when it seemed to JoAnn that she could stand no more of his bittersweet torture, he proved her wrong. When he released her mouth from his hungry imprisonment to trail tiny, searing kisses down her throat, across her collarbone, then down again until he finally reached her aching breasts, her passions soared higher still. Too eager to share with Adam that which she had denied herself for far too long, JoAnn took as much of his sweet torment as she could before tugging frantically at his shoulders, letting him know the time had come.

When Adam finally liberated her breasts from his gentle assault and moved to take her mouth in one last soul-shattering kiss, she arched her body to remind him of her urgency. Inside she was ablaze with need, and she wanted desperately to pull him into the flames.

Slowly, Adam rose and looked down at her beauty one last time. He gazed first at her flushed face, at the enticing way her eyes had closed and her mouth was parted, then he saw her swelling breasts straining forward, a result of the inferno that blazed inside her, and knew the time was right. Eager to feel her warmth, he took only a moment longer to gaze at her beauty, then lowered himself to her once more, gently, still thinking it her first time.

Flames of white-hot pleasure seared every fiber of JoAnn's being when he finally moved to claim her. At last, the man she loved, and would continue to love for the rest of her life, was a part of her. It was an exquisite, almost indescribable feeling of completeness. A rapture beyond any she had ever believed possible. And, incredibly, the overwhelming feeling of joy continued to build with each movement that followed.

JoAnn's breath, shallow and gasping, grew stronger and more rapid as she reached higher and higher for the pinnacle—until finally, in a glorious burst of ecstasy, she cried aloud Adam's name. Adam responded to her outburst of pleasure with a deep, shuddering groan that racked his entire body again and again. Never had lovemaking been so all-consuming to either of them.

Fulfilled at last, they both lay quietly on the sofa for a long moment, their bodies still entwined, their energy spent, languorous in the aftermath of their love.

It was Adam who first broke the warm silence that filled the room. "I want you to know I love you."

Despite the fact he had just discovered she was not the virgin he had believed her to be, he still loved her with all his heart. Before continuing with what he had to say, he rose up on one elbow so he could better gaze at her beautiful face. "And I want to marry you."

JoAnn's eyes widened with instant regret, aware for the first time she was not the only one who was about to be deeply hurt by what they had just done. A cold, sickening feeling snaked its way into her stomach, making her flinch with pain. Why hadn't she realized he could be hurt, too? "You can't possibly mean that."

"Oh, but I do," he replied and lifted his free hand to trace the soft curve of her cheek with his finger, wondering why her body had tensed so suddenly. "I want you to be my wife. I want what we just shared to be ours forever."

Tears filled her heart then spilled over into her eyes. She had been so overwhelmed with what she was feeling toward him, she had not realized the depth of his feelings for her.

"But I can't marry you." Ashamed that she had not considered his true feelings at all, that all she had thought of were her own selfish needs, she sat up and turned away from him. Needing something to help console her, she reached for a ruffled pillow that had been knocked to the floor and clutched it to her breasts. "As much as I love you, too, and I do love you, Adam, I can never be your wife."

Thinking she was ashamed because she had not come to him a virgin, and remembering that she had already admitted having loved another to the point of having planned to marry him, he, too, sat up then rested his hand on her shoulder reassuringly. "If you think it matters to me that I was not the first man in your life, you are wrong. Whatever happened before you met me is none of my affair. All that really matters here is the fact that I love you and because I do love you, I want to share the rest of my life with you. JoAnn, I know I can make you happy."

The pain that tore at JoAnn's heart became so intense, she was not certain she could bear the onslaught. Tortured by the candor in his voice, aware he was telling her exactly how he felt, she buried her face in the pillow and wept bitterly. This was not supposed to happen.

Chapter Sixteen

Baffled by such a distraught reaction to his proposal of marriage, especially after what they had just shared together, Adam gently stroked JoAnn's dark hair and continued to reassure her. It truly did not matter to him that she had had another man in her life. He loved her too much to be bothered by past mistakes. All that really mattered was that she agree to marry him and promise to make him the only man in her life from that day forward.

"JoAnn, I really don't care about your past. Please believe that, and tell me that you will marry me."

When all she could do was shake her head no while she continued to weep uncontrollably into the sofa pillow in her lap, it felt as if his heart was being torn into tiny pieces. Why didn't she believe him? "It's true. I love you enough to forgive *anything* from your past. Please, JoAnn, just say that you will at least consider marrying me."

Unable to believe his generosity, JoAnn sucked in a deep, sobbing breath and lifted her head away from the pillow. She had cried so hard the pillow was wet and her eyes were rimmed red. "I already told you, I can't marry you. Our lives are too different."

"Our lives themselves may have been different up

until now, but we are very much alike," he countered and slipped a finger beneath her chin to keep her from returning that beautiful face to the tear-stained pillow she now clutched against her breasts. "If it is a medical practice that worries you, then don't let it. I can help you establish a practice right here in Cambria County. As fast as Johnstown has been growing these past several years, it is in constant need of another doctor."

When her only response to that was to let her lower lip tremble while she blinked back a fresh rush of tears, he felt encouraged and hurried to explain. "You could start by working out a partnership agreement of some kind with my father. It's pretty obvious he will be needing some help now that his health has started to give him problems. You could work with him for however long he continued to work, knowing he won't be able to keep up his practice forever. Eventually he will have to retire and let his patients go to other doctors. Why not be the doctor he recommends? Why not be the one his patients are already accustomed to?"

JoAnn's whole body trembled when she saw the hope reflected in his glimmering blue eyes. A very real desire to stay right there with him speared her heart and became pitted against another need just as real and just as vital, the need to return to her own time. The battling emotions caused all manner of havoc to stir inside her, making her feel as if she were being pulled in all directions at once. "Oh, Adam, I wish I could do all that. I wish I could make a life for myself right here with you. I truly do. But I can't. It just wouldn't work."

"Why wouldn't it?" he wanted to know, hurt now by her continued refusal. His expression hardened when he pulled his hand away and placed it on the sofa behind her. "It's not as if you already have a practice established somewhere else," he said, his tone bitter. "Nor are you presently on staff at any of the licensed hospitals in Pittsburgh. I've checked them all and none of the supervisors at any of the hospitals has ever heard of you. Nor could you have much of a practice established anywhere—or you would never be able to come and go as freely as you do."

When she looked away from him, her pain clearly evident in her tear-filled brown eyes, he felt ashamed by both his words and his cruel tone and hurried to rectify the damage done with a more soothing voice. "Don't take what I just said the wrong way. I'm not trying to make you feel like a failure. The only reason you have not been able to establish a successful medical practice in Pittsburgh is because, like in Johnstown, the people there are having a difficult time accepting you as a real doctor. And obviously the hospitals are, too."

"You checked with *all* the hospitals in Pittsburgh?" she asked, amazed that even after having found out what had to look to him like a pack of deliberate lies, he still wanted to marry her. "When?"

"Weeks ago, but only because I care about you and wanted to know more about you." He wanted her to understand it was not because he did not trust her. "I was worried about you."

"Worried about me? Why?"

"Because whenever I tried to get you to talk about yourself, you'd suddenly look troubled then you would change the subject immediately. It was obvious that you were afraid to talk about yourself, which made me think you might be trying to hide from something or someone. I was worried that you have run away from something or someone who was out to harm you. If

337

you were in some sort of danger, I wanted to know so I could help protect you. But now I understand the reason you were so reluctant to talk about your work or where you lived. It had nothing to do with you being in any danger. You did not want us to think you were a failure. But don't you see? It isn't *you* who is a failure; it is all those people who have refused to accept you as a competent doctor. They have failed to look beyond their own prejudices to see what a qualified doctor you really are."

JoAnn could not believe the compassion nor the generosity that was so much a part of Adam's character. If only more men could be like him. For a brief moment she pushed all other thoughts aside and fantasized what it might be like to stay and be married to him, to have such a wonderful man at her beck and call for the rest of her life. But all too quickly the reality of their situation returned and she knew she could not allow him to be deluded by such fraudulent hopes any longer. "Even so, I can't marry you."

"But *why?*" he demanded, so filled with frustration and anger, he slammed his hand against the back of the sofa. Not knowing what else to do, he stood and started snatching up their clothing, tossing hers toward her when he came to it. He was too furious by her continued refusal to pay much attention to the strange garments she had worn beneath her clothing. All he could see at that moment were his hopes slowly slipping away from him.

"You haven't answered. Why can't you marry me?" He turned and waved the shirt he had just grabbed from the floor to emphasize his words. "You've already admitted that you love me. And you told me several weeks ago that there is no longer another man in your life."

Another tiny piece of JoAnn's heart tore off and fell away, causing a hurt so severe, so all-consuming, she never would have believed a person could experience such pain and still go on living. If only he had not fallen in love with her, too. It would have made this so much easier.

"That's true," she said, forcing the words past the painful constriction that held her throat while she hurriedly slipped into her underclothing and tried not to look at him while he jammed his legs into his own. "I do love you, and there is no other man in my life. But still I can't marry you."

"That still doesn't explain why." He paused while pulling on his clothing long enough to look at her, only vaguely aware she already had her dress on and was frantically working with the buttons behind her. "Why can't you marry me?"

JoAnn was so filled with anguish, her blood felt cold beneath her skin. "Because I can't."

More visions of what it would be like to be Adam's wife drifted before her while she finished with her dress, making her aware of how much simpler life would be if she stayed. The only thing she would have to worry about was making Adam happy. But just as quickly as those fanciful visions had formed, others moved in to take their place.

She would never be happy living a life like that. She was a doctor. She had to have her medical career. And playing second fiddle to another doctor who had far less education in hopes of one day taking over a small part of his dwindling practice was not enough. Not when she knew her name was due to come up for the job of Medical Director of Emergency Services when Dr. Sanford left for California in August. And not when she realized she would be practicing without an actual license if she stayed. Unlike the twentieth century, she would not be a legitimate doctor in the year Eighteen eighty-nine.

Adam watched a wide range of conflicting emotions flicker across JoAnn's face and realized that although she continued to refuse him, a tiny part of her wanted desperately to accept. Clinging to the hope that tiny part of her would eventually win out over the rest, he knelt before her, his blue gaze level with hers. "I realize my proposal was awfully sudden, too sudden for you to make a knowledgeable decision just yet. That's why I'm asking you to wait until you've had more time to think about it before making up your mind. Will you at least agree to do that much? Give it more thought before making any final decisions?"

Knowing she would be able to do little else but think about his generous proposal, JoAnn nodded. "All right, Adam. I'll give it more thought. But don't go getting your hopes up too much. It is very unlikely I'll change my mind about marrying you. We really are too different for something as lasting as marriage to ever work." If only he could know *how* different. If only she could truly believe what he had proclaimed earlier, that it would not matter to him if she had secrets in her past.

But the truth was her secrets would matter. If she were to tell him the truth about who she really was and where she was from, he would think her deranged. And even if she could finally convince him of the truth, it really would not change their situation any. They would still be from two different worlds — from two different *centuries*. A future together was hopeless.

For the next few hours, nothing else was said about

340

Adam's unexpected proposal or that they had willingly given into their passions and made love right there in the parlor. It wasn't until Adam yawned and the late hour became apparent that any reference was made to what had happened.

"I want you to come with me to my bed," he said, extending a hand to her as he met her gaze directly. "I want the chance to show you what it would be like if you agreed to marry me." He stood in front of her, waiting for her response.

JoAnn knew she should refuse, but the desire to be in his arms again was too great. She would rather put aside her heartache for a moment and pretend the future really was theirs. She knew it was the only way she would be able to get through this last weekend with her mind intact. "As long as you understand that whatever happens tonight will not influence my decision in any way."

"But how can it not?" he asked, searching her face intently while his hand closed possessively around hers. But without waiting for an answer, he dipped forward and placed a delicate kiss on her cheek, near her ear, and heard a sharp intake of air.

"It's just that I don't want you to be further disappointed if I don't change my mind about marrying you," she said and reveled in the wild array of sensations that sparkled through her.

"But you promised to think about it. That's enough for me." He pulled her toward him with a gentle tug. Again he bent to place another tantalizing kiss on her cheek, this one even closer to the sensitive lobe of her ear.

JoAnn's eyes fluttered shut while the sensations bubbling inside her played havoc with her senses. "As long as you understand how I feel," she said in a wispy voice, already breathless in response to the need arising inside her. Then offering no further mandates, she went with him up the stairs and into his darkened bedroom where she waited just inside the door while he hurriedly crossed the room and lit a small table lamp near the bed, creating a soft island of light that touched all corners of the room.

While he pulled back the covers, JoAnn scanned her surroundings. It was the first time she had been in Adam's bedroom and she was pleased by the solid but elegant furnishings, so very like Adam himself. It was a much larger room than the one where she slept, with a full set of bedroom furniture at one end and a small sitting arrangement at the other.

"Close the door," Adam said. "Then come here." He opened his arms to her and waited for her to obey, eager to show her yet again how very much he loved her.

Eager to comply, JoAnn eased the door then rushed into his arms. Within minutes, they were again unclothed and in bed, basking in the warmth of each other's lovemaking. Only this time, no words were spoken afterward to break the magical spell that lingered and JoAnn chose to stay what was left of the night in his bed pretending for the sheer pleasure it gave her that there were no barriers ahead for them, that she could indeed one day become his wife.

Not until the first blush of daylight drifted through Adam's bedroom window did she slip out from beneath the covers, walk quietly across the floor, and into her own room, for the first time using the door that divided the two. She would have loved to stay and watch Adam wake, for it was a sight she knew would thrill her, but she did not want Doris or the boys to know what had gone on between them and was not

342

sure if Doris came upstairs to urge him awake each morning or whether he awoke on his own.

When Adam stirred the following morning, he was disappointed to find himself alone beside a dented pillow, and for a moment worried that she had left his bed for all the wrong reasons. But when he then remembered how incredibly she had responded to their lovemaking and how sincere she had sounded when she'd declared her love, he decided not to let her disappearance dampen his hopes. He and JoAnn were meant for each other and he would do everything within his power to convince her of that fact.

JoAnn spent the following day reliving those wondrous moments in Adam's arms again and again, and was not upset nor surprised when Adam entered her bedroom that night just as she was getting ready for bed. And because she loved him so dearly and knew their time together was now painfully short, she did not ask him to leave. Instead, she pulled back the covers on her bed much like he had done to his own bed the night before then blew out the only lamp burning in her room and welcomed him with a fiery kiss.

Later, while lying in the crook of his arm, sated and complete, it suddenly dawned on her that she had taken no precautions against pregnancy. She had no idea why that consideration had not occurred to her earlier and wondered what she would do if after she returned to work, she discovered she was pregnant with Adam's child. Blinking at such a startling thought, she rested her hand on her stomach and smiled, knowing she would keep the child and raise it with all the love Adam would have wanted.

343

When JoAnn finally drifted off to sleep that night, with Adam still at her side, visions of motherhood danced happily in the back of her mind. A baby would certainly be something wonderful to remember him by.

That following morning, JoAnn was the one who awoke to find an empty bed—except for a small yellow flower that lay on the pillow beside her. Lifting the flower gently, she held it to her nose and even though the petals offered no fragrance, she smiled, pleased that in addition to all his other amazing qualities, Adam was also a romantic.

That night, knowing it was to be her last night in the year Eighteen eighty-nine, JoAnn decided to make the most of it. Rather than wait for him to come to her room as he had the night before, she gathered her courage and went instead into his. She forced aside all thoughts of what would happen the following morning when it came time for her to return to her own century and concentrated instead on this last chance to be with Adam.

With the desperation of a woman who knew she would soon be denied that which she wanted most, JoAnn encouraged Adam into their most passionate night of lovemaking yet. With all abandon tossed aside, she led them into ecstasy time and time again, forcing herself not to dwell on the fact she would soon have to tell him goodbye forever.

That night she did not leave his bed except once and that happened shortly after he fell asleep. Without making a sound, she returned to her own room, found her camera, then tiptoed back to chance taking a picture of Adam while he was asleep, the whole time praying the sudden light would not wake him. To her relief all he did in response to the blue flash was rub his face with the back of his hand and roll from his side onto his back. She thrilled at the realization she would have a close-up of his face when she returned — a photograph to treasure in the lonely nights to come, one to show their child one day should she actually be pregnant. And now she fervently hoped that would be the case. When she left, it would be like taking a tiny part of Adam with her.

Aware now that Doris rarely came upstairs until after breakfast, allowing Adam to awaken on his own, JoAnn returned the camera to her room, buried it inside a pile of clothing, then hurried back to his side. She spent the rest of the night snuggled against his sleeping body, feeling the steady rise and fall of his chest beneath her cheek.

The thoughts of their lovemaking made her whole body feel deliciously warm; but when she later remembered how short lived their relationship was to be, the warmth faded into a dull, cold ache near the pit of her stomach. They had shared their last night together.

When Adam awoke the following morning to find JoAnn still in his bed, his heart filled with hope.

"Does this mean I've started to wear down your resistance?" he wanted to know after he'd opened his eyes to find her propped on her elbow, staring at him with the most peculiar expression, her long brown hair cascading over her bare shoulder like that of the seductress he now knew her to be.

"No," she answered honestly and shook her head sadly. Now that he was awake, the time of reckoning had come. "This means I am heartbroken over the fact I have to leave you today."

345

Adam sat bolt upright, his face stricken. "You what? You never mentioned that you planned to leave today."

"That's because I didn't want to upset you," she told him and quickly looked away, knowing if she didn't she would end up in tears and he would realize this goodbye was permanent. She did not want him knowing he would never see her again until it was time for her to leave. "But I do have to go today."

"Why?" Adam wanted to know, his voice as pleading as it was baffled. He was not ready for her to leave. He had not yet convinced her to marry him. "Why do you suddenly have to leave?"

"It's not sudden. I've known for several days that today would be the day. I have to go back to work," she said, knowing it was true. She did have to go back to work, even though certain feelings of inadequacy still plagued her and the loss of her parents still hung heavy over her, she had to be in ER ready to go to work that very afternoon.

"But where?" His eyebrows dipped low while he tried to make sense of this sudden decision to leave. "I've already checked with all the hospitals in Pittsburgh. Remember? And I was told you don't work for any of them."

"There's one hospital you obviously overlooked," she said, then tossed back the covers and hurried to slip into her gown, not wanting to explain further. "It's nearly six-thirty. Doris will be wondering what happened to us. I'll tell you more about my plans after I'm dressed and have come downstairs." Then giving him little chance to say more, she hurried through the door and into her own room.

Although she did not want a pair of red, swollen eyes for Adam to remember her by, she was unable to

346

keep from crying while she hurried to dress. Within a very few hours, she would have to pack what dresses she wanted to take back with her and then leave Adam forever. Just knowing their time was so short hurt beyond belief.

But if she was to be at work by four, she needed to be out of the year 1889 long before noon so she could get on to her parents' house. She had not yet packed her things so she could return to Pittsburgh, nor had she brought any suitable working clothes with her to Woodvale. Therefore, she would need to leave her parents' house in time to stop by her apartment and change before going on to work; and knowing it was at least an hour's drive to Pittsburgh, she needed to leave Woodvale no later than two o'clock.

When JoAnn entered the dining room shortly after six-thirty, her tears were again under control but Adam could easily tell she had been crying. Her eyes were puffy and her eyelashes still damp. Rather than make her parting more painful, he decided against trying to pressure her into staying. Instead, he accepted the fact she felt she had to leave and waited to find out exactly when that would be, hoping they might still have most of the day together. He was disappointed when after they finished their meal, she excused herself and hurried back to her room to pack her things.

Shortly after nine o'clock JoAnn was back downstairs with her two bags, ready to leave. She found Adam in the parlor staring out an open window, looking so dejected. Trembling despite her effort to show an outward calm, she walked over to stand beside him. "I'm leaving now."

Adam came to with a start, so lost in thought he had not heard her enter. "But I still have to get the

347

carriage ready." He looked at her two bags questioningly, surprised at how quickly she had gathered her things. Most women took all day to pack, even if traveling for only a few days. But then again, JoAnn was not like most women. She was different in every way. Special in every way. Which is what made her leaving hurt all the more. "I did not realize you'd be back down so soon." He headed toward the door. "It'll just take me a minute."

JoAnn rested a gentle hand on his shoulder and fought the pain of knowing it would be the last time they ever touched. "Don't bother with a carriage. I'd rather walk."

"But I can't let you do that," he argued. "It's nearly five miles into town and the roads are still muddy from that last rain."

Which was exactly why she did not want him to take her into town. It would be nearly an hour's ride there and another hour back, and to that time would be added the half hour she would have to spend arranging the transportation back. She did not have time for all that. She had already stayed too long. "Please, Adam." She took her hand off his shoulder and dropped it to her side. "Just let me say goodbye now."

Adam's facial muscles hardened while he studied her determined expression. "You made that sound like you're never coming back."

"I'm not sure that I am," she said, feeling it pointless to give him any false hope. She wanted him to put her out of his mind as quickly as possible and get on with his life. It would do neither of them any good to have him pining away, waiting for her return. "I think that possibility should be clear."

Adam's hands curled into tight fists as a cold fear

348

curled around his heart. Suddenly he knew. She *was* leaving him forever. Swallowing around the lump lodged in his throat, he grabbed her by the shoulders then peered beseechingly into her overly large brown eyes. He could tell by looking at her that this was not what she wanted — *not entirely.* "Please don't do this. Don't leave me yet. Stay on just a few more days. Please. Just a few days longer. You have to give me a better chance than this to convince you to marry me."

JoAnn could not stand the bitter anguish she saw in his eyes. She trembled beneath his touch. "I can't stay. Not even a few more days. And even if I could, it wouldn't make any difference." The hurt she felt as she pulled herself out of his grasp was so intense she was not sure she could stand it much longer "I have to go."

"Then at least give me an address where I can find you," he said, already headed across the room for a piece of paper and a pencil. "You can at least do that."

JoAnn bit back another quick stab of pain and, unable to bear the hurt evident in his blue eyes any longer, she turned away. She knew how he felt, remembering the emotional devastation Thomas had dealt her so many years ago. "No, I can't."

"But why?" Adam asked, his hurt roiling into anger, furious that she had yet to give him an acceptable explanation for what she was about to do.

"Because I need time to think," she lied, believing that the easiest way out. "And the only way I can have that is to get away from you for a while."

"That's not true," he argued, again looking pleadingly hopeful. "You can have all the time you could possibly need to think right here. I'll leave you alone for as long as you want. I have plenty of work I could do. I'd stay in my study and give you free reign of the place."

"Adam, don't make this any more painful than it already is," she pleaded. Her whole body trembled as she headed back across the room to where she had left her two valises. How could she ever get through these next few minutes?

"Why not?" Adam's voice had turned angry as he hurried to follow. "You are certainly not concerned with how painful you are making this for me."

"That's not true," she sobbed, losing what grip she had on her emotions as she bent to pick up the valises, wanting instead to turn and flee into his arms one last time. "It's just that there is no other way to do this than to just do it."

"You can at least let me drive you."

"It will only make it harder for me," she said and headed toward the door, her back stiff, her arms quaking from the weight of her bags.

"I'll come after you," he warned. "I'll give you just one week in which to do all your thinking, then I will come after you. And I will find you."

JoAnn closed her eyes and drew in a long, quivering breath before opening them again. With emotions so raw and strained it felt as if her heart was in very real danger of collapsing, she turned to face him one last time. "Goodbye, Adam."

Another sharp pain pierced her when she saw the look of anguish and betrayal on Adam's face, knowing it was an image she would take with her for the rest of her life. Spinning around and stepping blindly away, she hurried out of the house. She could not bear the torment a moment longer and did not glance back to see if he had followed until she was well down the road.

When she did look back and saw that he had not followed, she slowed her steps but went directly to the clearing where she had left the pile of stones, certain they still marked the opening that would take her back into the twentieth century.

After locating the exact spot, she tossed the two valises through then she paused for just a moment to give her surroundings one last look, severely tempted to go back and beg Adam's forgiveness. Convince him that she had changed her mind about going. But she was far too much a realist. She could never fit into his world any more than he could fit into hers—not completely. At least this way she still had her career to cling to, and the possibility that she might be carrying his child.

"Have a good life, Adam," she whispered softly then, with tears blinding her vision, she lifted her slippered foot and stepped into the time opening, further saddened when she had to duck low and pull in her elbows to get through. She knew that one day very soon, probably within the next couple of weeks, the hole would be too small for human passage, and would eventually disappear all together. She would never see Adam again.

Spotting her car exactly where she'd left it, she picked up her bags and slowly headed toward it, leaving the past behind, and without ever once having hinted to Adam that she was from the future. She knew that telling him the truth would have been counterproductive because rather than be convinced that she was from another era, he would have either thought her a deliberate liar who he never should have trusted—or else he'd think her a first-class nut.

Knowing that one day his anger would abate, she wanted his memories of her to be fond and flattering. By having handled it the way she did, he could eventually have just such memories. By having left without trying to sell him on the idea that she was from another time, there would come a day when he would be able to smile when he sat back on some lazy summer afternoon and wondered whatever had become of her. And it was important to her that one day he think of her with just such a smile.

Patting the camera she had tucked away inside her pocket, she knew the day would come when she would be able to smile again, too, and felt grateful she would have more than a few fading memories to sustain her in the long, lonely days ahead.

Chapter Seventeen

After Jean had finally gotten over being angry with JoAnn for her thoughtless actions during the past several weeks, she took much time to assess JoAnn's unusual behavior. Realizing how unstable JoAnn was at the moment, Jean had begun to treat her much differently than she ever had.

Jean became more cautious of everything she said or did around JoAnn, behaving as if she thought JoAnn were very close to losing what little grip she still had on reality. Jean had become so strangely solicitous that it made JoAnn feel as if she were a small child being constantly coddled and watched. Finally it had reached the point where JoAnn felt smothered, making her want to strangle her own best friend for treating her so strangely. *She was not losing her mind!* And she now wished she had never told Jean where she'd been those past few weeks.

Although JoAnn had not expected Jean to believe everything, she had certainly not expected her to start treating her like a lost child. Nor had she expected the people she worked with to act as if she were just one tiny step away from an emotional breakdown. Everyone was walking on eggshells and she was tired of it.

True, at times she walked around in a half daze, her thoughts so focused on Adam and what he might be doing now that she was gone from his life, that she was not always aware of what went on around her. It did not mean she was headed for the deep end. It just meant she missed him. Missed him every bit as much as she missed her parents, and rightfully so. He was just as gone from her life as they were, which left her feeling lonely and depressed. Plus she was still haunted by how truly devastated he had looked that day she left.

She had never wanted to hurt Adam any more than she had wanted to hurt herself. And hurting she was, down to the very pith of her soul. The pain became so severe at times she could hardly eat and rarely did she manage a full night's sleep. She constantly wondered if he had yet gotten over the pain, or if he had carried through with his threat to try to find her.

And if he did carry through with the threat, she wondered how long until he finally gave up the search. Would he engage another investigator or take off on his own? Would his inability to find out where she'd gone make him feel like a complete failure? She hoped not. She hated the thought of him suffering like that: wondering where she could have gone and why she never bothered to return. She hoped he would not wrongfully conclude that he had done something wrong, that he had driven her away somehow. Not when her leaving had been foreordained and had had nothing to do with him. It broke her heart to think of the misery he'd suffered.

Another reason for JoAnn's deep sorrow had come with the discovery she was not pregnant with Adam's child. That and for some reason the film she had brought back with her still inside her camera had somehow become overexposed. She had so wanted something tangible to help her through the long years to come, something she could actually touch; but now realized she would have to rely solely on what she held in her memory.

That was why she did her best to keep his image constantly before her, for fear if she didn't she might one day forget some tiny detail. She was constantly remembering him and all the others she had met during her sojourn in the past, though she tried not to dwell on the horrors that lay just ahead for her new friends. Just knowing that their hour of reckoning was so close caused a deep, sickly feeling to twist through her gut that grew stronger with each day's passing until, at times, the agony reached unbearable proportions.

"I don't suppose you are hungry."

Not having heard Jean enter the apartment, JoAnn gasped when she looked up, startled to find her standing just a few feet away holding a large grocery sack in one arm and her set of keys to JoAnn's car and apartment in the other.

"What are you doing here?"

"At the moment asking if you are hungry."

Befuddled to have been drawn out of such absorbing thoughts so suddenly, JoAnn blinked several times in an attempt to clear her mind enough to focus on what Jean had to say. "Hungry? Why? What's in the sack?"

"A couple of two-liter bottles of diet Coke and a half gallon of rocky road ice cream."

JoAnn looked at her with obvious suspicion. "You bought rocky road ice cream? *You?* The queen of yogurt who claims that the partaking of ice cream is the same as asking your arteries to fail and your thighs to balloon out to twice their natural size? What happened to that diet you said we were on?"

"Not only do I have your favorite ice cream here, I've ordered pizza," she said, ignoring the question while she walked across JoAnn's roomy ground-floor apartment to the small dining area that divided the living area from the kitchen. She set the large sack on the octagonal table, then reached inside. *"With* jalapeños."

"Now I *know* something is wrong," JoAnn said, narrowing her gaze while she watched Jean carry the carton of ice cream on into the kitchen where she slipped it into the freezer unit of her refrigerator. "Just what are you trying to pull here?"

"Pull? Is it a crime for me to want to spend the evening with my best friend?" Jean asked and splayed her hand over her heart as if offended by JoAnn's calloused remarks.

"This happens to be Saturday night," JoAnn reminded her as she pushed away from the gray couch and moved across the carpeted floor to join her. "Why aren't you and what's-his-name going out to-night?"

"Because *John* is in Minneapolis this weekend and I am stuck here without him," she answered, then shrugged when she saw the accusing look. "Can I help it if I don't like to be alone on Saturday night?"

JoAnn continued to study her friend suspiciously while she leaned against the narrow wall abutment that divided the dining area from the living area. "Why is it you suddenly seem to have so much free time to spend with me — and have ever since I came back about a week and a half ago?"

"Because it's the end of May for one thing," she

said as if that should have been understood. "It's amazing how much better my patients claim they feel just about the time summer approaches. From the end of May till about the middle of July has always been a slack time for me, which is why I almost always take my vacation the latter part of June."

JoAnn stiffened against the sickening wave of foreboding that washed over her at Jean's reminder of the date. It was indeed the end of May. May 30th to be exact. Which meant tomorrow, would be the 31st. Back in 1889, May 31 was the day the dam would break and the ensuing flood would destroy Johnstown. Her stomach constricted and her blood felt thick and cold.

She tried to push the agonizing thought aside before it made her physically ill. "How long until the pizza arrives?"

Jean glanced at her watch, then pushed her short bangs off her forehead with a quick flip of her hand. "I'd say in about five minutes. Why don't you go ahead and put ice into the glasses while I bring out the napkins and a couple of paper plates?"

Not really wanting to be alone, at least not tonight, not with such a strong feeling of impending doom hovering over her, JoAnn hurried to comply. She had just finished pouring the diet Coke into glasses when the doorbell sounded.

"That must be the pizza," Jean said, already shoving her left hand into her pants pocket as she headed for the door. "I hope you are hungry. I ordered two of the largest ones they make."

"Two? Why on earth would you order so much?"

"Because you are not eating right. You look like you've lost five pounds since you came back. Jo, dieting is one thing, but you have to eat something to stay alive. And eat you will."

When she opened the door, she was greeted by a pretty teenage girl with blond hair and blue eyes dressed in a red and white checkered jacket holding two large, flat boxes. "Pizza. Fresh and hot." She then glanced at her multicolored watch and smiled. "And on time."

Jean hurriedly paid the girl, then carried the pizza across the room and placed it in the center of the table. To JoAnn's surprise, as soon as she bit into her first slice, her appetite returned and she quickly wolfed down four large slices. It wasn't until she sat back in her chair and moaning from the pressure around her middle that Jean decided they could at last retire to the living room.

"We'll save the ice cream until after the movie comes on," she decided as she picked up JoAnn's remote control and clicked on the television set. She then sank into her usual place on one end of the couch while JoAnn settled into the other, both pulling their feet up under them to make themselves more comfortable. They were definitely creatures of equal habits.

"What movie are we going to watch?" JoAnn asked, glancing around for the *TV Guide* but not finding it where it should be, which was not unusual considering her recent frame of mind.

"*Casablanca* is supposed to come on tonight right after the local news," she answered, jumping to the correct station but keeping the volume down, waiting until the movie actually came on. "You don't really want to listen to the news do you?" she asked, already setting the remote on the couch between them.

"No," JoAnn answered, suddenly sad again. "The news would probably just end up reminding me what tomorrow is."

"What? That it'll be a Sunday?" Jean asked, looking confused.

"No. Not that it'll be Sunday," she said with a somber shake of her head, her heart already aching again. "Tomorrow is the day the flood hits Johnstown." She turned her tearful brown eyes to her best friend. "Sometime tomorrow afternoon, over two thousand people will be killed."

Jean sat forward, clearly concerned as she met JoAnn's gaze. "No, JoAnn. You are wrong. Tomorrow is the *anniversary* of the day the flood hit. Those two-thousand-plus people died well over a century ago. What is it with you and the year eighteen eighty-nine? It's as if you have some sort of personal fixation on that one year."

"I told you. That's the year I entered when I went through that hole."

Jean rubbed her face with her hands, wondering how she should handle the situation. She did not want to provoke irrational behavior from what was already an irrational mind. "JoAnn, you know as well as I do that trip of yours happened only in your mind. It is impossible for a person to travel back and forth in time."

She reached forward to rest a hand on JoAnn's arm, glad that JoAnn did not pull away. "I really do wish you would get into therapy. If not with me, then perhaps with Doctor Alfonsi. Alex is an expert when dealing with delusionaries. There has to be a reason you are so determined to believe in that fantasy world you created and if you don't come to terms with what all is happening inside your head

359

and soon, you will lose any chance you may have at being appointed Doctor Sandford's replacement. Don't risk your one big chance to be the new Medical Director of Emergency Services."

"It wasn't a fantasy," JoAnn insisted. Her expression hardened with resentment while she reached for the remote. "And I really don't want to talk about it with you or Doctor Alfonsi."

"But talking about it might help you to see it for what it really is."

"I already do," she answered, then pressed the volume-up button until the sound was loud enough to drown out whatever Jean might say next. She refused to be told again that Adam was not real, nor that the very deep pain she felt from having had to leave him was not real.

Jean studied her friend's troubled expression for a long moment, then decided not to press the situation just yet. Instead, she pushed herself up off the couch and padded barefoot toward the kitchen. "I'm headed to get my drink. You want something while I'm up?"

Just to get over the heartache of missing Adam, she thought as she blinked back tears; but what she actually said aloud was, "Yes, bring my drink, too. But you'd better hurry because the news is already over. That means the movie is about to start."

Because *Casablanca* was followed immediately by yet another of their all-time favorites, *African Queen*, and because neither woman felt all that sleepy despite their long hours at the hospital earlier, Jean stayed at JoAnn's until three-thirty that morning. When she finally stepped outside to head back to her own apartment, the night was pitch black and an eerie mist hung in the air.

"John is due back early tomorrow afternoon. If I don't see you before then, I'll see you sometime Monday."

"Or, Tuesday, when I return to work," JoAnn added as Jean started down the sidewalk, wanting her aware she did not have to baby-sit her the two days they were off. She sighed when she turned to go back inside. The thought of returning to work Tuesday did not appeal to her. Truth was, at that moment nothing appealed to her.

As had become their custom, JoAnn waited by the telephone until Jean had called to let her know she was safely inside her apartment. But despite the late hour and the fact she had had so little rest the night before, JoAnn still found it impossible to drift off to sleep. She could not let go of the painful realization that tomorrow was the day the terrible flood struck Johnstown.

She thought Adam should be safe enough because during the summer he normally spent at least three days during the end of each week at his own house because there was more work to be done then and the flood would be on a Friday. But she still worried about Park. Park's house was right in the center of what was called Johnstown proper, and if her memory served right, that was the area the disaster claimed its worst damage.

If only she had done something to be sure he would not be home that day. She should have suggested to Adam that his father start spending more time with him at his farm, for his health's sake. But she hadn't because when she left, she had still believed it not her right to interfere with fate.

But now that she was safely tucked away in the twentieth century with plenty of time to think about it, she was not so sure she had done the right thing. Not when she cared about Park as much as she did and truly wanted him out of harm's way, as she did his prattling housekeepers, Sheila and Shelly. She also hated to think of any harm coming to Adam's friends Anthony Alani and Andrew Edwards, who had fought so hard to make everyone see the very real danger hanging over their heads. Or to Jeanne and Harrison Rutledge, who had helped the men when they could.

After having spent more than five weeks in the year 1889, JoAnn had met at least a dozen people she hoped would survive the flood. If only there had been some way to assure their safety before she left. But there hadn't. Not without changing fate and causing dramatic changes in her own time.

Even had she tried to persuade them to take measured precautions, her words would have fallen on deaf ears, especially after explaining to them how she happened to know about the flood. The moment she'd mentioned having come to them from another century, they would have immediately discredited everything she'd ever said. But still, she could have tried to save Park from the horror of being caught up in such a destructive flood. Whatever changes that might have incurred would have been worth it.

With so many distressful thoughts to torment her, it was nearly daybreak before JoAnn finally drifted off into a deep, fitful sleep. She didn't open her eyes again until eleven-thirty.

When she did finally come awake, she felt so heavy-headed she did not bother to climb out of bed right away. Instead, she buried her face beneath both pillows and tried her best to go back to sleep. But it became obvious that mindless state was not going to return and eventually she forced herself out of bed.

Having no special plans, she pulled on a comfortable pink and white summer-weight warm-up suit and a pair of canvas shoes, then stumbled into the bathroom where she washed her face with a cold cloth, brushed her teeth, then brushed her hair back away from her sleepy eyes. Without glimpsing her reflection for fear of what she might see after having slept so hard, she headed toward the kitchen for her first diet Coke of the day.

She then went to open the door to pick up her newspaper. Stepping back inside, she rolled off the rubber band and headed for the dining table where she could spread the sections out before her and enjoy the next hour or so catching up on current events.

Because JoAnn rarely read sports, she immediately tossed that section aside, and picked up the regional news section. Leaning back in one chair with her feet propped in another, she scanned the different headlines first. Her heart froze when she realized the regional focus this Sunday was on the Johnstown Flood of 1889. The entire front page of section D was sheathed with retrospective articles describing the flood and explaining its far-reaching aftereffects.

While fighting a sudden feeling of dread so intense it reached down and pulled at her lungs and throat, her gaze was drawn, as if guided by some unseen force, to a sidebar shadowed in pink that ran one column the length of the page and was continued on pages four and five. The words were in very

363

tiny print and listed according to the cemeteries where buried, the names, ages, and general addresses of the 2,209 original victims of the Johnstown Flood, of which it was stated one out of three were never positively identified.

Among the different lists making up the side story was a fairly extensive group of names for which the bodies had been positively identified but the cemeteries where they had eventually been buried were not known. Despite the efforts at the time to keep efficient records of the many burials during the days following the flood, some burial sites had not been properly documented.

A foreboding chill curled down JoAnn's spine and settled deep in her abdomen while she scanned that list because about a third of the way down, she saw the listing: Adam Johnson, 36, Woodvale.

Knowing Adam's home was far closer to Woodvale than Johnstown, and aware the age was about right, a sharp stab of fear pierced her heart, making it suddenly very hard to breathe. According to this listing, Adam *would* die in the flood.

Overcome with panic, JoAnn tossed the paper onto the table in a wadded heap. All thought of not doing anything that might in any way alter the past vanished instantly. She had to go back. She had to warn Adam.

"No, Adam, not you!" she cried while she frantically tried to remember what she had done with her purse. She refused to let Adam die such a violent and senseless death. Not Adam. She could not let the man she loved more than anything end up in some obscure, unmarked grave. She had to go back and find him. That's all there was to it.

While tossing items around frantically, she finally

spotted the purse in a chair near the television. While headed in that direction, she glanced at the clock on the VCR and saw that it was already after twelve-thirty. Aware how little time that left her, she snatched up the purse, jammed her hand inside, and retrieved her keys.

Not needing anything else from the purse, she quickly tossed it aside and headed back for the dining-room table. Gripping the keys with such force her knuckles turned white, she quickly smoothed out the discarded newspaper with her free hand, then ran a finger down an article that described the events before the flood until she finally located the information she wanted: the time the floodwater should hit the borough.

"... the 60-foot wall of water and debris struck Johnstown about 4:10 that afternoon ..."

Taking daylight savings into consideration, remembering the hour difference she had discovered upon her return, JoAnn quickly calculated exactly how much time she would have to try to save Adam and wondered if it would be enough. She had barely over four and a half hours to drive to Woodvale, find the passageway that would let her return to 1889, and travel by foot to the already flooded and disoriented city of Johnstown. She would then still have to find Adam and Park in all the confusion and somehow convince them both there was a legitimate reason to run for their lives.

Without taking the time to see if Park's name was also listed somewhere on those pages, knowing even if it was not, he could still be among those who were never identified, she rushed immediately out of the apartment. She did not take time to change her clothes nor her shoes, nor even lock her door.

While headed along the absurdly crowded highway at breakneck speed, it occurred to JoAnn that over eleven days had passed since her return. By now it was quite possible the passageway had shrunk enough she would no longer be able to fit through it. And at the same time, she realized that even if she did manage to slip through, with that hole continually shrinking while she was gone, she could very easily become stuck on the other side. In the time it would take to find Adam and Park, warn them of the danger, then return to the clearing, the hole might have become too small for her to wriggle back through. There was a very real possibility she could end up trapped in the year 1889. Something she should *well* consider.

But at the moment her concern for Adam was too great. It overrode any regard she might have had for herself. And without taking the time to lock her car or even pull her keys out of the ignition, she hurried to the hole and found it had shrunken to the point she had to squirm through headfirst. It was obvious she would have to return to the opening immediately after she'd found Adam and Park or chance the hole becoming too small to accommodate her.

With the knowledge that Adam was indeed destined to die in the flood, JoAnn knew he had to be somewhere within the path of the water when it struck, which would put him somewhere in the valley. Setting her watch back an hour to help her keep track of the actual time now that she had returned to 1889, she hurriedly tramped her way through the mud and mire that covered the rain-soaked countryside, headed for Johnstown.

366

Although the sky was a threatening gray and the clouds churned in wide, circular motions just above the trees, she was glad that for now it was not raining. She had enough trouble trudging through the narrow bog that had once been a travelable road.

After discovering that the carriage bridge she had hoped to use to get across the Little Conemaugh had already collapsed on one side, and seeing that the water was moving too rapidly to try to swim across, she left the roadway and followed the flooded river westward until she finally found a small footbridge still intact. The river, which was now the color of rich, creamed coffee, had become so swollen from the rash of recent storms, the surface thrashed violently against the bottom of the narrow bridge while she hurried across. She wondered how much longer that bridge would hold against such abuse and decided even with its stout timber and iron framework, the tiny bridge would not have a chance against the huge mountain of water that would wash over it shortly after the dam broke.

With her heart still hammering savagely against her chest and her legs aching from having plowed through all that mud, JoAnn continued toward the lower part of town. At that hour she expected to find Adam in his office at Cambria Iron, which was just the other side of Johnstown. But she had no idea where she might find Park.

An unseasonably cold wind spat haughtily in her face and her mud-caked clothing slapped painfully against her tender skin while she hurried along the crowded streets, unaware yet of the curious stares her strange clothing brought her.

Running as swiftly as the crowded streets and her

wet clothing allowed, she soon neared the area of town where the Little Conemaugh joined with Stony Creek to form the Conemaugh River. There she found that the entire lower part of Johnstown was already under water, just from the natural runoff of the many creeks and streams that fed the rivers above them. The muddy water had already spilled two feet over its riverbanks, making the area look like a small, moving lake.

JoAnn skirted the area and headed for the huge stone bridge that crossed the river at the farthest end of town, knowing it was the only way to get to Cambria Iron from there.

It was nearly three o'clock by the time she had entered the main office building at Cambria Iron and discovered no one there. Everything on the lower floor had been elevated several feet by using stacks of bricks and small wooden crates to boost them, but not a single worker was in sight.

She chewed nervously on her lower lip while she wondered where everyone could have gone and eventually remembered something from her high school history about the entire plant having shut down sometime that morning so its workers could go home and help their families and friends prepare their homes and businesses against the rising floodwater. Only a few men were left behind and most of them were in the open-hearth area, maintaining the furnaces and ineffectively keeping intruders out.

Spotting just such a worker as he came out of one of the larger buildings some distance away but already headed in her direction, she hurried to meet him halfway.

"I'm looking for Adam Johnson," she said as a way of explanation when the two neared each other. "Do you have any idea where he might be?"

"Nope," he said, then glanced down at her clothing with a curious expression. "But I imagine he's gone home like the rest to help get his house ready for water in case the rivers get much higher."

"But he lives five miles up in the mountains. There would be no need for that," she said, wondering just how much this man knew about the people he worked with but then realized thousands of people worked in that plant.

The man pushed back his black-smudged worker's cap to scratch his balding head and shrugged. "Then I don't rightly know where your Mister Johnson might be. All I do around here is work the furnace. I don't keep up with what goes on in the other areas. But I could go ask my friend, Ray, if you want. He knows a lot more about who does what around here than I do. But you should keep in mind that over seven thousand men work for Cambria Iron. It's impossible for all of us to know each other."

Aware time was rapidly running short and already having a pretty good idea where Adam might be, JoAnn shook her head. "No, that won't be necessary. I'll just be on my way." Then in afterthought, she added, "But if you do happen to see him, tell him I'm looking for him. My name is JoAnn Griffin."

"Will do," the man said, still looking at her clothing with a raised brow while he made a mental note of her name.

It was then JoAnn realized what she had on; but as she headed back toward the huge railroad bridge that she knew would eventually become one massive funeral pyre where hundreds would die, she felt such inappropriate attire was the least of her worries. With panic still her driving force, she hurriedly

369

made her way back around the flooded area, headed toward Park's house.

While she rushed past the small clusters of people who stood along both sides of the streets that led down the flooded area, she caught quick snatches of conversations that made her realize that even with the water higher than it had ever been before, the people of Johnstown were still not concerned with the possibility of that dam finally giving way.

"Is the water still rising?" she heard one woman ask of a man who had obviously been down to the flooded area because his trouser legs were soaked to the knees. The woman, dressed in her afternoon finest, stood at the side of the boardwalk only a few yards ahead, talking as casually to the approaching man as if they discussed Sunday dinner.

"Appears to be," the man answered, then gave an enthusiastic chuckle. The chuckle had been just loud enough for JoAnn to hear while she continued toward them, her legs numb from exertion and her heart burdened with fear.

"If it keeps up, my dear, there could be fishing in the city park by late afternoon. Why there's already talk of the dam breaking." He shook his head at what he obviously considered a ludicrous thought, then frowned when he glanced up to see JoAnn headed their way. "I wonder why it is that every time either of those rivers overflows its banks, someone invariably brings up that old wives' tale about the South Fork dam. Don't they realize that thing has now withstood over forty years of just such flooding with only one little mishap worth mentioning?"

"But isn't this the worst it's ever been?" the woman asked, then turned to see what had captured his attention so completely. Her eyes rounded to their limits when she spotted JoAnn now only a few feet away.

"I guess it is," the man relented, still keeping a close watch on JoAnn. "In all my fifty years of living here, I don't recollect ever seeing the water quite as high as it is today." He waited until JoAnn had passed before he added in a quieter voice, but not so quiet JoAnn could not hear him. "Did you see *that?*"

"Some women have no shame," the woman replied in a sharp, scornful voice. "Just look how everyone is staring at her. Women like that should be locked away in an institution somewhere."

Whatever was said beyond that, JoAnn did not hear, nor did she really care. She was in too much of a hurry to reach Park's house. Her only concern was finding him and Adam, and getting them out of the flood's path before the water struck. She glanced at her watch and felt another surge of panic burst through her soul. It was already fifteen minutes after three. She had less than an hour.

Several precious minutes later, just as she headed down Main Street, thunder sounded in the distance and within seconds it started to sprinkle again, causing many of the people who had been standing around talking to rush indoors to avoid getting wet. When she neared Park's house, she noticed that the backyards of the houses across the street were already flooded. That meant at least a half-dozen streets were now under water.

Pushing her rain-soaked hair out of her face, she went straight to Park's front door and rang the brass bell but did not wait for anyone to answer. After discovering the door unlocked, she let herself inside and called out to anyone who might be near enough to hear her.

"Adam? Park? Is anybody home?"

She heard noises from one of the back rooms and headed in that direction even before she heard the shrill female voice she recognized as one of the housekeepers. "I'm in Doctor Johnson's study."

"Where is everyone?" JoAnn asked when she entered the room and found the small woman busily packing a stack of medical journals into a large wooden crate. Her usually immaculate, starched apron was rumpled and streaked while long strands of dark hair had come loose from whatever held it in place beneath the large white mob cap and now hung in precarious spirals down her back. "Are you here alone?"

"For now." The housekeeper glanced from her work and noticed JoAnn's disheveled appearance. Her eyes widened with obvious surprise. "The doctor has taken the carriage over to the part of Washington Street that isn't yet under water to see if he can bring back a strong helper or two so the carpets and some of the heavier furniture can be moved upstairs. With the water rising as quick as it is, already up to the windows in those buildings nearest the point, and with reports that rain is still falling higher in the mountains, he seems to think that river is not through with us yet. He says the water might rise up high enough this time to do some damage even in this area."

"And *no* one else is here?" JoAnn listened for evidence of someone else in the house, hoping against hope that Adam might be working in another area.

"Not at the moment," she replied, never pausing in her work, though she did continue to glance at JoAnn intermittently. "My sister went over to Mar-

372

ket Street to see if she can talk a storekeeper out of a few more empty crates." She then glanced at the many books, magazines, and trinkets that were scattered about the room. "We've decided to store some of these items in the attic for a while. Doctor Johnson doesn't need all this clutter around him all the time. And it just gives us more to dust."

"But what about Adam? Where is he?"

"I don't know where Mister Adam is. He hasn't been here since early this morning," she explained, then when she noticed JoAnn's worried expression, she quickly added, "But you might try asking over to the bank. He is probably there helping get the main floor ready for high water. Since they are two streets over, they will get the high water long before we do."

Considering that was her next choice anyway, JoAnn nodded in agreement, then thanked the busy woman before turning toward the hall.

"And Miss Griffin?" the housekeeper called out in an uncertain voice as if not quite sure whether she should say what was on her mind. When JoAnn glanced back at her with a questioning brow, the woman nodded toward her wet clothing with a cautious expression. "You might want to get out of your nightclothes first. I can lend you a dress if you like."

"I don't have time to change," JoAnn informed her, knowing how long it would take to peel out of her wet clothing and slip into a dress about two sizes too small. "I have to find Adam right away."

Again headed toward the door, she glanced at her watch. It was now past three-thirty. She no longer had enough time to find both Adam and Park. Frowning with frustration, she looked back at the housekeeper though she continued toward the door. "When Doctor Johnson returns, tell him that the

373

dam has already broken and that a huge mountain of water as tall as this house is already on its way down the valley. It should reach Johnstown just after four o'clock."

Then not certain if she was talking to Sheila, the scatterbrain, or Shelly, the pragmatic, she paused long enough to make herself very clear. "You, your sister, and Doctor Johnson have until just a few minutes after four o'clock to get out of this house and to the nearest hill. Make sure Doctor Johnson understands that."

She did not wait for the questions she knew would follow. She now had barely half an hour to find Adam and convince him to leave with her. If he was at the bank, she had just enough time to save him. But if he wasn't there—she refused to think about it.

The rain was coming down in thick silvery sheets by the time JoAnn arrived at the bank and was told by those who had stayed behind that her Adam had already been there, secured his office, and left. They had no idea where he had gone, but did tell her he was in his carriage so she would have something definite to look for.

JoAnn next headed for the Davises to see if he might have gone there to help Constance prepare her house for water and when she saw he was not, she began asking total strangers if they knew where Adam Johnson might be.

Most people thought he should be at the bank, but finally she found a man who claimed to have seen him traveling down Mockingbird Street not an hour earlier, probably headed for the Morrell Institute to help move some of the desks and papers from the lower floors to the upper floors where it was presumed they would be safe from damage. Aware

374

she barely had fifteen minutes left, JoAnn raced through the rain-filled streets, headed in the direction of the Institute, running as hard and as fast as her wet, sagging clothes would allow.

While hurrying along the puddled streets, she wove her way through the cautious few who struggled to get their children, livestock, and their more precious belongings to higher ground. Struggling with carts and wagons piled to the hilt with furniture, small animals, and boxes, about two-dozen families battled their way through the flooded streets toward the rain-drenched hills that surrounded Johnstown while the children and larger animals followed closely behind.

Aware the vehicles were moving too slowly to make it to safety by 4:10, she wondered just how accurate that newspaper article had been. She wondered if *about* 4:10 meant a leeway of only a few minutes, or several.

With the institute now only blocks away, she prayed that the crushing wall of water would not strike the town for several more minutes. Again she glanced at her watch though she continued to run as hard as her numb legs would allow. 4:03. Her heart hammered with renewed fear while she forced legs she could no longer feel to run harder still.

When she rounded the next corner, she saw the front gate of the Morrell Institute and knew she was only minutes away. She prayed that Adam would be there and would not stop to ask any questions after she'd suddenly appeared out of nowhere, dressed like an outcast, begging him to go with her to the nearest hillside.

With lungs burning as if on fire and her long brown hair plastered across her face blinding her while the heavy rain continued to pelt her body with relentless force, she bent forward to put her last bit of energy into that final sprint. Her wet clothing flopped against her body, pulling against her legs. Still, she continued to force one foot in front of the other, knowing in less than five minutes, Adam's fate would be sealed.

Conscious of the equal risk to her own life, she continued toward the front gate of the institute. She was only several dozen yards away from the entrance when the rain slackened to a light drizzle. Seconds later, she heard the unbroken blast of the Cambria Iron whistle, warning the citizens of some untold danger to which no one knew how to react.

The citizens of Johnstown started shouting and darting about in the drizzling rain, calling to each other with panic tearing at their voices. They had no real direction because they had no idea of what the impending danger might be.

But JoAnn knew. Someone had finally paid attention to the messages being sent down the valley from telegraph stations along the way. The dam had broken. The twenty million tons of water and wreckage had established its course.

JoAnn was nearly to the front steps when she heard the loud, steady rumble of the approaching water. It sounded like nothing she had ever heard. The ground beneath her vibrated from the coming assault.

With a combination of fear and disbelief, for she had truly believed there would be time to save Adam, she turned to watch the towering black wall of death while it crashed through the valley like a rolling avalanche, taking whole buildings in its wake.

The incessant sound of people screaming was broken only by the earsplitting crashes of buildings going down and the brays of animals crying their last. Glass shattered as whole houses were ripped from their foundations, making the scene before her more terrifying than any of the accounts she had read in books. The water was more violent and the destruction more devastating than anything she had imagined.

Helpless to save herself, she stood there, gasping for air, her lungs still throbbing with the want of oxygen while she watched the giant avalanche devour house after house, sucking the remains into its craw like a child sucking Jell-O. She heard the frantic screams of the people still desperately scrambling to get out of the water's way, yet finding no safe haven.

The hills were too far and even the tallest trees offered no refuge to those agile enough to climb them — not from a mountain of water forty feet high.

Horrified, JoAnn watched while the wall of death rolled steadily toward her. She did not turn away and run like the others. Nor did she scream. She simply stood there, facing the torrent, frozen with the realization she had lost her race against time.

Having accepted her fate, her last thoughts were of Adam.

Chapter Eighteen

The closer it came to four o'clock the more frantic Sheila's pleas became. "Sister, come with me to Green Hill," she cried, already clutching her cloak and umbrella. "It's nearly four o'clock. We have only a few minutes left."

"I have too much work to do right now to be wasting my time running away from something that is not going to happen," Shelly responded, sounding very annoyed with her addle-brained twin for continuing to insist she do something so foolish. "This is not the time to be running away. The water is now only a few yards away from the house and with the rain we've had this afternoon, it will probably go much higher."

"But we've already cleared most of his things," Sheila argued. "What's left is not really all that important anyway."

Shelly sighed and waved a work-worn hand. "You run on if you're really that frightened, but don't stand there trying to talk me into running with you. I'm staying right here until I have the last of the doctor's things packed and carried upstairs. And when I'm finished with that, I plan to go into that kitchen and reheat what's left of yesterday's stew for Doctor Johnson's supper. As hard as he's worked today, he'll be one hungry man by then. Besides, he said we'll all be headed for Mister Adam's house just as soon as our work is done. You know that."

"Please, Shelly," Sheila begged, curling her worn hands into fists while pressing them over her heart. "That will be too late. Come with me, now. Miss Griffin said that water is to be as tall as this house. You'll drown for sure if you stay here. You don't know any more about swimming than I do."

"I happen to put more store in what Doctor Johnson said," Shelly responded with her usual stern expression. "There is no cause for such alarm. The dam has not broken and the lake is not washing down upon us. If we were in danger, a warning would have been sent and the city bells would have sounded by now."

"But what if it's true? What if the water is already on its way and a warning has been sent but, like you, no one wants to believe it's true?"

"It seems pretty obvious that Miss Griffin has let a few of the local louts fill her head with that usual nonsense about the dam breaking. The only reason she took what she'd heard to heart the way she did is because she is so new to the area. Like Doctor Johnson said, she simply doesn't know any better. She hasn't been here long enough to know how every time it rains, some half-wit tries to convince everyone that the dam has burst. That happens because there are always a few who will believe them and those louts think it is great sport to watch those few people panic from the thought of drowning at the bottom of a lake." She shook her head as if bored by the subject. "Every year it happens. Some oaf runs around shouting: 'The dam is about to go! The dam is about to go! Run for your lives!' And every year there is someone who actually does."

"But Miss Griffin said the dam had *already* burst. She said the water was already on its way. She said it will hit here shortly after four."

"And you know what Doctor Johnson had to say about that," Shelly said, her tone as flat as her expression, then turned her back on her sister to resume putting what few items were still scattered about into the wooden barrels and crates she had brought back earlier. "Even if the dam did break, it would be impossible for her or anyone else to know an exact time. There'd be no way to predict how long it would take that much water to spread out as far as Johnstown. Whoever told her such a tale was shining her from the start. Run away to the hill if you want. Sit out there in the freezing rain until you turn blue and catch your death. But leave me to my work."

"Please," Sheila tried one last time, tears filling her dark eyes, undecided what she might do to convince her sister to go with her.

"No." Shelly spoke with such finality, Sheila knew there would be no changing her mind. "Be gone with you, Sis. I don't have time for this nonsense."

Not willing to take any chances, having heard the frantic tone in JoAnn's voice earlier, Sheila hugged her twin sister one last time, then left to do exactly what she had been told. After running through the rain-soaked streets as quickly as her heavy skirts would allow, she arrived on the side of Green Hill just in time to turn and see the huge black mountain of water and wreckage as it took the Gautier Wire Works with an explosive hiss. She watched with dumbstruck horror while the immense giant rolled forward, on toward Johnstown, kicking up a dark black mist in its wake.

Because of the steady friction caused by the rough terrain along the rugged valley floor, the bottom of the monstrous mass moved at a much slower rate than the top. The slower advancement near the bottom allowed the unfettered water near the top to roll forward at a faster rate, which caused the top layer of water to slide constantly over the front of the advancing wall. The tumbling forward created a violent downward smashing of water and debris that literally crushed everything that stood in its path. Trees were snapped like matchsticks and houses collapsed as if made of paper.

With hands clasped to her throat, Sheila watched the rolling mass as it enveloped the small borough of Conemaugh, then fanned out to cover the widened area of the valley where Johnstown lay. Somewhere below a whistle sounded, then two, then finally a church bell. A warning had been issued but too late to save her dear sister.

Knowing there was nothing that could stop the angry rush of water nor could anyone possibly survive its onslaught, Sheila riveted her gaze to the dark roof of her employer's house—the house where she had last seen her beloved sister. She wondered if Shelly had heard the whistle. And if she did, would she have time to say a prayer before gasping her final breath? Would her final thoughts be of her? Would she wonder if she'd made it safely to the hill? Or perhaps her last thoughts would be of their dear mother, rest her soul. Or would the water catch her by such surprise, she'd never know what hit her?

With tears brimming, Sheila prayed that last

thought be what happened. She hated to think of Shelly being that frightened even for those last few seconds.

The pain that crushed Sheila's heart at the mere thought of what her twin was about to have to go through was so severe, it took the very breath out of her. Still, she did not close her eyes against the horror nor did she lift her gaze to something less frightening — not even when the water washed over the house, obliterating all but the four chimneys from her sight. Nor did she close her eyes when she heard the terrified screams that pierced the cold air around her.

She stood paralyzed by the shrieks and wails that bellowed from both man and beast. Some of which had come from the ravaged valley below, others from those who had sought refuge in the thick forest around her. Still, she did not close her eyes, not even when she realized the loudest of those ear-shattering screams had risen from her own throat.

Adam looked up when he heard the unbroken screech of the Cambria Iron whistle, aware the sound meant there was trouble somewhere. He glanced at young George who had just brought another box of his aunt's personal belongings into the room but had not yet found a place to set it.

"I wonder what's wrong," George said, frowning as he put the box in the middle of the floor and hurried to the window to see if there was smoke or something else that might indicate a problem. He scratched his blond head questioningly when he saw nothing in the air but a slight drizzle.

"I don't know," Adam admitted. He moved the box

to a pile of others so they would not trip over it, then followed George to the window. From the attic window of Doris's sister's small frame house, they could see for several blocks, but the only movement visible was that of the men wading through the shallower areas of the rising water waving their hands and shaking their heads as if discussing the damage the water had done thus far. "But whatever is wrong, we'll have to let someone else handle it. We still have a room of furniture to move and very little time to move it. Look over there to the right. The water is already in the neighbor's yard and with the rain still coming in quick bursts like it has, it will probably reach this house within the next few hours."

"It's a good thing I spotted you when I did," George said as he hurried to comply. "We'd never have that bottom floor cleared in time if you hadn't stopped to help us. Not after Cyrus hurt his arm the way he did tryin' to lift that sofa all by himself." George's eyes rounded with remembrance. "Momma is still angry with him for such foolishness. Says we are guests here and should be tryin' to help Aunt Veronica, not cause her more concern."

"Well, at least he didn't break a bone," Adam said, knowing that Cyrus would not be able to maneuver his hand quite so easily if he'd broken a bone in his arm. With yet another room of items to move into the attic, Adam started stacking what they had brought up thus far into taller heaps. "I'll take him over to Father's house to have it examined right after we've finished here. If we hurry, we should be there before the water has his street blocked."

"But I thought you were headed to that school where you teach to help them a while," George pointed out.

"They'll just have to get along without me," he said, though he had wanted to be sure his papers were moved to the third floor. Knowing there was always the possibility the dam could break, if it hadn't already, he was afraid there might be as much as ten to twenty feet of water during however long it took the lake to pass through. That would not only damage items on the ground floor but could also soak everything on the second floor. He did not want anything of his left on the second floor. He just hoped whoever had gone to help at the institute would show enough good sense to evacuate both floors but had a feeling they would quit after having cleared only that lower floor.

Adam frowned when he heard a second whistle merge with the first and over that, the faint clanking of church bells. But he said nothing of the fear those sounds caused him, aware this was not a typical emergency. "Cyrus's arm has to come first. Just like your hand had to come first when you cut it a couple of months ago. Remember?"

"Then we'd better hurry," George said, then spun about and bounded toward the door with his usual youthful exuberance. He paused after only a few feet then turned toward the window with a bewildered expression.

Then Adam felt it. The whole house shook, as if it were right next to the railroad tracks. Next he heard a deep, rumbling sound. Something like a train coming at them, but not quite.

"What's that noise?" George wanted to know. His face twisted with confusion when he looked to Adam for an explanation.

"I don't know," Adam answered honestly, also turning his attention toward the window where a sudden wind prodded the curtains. The roar outside reached deafening proportions, causing George to throw his hands over his ears. Frowning at such a loud, bizarre noise, Adam headed toward the window to have a better look but made it only a few feet before the entire wall suddenly exploded.

There had been a thunderous roar, then pain, then suddenly JoAnn was under water, struggling, being yanked back and forth in the murky depth until her lungs ached with the need for air. Knowing she could go only so long without oxygen before her brain would shut down forcing her to pass out, she fought to swim to the surface, though she had no way to know which direction that might be.

There was no light to guide her, nor any sensation of her body rising in the water. Instead, it felt like she was inside some huge washing machine, being sloshed back and forth with all the other debris while some unseen agitator worked hard to keep her under.

Though the filthy water was abrasive, she kept her eyes open, even after something sharp struck the side of her head and sent a sharp pain piercing her skull. Odd visions of white light danced crazily in front of her, but she fought to stay conscious, knowing if she didn't death would be immediate.

While she continued to be yanked around by the raging water, she spotted something large and shadowy come within inches of her face. Instinctively, she reached out and grabbed it with both hands, more in an effort to steady herself than to keep it from striking her — or more likely to keep *her* from striking *it*.

Finding renewed strength from clutching something solid, she pressed her eyes and her mouth closed and fought with all her might to keep from taking the breath she so desperately needed while she tried to decide where the surface was.

But the need for a breath became too great, the ache in her lungs too overwhelming. Finally she opened her mouth, knowing she was about to let her lungs fill with the turbid water. But at least it would be over. Odd, she thought, how she had come to save Adam from being buried in a common, unmarked grave and yet that was exactly where she would now end. The chance of her being identified in the year 1889 were practically nonexistent. Most of the people who might recognize her were still back in the twentieth century. Never to know whatever became of her.

At the same moment she decided to let her lungs have their fill, whatever she held on to broke the surface and plunged into the air like a winged projectile, taking her with it.

Stunned when her lungs filled with air instead of water, she opened her eyes just when she and whatever she held on to splashed back into the water; but this time the object managed to stay afloat and for the first time she could make out what it was. It was the wooden bed of a large wagon. One of the sides had been torn away, which caused it to float at an awkward angle, and all four wheels were gone; but the tongue was still attached as was a wooden seat near the front.

Gripping the rim for dear life, JoAnn struggled to pull herself higher onto the wooden structure but the swift undercurrents continued to tug sharply at her legs, making the task impossible. All she could do was hang on to the side and pray the wagon stayed afloat and that it did not carry her into the acres of wreckage she knew would accumulate near the base of the old stone bridge, one of the few bridges to withstand the onslaught.

JoAnn knew the massive tangle of debris and human bodies would become so large and so compact it would function like an artificial dam, causing the water to form another huge lake over the town. She also knew that later, when the huge heap caught fire, it would become a death trap to those who had ended up there still alive.

Instead of becoming a part of that massive funeral pyre, she prayed the wagon she held onto would eventually carry her to the outer edges of the water where she could swim to safety. Or else she hoped it would pass near one of the few buildings she knew had withstood the onslaught.

But such was not to be the case because just seconds later, something hard and jagged slammed into the small of her back, causing her body to jerk with pain. As a result, she lost her hold and was sucked back down into the black water. But this time she managed to thrash her way back to the surface within seconds.

Knowing she needed to find something solid and buoyant to hold on to, something that would help her keep her face above the brackish water, she made a wild grab at a large telegraph pole as it charged past her, but missed the thing by inches, leaving her to flounder again against the varying water currents. Finally, a large piece of a building broke the surface of the water like an emerging submarine only a few dozen yards away and already two other people were headed toward it.

Aware the structure looked large enough to hold the weight of quite a few people, JoAnn also began a frantic swim toward it. Several harrowing minutes later, she reached for the jagged edge and was relieved when her hand finally made contact. Although she no longer had the strength to pull herself up onto the massive platform that looked like the side of a large house, someone else did. She felt large hands grab her by her wrists and lift her out of the water, then plop her over toward the center of the makeshift raft.

Coughing spasmodically from the filthy water she had swallowed, she lay there in a wet heap for several seconds, unable to believe she was still alive. At least for now.

After she stopped choking long enough to suck in several deep breaths, she lifted her head and pushed her thick mat of wet hair away from her face. When she did, she saw a huge black man on his hands and knees beside her, scanning the area ahead of them, his clothing torn completely from his body.

Used to seeing the naked male body, JoAnn did not turn away. Instead, she smiled gratefully and called to him. "Thank you," was all she had the strength to say.

It was all she needed to say.

"You're welcome," he answered in a deep, cultured voice and flashed a brief smile before he bent over to help yet another hapless victim onto their strange craft.

Soon there were four of them clutching that small section of building as it was propelled first in one direction then another. JoAnn knew the reason they kept shooting off in so many different directions was because of the backwash that had been created when the water had eventually struck the side of the mountain that stood just the other side of Stony Creek. The mountain, which was positioned near the bend in the river, had worked like a mighty backboard, forcing the water to splash back into itself.

After that, the water lost part of its forward thrust which was why it had failed to collapse the huge stone bridge just below town. It was in the arches of that massive bridge that the larger pieces of debris would become lodged and gather into an obstruction so large and so compact, when it finally caught fire, it would burn for days. In that time, hundreds would burn to their deaths. JoAnn prayed she and her new raft mates would not be among them. She prayed they would find their way off the massive lake that would eventually settle over Johnstown, knowing they could spend days drifting aimlessly if they did not.

Powerless to maneuver their flat craft against the twisting currents, the four watched helplessly while whole houses or just mangled parts came crashing into their vessel, each time splintering off tiny pieces of wood before sending them in a new direction.

JoAnn wondered how much longer their dwindling link to survival would last before it crumbled entirely as she had seen so many others do. Her arms ached from having fought the current, then having held on to the narrow indentations in the lapped wall for as long as she had. To her it felt like an eternity had passed, but in truth they had fought the violent current only a few minutes. She knew the catapulting could go on for half an hour before the water finally settled enough to be able to maneuver in it.

389

While the raft continued to hurl back and forth among the ruins, she focused on the other occupants of the unusual raft. The large black man who'd saved her had captured a mangled piece of what looked like it had been a curtain rod and was using it to try to snag a piece of clothing from the debris floating around them. A frail-looking woman with matted white hair who looked to be in her sixties lay in a rumpled heap near the center. Her eyes were pressed tightly closed and she had her face turned away from the black man as if desperately trying not to look at his nakedness.

Beside the older woman was a red-haired young man with pieces of leaves and grass stuck to his face. He looked to be about seventeen and lay on his side, curled into a tight fetus position. He held his right arm pressed against his ribs as if to protect an injury. Although he didn't move, he lay watching the black man with a curious expression.

Aware there was little she could do for the boy until the craft had settled more, JoAnn next focused on what was happening beyond their small craft. She felt a sharp pain clamp her gut when she saw the panic and chaos. People were struggling and dying everywhere. And there was absolutely nothing she could do to help them. Not even when a face would suddenly surface in the water beside them, its eyes rounded with the knowledge death was near. Then before any of them could reach to help the person, the face would be gone again. As if it had never existed.

Other people, just as desperate, floundered helplessly in the water or clung to whatever floated, striving to keep their heads above the water, never knowing when the churning mass of littered water would suck their only handhold on life into its dark depth as it had so many others, or send them crashing forward over the front wall to a sure death. Or simply knock them from their perch into the grinding debris to be crushed to death.

The water around them had become a littered mass made up of mangled railroad cars, twisted rails, splintered railroad ties, broken houses and barns, whole trees, parts of trees, household items of all kinds, telegraph poles, telegraph wires, barn implements, children's toys, plant roofs and factory equipment, as well as the miles and miles of barbed wire that had come from the Gautier Wire Works only a mile or so upstream.

Whole bodies and parts of bodies, both animal and human, bobbed around them like corks. Many of them, such as the black man beside her, had been stripped by the swift tides of all their clothing while others had been stripped of their arms and legs. Even to a doctor who had supposedly seen the worst, it was a gruesome sight, one that made her stomach reel.

Fighting the compulsion to empty her retching stomach of all the foul water she had swallowed, she took several deep breaths and again turned her attention to those on the raft with her.

Seeing that the boy was biting his lower lip in an attempt to fight the pain while he continued to watch the black man make failed attempt after failed attempt to snag a piece of clothing, JoAnn decided to try to rise up on her hands and knees but was knocked flat again when suddenly they struck a floating boxcar. She waited until the craft had settled into its new current before lifting her head again.

"What happened to your chest?" she called to the

boy as she tried again to sit, finding it was still a precarious thing to do. They continued to bump into things at an unpredictable rate, causing her to be constantly off balance. Finally she managed to wriggle closer to where the woman and boy lay.

"Don't know," he answered, then grimaced when he rolled over onto his back and started to unbutton his ragged, wet shirt with his mobile arm. "Something hit me when our house collapsed."

JoAnn supposed the boy wanted to unbutton his shirt so she could have a look at his injured ribs. She balanced herself as best she could on her knees, then leaned over the older woman still cowering between them to help him with his buttons. But rather than simply part the shirt so she could examine the injured area, as soon as she had finished with the last button, the boy proceeded to peel out of the shirt one arm at a time, despite the severe pain each movement caused him. He then pushed himself onto one elbow and turned toward the black man. His eyes wavered with pain when he held the shirt out to him.

"Here, mister. You can tie it around your waist," he said between raspy breaths, then offered a smile that quickly turned into another pained grimace when they bumped against a broken piece of roof that had been floating just ahead of them. He fell instantly back against the side of the building but continued to hold the shirt out.

"Thank you," the black man said with a catch in his voice that revealed how truly touched he was by the young man's gesture. Bracing his knees against the tossing movements of their craft, he shook the shirt open and quickly tied the sleeves around his waist so that the bulk of the material hung down to cover him.

Aware there was no reason now for the woman beside them to continue to lie there with her eyes pressed closed, JoAnn nudged her gently, but she refused to open her eyes. At first, JoAnn feared the woman dead and reached to feel for a pulse. When she felt the steady heartbeat she realized the woman was keeping her eyes closed in a futile attempt to withdraw from everything happening around her. And who could blame her?

Rather than continue trying to coax her to open her eyes and chance the woman becoming hysterical, JoAnn decided to leave her be. There was enough madness to contend with at the moment.

"Look, over there!"

JoAnn followed the direction the black man pointed and saw that Alma Hall, one of the largest buildings in Johnstown at that time, was still standing. It was only a few hundred yards away, close enough to see people hanging out the second- and third-floor windows attempting to rescue anyone who came close enough. *And they were headed right for it!*

Thinking salvation was at hand, she sat forward and watched. "They're throwing out ropes. We have to catch one."

As soon as they had drifted closer to the building, JoAnn rose up on her knees and waited for someone to toss them a rope. She was surprised when she scanned the different windows and recognized one of the men. It was Andrew Edwards, Adam's preacher friend who had tried to warn everyone that just such a disaster was possible.

For the first time since the water had struck, JoAnn felt hopeful.

"Here, catch," a man who had leaned out the window beside Andrew called just before the end of a rope was tossed toward them.

"It fell short. Try again," the black man shouted. "I'll get it this time."

While they hauled the rope back in for a second attempt, the injured boy rolled to his knees to help. He, JoAnn, and the black man knelt poised, ready to catch the rope if it should strike near enough this time.

"Here it comes," Andrew called out to them, then leaned back to give the other man more room to make his toss.

This time the rope sailed out high above their heads and it was the boy who made a wild lunge for it.

JoAnn screamed when at that exact moment, they bumped against a huge desk and instead of catching the rope, the boy stumbled sideways into the water while they moved quickly away.

Unable to swim and with nothing around for him to hold on to, he floundered helplessly, crying out in a combination of stark fear and overwhelming pain.

In an instant the black man was in the water, swimming frantically toward the boy.

"Hold on. I'm coming to get you."

JoAnn held her breath while she watched, praying he would make it in time, then released the breath with a shout of relief when the black man finally reached the boy and held him steady in his arms.

Everyone shouted with elation while the two worked their way toward the building, then screamed in terror when they heard a sudden explosion. A nearby tanker car had caught fire and the flames were spreading across an oily patch in the water directly toward the two men.

JoAnn watched in helpless horror when seconds later the flames reached the pair and surrounded the two instantly. Letting out a bloodcurdling curse, the black man pulled the boy under and the surface thrashed for several seconds before it went calm again. JoAnn watched the area surrounding the large patch of flames, praying the two would surface again, safe and ready to be rescued by those in the building.

But the explosion had caused such a ripple in the water, it had sent the raft scooting in the opposite direction and soon she was too far away to know for certain if the two ever surfaced, and too far away to hope that the men at Alma Hall could still save her.

Sadly she turned away from where the flames still licked the water and looked in the direction she and the older woman were headed to see if there might be other such buildings ahead. Her heart sank when she saw that the closest ones still standing were quite a distance away and not at all in the direction they were headed. Yet, as fate would have it, a few seconds later the raft bumped against a small shed that altered their course just enough to send them in the very direction they needed to go.

Laying flat again, JoAnn placed a supportive arm around the trembling woman and waited to see if they would actually end up near one of the buildings ahead or bump into something else and head off again in the wrong direction.

Several endless minutes later, they floated close enough to one of the buildings to see men leaning out of windows, making similar rescue attempts to those at Alma Hall. It was not until someone had tossed her the end of a rope and she had caught it that it dawned on her that the building was what remained of the Morrell Institute.

After having been washed all over Johnstown, she had ended up back in the very same area where she had been when the water hit.

"Wrap the rope around something so we can pull you over without yanking you off," the man from the window shouted. "Do it quick. You are drifting pretty fast."

Glancing down, JoAnn spotted a loose board that protruded slightly and hurried to comply.

Chapter Nineteen

"Are you sure she even wants company?" John Boswell asked when JoAnn did not immediately answer Jean's knock. "Maybe we should wait and come back later."

"It doesn't matter if she *wants* company or not," Jean replied, already reaching into her slacks pocket for her key to JoAnn's apartment. "Jo *needs* the company. She needs someone to help her keep her mind off the death of her parents. You have no idea how very odd her behavior has been lately."

"But what if you're wrong? What if what she really needs is simply to be left alone awhile longer?" John asked, but did nothing to stop Jean from opening the door and entering JoAnn's apartment.

"I'm not wrong," Jean responded in a low whisper, wanting only John to hear. "You should have heard her yesterday. She was so confused it was frightening. She can't seem to separate the past from the present — and by past, I'm not just talking about events that happened last week or even last year. I'm talking about a part of the past she never even knew. That poor girl needs a lot of help and being her best friend I fully intend to see she gets it. Why, that woman doesn't even have enough wits about her right now to remember to lock her door. I really didn't need my key." She shook her head and her frown deepened. "There's no telling what sort of riffraff might take advantage of that."

"No telling," John commented, wondering if they qualified as riffraff.

Quietly, she moved further into the room and motioned for John to follow before she lifted her voice loud enough to be heard at the back of the apartment. "JoAnn. It's Jean and John. We've stopped by to see if you would like to go have supper with us. John's treating us to seafood." When John's eyebrows shot up questioningly, she pressed her fingertip against her lips to silence him, then looked perplexed when there was no response from JoAnn's bedroom. "JoAnn? Where are you?"

John remained near the front door while Jean hurried to the back of the apartment looking for JoAnn. "Looks like she left most of her lights on so I doubt she went far," he commented after she'd returned to the front looking every bit as bewildered as before. "Did you notice if her car is in its usual slot?"

"No, I didn't," Jean admitted. Her gaze darted about the room as if searching for something that might explain where JoAnn had gone. "Maybe she left to get something to eat," she suggested in a hope-filled voice. But when she spotted JoAnn's purse lying on the floor with its contents scattered, including her wallet, which held her money and identification, she knew that wasn't the case. She would have needed the wallet to pay for the food and would have taken her license in case she were stopped for speeding again.

Jean hurried over to pick up first the purse, then the wallet. Her eyes widened with growing bewilderment when she opened the wallet to see if JoAnn's driver's license was inside and found that it was. While still kneeling, she searched the wallet for other clues that might indicate where JoAnn had gone. When she opened the change purse, her frown deepened immediately.

"Look at this," she said and held several strange coins out for John's inspection.

"Antique coins." He knelt beside her. "And in mint condition." He picked one up and turned it over, looking very impressed. "I'm no expert, but I think these coins could be worth several hundred each. She shouldn't just carry them around with the rest of her money like that. She'll damage them."

"Look at the dates."

"I did," John replied with a quick nod, not understanding the significance. He nudged the coins still in her hand with the tip of his finger, turning them all to face up. "Four are 1888 and two are 1889. They are all over one hundred years old with hardly any scratches on them. That's why I think they could be worth quite a lot."

"But don't you see? That's the same time period she keeps trying to convince me she visited while she was at her parents' house." Jean's eyes filled with renewed concern. She stared at the coins for a long moment, then looked at John again. "Why would she go to the trouble to buy coins from that same time period — unless she's trying to collect a lot of items that might eventually link her to that fantasy world she's created."

She shut her hazel eyes as if admitting defeat. When she opened them again, she slowly closed her hand around the coins. "Her condition is far more serious than I thought. She really has gone over the edge."

John looked at her, his thick eyebrows drawn, as if not knowing what to do next. "Where do you suppose she's gone?"

"I don't know," Jean said, then stood and headed for the telephone. "But I sure as hell intend to find out."

By nightfall the water and ruin had settled into a large, filthy lake that covered most of Johnstown and parts of Kernville and Conemaugh. Even though the water itself was now calm, it was still too dangerous for anyone to venture outside the building. The debris-choked water that surrounded them on all sides continued to grind and creak like some massive machine eager to devour anyone who made the mistake of entering its jaws, stranding all one hundred and seventy-five people who had taken refuge inside the Morrell Institute.

Darkness came early for Johnstown that night while churning black clouds still hovered low over the flooded city. But because of the oil and kerosine that coated many of the people as well as the threat of natural gas leaks, no fires were allowed inside the institute that Friday night, not even a candle. The only light they had was the eerie glow that seeped through the broken windows and where a large section of wall had been sheared away during the flood. The dull, amber light came from a huge fire near the stone bridge at the lower end of town.

Occasionally smaller fires flared in other locations across the flooded borough, giving off additional streams of light for brief periods; but mostly the area inside the large building was dark and only those people nearest the windows had enough light to see more than black shapes.

Because of such a shortage of light and the fact that several men still hung out the windows hoping to catch a few more stranded souls, JoAnn had no way to know how many people might have taken refuge on

400

the third floor of the Morrell Institute that night. But judging by the number of moans, groans, and frightened murmurs that drifted in the darkness at any given time, she felt there had to be at least one hundred people in the many rooms around her.

If only one of them had been Adam.

But she had already asked and found out that Adam had not gone by the institute after all. Even if she had been awarded those few extra minutes she had so desperately longed to have just before the flood hit, it wouldn't have made any difference. She still wouldn't have located Adam in time. The outcome would have been no different: because she had been unable to warn him as she had wanted, Adam was dead.

And because of that, JoAnn felt as if she had no reason to go on with living. No reason to draw her next breath.

Yet she did.

Despite the foul odor of mud, sweat, filth, and blood, she continued to take breath after breath. But because she was still in such a state of shock, breathing was about all she could do. That, and stare idly into the darkness wishing the pain and horror of everything she had witnessed that day would go away.

She was wet, filthy, and numb from exhaustion but she could not sleep. Instead, she sat on the soggy floor with her back against a large wooden desk and her legs stretched in front of her while her mind replayed every horrible incident.

If only she had been able to find Adam in time. But she hadn't. She had accomplished nothing in the hours she'd been back that could have changed Adam's fate in any way. Perhaps it was inevitable he drown in the flood. Perhaps nothing she could have done would have saved him.

Still she could not stop herself wondering, from

playing with what might have happened had she found him—not even while she sat there listening to the macabre sounds around her, nor while trying to remember if the Morrell Institute was one of the few buildings that would last the night.

As the enormous weight of the water and the mountains of debris packed against the building continued to shift steadily back and forth, JoAnn knew there was a very real possibility the building could not take the strain and would eventually collapse. Like they had heard so many others do that night. Each time accompanied by piercing screams. *Death screams.* Screams that would be with JoAnn forever. And all she could do was sit there and listen. And wonder if Adam had been among them. Had he survived the cruel flood only to be crushed to death by a falling building?

"Does anyone know what's burning?" a man only a few feet from where JoAnn sat asked. It was the first time in hours someone had spoken in such a strong voice and it had sounded stark against the muted whispers and gentle sobbing of the others.

Although JoAnn had heard the question and knew the answer, she was still too despondent to speak. She waited to see if anyone else knew.

"I have no idea," someone several yards away finally answered. "But whatever it is, it must be plenty big. The whole area near the point is a bright orange."

"Looks to me like a train or something else big like that caught fire on top of the old stone bridge," came a suggestion, this time from the area where part of an outer wall had been torn away. From there the enormous amber glow could be seen clearly. "But it's hard to tell with all this fog rolling in."

"It's not a train," JoAnn finally answered, not realizing she had no reason to know such a thing, that it was information she had brought with her from the

402

future. "It's a huge pile of rubble that gathered against the base of the bridge."

"What rubble?"

"Some of the wreckage floating in the water was so big it could not fit through the arches beneath the bridge and became lodged. And as more water carrying yet more debris tried to pass through, the wreckage began to pile up one thing on top of the other. That's why the water has not gone down much outside. It's being held back by a huge mountain of rubble jammed against the bridge. And when oil from an overturned tank car spilled into a still-burning cookstove, it caught fire and the wreckage has been burning ever since."

"You mean that bridge is still standing?" Whoever asked that clearly found it hard to believe.

"Yes. Because of the sharp bend just this side of the bridge, most of the water smashed straight into the side of the mountain, which broke the force considerably."

"How do you know all this?"

JoAnn's eyes widened when she realized the answer and quickly sought a more believable explanation. "Ah, because the makeshift raft I was on went very close to there and I saw for myself what was happening."

"You were that close to the front? You're lucky to be alive."

Am I? JoAnn wondered, thinking life without Adam held little meaning. Then she realized she might yet be able to make it back to the twentieth century, and she finally had to agree. As long as there was a chance that she might make it back yet, there was still a chance to find happiness again, at least to some degree. "Yes, I am. Very lucky. So are all of you."

A strange silence followed that remark, broken only by the gentle sound of a woman singing a lullaby, obviously to comfort a small child. JoAnn leaned her head against the desk and closed her eyes, wishing the song would lull her to sleep as well. But it didn't. Nothing could bring her sleep that night. There were too many thoughts, too many horrors racing through her mind.

She was haunted with the realization that as long as she remained stuck in that building, waiting for the water to slowly seep its way through the wreckage at the bridge, the passageway back into her own time was steadily shrinking and would soon become too small for her to wiggle back through. If she did not find some way to get back there and soon, her destiny would be forever changed. She would be forced to remain in the year Eighteen eighty-nine for the rest of her life. Which would not seem quite so dreadful if Adam were still alive. But he was not.

She had failed to save his life, in much the same way she had failed to save her own parents' lives — through her own incompetence. That meant if she did end up forced to spend the rest of her life surviving in Adam's world, she would no longer have Adam's love to comfort her.

Morosely, JoAnn stared at the dull amber reflection flickering on the ceiling while her mind carried her back to the precious few weeks she had spent with him. Although the thoughts were now painful, her mind recalled the memories of those special times: those first stolen glances, the first lingering touches, the shared laughter, and most vividly, she recalled their passionate lovemaking. Bittersweet tears burned her eyes and spilled down her bruised cheeks when her mind replayed the night he'd told her he loved her.

Dashing the wetness away with the back of her

battered hand, she next turned her thoughts to that world she might be forced to leave behind forever and focused for the moment on her best friend, Jean. For now, Jean was probably merely irritated with her for having gone off again without telling her where, and for not responding to the messages she had surely left on the answering machines at both her apartment and her parents' house.

But after JoAnn missed work Tuesday and did so without bothering to telephone an excuse, Jean's annoyance would progress steadily into outrage. Then when the outrage finally wore off, Jean would decide something terribly wrong had happened and she would become extremely worried. Eventually, Jean would become worried enough to make the drive to her parents' house to search for her, only to find out from the neighbors she had not been at the house in nearly two weeks. JoAnn speculated how long it would take the neighbors to discover her car in the woods nearby and what conclusions would be drawn from finding it unlocked and the keys still in the ignition.

Sadly, JoAnn wondered how long after her car was found until Jean accepted the fact she was gone forever. Would she ever accept it? Or would she always be looking for her around the next turn? Waiting for the chance to lecture her but good. But the way things looked now, Jean would never get that chance. She would spend the rest of her life wondering what became of her best friend.

JoAnn then wondered if such a complete and unexplainable disappearance would result in her being included in one of those "Unsolved Mysteries" type shows that had become so popular in recent years. She could visualize it now: Jean Gallagher trying her level best to get the entire world involved in the search for Dr. JoAnn Griffin. Jean was the type not to give up until every option had been tried, especially if the quest involved something or someone near and dear to her.

A deep, pulsating ache formed deep inside JoAnn when she realized that she had now managed to lose *everyone* she had ever held dear: first Tom, then her parents, then Adam, and now Jean and all her other friends who worked at the hospital. If she did not make it back to the twentieth century, not only would she be forced to face a life without modern medicine, she would have to face that life *alone*.

During the next few hours, while JoAnn continued to dwell on the true gravity of her situation, another section of outer wall gave way. Most of the bricks and plaster collapsed inward, landing on the dozen or so people who had taken refuge on the floor nearby.

Although the building had become relatively silent during those early morning hours, the pitiful screams of horror and pain were immediately revived as was the fear that the whole building was about to cave in and kill them all.

JoAnn snapped out of her mournful reverie and let the doctor in her take over. Suddenly, the resolve to be little more than an interested observer while visiting in the past meant nothing to her. These people needed her help.

Though her whole body ached from the abuse it had taken earlier, she could no longer sit back and allow these other people to suffer any longer. She had the knowledge and the talent to help them and she now saw no logical reason not to do just that. Moving into the dim light let in through the new gaping hole, she did what she could for the injured.

She started with the people who looked to be in the most pain, then moved next to the ones who had not yet realized the extent of their injuries. Some had become so traumatized by the horror of what had happened, they had yet to feel the true magnitude of their injuries. Still, if she saw the need to do something for any of them, she did it. Soon, it became apparent she was helping herself as much as she was helping them. By keeping busy, she had no time to dwell on her own misery. Having so much to do turned out to be a godsend.

Working quickly, more by touch than by sight, JoAnn tore what curtains were found still hanging from their curtain rods and what clothing the people around her had contributed into narrow bandages, then bound the wounds as best she could. She broke up what few chairs had not been washed out of the building and used the smaller pieces for splints. Fifteen minutes later, someone produced an unopened bottle of whiskey from inside one of the desks and she used the alcohol to cleanse the more serious wounds.

Those around her who could, helped. Those who could not, remained quiet and out of the way, grateful for what little she could do for them.

By five o'clock, when the first dim shapes emerged from the darkness, JoAnn was too busy with her work to take much notice of the subtle changes around her. Eventually the room brightened enough she was able to see the people with her. It was heartbreaking to discover that the woman who had been calming them with soft lullabies had sat all night in a dark corner, desperately rocking a dead child.

When the woman pleaded with JoAnn to do something to help her beloved granddaughter, she looked so lost, so pitiful, JoAnn pretended to bind a wound on the toddler's leg, then assured the woman that was all she could do for now. The woman tearfully thanked her for her help, then resumed rocking the dead child, singing softly against her cheek.

By seven o'clock, the ribbons of mist from the previous night's fog had cleared enough to reveal that the water had gone down considerably at their end of town. Several of the men decided to venture out onto the piles of body-littered debris and, after finding much of it solid enough to hold their weight, others soon followed, many without shoes and most wearing clothes that were tattered and torn. All looked bruised and battered—and badly bewildered.

At first many of the survivors who walked around outside did little more than stare, too deeply in shock to respond to the mountains of death and destruction that surrounded them. Desperately, they tried to understand what could have happened to change their world so dramatically.

Others seemed oddly fascinated by the quiet. The valley was suspended in an unearthly stillness. All the usual harsh noises that had become such a normal part of their lives—the screeching mill whistles, the clanging of machinery, the clattering of wagons and carriages as they bounced along the cobblestone streets, the rumble of the cumbersome coal trains that barreled past day and night—all had stopped. Absolutely every one of them.

Except for the hourly chime of the Lutheran church and an occasional creak or groan from the piles of debris whenever the weight shifted, there were no outside sounds at all. After daylight had revealed to them the true extent of what had happened, no one spoke. Not even a bird found reason to chirp in the macabre scene of death and devastation that surrounded them.

With so many people leaving the institute, JoAnn saw little reason to stay on. She made certain someone planned to stay with those too injured to leave until help could arrive, then by noon she, too, had left.

Still feeling defeated and emotionally ravaged from

having failed to save Adam from such a violent death, she started off for the improvised morgues she remembered had been established at various locations. While carefully picking her way around the fetorous heaps of wreckage and the filthy pools of stagnant water, she tried not to focus on the pain she felt, though the entire side of her head throbbed and almost every major muscle in her body ached from the previous day's dilemma. Nor did she allow herself to concentrate on the hundreds of dead lying either wholly or partially buried in the rubble around her.

With most of those milling about now dressed in rags and others in just their underwear or in clothing that had been found floating in the water after having had their own torn off, JoAnn no longer felt quite so conspicuous being dressed in a pair of muddied warmups and did not give her clothing a second thought while she maneuvered across the wreckage. Nor did the people around her. Such matters were no longer important.

At that moment, all that mattered to JoAnn was finding Adam's body. She remembered from pictures she had seen and stories she had read during her youth that the main emergency morgue was to be established at the Adams Street School. Other morgues were to be established in a saloon in Morrellville and in a few of the churches that had withstood the onslaught, but knowing the one on Adams Street was to be the central location, she decided to go there first. Somehow, it seemed appropriate Adam would end up at a school that bore his same name.

But locating the building without the usual landmarks to guide her proved impossible. Some areas were heaped so high with banks of wreckage that even the steep mountains surrounding Johnstown could not be seen beyond them. Yet other patches had been left so void, they looked as if they had been hosed down to raw earth.

Human and animal bodies, and the body parts of both were strewn everywhere as were the broken bits and pieces of what had just the day before been a thriving industrial valley.

Splintered furniture, twisted rails, broken tools, and shattered toys had mixed together with books, dishes, carpets, curtains, pickle barrels, sections of steps, chamber pots, bicycle wheels, trunks, candlesticks, telephone poles, telegraph wire, chunks of machinery, shredded trees, leather harnesses, ragged bushes, nail kegs, torn linen, utensils, clothing, and all manner of building materials. The wreckage had been thrown up into odd-shaped heaps ten, twenty, and even thirty feet high, some acres wide — or it lay gently shifting back and forth in the huge pools of murky water that still covered the valley floor.

By noon, many of those who had survived the cold, wet night had ambled down from the mountainsides and out of what few buildings remained, joining others in their dazed search for loved ones, still trying to grasp a reason for what had happened. Although occasionally eyes met and bodies touched, hardly anyone spoke — other than to ask if the other person had seen a particular loved one. The city was still too deep in shock for conversation.

But by early afternoon, the mood of the city gradually changed. Rescue efforts had begun in earnest with almost every able-bodied person helping dig survivors out of crushed houses and pull the marooned off the rooftops or down from the few mangled trees that had endured the water.

Small groups of men and women had banded together to search the larger piles of rubble for signs of life, of which there were few, while others struck out on their own in search of their missing families and loved ones.

For as far as the eye could see there was destruction but no way to know how the rest of the valley had fared from the mishap. Every telegraph and telephone line to the outside world was down. Bridges were gone without a trace; the roads impassable. The railroads, which had run along the valley floor next to the river, were all but destroyed.

Buildings still crumbled and fell with horrific suddenness, crushing anyone who had sought shelter from the unseasonable cold. Large piles of debris suddenly shifted and collapsed or caught fire for no apparent reason, making the rescue efforts all the more treacherous. It was slow, tedious work, but those who searched for their friends and family remained undaunted by the danger and dead that lay everywhere.

Now that JoAnn moved through the center of the retched bayou of destruction, she found the putrid stench of mud and death much stronger than she had imagined, and growing worse by the hour. There was no food left worth eating and no clean water with which to wash or drink. Soon disease and hunger would become a major concern.

Because there was no real order to what went on, no organization, and not much sense to what was being done, JoAnn had a hard time finding her way through the torn city. Whenever she stopped to ask someone for directions, the most she received was a sad, hollow-eyed shrug. With so few landmarks remaining and so much activity going on around them, it was impossible even to guess where anything had once stood.

But she was determined to find Adam's body. She refused to let him spend eternity in some unidentified grave. She may have failed to save his life, but she fully intended to see that he had a proper, Christian burial and a headstone with his name.

A problem arose though when she finally located the Adams Street School and she discovered it had not yet been put to use as an emergency morgue. A few injured people had taken refuge there, but the town had not yet held the assembly in which the leaders attempted to organize the rescue efforts while setting up a more systematic method of accounting for the dead.

With little choice but to await such a meeting, JoAnn decided to grapple her way back over the battered ruins to see if Park's house had withstood the flood, thinking the others might do the same. Since there was nothing she could do about rescuing Adam's body just yet anyway, she decided to find out if Park and his two housekeepers had made it to the mountainside safely. She thought it would be wise to be with Park when he first found out about his son's death.

Her heart wrenched at the thought of Adam actually being dead, but she refused to give in to the deep feelings of grief just yet. She had too much to do. There would be plenty of time for tears later. For now she barely had time to think.

Since Adam had not been at the institute as she had thought, JoAnn realized he might have been on his way to his father's when the water struck. Even though the possibility of finding him was slight, she walked slowly after she neared what looked like it might have been the Main Street area.

Carefully, she scanned the filthy pillars of ruin for evidence of his body while she continued toward the area where Park's house had stood. She gave each male body careful scrutiny, hoping to locate Adam's herself. She knew by doing so, he would be assured a proper burial because she would stay with him until his body was placed in the ground and a proper marker set — even though such a delay meant an increased risk of being trapped in the past forever. But there was nothing she could do about that and she was determined to see her quest through.

Despite her years of doctor's training and all the blood and gore JoAnn had seen while working in trauma services at McCain Hospital, her stomach clenched into a rigid knot whenever she spotted a particularly mangled piece of human body. It forced her to have to stop and take long, deep breaths to steady the queasy feeling that sometimes followed.

But stopping to take breaths only made matters worse when the putrid-smelling smoke from the still-smoldering bridge mixed with the smell of wet decay and filled her senses. But she refused to let the temporary bouts of nausea and light-headedness overcome her — even when she came across the twisted body of a frail four-year-old dressed in dirty pink ruffles and lace as if she had been headed for a party.

Although JoAnn had yet to find Adam's body, she felt inordinately pleased when she rounded a particularly large pile of rubble and discovered Park's house still standing in the distance, though severely damaged. Plodding through the thick layer of mud that had settled around the house, she trudged her way to the front door. She overcame a ridiculous desire to knock, then pushed against the front door, which had stood half open, and stepped inside the muck-filled house.

She felt disheartened to see so little furniture left inside. Even on the second floor, where most of Park's belongings had been taken to avoid the rising water, there were very few pieces of furniture left. Most had been swept away by the same angry tide that had broken out a large hole in the wall and every window but one on the first two floors yet had left the windows on the third floor amazingly intact.

While stepping cautiously through the mud and water that lay six inches deep on the second floor, for fear huge pieces of broken glass could be hidden inside, she repeatedly called out Park's name. When that brought no answer, she called out for Shelly then Sheila. Still no answer.

Aware they had not yet made their way back from the hillside, she looked around for something with which to leave a message. Spotting Park's desk embedded in a large stack of broken furniture pressed against the far corner, she hurried to see if there might still be a pencil inside. It was while she rummaged through the top drawer, finding both a broken pencil and water-stained paper, that she first glimpsed a human leg protruding from beneath the desk. A closer look revealed it belonged to one of the housekeepers.

A strong wave of repulsion washed over JoAnn while she slipped the paper and pencil into her only pocket so she could pull the twisted body from the mire. She wondered why the foolish woman had not heeded her warning and gone to higher ground as she looked around for sight of the other housekeeper, but found nothing else that in any way resembled a human body.

After dragging the mud-caked body down the now-rickety front stairs, then outside onto the veranda where it could be more easily discovered, JoAnn pulled back the woman's sleeves to see which of the twins she had found. When she saw no burn scar on either arm, she slipped the rumpled paper out of her pocket and tore it in half. Using the broken pencil, she wrote the name Shelly Drum in bold letters on the paper, then slipped it into the woman's pocket.

On the other part of the paper, JoAnn wrote a brief

414

note informing Park and Sheila that she had been by looking for them and would eventually return. She placed the note on a mantel where it would be easily seen, then left the house, anxious to continue her search for Adam's body.

While wandering about what had at one time been one of the most prominent neighborhoods in Johnstown, she noticed a large black dog laying high on a bulky heap of shattered wood and twisted metal. Even with his black coat matted with mud and littered with shredded leaves, she recognized the animal.

"Shadow!" she called out, feeling inordinately pleased to see him. Stumbling over the wreckage that lay between them, she worked her way closer, then held out her arms to the animal. When he did not immediately respond, she noticed he held his right paw tucked under him as if it had been injured.

"Shadow. Come down. It's me. Come here, boy."

Shadow whimpered pitifully when he recognized her, but despite her desperate pleas, he refused to come down off the jumbled heap and was perched just high enough she could not reach him to pull him down.

"Please, Shadow. Come down. I can see you are hurt, but you have to come down." Bracing herself against a broken telegraph pole that stuck out of the ground at an awkward angle, she ignored the slick feeling of slime against her bruised palm and took yet another step toward him.

"Shadow. Come on, boy."

Thinking he must be in too much pain to come down on his own, she decided to climb higher so she could help him down. When she stretched her hand to pull herself up, she noticed an arm protruding from the rubble with fingers outstretched, as if seeking her help. Fighting the sudden, cold feeling of revulsion then panic, knowing Shadow rarely left his master's side, she quickly yanked away several broken boards and a large piece of what looked to have been the leather top of a carriage until finally she had the shoulder and face uncovered.

"Oh, dear God, *no!*" Her worst fear was true. The outstretched hand belonged to Park.

She stared at him in stunned horror. From what she could tell, he was wearing only a coat sleeve, a pair of trousers, and one boot. His other boot, the rest of his coat, and the shirt he'd worn beneath had all been torn away. Yet oddly enough, except for a dozen or so tiny cuts and bloodless scratches across his chest and upper arms, his body looked relatively undamaged. None of the cuts appeared to have been serious in nature, which meant he must have died early on from another heart attack.

Apparently, the flood had caught Park and Shadow while they were in the carriage. The vehicle must have somehow withstood the initial onslaught and carried them for a while before finally ending up caught in the rubble, which would explain how Shadow had survived. It also explained why the housekeeper had not taken her advice to leave the house. Park had never returned home to receive the message and the housekeeper had stayed on in hopes she would yet be able to warn him.

Unnerved by the discovery, and with the body still partially buried, JoAnn shouted and waved her arms frantically, hoping to attract the help of two nearby men. Without stopping to discuss what should be done, the three hurried to pull more of the wreckage away.

Although Park's skin was already a deathly blue and his body immobile, JoAnn took a deep, hopeful breath and checked his pulse the moment they had him free. There was none.

Sharp pains shot through her like burning arrows and her legs felt instantly weak. For the first time since having left the institute late that same morning, her emotional barriers were broken and she fell to her knees in loud rasping sobs. Not only had she lost Adam to this horrible flood, she had lost Park, too. How much could one heart take and still go on beating?

JoAnn covered her face with her hands to hide her agony when she realized she had earlier saved Park's life only so he could end up dying a far more violent death. She had not done him a favor after all. If anything, she had done him an injustice. Instead of having the sort of funeral a man of his caliber deserved, he would now be buried in mass, along with over two thousand others.

Morosely, JoAnn watched while the two men who had come to her aid carried Park's body to a less cluttered area where it would be more easily found. Shadow followed a few feet behind, limping slightly from the injury to his front paw.

"Won't have no problem identifyin' this one," the larger man said with a sad shake of his head. "Everybody in town knowed old Doc Johnson. He delivered all four of my children and saved my youngest from dying of scarlet fever just last year. Sure am going to miss him."

Not wanting to think about Park's death any longer, JoAnn hurried to her feet. She allowed herself only a moment to get over a sudden wave of light-headedness before she tried to coax Shadow into leaving Park's side, afraid the injured animal would only get in the way of further rescue efforts. But Shadow flatly refused to follow her. Instead, he settled down beside

417

Park's body with his injured paw still tucked up under him.

"Please, Shadow," she pleaded, now in tears. The dog's devotion was heartbreaking. "Come with me. I'll find someone to take care of you." She thought perhaps Sheila might still be alive, and if that were true, the remaining housekeeper might be willing to take Shadow in. "Come on, boy. Let's go back to the house. You can wait there.

Shadow lifted his head and looked at her with sad brown eyes but did not budge. Finally, he turned away and rested his chin on Park's leg, clearly intent on staying.

"Well, I can't stay here with you," she said, as if expecting the animal to understand. "I still have to find Adam."

Wiping away the tears, she checked the clock in the tower of the Lutheran church, which to everyone's amazement still worked, and saw that it was nearly four o'clock. Aware several hours had passed, she decided to try the Adams Street School again. Surely by now the town had gotten itself organized. The dead had to have somewhere to go, as did the living.

But she needed to hurry. Time was running out.

Chapter Twenty

It was dark again by the time JoAnn had the Adams Street School in sight, but there was enough light from the lanterns scattered across the front to see that the building had finally been put to use.

Despite the continued threat of gas leaks, it had been decided to use artificial light where it was most needed. Time had become too important because even though the temperatures were still unseasonably cool for June, there was no way to know how long that could last. Already some of the bodies smelled of decay.

Their only recourse was to work right through the nights. Bodies were already being brought to the emergency morgue in rapid succession. They were being carried in on planks, doors, torn sections of roof, and anything else that could be used as a stretcher. With no wagons or horses yet on hand, not having been brought down from the neighboring farms yet, there were no conveyances to help them transport the dead. Each new body found had to be carried over the mountains of muddied rubble to the nearest temporary morgue by individual workers.

But because Adams Street School had been declared

the principal morgue and was located more centrally than the others, JoAnn knew more bodies would end up being brought there than all the others combined. She also knew that eventually a master list of the dead would be established here and would be updated regularly with information from the other morgues.

Spotting two haggard-looking men seated at a small uprighted table near the front door of the pale-brick building, JoAnn headed there first.

"Sirs, could you help me?" she asked when she had come close enough to see that they were both busily writing something on large scraps of paper that had been scavenged from the debris.

As if already knowing what her request would be, the larger of the two men gestured to the pages before him. "First look through these here to find out if the person you want has already been identified. If not, then go on inside and look over any of the bodies that are tagged with numbers but ain't been identified yet to see if whoever you're looking for is already here. If the person you want isn't in there, come back in a few hours and look again."

He then turned his attention to a tall, brawny man who had come up behind him. "Got me another one?"

"Yep. Number nine. One of the first ones brought in. Turns out she was Carla Beth Morris. Lived over on Walnut Street. Her age was twenty-seven. She was just identified by her older sister, Patricia."

The clerk turned to the appropriate page and with a dull look, glanced at a watch that lay on the table, then began writing.

Aware she had been left to look over the small makeshift ledgers on her own, she picked up several of the pages and saw that they held the names of those who had been identified as well as the descriptions of those who were as of yet still *unknown*. And that every

420

body, whether known or not was being tagged with a number. It was the only way they had of bringing any order to such chaos.

Running her hand down the center column, JoAnn read the names that had been filled in each time a body was positively identified. On the second page, her finger stopped. Her heart slammed against the walls of her chest with such force when she noticed Adam's name, it left her temporarily numb, unable to conceive any rational thought other than the fact she had just found Adam. Even though she had known to expect it, a tiny part of her had held on to the hope that something had happened to save him.

"You find who you were looking for?" the man asked when JoAnn did not immediately move away from the table.

"Yes. I did," she said, her voice strangely calm while she continued to stare at the neatly penned entry with dumbstruck horror.

According to what was written, Adam had been brought in sometime that afternoon and logged as another "unknown." About an hour ago, he had been positively identified by someone named Wilson Kilburn.

The entry also offered a brief description of his clothing and general appearance, and stated that his body had been tagged with the number 116. Although his body had been identified, it had not yet been claimed by family, nor had it been carried to one of the cemeteries.

"He's number one hundred and sixteen," she told the man in what remained an amazingly strong voice.

He took the page from her and ran his finger down the list until he found it. "Body still unclaimed." He looked at her. "You some sort of family?"

"No. Just a very close friend."

421

"You want to see the body?"

Though her gut clenched at the thought of seeing what the flood had done to him, she knew she had to. "Yes. And if his body is not claimed by a member of the family by morning, I plan to claim it for burial." Suddenly it was clear to her. She would find some means of transportation and see that he was buried on his own land, beside his late wife and son, with a marker that clearly stated who lay below. And if possible, she would relocate Park's body and claim it, too, and see that father and son were reunited. It was the least she could do for the two people she had held so dear.

The man keeping up with the lists obviously did not care who claimed the body because he nodded agreeably while he touched a small piece of a candle to the small lamp on his table until the wick had caught fire, then handed it to her.

"I'll make a note of your name when you come by on your way out. For now, go on through those doors behind me and into the big room on the right. The bodies that have already been identified but not yet claimed nor taken off to be buried are in there. I figure you should find about nine or ten rows of them by now."

With trembling hands, JoAnn accepted the candle and turned to enter the dimly lit building. When she first stepped inside, she noticed a lot of movement to her left. She glanced to see what it might be and noticed bodies that had already been tagged with small pieces of paper were being piled in a heap like sacks of grain while others were being taken off the pile and carried to a different spot. The thought of Adam having been handled in such a manner made her blood run cold.

Turning away, JoAnn clenched her jaw and entered

422

the room to the right. She was further appalled to find yet more bodies lined across the floor, side by side, warehouse style; but in no particular order. Because there was only one lantern burning inside that particular room and it hung in the far corner, she raised her candle high to provide more light while she slowly passed down the aisles, no longer certain she had the courage needed to see this through.

The sight of so many dead bodies having been laid out for display like so much damaged merchandise was worse than she had imagined. Although it was obvious that the bodies had been washed and straightened as best they could, they still looked dirty and disheveled — even though someone had taken the time to comb the hair of the women and children, and those without clothing had been carefully draped with pieces of tattered cloth or paper, as had those with missing or mangled body parts.

Fighting back the bile boiling in her throat, JoAnn proceeded down the aisles of dead until, on the fourth row, she finally spotted a body with the number 116 pinned to a pant leg. Horrified that she had found him, her hands folded over her mouth. All the strength left her body as she sank to her knees beside him.

She was close enough to touch him, but did not have the fortitude. Never had she felt such body-wrenching pain. It drove right through to the very core of her, crushing and twisting as it bore first through her heart then down into her very soul.

Her whole body ached with such intensity, it was hard for her to speak aloud, but somehow she found the stamina to call out to a man who had just set another body down, that of a small child.

"I want this body," she said to him, her voice quaking with grief. "I don't have transportation for it yet, but I plan to take it out of here before morning." She was still determined that Adam have a Christian burial even if she had to dig the hole and speak the words herself. "I don't want anyone touching it until then."

The man, who had knelt to smooth out the clothing of the little boy he had placed nearby stood and looked at her as if wondering what she thought he could do about it. "I'll tell Mister Cowan."

"Thank you," she said, not knowing who Mr. Cowan was but aware he must be someone with authority.

Because the body had been draped with what looked to be a muddied parlor curtain, hiding the upper portion of Adam's body from her view, JoAnn leaned forward and with trembling hands, reached for the edge of the veil. She knew a veil meant there had been extensive damage to that area of his body and until she looked beneath it, she would not know how badly Adam had suffered.

Although she was not completely certain her heart could stand what she was about to see, she had to look just the same.

With all the courage she had left, she tossed the drape back and peered down at his contorted face. All the air rushed from her lungs when the realization of what she saw struck her.

The body was *not* Adam's.

Weak and almost giddy with relief, she fell forward onto her hands and knees and stared at the man who bore Adam's tag. Although she saw several similarities, this man was definitely not Adam.

"It's not him." Stunned, she looked at the man whom she had called to just moments before. "This is not Adam!"

The man stepped forward and looked at the body, then frowned. "I'm afraid you are wrong," he said with a consoling shake of his head. "I happen to know Adam. He was president at the bank where my wife and I kept our money."

"*President?* No, that's wrong. Adam was *vice* president." Then JoAnn remembered Adam having told her about a second cousin with the same name. Her heart soared to new heights when she realized that the Adam Johnson she had spotted in the newspaper was not necessarily *her* Adam Johnson. It could have been this man. And if that was true, her Adam Johnson could still be alive. He might not have even been in town when the water hit. He might have decided to go on home and could be safe and sound in his own house at this very moment. Or he might be at Park's house waiting for someone to show.

With every reason to believe her Adam still alive, JoAnn left the morgue in much higher spirits. After stopping by Park's house to find it dark and still empty, she continued her search for Adam for several more hours.

Still, every couple of hours she returned to the morgue to check their lists just in case. Although she no longer expected to find him there, it was the only thing she knew to do until finally she learned of a special registry bureau that had been established at the corner of Main and Adams. Unlike the morgue, the registry's sole purpose was to keep a running tally of the living. But to her dismay, Adam's name was not on that list either.

By four o'clock that following morning, JoAnn was too exhausted to continue walking around and decided to check back at Park's house one last time, still believing that Adam would eventually go there.

When she entered the house, there was just enough light from a large fire someone had built down the street to make her way across the room without stumbling over the clutter.

She headed immediately for the mantel, hoping to find that her note was gone, or better yet that a second notation had been scribbled beneath it in Adam's handwriting. But the piece of paper was exactly where she had left it, and when she carried it to the window so she could see what was written on it, she found the message unchanged.

Knowing she had to have rest if she was to continue her search at the first sign of daylight, JoAnn pulled a curtain off the wall, then spread it across the muddied floor to make her bed. Still warmed with the hope that Adam was alive, she folded the curtain over her and immediately fell asleep.

Because of her near exhausted state, JoAnn slept far longer than she had intended. The sun was well into the morning sky when suddenly she was awakened by a loud, piercing scream.

"Oh, no! She's dead!" came the horrified words that followed.

Recognizing Sheila's voice, JoAnn sat bolt upright and looked around in momentary confusion. "Who's dead?" She remembered that Shelly's body had already been removed and she had not noticed anyone else inside the house the night before. But it had been very dark.

Upon seeing JoAnn rise from what she had thought was the dead, Sheila clutched her throat with both hands and screamed again. After her lungs eventually ran out of air, her eyes rolled to the top of her head and she crumpled to the floor.

"Sheila, wake up," JoAnn cried as she scrambled to the woman's side and hurried to revive her, aware now what must have frightened her. "It's me. I'm okay."

It was several seconds before Sheila responded to her voice and when she did, it was with noticeable fear. "You aren't dead?"

"Not that I can tell," she answered and grinned into the rounded eyes of the still prone woman.

Sheila blinked several times, as if testing her vision for credibility. "But when I saw you lying there on the floor covered with mud like that, I thought — I thought —"

"I know what you must have thought, but as you can see, you were wrong. I am still very much alive. Just in dire need of a bath."

Sheila pushed herself up on one elbow. "And what about my sister? And Doctor Johnson? Are they still alive, too?"

Aware there was nothing to be gained by lying to her, JoAnn waited until she was sitting then told her the truth. "No, neither of them survived."

Sheila closed her eyes and bent her head, looking vulnerable and defeated. "I tried. I tried to make them listen. I tried to convince them what you told me about that dam breaking. But they wouldn't believe me."

JoAnn looked at her, confused. "But I thought that was your sister I talked to. That was you?"

She nodded while an indescribable sound of anguish gurgled inside her throat. It was a few seconds before she could speak again. "Yes. That was me. And I did what you said. I told them they needed to leave. I told them to get themselves up to the hill because that dam had already broken and the water was on the way. But they wouldn't believe me. After all these years, they both refused to believe it had actually happened."

"But why? That doesn't make sense." Park knew the dam was in ill repair. He of all people should have realized the possibility.

Sheila looked at her tearfully. "Because practically

every spring since that dam was rebuilt in 1879 that very same warning has been made. Over and over. It's like that boy who cried wolf. It was said so many times, no one believed it anymore. And when on top of proclaiming the dam had already broke, you claimed to know the exact time that water would hit, Doctor Johnson thought it especially ludicrous. He said there was no way for anyone to know how long it would take the water to travel from there to here. He said that even if the dam did break it would take hours for the water to find its way this far."

JoAnn stared at her, angered and saddened to realize Park had been warned but, like the others, had not heeded that warning.

"He thought you was being gullible," Sheila continued with a loud sniff. "He decided it was because you were so new to the area that you had overreacted to all those tired old rumors. Still he had every intention of getting us all on up to the hill just as soon as he had everything of importance moved up onto the second and third floors, because he agreed that dam could give way before it was all said and done. But because you seemed so sure of an exact time, he decided you had been fed a lot of the same old rubbish by some of the old-timers who liked to see just how excited newcomers could get at hearing the dam had burst. That's why he figured there was still plenty of time."

"But you obviously believed me," JoAnn said, noticing Sheila's clothing was muddy in places but otherwise undamaged.

"There was just something about your voice," she said, shaking her head while she remembered back. "I could tell you meant what you said. I tried to convince my sister of that, tried to get her to go with me, but she refused. Said there was too much work to do. But I decided not to take any chances. I'm afraid of the water. I took off for Green Hill just a few minutes before — before —" She either did not know how to describe what happened or could not bring herself to say it aloud because she left the sentence hanging.

"So you spent the night up on Green Hill?"

"With thousands of others. We watched from beneath the dripping trees while the fires burned eerily through the night. Nature's funeral pyres, one man called them."

"But what took you so long to finally come back here?"

"At first we couldn't come back. There was too much water. But even after the water went down some, I was too afraid to come back. I knew what I would find out if I did. You see, my sister and I couldn't swim. Never learned how, though Shelly always said one day she wanted to," Sheila said then fell silent, lost to her thoughts. JoAnn did not disturb her again until it was time for her to leave.

"Sheila, I am going out for a little while. I still have to find Adam. But I want you to stay here in case he comes by looking for his father. If he does, I want you to tell him I've returned and that I'm out there looking for him. Will you do that for me?" she asked, remembering Sheila was scatterbrained enough without all this other to occupy her thoughts. "Do you understand what I'm asking?"

Although Sheila did not respond verbally, she turned her doleful gaze to JoAnn and nodded that she understood. When JoAnn left a few minutes later, Sheila sat in a small, straight-back chair they had unearthed from the rubble, staring absently at the front door, as if waiting for her life somehow to return to normal.

Since the registry for those still alive was just down the street from Park's house, JoAnn went there first.

She hoped to learn that in the past few hours Adam had been by and put his name down. Although she would still face the impossible task of finding him in all the confusion surrounding them, she could do so knowing he was alive.

Since Adam would not be watching for her name anyway, yet unaware of her return; and still hoping to get back to the time passage before it became too small, JoAnn declined having her name listed among those living. She did, however, take the time to go over the many names written under the letter J to see if Adam had registered yet. He had not.

Then just when she set the pages down and prepared to leave, she happened to glance at a page with the H listings and noticed the names of Cyrus and Doris Hess. She stared at the names, puzzled. Why were they in town that day? And why wasn't George's name listed, too?

Baffled by what she had learned, JoAnn was lost to her thoughts when she started toward the front of the building but not so lost she did not notice the one familiar face in the crowded room.

"Doctor Lowman," she called to a man who had just written his name on one of the L pages and had turned to leave. When he glanced around to see who had called his name, she waved her hands to be sure she caught his attention.

"Doctor Griffin," he responded. His eyes widened with something akin to relief when he headed toward her. "I thought Park told me you'd gone back to Pittsburgh."

When he came closer, JoAnn was struck by how extremely exhausted and tormented he looked. His clothing was torn and there were slanted, dark patches under his eyes, making the fact that he had not shaven all the more noticeable.

"I had, but I decided to come back," she said and left it at that. "I'm here looking for Adam. Have you seen him?"

"No. Not since Memorial Day when I ran into him and that youngest boy who works for him at a lemonade stand in the park. He was buying them each a cold drink to go with their peanuts."

JoAnn's body stiffened. So George had been in town the day of the flood. Then why wasn't his name on the list with the rest of his family?

"Haven't seen Park either," Dr. Lowman went on, unaware of her concern for the boy. "But then I've been pretty busy since the flood."

"I can imagine," she responded, knowing how hard-pressed the doctors must feel to help the injured. He looked as if he hadn't slept a wink since before the disaster struck. At least she had managed to get a few hours rest.

"As you probably know, the hospital was completely destroyed by the flood, but a temporary hospital has been set up over on Bedford Street." He grabbed her by the arms and looked beseechingly into her eyes. "So far we have located only four of our doctors. Doctor Matthews. Doctor Rutledge. Doctor Pyle. And me. We need more help. We need *your* help. Please, Doctor Griffin. Come with me and help. You can't imagine how many people are being brought in. There is no way for the four of us to keep up."

Remembering how many injured there had been just inside the institute alone, JoAnn shook her head to indicate he was wrong. She could well imagine the vast number of injured they faced. "But I was hoping to find Adam. I have to know for sure that he's still alive."

"But we need you. Desperately," he said, not about to give up. "Besides, once he finds out about the

431

temporary hospital, that will probably be one of the first places he'll go. He'd want to find out if his father was still alive. Park, too. Just as soon as Park finds out about the work we are doing, he'll come there demanding to help."

Aware Dr. Lowman had enough problems, JoAnn decided not to tell him about Park yet. "But what if he doesn't hear about the hospital?"

"He will. The word has been getting around too quickly for him not to. Please, come help us. Just for a few hours."

Despite the inner naggings not to allow herself to become further involved in matters that were not even of her time period, JoAnn could not refuse this man's earnest pleading. She had an ingrained need to help. It was that same need that had made her want to become a doctor in the first place. "Okay. I'll help out for a few hours. But keep in mind, if Adam has not shown up there by midafternoon, I'm setting out to look for him again."

"Agreed. We'll gladly take whatever amount of time you are willing to give to us," Dr. Lowman responded, truly grateful, then took her hand and pulled her toward the door as if afraid she might yet change her mind. "Let's get you right on over there."

Within ten minutes, they had worked their way to Bedford Street where Dr. Lowman pulled her through the back door of a large building that looked to have at one time been a school. Once inside, JoAnn was handed a small bowl of water to wash with, then a small damp towel to wipe her face, arms, and hands.

When Dr. Lowman noticed how JoAnn had let the damp rag linger over her mouth when washing her face, he cautioned her not to take a drink. "The water's been boiled, but I really don't think it's fit for consumption," he explained. "But take heart. We've

432

sent a man out to fetch us fresh water. Someone told us that people are bringing it down from the mountains in large barrels and passing it out over near the stone bridge. If that's the case, we should have drinking water soon."

JoAnn closed her eyes. It had been two days since she'd had anything to drink. The memory of the ice-cold diet Coke she had left sitting on her kitchen table was unbearable. "How long until you'll have food and supplies?" She remembered that eventually relief items poured into the city by the trainload, but she could not remember how long until that happened.

"There is no way to know. Although I've heard rumors that the railroad tracks near the west end of town are being repaired, there's no telling how long it will take before they can get a train through. Someone said they heard that one arrived just a few hours ago, but if that was true, I think someone would have brought us medical supplies by now. Truth is, it could be days before any of the promised relief can get through to us." He waited until she had set the towel aside and looked a little more prepared for what she was about to see before gesturing toward an inner door.

"Ready?"

"As I'll ever be," she replied, then followed him into a large room that had been rigged for examinations and treatment. Three other doctors, one wearing bandages of his own, ignored the need for rest and worked steadfastly to take care of the patients either seated or lying on the long tables in front of them. What few supplies had been scavenged from the ruins or from people bringing what they could spare from their homes higher in the mountains were spread out across other tables that stood centrally located to all.

"Gentlemen, this is Doctor Griffin," John Lowman

said as a way of explanation to the other men, who had barely taken notice of his return. "She's here to help."

Of the other three doctors, JoAnn recognized only one. Despite his haggard appearance, she recognized Dr. Harrison Rutledge from that Saturday picnic in the park when he and Adam had signed Andrew Edwards's and Anthony Alani's newest petitions.

The other two men were strangers. But if either was alarmed to find a woman working alongside him, he did not show it. Instead, the men nodded gratefully, then paid little attention when she headed toward a table on which lay a pale young woman who had had part of her hand torn off during the flood.

Taking into consideration that over forty hours had passed since the disaster and that the hand was still oozing bright red, JoAnn could imagine how much blood the woman had lost.

Working quickly and with the crudest of implements and supplies, she repaired the hand as best she could, then dowsed it with whiskey and wrapped it in a skimpy dressing. Having learned that only the most critical patients were being kept for observation either in one of the adjoining rooms or at Dr. Lowman's or Dr. Pyle's houses where their wives were nursing them back to health, she had no choice but to send the woman on her way.

"Who's next?" she asked, turning to Dr. Lowman who was bent over a young boy with a piece of stained glass embedded in his cheek.

"Ask Nurse Bunn. She's keeping an eye on the patients still waiting their turn. You'll find her in the front room." He gave a sideward wave of his head. "Other side of that door."

JoAnn headed toward the door he had indicated but was unprepared for what she was to face. The room

434

was very large and filled with bruised, battered, and bleeding people who sat slumped in undersized chairs or on school benches, or else lay directly on the floor waiting for a doctor or nurse to help them.

Maimed and disoriented, many waited in silence while others moaned aloud their agony, making her aware of just how excruciating was their pain. If only there was medication to give them. But there was none. She could not even offer them a gulp of whiskey to help dull their senses because what liquor they had was needed for cleansing wounds. Seeing that many people, and all of them with serious injuries, for the less injured had already been weeded out, was all a little too overwhelming. For a brief moment, JoAnn wondered what good she and these four other doctors could do against such a tide of injuries.

Having spotted JoAnn the moment she had entered, Nurse Bunn motioned for her to go back into the treatment room and within seconds another patient was brought in by two men who had already seen the doctors but had stayed to help.

Because of the vast multitude of injured and the lack of medical help, JoAnn ended up working well past mid-afternoon. Although her thoughts constantly strayed to Adam, wondering if he was alive or dead, there was little she could do. These people needed her more than she had ever been needed in her life. She found it impossible to turn her back on them.

Chapter Twenty-one

"So there you are," Andrew Edwards said when he spotted JoAnn busily stitching a long, jagged cut on an older man's shoulder. "I *thought* I saw you right after the water hit Friday. But I wasn't sure it was you because Adam had told me about a week ago that you had gone back to Pittsburgh for good."

JoAnn looked up to see who had spoken and was surprised and a little relieved to see a familiar face.

"I did go back," she explained while she tied off the last stitch, then reached for a strip of cloth to cover the wound. "But I returned to Johnstown Friday afternoon just a few hours before the flood hit." The moment she had the cloth in place, she helped the man back on with his shirt.

"Bad timing, I'd say," Andrew commented with a brief smile, then stepped aside to let Dr. Rutledge pass, knowing he was on his way to the supply table for more bandages. "Hi, Harrison. How are things going here?"

When Harrison turned to look at him, it was a moment before his tired face registered recognition. "About what you'd expect considering the circumstances, which are certainly not the best."

"I brought more provisions," Andrew inserted quickly. "Mrs. Mack from up on Prospect Hill brought down two unopened bottles of carbolic acid and a whole box full of clean towels and linens that can be torn into bandages. I set them over there on that table behind Doctor Lowman."

"Thank you." Harrison looked in the direction he'd indicated then when he turned back to look at Andrew again, he appeared puzzled. "You certainly are in a better mood. Where'd you ever find a razor?"

"Tom Porterfield had one and let me use it. Said he didn't much like the idea of a Methodist preacher walking around looking like the very devil. And you are right. I am in a better mood. It just so happens I found Laura Edison's husband about an hour ago — *alive*. I've already taken him to see her. In fact, I'll wager he's still in there with her right now." He nodded toward one of the several classrooms that had been cleared out to hold the more critically injured.

"Probably won't leave until we run him off," Harrison said, then forced a smile that proved short-lived. It was as if his face was too exhausted to hold any expression for long. "I'm glad you found him. It's bad enough she lost her baby. I don't think she could have stood losing her husband, too."

"I also found out that a relief train from Pittsburgh has made it to the edge of town. Rumor has it there are medical supplies on board, although probably not enough to take care of everyone who was hurt. After all, there are thousands of injured who refuse to even come close to the hospital right now. Too busy looking for loved ones. Still, whatever supplies that train has brought us, it's a definite step in the right direction."

"I wish they'd send more than just supplies. I wish they'd send doctors to help take care of all these injured," Harrison muttered, then glanced toward the room where hundreds waited.

They do eventually remembered JoAnn, but knew better than state that fact aloud. If she as much as hinted about knowing what lay in store for them over the next few days, they would decide she was either a witch or a nut.

"Heard there's also clothing and blankets on board that train," Andrew went on. "Food and fresh water, too. Won't be too long before they get everything organized and start handing it all out. Oh, and I found out your other sister-in-law is still alive. So things *are* starting to look up."

"I know about Patricia. She was by earlier hoping to find Jeanne here helping with the injured," he said and let out a troubled breath. "I had to admit to her that I hadn't seen my wife since before the flood hit."

"You want me to check at the registry for you again?" Andrew asked. "I was headed that way anyway. I'm still trying to find out what happened to Faye. We could certainly use the calming effect of a nun around here, especially with so many of the injured being Catholic. While I'm there checking on Faye, I would be happy to look on the list for your wife's name."

"Would you check at the morgue, too?" Harrison asked, then closed his eyes for a moment. When he opened them again, tears had collected at the outer corners making him look all the more haggard. "And if by chance she is there, do what you can to see that she's taken to the Grandview Cemetery. That's where her mother is buried and as I understand it, that's where they are taking her younger sister, Catherine." He then looked at JoAnn, who stood quietly to one side listening to their sad conversation. "And while you are looking, check to see if Adam Johnson's name is either at the registry or the morgue. JoAnn has been beside herself with worry."

JoAnn smiled, grateful to have someone go check. She was not certain of the hour, but knew it had to be late afternoon by now. That meant two days had passed since the flood. Two days since she had last wiggled through the passageway. She did not know how much longer she dared wait for Adam, though she knew in her heart she could not leave until she knew his fate.

Andrew promised to do what he could to find Adam

and Jeanne, then left immediately. Within minutes after JoAnn and Harrison had returned to work, a man with an armful of clothing entered unannounced through the back door, proclaiming to have brought clothes for everyone. In addition to assorted shirts and trousers for the male doctors, he had a clean dress made of dark blue cotton trimmed in white lace for JoAnn. He smiled when he handed her the clothing and JoAnn recognized him as a man she had sewn up earlier that afternoon.

"When I found out they was passin' out clothes up at the train station, I decided to see if they would let me have enough for all of you," he said with a pleased grin. "When I explained about the hospital and all your work, they also sent over a box of food and water for you, which I had to set down outside so I could open the door. Those people at the train said to tell you they'd send more later. That this was just a start because more trains are due in later this evening."

"But what about medical supplies?" Harrison asked, clearly worried. "I was told there were medical supplies on that train."

"There were. They were piling it all onto some man's wagon when I left. Said they'd be bringing you a whole wagon load of supplies in about an hour. That should give you just enough time to change clothes and eat some of the food I brought."

By the time JoAnn and the other doctors had bathed with a damp cloth and changed into the clean clothes, the nurses and the volunteers acting as nurses had unpacked the box the man had brought and for the first time in two days, they had fresh water to drink — and cheese, ham, and bread to eat.

After taking a few minutes for a quick meal, the doctors went immediately back to work. There were too many people still needing medical attention.

When another hour passed and neither Andrew nor

Adam appeared at the hospital, JoAnn thoughts took a downward turn and she started to believe the worst. It seemed to her that if Adam was still alive and unhurt, she would have heard something by now. It had been two days since the disaster struck. Plenty of time for him to have surfaced and started his own search.

The thought that perhaps Adam had not survived started to nag at her and would not go away. Perhaps the flood had caught him so completely unaware he had no opportunity to save himself. Perhaps his fate had been taken so far out of his own reach, he'd never had a chance.

Eventually she could think of little else and after another hour of watching people come and go, yet none being Adam, JoAnn became frustrated to the point of fighting tears. Where was he? Where was her beloved Adam? Why didn't he come to the hospital looking if not for her then for his father?

He would not immediately know that his father was dead; therefore logically, he would either have come straight there to the hospital, thinking his father would be among those helping, or else he would have gone to his father's house. In either case, at the same time he learned of his father's death, he would have found out about her return. He would have been told that she was in Johnstown looking for him. So why didn't he come there looking for her?

Suddenly the flaw in that line of thinking dawned on her. Had he gone by the house searching for his father, *all* he would have been told was that she was out there somewhere looking for him. Because she had not thought to send a message letting Sheila know where she had gone, that was all Sheila knew to tell him. And if Adam had gone by there first, he would have already been told about his father and, therefore, would have no reason to come on to the hospital looking for him. He would have then taken to the streets looking for her. She felt sure of it.

But why had that not occurred to her before now? Was she so near exhaustion that she could no longer think straight?

She had to go look for him once more. It was the only way to relieve the agonizing doubts that tormented her.

JoAnn was unable to find Dr. Lowman to tell him she needed to leave for a while because he and Dr. Pyle had gone to their respective homes to take their wives some of the food and check on the patients there. She finally told Harrison that she would be gone for an hour or two. She had to know if Adam had been by the house, or if his name had turned up at the registry. She could not wait for Andrew to finally return.

"Maybe by the time you get back, we'll have those medical supplies," Harrison said, sounding hopeful despite his exhaustion. "And maybe by then we'll have clean sheets and blankets for our patients."

After seeing how haggard Harrison looked, JoAnn felt guilty leaving, knowing that if she was fortunate enough to find Adam still alive while she was out, she would not be back. She would make sure that he was okay, then head immediately for the passageway. And with Dr. Matthews starting to show signs of light-headedness, probably due to his own injuries, the number of working doctors would soon be down to three. But she could not let that bother her. Time was running out for her.

When JoAnn returned outside, all the activity confused her. Twice as many people were now working to find the dead and clear away the ruin, many of them dressed in freshly laundered clothing. It was then she remembered that the relief trains had not only brought needed supplies, they had also brought workers. Lots of workers. Most of which had been sent by the Pennsylvania Railroad. Unfortunately, the trains had also brought curiosity seekers who had no intention of working, but wanted to see as much gore and death as possible while there.

Holding the sleeve of her new dress against her nose to block out part of the stench, which was far worse than it had been that morning, JoAnn lifted her skirt with her other hand but for a moment could not remember in which direction she would find Park's house.

She was too exhausted from all the work she had done, so much so that whenever she closed her eyes for very long, she felt a heavy pressure against her eyes and forehead, like a giant hand pressed into her skull. It was painful enough to make her dizzy, but as long as she kept her eyes open and her body moving, she was fine.

Finally, she spotted the Lutheran church and she headed in the direction of Park's house.

Due to a network of narrow paths that had been cleared while JoAnn was busy at the hospital, it took only ten minutes to cover the distance to Park's house. Thinking she was about to hear good news at last, she lifted her skirt higher still and ran the last part of the way. When she burst through the front door seconds later, she found Sheila still seated in the same chair as before, lost in dark thought.

"Has Adam been by yet?" she asked, looking at the woman worriedly. She wished now she had thought to bring food and water with her.

"No. I haven't seen him," she answered, without looking at JoAnn directly. "Haven't seen nobody."

Her face twisted in anguish. She had so expected to hear that he had been by there and was now out searching for her that she had a hard time accepting anything different. "Are you sure?"

Sheila nodded once.

Worried by Sheila's despondent behavior, JoAnn knelt beside her. When she peered into Sheila's eyes, all she saw was a vacant stare. "No one has been by here at all?"

"No one I recall," she replied, then frowned while something from her memory surfaced, though her eyes remained empty. "Except for one little girl. She was looking for her mother. I told her I didn't even know her mother. Told her to keep looking, though."

"Haven't you been out to get any food? Relief trains have arrived and there is food and water now, though not much."

"You told me to wait here," Sheila reminded her and for the first time, her gaze focused on JoAnn's face. "You told me to wait here for Mister Adam."

JoAnn sighed. A part of her wanted to tell the woman to go on to the railroad station and get some of the food being handed out while another part of her was afraid to let her leave for fear Adam would come by in that time and find no one there.

"Tell you what. I'll have someone bring you something. But you can't just keep sitting in that chair." She needed something to occupy her mind. "There's too much work to be done. There are too many people with no place to stay. No way to get out of the weather. You know if you could get this floor cleared out, you could invite some of them to stay here." She thought of suggesting they stay on the upper floors, too, but remembered the stairs had been weakened until they were no longer reliable. "You could offer some of the homeless children out there a sheltered place to sleep."

It was as if a light went off in Sheila's eyes and she turned to look at her surroundings as if assessing how much work that would take. "That is a good idea. And if I could get someone out there to come in and help me, I could board up those windows and have this place livable in no time. Why, I could have this room ready in less than two hours."

By the time JoAnn had left Park's house to continue her search for Adam, Sheila and two children whom JoAnn had found hiding on the back porch were busy scraping mud off the floor with broken boards and dented pans.

Because JoAnn was not ready to face the horrible scene at the morgue again, she headed first to the train station to get Sheila and the children some food and water, then as soon as she had delivered that, she went on over to the Registry Bureau on Main Street. There she looked not only for Adam's name, but for George Hess's name, too, and was disappointed to find that neither had registered yet. Nor had Jeanne Rutledge. Where were these people?

With nowhere else to go besides the morgue, and knowing Andrew would have already gone by there and checked, she decided to head back to the hospital, determined to keep busy until word finally arrived concerning Adam.

Staying within the pathways that had been cleared earlier, JoAnn glanced at all the activity going on around her. Another wave of hopelessness washed over her when she saw how very many bodies were still being pulled from the wreckage and put into wagons to be carried to the nearest morgue. While the brackish water continued to go down, it relinquished more and more of its dead.

JoAnn tried not to think of Adam's body being unearthed in much the same way she had unearthed Park's earlier. Instead, she focused again on the fact that Adam was such a strong, capable man. If anyone had the strength to survive such a terrible ordeal, it would be Adam. She refused to consider that men just as strong and just as capable had died by the hundreds.

Instead, she forced her attention back to her surroundings while she continued on her way. When she did, a tiny splash of brilliant red caught her eye. Attracted by such a vivid color when everything else looked so drab and gray, her eyes widened with wonder. There just off to one side was a single, perfect red rose floating atop a littered pool of black water. It felt odd to see an object of such flawless beauty floating unmarred in such a vast sea of death and devastation.

Slowly, a tiny ray of hope entered JoAnn's heart and warmed away the chilling fear that had settled there. If something as delicate and beautiful as a rose could come through such a horrible disaster unharmed, then surely Adam could, too.

A few minutes later, when she entered through the back door of the hospital, JoAnn was in much better spirits.

But her lighthearted mood lasted only until she noticed Harrison and Dr. Matthews vigorously arguing that Dr. Matthews needed to go to Dr. Lòwman's or Dr. Pyle's house for a few hours of rest.

"You nearly passed out a few minutes ago," Harrison said, raising his voice in anger, too tired to deal with any more frustration. "You need your rest. You haven't slept since the flood hit."

"Neither have you," the handsome young doctor countered with a determined thrust of his jaw.

"But that's different. I don't have three broken ribs to worry about. I came through the flood virtually unharmed."

"I feel fine."

"That's a lie. You are in so much pain you can barely focus on my face and I can tell by looking at you that you are running a fever. Just what good do you think you will be to us dead?"

"I just need a little more of that cheese and ham over there and another drink of water. I'll be fine."

"You need more than food and water to get *your* strength back," Harrison insisted, then noticing JoAnn, he gestured for her to come closer. "Don't you agree? This man needs some rest."

"You both look like you could use some rest," she admitted, knowing she could do with a little herself. She was so exhausted from everything she had gone through during the past few days, her arms felt like lead weights at her

445

sides. "But I have a feeling neither of you will as much as close your eyes until your own bodies finally rebel against you and force you to."

"So we might as well get back to work," Dr. Matthews added, then gestured toward the room where hundreds still waited for treatment.

None of the three doctors was aware that someone had come up behind them and now stood only a few yards away waiting for a break in their conversation.

"Where do you want him?" a male voice asked when he saw the opportunity to speak.

When JoAnn turned around to see who had spoken, her attention focused immediately on the sagging body of a boy and not the man carrying him. Stepping closer to the child, her eyes widened with immediate recognition. It was George Hess—unconscious, filthy, and mangled, but definitely George Hess.

"Take him to that table nearest the window," she said, all her earlier fatigue instantly gone. Barely noticing how stiffly the man moved while carrying the boy, she and Dr. Matthews followed him to the table and as soon as he had set the boy down, they began an examination to determine the extent of his injuries.

"Why are you here?" the man who had brought George in asked in a feeble voice.

Not knowing which of them he had spoken to, JoAnn looked at the haggard man who could barely stand and felt her whole body tense, then turn instantly weak.

It was Adam. He was covered in dried blood and streaked with oil and mud and looked too exhausted to stand a moment longer, but he was still alive. Still so very much alive.

With tears brimming, JoAnn rushed to embrace him, but because the unexpected embrace caught him off guard, he stumbled against her and she felt something sharp press into her ribs.

446

It took a moment for him to stand upright again. After that he looked down at her, half dazed while she pulled the front of his tattered shirt apart. She gasped at the jagged piece of wood protruding from his body, just inches below his rib cage, near his waist. The wood was round though badly pitted and looked to be a little more than an inch in diameter, the right size to have been a curtain rod or maybe the spoke on a baby's bed or the bracing of a bench.

"Oh, Adam," she said, staring at the injury in horror. With panic filling her heart, she lifted the shirt up higher and peered around at his back. She grimaced when she discovered the wood had lanced him through like a spear. Knowing the pain he must feel, her throat constricted until she could hardly swallow. "What happened?"

"I'd have pulled the blasted thing out myself," he babbled, looking down at the bloodied piece of wood with disgust. "But I was afraid what might happen. Afraid it might cause me to start bleeding more that I already was. Or worse. I was afraid I'd pass out again." He looked at her and blinked several times, trying to focus. "I couldn't let that happen. If I passed out again, I wouldn't be able to help George. And he was trapped."

"Trapped? Where?" she asked, glancing only briefly at the unconscious child for her main concern was with Adam. It amazed her that he had survived such an injury for as long as he had.

"U-under an overturned tree," he stammered. His voice had grown so weak in the time he had been there, it was little more than a rush of air past his lips. His body had started to weave, making JoAnn realize he was about to faint, but he continued to babble. "Had to get him out. He's like a son to me. I had to get him some help."

"And you did. Doctor Matthews is helping him now," she assured him, though she didn't know how much help Dr. Matthews could be. In the brief examination she'd made, she noticed most of the bones in the lower part of his body were broken and with no X-ray equipment on hand, there was no way to know what the internal injuries might be.

"Adam, I want you to sit down, before you fall down," she coaxed, her stomach in knots while she looked to find a place for him and noticed Dr. Lowman's table was empty. When she reached to lead him by the arm, he stumbled but managed to keep from falling. Aware he might not make it as far as the table, her heart pounded with such painful force she thought surely it would burst. She knew if that spike caught on something when he fell, it could easily tear him in half.

"H-had to get George out of there," he continued while allowing JoAnn to lead him across the room. "Had to get him s-some help." Then suddenly his legs gave out from under him and he fell to the floor in a crumpled heap.

"*Doctor Lowman*," JoAnn screamed, feeling suddenly hysterical. She had spotted the doctor when he'd entered through the back door just seconds earlier. "Doctor Lowman, I need your help."

Chapter Twenty-two

"About all Doctor Matthews can hope to do for Adam's little friend is splint both his legs and make him as comfortable as possible," Dr. Lowman said while he helped JoAnn remove the wooden spear from Adam's waist. Because they had to be sure every tiny splinter had been removed before closing either entry or chance a very risky infection, the going was slower than they would have liked, especially with his pulse having become so weak.

"That's all Adam would expect of him," she said, bending low while she felt again for more wood fragments with the tip of her finger. Satisfied there were none, she reached for the carbolic acid to flush the area before closing.

"Here let me do that," Dr. Lowman said and took the bottle from her. "You go prepare a place for him and the boy in the other room. I'll finish here."

Rather than argue over who would do what, JoAnn nodded and stepped back. While wiping the blood off her hands with a damp cloth, she gazed at Adam and noticed the deep lines furrowed in his brow and knew that despite the fact they now had liquid cocaine to apply to the wounds, he was in severe pain. She also noticed how terribly pale he had become from having lost so much blood.

Fighting back her anguish, she wondered if he would last the night. If only they had the life-supporting equipment of her time. Then he would have a better chance. As it was, she could not even give him the antibiotics he needed to fight a likely infection because that particular form of drug did not exist yet. The best they could do in the year 1889 was sprinkle the open wound with a form of powdered zinc before closing.

Knowing that was not enough to assure Adam's return to health, she considered taking off for the passageway to see if she could get through to the medicine he needed, but knew there were no roads leading out of Johnstown at the moment, nor were there any bridges spanning the still swollen rivers. It would take her a full day to make the five-mile trek up the mud-slick mountain and another to make the slow trek back.

And even if she did manage to get through to the twentieth century, she would still have to drive quite a distance to find an all-night pharmacy before she could lay her hands on the right medicine. Chances were by the time she returned, the passageway would have shrunk enough, she might not be able to wiggle back through to get that medicine to him. The whole trip would have been for nothing, which meant it was better she stay right there and help him as best she could with the medications she had.

But knowing Adam would have to fight any infection that occurred without the modern medications she was used to administering, she had no idea what to expect.

"Better get going," Dr. Lowman said, aware she still stood nearby. He had already covered the area with powdered zinc and was busy making his first set of stitches deep inside the wound. "I'll be through here in just a few minutes."

Prodded into action, JoAnn hurried into a room where over forty critically injured people already lay and quickly spread out two blankets. Seeing that they now had plenty, she then spread two more blankets on top of the first ones, wanting to cushion Adam and George as best she could from the hard floor.

By the time she had finished making a special place for them very close to the door where it would be easier for her to keep a close vigil, Dr. Matthews was ready to carry George into the room. And by the time they had him settled in, Dr. Lowman was ready to move Adam.

While covering Adam's pale body with yet another blanket and wondering what else she could do to make him comfortable, JoAnn felt such a strong, overpowering wave of admiration wash over her, she had to smile. Despite her tears.

Adam was a truly remarkable man. As critical as his own injuries were, he had been more concerned for George's well-being than his own. He had selflessly put aside caring for his own injuries until he was certain George had been provided medical help. Her heart soared with pride. Not many of the men she knew would have behaved so honorably.

She reached up to wipe away some of her tears so she could see him better. How very much she admired and loved this man. How very hard it would be to leave him a third time. And what a great loss to the world if he should die. Which was why she intended to stay on in the year 1889 a while longer. She had to know Adam's fate.

Knowing there was nothing else she could do for either Adam or George but keep a close watch over their vital signs and pray that God would show them His divine mercy, JoAnn returned to the treatment room where she continued tending to the injured. She hoped that by keeping busy, she would be able to stay one step ahead of her emotions. But that had been asking for the impossible.

Being at the hospital that night was like being on an endless emotional roller coaster. While she worried constantly about Adam and George, news of the condition of others found its way to the hospital. No sooner was Harrison told that his wife was indeed still alive than it was discovered that two of Andrew Edward's closest friends, Anthony Alani and Faye Gifford, had drowned in the flood. Dr. Pyle also learned he had lost a brother, Eric, and that his sister, Veronica, had been found several miles downstream badly bruised but very much alive.

And before the night was over, Constance Seguin was brought in with a large piece of a mirror lodged into the side of her neck and when JoAnn turned out to be the one to have to remove the broken glass and stitch the wound, Constance did not once protest having a "woman" doctor take care of her. And although she seemed truly grateful that JoAnn was taking such good care of Adam, she seemed more interested in the fact that the handsome Dr. Matthews was so badly injured. She tried to convince him to go home with her and let her take care of him, but got no further with the suggestion than any of the others had.

During that time when news of loved ones kept everyone at the hospital in an emotional maelstrom, the doctors continued to work tirelessly through the night. And while they worked, JoAnn kept a close eye on both Adam and George, desperate to discover some evidence of improvement.

But each time she checked them, she found nothing that might give her hope, nothing to indicate that either would ever regain consciousness. Still, she refused to give up. As long as they both continued to breathe, whether that breathing was labored or shallow, she held on to her last vestige of hope.

Early that following morning, fourteen men arrived from Pittsburgh, each carrying large boxes filled with yet more medical supplies. The group entered through the front of the building and hesitated momentarily when they saw just how many people waited to be seen, some so near death they were barely breathing.

Having spotted JoAnn first, the group introduced themselves as relief doctors and asked her to point to the physician in charge. Because she had no idea where to find Dr. Lowman at that moment, not knowing whether he was still at the hospital or at his house taking care of those injured being kept there, JoAnn hurried to find him.

When she entered the large room closest to the treatment ward, she saw Dr. Matthews sitting on the floor between George and Adam, clutching his injured ribs, slumped forward in defeat. Her heart slammed hard against her chest when she looked from his quaking shoulders to Adam's lifeless form and noticed immediately that her beloved was no longer rasping for breaths and that none of the color had returned to his face. If anything, he looked even more pallid than before.

Paralyzed by her own rising fear, she took several deep, quick breaths, then forced out the question she did not want to ask.

"What's wrong, Doctor Matthews?"

The young doctor lifted his head and looked at her beseechingly with an expression like that of a lost child. Tears had filled his hollow eyes and his whole body shook uncontrollably. "I am doing the very best I can but they just keep on dying. No matter what I do, they just keep on dying. One by one. Death picks them off. And I *don't* know what to do to save them."

Certain her heart had stopped beating, JoAnn pressed a trembling hand against her mouth as again her gaze fell on Adam's lifeless form. His shallow cheeks looked stark white, almost blue in contrast to the dark hair spilling over his forehead and the tiny lines of pain were gone from his face. "Adam? A-Adam's dead?"

The pain that pierced her was so great, she was not sure she could bear its onslaught. Bent forward as if to protect herself from yet more pain, she bit the inside of her lower lip and prayed it was not true. The room filled with shadows that spun crazily before her, and before Dr. Matthews could confirm her worst fear and admit that the only man she had ever truly loved was indeed gone forever, the long days of exhaustive work finally exacted their toll and she sank obliviously into an ocean of darkness.

Thirty hours had passed before JoAnn surfaced from what felt to her like a drugged stupor. When she finally did awaken, her thoughts were disoriented and she had a difficult time focusing on any one object. The sunlight that streamed through a nearby window hurt her eyes, causing sharp flashes of pain to pierce her skull.

Squinting against the effect from such a harsh light, she stared at a gaslight fixture overhead until she was able to make out the intricate pattern of the plaster molding that held it in place. Once that had come into focus, she carefully turned her head and gazed at the antique furniture around her.

Blinking with confusion, she wondered where she was and tried to sit up to have a better look at the unfamiliar furnishings. To her dismay, she barely had the strength to roll over onto her side and even that provoked considerable pain. Every movement caused some part of her body to rebel. Her first thought was that she had been in an automobile accident, but she could not remember where or when such a thing could have happened. But then logic quickly pointed out that had she been in an accident, she would now be in a hospital and this was definitely not a hospital room. This was a bedroom in someone's home.

Still, it was not a bedroom she had ever seen before. That much seemed obvious.

Tossing back the heavy bed covers, she glanced down at her clothing and her forehead wrinkled with further bewilderment. She had on a long, white nightgown stitched with colored thread, and over in the corner of the room, draped across a medallion-backed chair was a full-length blue dress that looked like it had come out of another century.

Another century.

Her heart froze when suddenly it all fell into place. The dress was where it belonged. *She* was the one who had come from another century. Aware now that she was still in the year 1889, she glanced at a nearby clock. It was after three. How long had she been unconscious? Five? Six hours? Or had it been longer than that? Why were her thoughts still so hazy?

Remembering now the horrible ordeal she had gone through, that she had nearly drowned in the Johnstown Flood, she pushed her sleeves up to have a look at her arms. Several of her bruises had begun to fade, which meant days had passed since the initial disaster. But how many? And what had caused her to pass out? While she reached up to feel her head for further injuries, she suddenly remembered having gone into the back room in search of Dr. Lowman. Her heart pounded wildly, pushing a tight, throbbing pain into the base of her throat when she remembered having found Dr. Matthews slumped on the floor between Adam and George, sobbing because he had lost Adam, too.

Fighting an overwhelming rush of heartache and dizziness, JoAnn struggled to sit erect. She had to find out where they had taken Adam's body. She wanted to be sure he ended up buried on his own land. Along with his father.

Still wondering where she was and how she had come to be there, she slid off the tall, four-poster bed and onto her feet. Fighting a sudden wave of nausea, she slipped out of the white gown and into the blue dress she now remembered had been provided for her earlier. As soon as the dress was fastened, she looked around for her shoes and socks but did not see them. Although she did not like the idea of having to walk barefoot in all that ruin, she realized she had no choice. She had to get to the main morgue before Adam's body was processed, which she knew would be pretty quick.

Because of how rapidly the number of dead had mounted, bodies were no longer being kept for families to claim. Within hours after a body had been identified, it was carried off to one of the area cemeteries for quick burial.

Hoping to get her bearings back as soon as she had stepped outside, JoAnn gripped the door handle with every intention of turning it but was surprised when she felt it suddenly move of its own accord. She barely had enough time to step back out of the way before the door swung open and in walked a small woman who looked to be in her fifties. In her hands was a small metallic pitcher.

"Get back in that bed," she admonished in a sharp tone and quickly set the pitcher aside. "You are in no condition to be up and about again." She wagged a bony finger as a means of reprimand. "Why you are every bit as stubborn as that mule-headed husband of mine. I hear you nearly worked yourself to death, Doctor Griffin, yet here you are up out of that bed already."

"And who are you?" JoAnn asked, taking a cautionary step backward.

"Doctor Pyle's wife," she answered with a haughty lift of her chin. "This is my house. In fact, this is my bedroom. Although we're now up to keeping seven and eight people to a room in most cases, my husband wanted you in a room by yourself. He said you were to get special treatment. Said Johnstown needed to make sure it kept a talented doctor like you healthy and happy."

"That was very kind of him," she said, surprised by Dr. Pyle's appraisal of her work. "And I appreciate the half-day's rest I've had, but—"

"*Half* day? My dear, you've been here for over thirty hours," Mrs. Pyle informed her. "And even that is not enough rest for what you've been through. I can tell by looking at you that you barely have enough strength to stand. That's why I'm ordering you back in that bed. Now!"

"But I have to leave," JoAnn tried to explain only to be cut short.

"No you don't. There is no reason for you to have to leave. It just so happens there are now plenty of doctors helping with the injured. Doctors have come here from Pittsburgh, Altoona, and even New York and they have literally taken over at the hospital. You and the other local doctors have done your part. But I can't seem to convince the others of that. My husband and Doctor Rutledge are both right here helping me with my patients. They are the ones who gave me strict orders to see that you stay in that bed and get plenty of rest." She crossed her arms to show how determined she was to do just that. "Do I have to call my husband or Doctor Rutledge in here to force you back into that bed? I will if I have to."

"But I can't go back to bed," JoAnn tried again to explain. "I have to find out what became of Adam Johnson." Tears filled her dark eyes while she pleaded for

457

understanding. "I have to find out where they carried his body."

The woman looked at her with a peculiar expression, as if not quite certain JoAnn was lucid. "They brought his body here at the same time they brought yours. He's in the next room."

"You mean he's alive?" she asked. Her body filled with so much sudden hope she thought she would burst. "But how can that be? He was so pale and he wasn't breathing. How can he still be alive?"

"He was breathing just fine when they brought him in here," she said and continued looking at her oddly. "He even opened his eyes once just a few hours after they brought him here. Although he was only awake for a few minutes because he was still very sedated, you'll be pleased to know he asked for you by name and seemed deeply comforted to hear you were in the next room resting. He's been sleeping peacefully since then."

"Which room is he in?" she demanded, already headed for the door.

"Will you promise to lay back down and rest if I tell you?"

"I have to see him first."

"Then will you lay back down and rest?"

"*Which room?*" JoAnn asked, clearly frustrated by this game of twenty questions.

"The one to your left," Mrs. Pyle finally answered, aware she would get no cooperation until JoAnn had actually seen for herself that Adam Johnson was still alive.

Finding sudden strength, JoAnn hurried into the next room, relieved to tears to see Adam lying peacefully on a cot with a white sheet pulled neatly to his shoulders. Although he did not appear to have on any clothing, or at least not a shirt, someone had thought to comb his hair and had provided him with a small pillow.

"*Doctor Griffin!* What are you doing in here?"

458

She heard Harrison's stern voice before she actually saw him. He stood near a large double bed that had been pushed against the far wall to make room for more cots. He had leaned over to check one of the three young men placed on top.

"I came to see Adam," she said, already making her way around the other patients to kneel at Adam's side. Trembling with joy, she took his hand and pressed it to her cheek. His skin felt warm, yet not too warm. He was definitely still alive and at the moment running only a slight fever.

"Adam? Adam, can you hear me?" When he did not answer immediately, she lifted the sheet covering him with her other hand and was pleased to see he had on a clean bandage that showed very little seepage. He was no longer losing large amounts of blood. "Adam. It's me, JoAnn. Can't you hear me?"

"He was running a high fever earlier and was in a lot of pain so I had to sedate him," Harrison explained, already working his way through the cots to stand beside her. "But his fever has since come down and as you can see, his coloring is much better. He's one of the few who has been resting peacefully since sunup."

JoAnn glanced at the other men in the room, aware many of them were still restless with pain and she felt her heart go out to them. "Doctor Rutledge, I realize I have no right to ask this of you, but could you have Adam moved into the next room where I was staying? I'm much better now and I really would like for him to have his own room where I can take care of him privately."

"But Doctor Pyle wanted you to—" Harrison started to say, but then stroked his freshly shaven jaw with his hand while he thought more about it. "You aren't going to be able to rest again until Adam is completely out of danger, are you?"

"No, Doctor, I am not," she said, gazing up at him,

adamant in her answer.

"Then he might as well have that bed," he said and nodded agreeably. "I'll get someone from downstairs to help me move him."

"And can I have George Hess moved into the room as well?" she asked, thinking she might as well take care of both of them.

Harrison paused a moment, then reached out to rest his hand on her shoulder, causing a sharp pang of apprehension to cut through her.

"I'm afraid the boy didn't make it. He had too many internal injuries. We had no medical machines to work with so we had no way of knowing his lungs were steadily filling with blood. He eventually drowned."

A tiny piece of JoAnn's heart fell away as she looked up at Harrison and saw the sympathy glimmering from his eyes. George was dead. George, who had defended her simply because he liked her was gone from her life forever. She would never see his shy smile or hear his playful laughter again. Suddenly she thought of Doris and wondered how the poor woman would ever endure her grief. How could any woman ever overcome the heartache that accompanied losing one's own child?

"When did he die?"

"He died early yesterday morning. Just minutes before you and Doctor Matthews finally succumbed to exhaustion. The boy is probably already buried by now."

"Where is Doctor Matthews?"

"Just down the street at Doctor Lowman's house where I understand he's already up and around again, helping take care of the patients they took in there. It's amazing how little damage this house and Doctor Lowman's house sustained, considering that several other homes in this neighborhood disappeared completely."

"Does Adam know about George?" she asked, remembering that Mrs. Pyle had told her he was awake for

460

a while.

"No. We felt it best not to tell him just yet. It's pretty obvious he loved the boy or he never would have put his own life in such jeopardy to save him. We felt it would be better to hold such painful news until Adam was a little stronger."

"Then you do expect him to recover?" she asked, glancing at Adam's restful face with renewed hope.

"Yes, I do. His pulse is strong again, and his breathing normal. As long as his fever doesn't shoot back up, indicating renewed infection, I think he has a very good chance of recovery. In fact, I wouldn't put it past him to be up and out of here within the week."

JoAnn was very relieved to hear it. "How can I ever thank you for all you have done for Adam."

"You already have," he assured her. "You did that by working right alongside the rest of us when we needed you most. And just like the rest of us you continued to work until you eventually collapsed from exhaustion. I feel like you became a part of us during those last few days. The work you did was more than enough thanks for whatever we may have done for Adam. If anything, we should be thanking you. Which is why I'm having Adam moved right away." He turned and headed for the door. "It's my way of repaying a few of your kindnesses. I'll find someone to help me carry him and be right back."

True to his word, Harrison returned in a very few minutes with Dr. Pyle and a tall red-haired man. Together the three men lifted Adam into the air, cot and all, and transported him into the next room. Carefully, so not to put any unnecessary strain on his stitches, they transferred him to the bed and left the cot at the foot so JoAnn would have a place to rest.

"We'll be by to check on him regularly," Dr. Pyle promised before he and the red-haired man headed back downstairs to care for the patients on the first floor.

Harrison patted JoAnn on the shoulder reassuringly. "Shout if you need me," he told her, then returned to the next room to attend to his patients.

Although JoAnn realized there was a chance, however slight, that there might yet be room for her to slip through the invisible hole and back into her own time period were she to leave for the mountain right away, she stayed by Adam's side for the rest of that afternoon and all that night. In that time, she slept some, but maintained a vigilant watch over his vital signs and kept his fever regulated by bathing his face, chest, and arms with cool rags whenever he felt too warm.

With her emotions held in careful control, she refused to consider that her efforts could ever have been in vain. She refused to believe that the longer he remained unconscious the less chance there would be for a total recovery. Instead, she concentrated on the fact that a strong, caring man like Adam deserved a full and happy life.

Early the following morning, while waiting for Harrison to make his rounds, JoAnn poured fresh water into the large porcelain bowl that had been provided for her. Having spent the night awake and at Adam's bedside, exhaustion pulled at her brain and tugged at her body, slowing both her thoughts and her movements. She needed something to help bring herself back awake.

Focusing on her own movements, she slipped the small white face cloth she had been using on Adam earlier into the cool water and gently swirled it back and forth to mix in the few drops of body oil Mrs. Pyle had given her for her hands earlier. After squeezing out the excess moisture, she dabbed her face and neck with the cloth, then smiled at how good the cool water with a touch of oil felt against her skin.

Thinking Adam deserved that same wondrous sensation, she turned to place the wet cloth against his face and was startled to find his eyes fully open and staring at her questioningly, as if not quite sure he believed what he saw. Her heart soared with sudden hope.

"You *are* here," he said in a husky voice while he worked to focus on her beautiful face. When he finally had a clear view of her, he smiled and his next words were spoken a lot more distinctly. "I thought maybe I'd dreamed having seen you at the hospital."

"No, it was no dream," she said, smiling happily. As much pain killer as he had in him, she was surprised his voice had sounded so strong and that his speech was not a little slurred. But then he had been given a pain killer she was not familiar with so she had not known what side effects to expect. "I was definitely there."

"But you were supposed to be in Pittsburgh. When did you come back?"

"Just hours before the water hit." She set the cloth aside and stepped closer, eager to see that familiar sparkle in his pale blue eyes. "I tried to find you when I first arrived, but you were not at the iron works nor were you at your father's house."

Adam's expression turned thoughtful while he tried to recall what he had done that day. "I remember I was at the bank for a while, helping carry some of the files and furniture to the second and third floors," he said, then flattened his mouth to show his disgust. "A lot of good that did. I passed by the bank on the way to find the hospital and there was nothing left but the front steps and a part of a wall."

JoAnn nodded for she, too, had seen what little remained of the bank where he and his namesake cousin had worked. "But by the time I went to the bank looking for you, they said you'd already left. Where did you go after that?"

Adam's reflective expression returned. "I can't remember. I think I headed for the institute next. But I don't remember if I ever got there or not." His eyebrows dipped low while he tried to break through whatever barrier had blocked his thoughts. "I don't think I did."

"No, you did not. It just so happens I ended up there right after the flood struck and they told me you had not been there all day."

Adam's eyebrows lifted with sudden remembrance when he again looked at JoAnn. "That's because George saw me traveling along the street and waved me to stop. I can't remember much about what happened after the water hit, but I remember what happened just before. George and Cyrus needed help readying his aunt's house and shed for the flood." He looked relieved when it all became so clear again. "Doris had decided she and the boys should take advantage of being in town for the Memorial Day ceremonies last Thursday by staying with her sister for a few days after. They were still there at her house when the water started to overflow its banks early that following morning. Since Cyrus had hurt himself while trying to move something too heavy for one person to lift and wasn't of much help anymore, I thought I'd better stay and do what I could for them."

"Is that where you were when the water struck?

He nodded, then looked at her questioningly. "That dam finally broke, didn't it? That's what caused so much destruction, isn't it?"

JoAnn nodded, then quickly changed the subject for fear his next question would be to ask about George and she just wasn't ready to give him such heartbreaking news. "I guess you are pretty hungry about now. It's been at least five days since your last solid meal."

"Five days?" Adam repeated. Clearly, he found that hard to believe. "How long have I been unconscious?"

"Since Sunday. And this is Wednesday."

He thought about that for a moment. "If that's true,

then why aren't I more thirsty?"

"Because I've been dribbling water into your mouth with a wet cloth and you've been swallowing it out of simple reflex. I even managed to get a little broth down you using that same method. It was important to get as much fluid and as many nutrients inside you as possible, to keep up your strength."

"Then you've been here with me the whole the time I was out? The whole three days?" He tried to pull himself to a higher position on the pillows but grimaced and fell back after having only moved a few inches. His injury had left him with a lot more soreness than he had expected.

"Not exactly," she admitted, then bent forward to gently stroke his forehead with her fingertips, encouraging him to stay relaxed against the pillows. She smiled when she realized how right it felt to be comforting him. "It seems I spent about a day and a half of that time lying unconscious in the next room." She then thought about that answer and realized the mistake. "Well, actually I was in here and you were in the other room. But I had you moved in here shortly after I came awake and discovered you were in a room with at least half a dozen other injured men, most of whom were moaning and writhing with pain. You wouldn't believe how many injured people Doctor and Mrs. Pyle have taken into their homes over the past few days."

Adam studied her a long moment as if deeply puzzled about something and hoping to find the answer simply by looking at her.

Rather than face whatever questions he was about to ask, still fearing he might ask about George, JoAnn bent forward and placed a tender kiss on his cheek. A familiar warmth curled through her, encircling her heart, then trickling down to fill her soul while she took a moment to gaze at his devastatingly handsome features and reflected on what a truly extraordinary man he was. "I'd better get on downstairs and find you something to eat. You'll need more than the broth I fed you to get the rest of your strength back."

"Amazingly, I don't feel all that weak," he said and again tried to sit up, this time managing to lift himself much further onto the pillows. "My side hurts like all get out whenever I move, but I don't feel all that weak." What he felt was exhilarated. After having been told JoAnn had all but disappeared off the face of this earth, he had thought he would never see her again. "There's no need for you to rush off."

"I think you would realize how weak you are if you tried to get out of that bed and stand up," she assured him, then smiled. "If you're worried that I'm not coming back, then don't. I'm just going downstairs to see if Mrs. Pyle has any of that lamb stew left. I'll be right back."

"No, wait," he said, his voice urgent. When she paused to find out what he wanted, he searched her face with a probing gaze. "First there is something I need to ask you. Something I have to know."

"Can't it wait until I come back with the stew?" she asked, afraid the rest of his memory had returned and he wanted to know how badly George had been hurt.

"No, it can't," he said emphatically.

"You need to eat something," JoAnn insisted, but realized his question was too important to him to be put off any longer. Her heart ached at the thought of being the one to have to tell him. "Okay. One question. What is it you want to know?"

"Why you came back when you did," he answered, studying her facial response closely. "Is it possible you had second thoughts about having refused to marry me?"

Second and third and fourth thoughts, she mused, her heart racing at a ridiculous rate while she stared into his startling blue eyes, the same eyes that had haunted her dreams for days.

Even as pale and as thin he had become, he remained the most handsome man she had ever met. If only it was possible for me to stay, she thought sadly, knowing she would have to leave for the mountain immediately. Then, in that moment, while she gazed longingly at the man she had come to love so dearly, she knew what lay in store for her. Suddenly, she knew she could never leave this man again. She could never survive the heartache a third time. And, too, by now staying could be her *only* choice. It had been five days. It was possible the passageway to her time had shrunk until she would have no other choice but to stay.

"What would you do if I said yes? That right this very minute I was having just such second thoughts about marrying you? That I loved you too much to want to spend another minute of my life without you?"

"Then I'd say I was a very lucky man." He smiled a smile so deep it reached into the depths of his sparkling blue eyes, then winced only slightly when he held his arms out to her, indicating he wanted to hold her. "Is it true? Are you having just such second thoughts?"

JoAnn blinked back the tears, for it was very true. Despite the many hardships she knew lay ahead, she wanted to spend what was left of her life with Adam. "During the past few days, I've had a lot of time to think about things and in that time, I wondered repeatedly what it would be like to be married to you."

"And that didn't frighten you away?" he asked and continued to watch her closely while he waited for her to enter his still-waiting arms.

"Obviously not." She laughed and leaned across the bed in a way she could embrace him without putting unnecessary pressure on the wound at his waist. "Adam, I love you too much to ever again be without you." It was true. Despite the lingering uncertainty that she would ever fully adapt to such a different time period, she was willing to try. For Adam. And for herself.

She would stay and become Adam's wife. And she would do so without bothering to make one last trip to the time passage to see if it was still possible for her to return to the twentieth century — to what was a much easier way of life. To a time when a woman was more readily accepted in a man's world.

Now that she was faced with making a final decision, she knew she could not leave. And it had nothing to do with the possibility the time passage had become too small to accommodate her. During the past couple of months, and more especially during the past several days, she had grown to love Adam too much. Even if she left, her heart would always be back here with him and what sort of life would that be?

Even as a doctor, she felt more needed in the year 1889 than she had ever felt needed during the twentieth century. Especially with so many injured people still needing treatment and the knowledge that a typhoid epidemic was only weeks away.

The truth was that at some point during this final trip back — and she had no idea exactly when the change had occurred — she had not only regained confidence in herself as a doctor, she had allowed herself to become a very real part of what had at one time been nothing more than a part of the past. She no longer cared that she had made unwarranted changes while in *the past* because she had already started to think of the year 1889 as *the present*. She no longer worried that having made changes while in the year 1889 could eventually affect the 1990s because that later time period no longer existed for her. The last decade of the twentieth century was now as remote to her as it was to anyone else living in the year 1889.

Smiling, she slid onto the bed beside Adam so she could stay within the crook of his arm without causing him any unnecessary pain. When she did, she realized how easily she moved about in what had at one time felt like very awkward clothing. "I'm finally where I belong."

Adam nodded that he agreed. "I am so glad you finally believe me. I really *don't* care about anything that might have happened in your past." He leaned closer so he could gaze more readily into her glimmering brown eyes. "I love you too much for that."

Tears sprang to her eyes when she realized he spoke the truth. "Adam, I do think there is one thing I should tell you about myself. . . ."

Adam reached out to rest his fingertip against her lower lip to silence her. "I already told you, the past does not matter. All that matters now is the future. Our future."

"And what a future that will be," JoAnn admitted, then blinked away yet more tears of happiness as she leaned forward for the kiss that would seal her fate. Her heart soared for she had never been happier.

After a few seconds, Adam pulled away just far enough to let her see the love shining from his blue eyes. "Our life together will be like nothing you have *ever* experienced. That I promise."

And what an easy promise for him to keep.

Epilogue

July 17, 1889

In the seven weeks that had passed, over fifty doctors had come from all over the world to help take care of the thousands of people who had been injured in the Johnstown Flood as well as those hundreds more who eventually contracted typhoid due to the unsanitary conditions that had immediately followed the disaster.

Because so many of the people were already on the mend and there were so many outside doctors still there, Dr. JoAnn Johnson was no longer as needed as she had been during the earlier part of June. Nor was her husband, Adam, for the relief trains had continued to bring temporary workers by the hundreds and the massive restoration of Johnstown was now well underway.

At her new husband's encouragement, JoAnn finally agreed to leave her new town to the other doctors and go with him to the farm for a much needed rest. On the second afternoon there, Adam and Cyrus had gone back down to check on the repairs to Park's house which, at Sheila Drum's suggestion, was being turned into an orphanage for the many children who had been left homeless by the flood. After the first few days following the

471

flood, Sheila had transformed into an entirely different person, finding a confidence in herself she had never had before. Although she had no experience in management, she was looking forward to being the headmistress of the new orphanage.

While Adam and Cyrus were gone, JoAnn told Doris she was planning to take a long walk. First she stopped by the small cemetery not far from the house where Adam's first wife and his stillborn son lay. There, she placed fresh cut flowers on their two graves as well as on the graves of George and Park, whose bodies had been moved at Adam's request just a few weeks after the flood. Adam had wanted both his father's and George's graves near him, claiming George had been too much like a son to allow him to lie alone in the Grandview Cemetery.

After arranging the flowers just so and giving Shadow a friendly pat for the dog rarely left his master's gravesite, JoAnn gathered the other items she had brought with her and headed for the area where the time passage had been. She was pleased to see the spot still marked by the pile of stones she had left there months earlier. After checking to see that the hole was still there, though now only inches in diameter, she pulled an envelope out of her skirt pocket and unfolded the paper inside. She wanted to read the message one last time.

The envelope was addressed to Dr. Jean Gallagher and the letter inside was JoAnn's way of reassuring her dear friend that her sudden disappearance had not been the result of foul play.

". . . and please see to it that my two aunts in Texas receive full and legal title to any and all of my parents' property including the house in Woodvale Heights and my father's old pickup. I also want it made clear that you, Jean Gallagher, are to have

472

my car and all the rest of my personal belongings, including that antique hutch you have coveted all these years.

"I also want it made clear that I am under no duress while writing this. I have finally found my true place in this world but, because of certain circumstances, I will never be coming back there. Not even for a visit. I will miss you dearly, but please believe that I am happier now than I've ever been in my life. Give what's-his-name a big kiss for me and tell him I said he had better be good to you because you deserve to be every bit as happy as I am right now.

Your friend through all time,
Dr. JoAnn Griffin, M.D."

Originally, JoAnn had dated the letter July 17, 1889 and signed it Dr. JoAnn Johnson, but had immediately changed both so Jean would not have as much trouble convincing her lawyer the letter should be considered a legitimate document decreeing what was to be done with her and her parents' properties.

As a way of letting Jean know exactly what had happened to her, though she knew Jean would be skeptical at first, JoAnn carefully folded the letter around a two-and-a-half-dollar gold piece stamped 1889 and two newspaper articles mentioning her name. One was written about the rescue efforts after the flood and the other announced her marriage to Adam and her plans to take over Park's practice. After having taken the necessary exams to prove her medical knowledge and obtain the proper certification, she could now in good conscience act as the doctor she was and continue serving the people she had come to care for so deeply during the aftermath of the flood.

To be certain the letter was easily noticed — figuring

by now someone had found the car which would bring Jean back to that area again and again while searching for clues that could explain what had happened to her — JoAnn placed the letter back into the envelope, folded it, then put the folded envelope inside the pocket of the freshly laundered sweatshirt she had worn on that day she had left the 1990s for the last time. Rolling the shirt into a tight ball until it was small enough to fit into the six-inch hole, she stuffed the garment through, until it and her hand disappeared completely from her sight.

After a second, she dropped the garment but let her hand remain on the other side for several seconds. She wiggled the fingers she could no longer see while she called out a soft farewell to the dear friend she had left behind. But despite the sudden sadness she felt, knowing she would never see her friend again, when she pulled her hand back, she smiled. She felt little regret for having chosen to stay with Adam for she truly believed her happiness lay there — in that amazing year 1889.

ABOUT THE AUTHOR

ROSALYN ALSOBROOK is a bestselling author whose novels have sold more than a million copies worldwide. A resident of Gilmer, Texas, Rosalyn married her high school sweetheart Bobby. She has two sons and one grandchild—but, she adds, she's a very *young,* grandmother! Rosalyn enjoys doing intricate research for the authentic details she includes in her historical romances. Her many bestselling Zebra historical romances include PASSIONS BOLD FIRE, ENDLESS SEDUCTION, WILD WESTERN BRIDE, and MAIL-ORDER MISTRESS.

Rosalyn would like to hear from her readers. Write to her c/o Zebra Books, 475 Park Avenue South, New York, N.Y. 10016. Please include a stamped self-addressed envelope if you'd like a reply from the author.

PINNACLE BOOKS HAS
SOMETHING FOR EVERYONE—

MAGICIANS, EXPLORERS, WITCHES AND CATS

THE HANDYMAN   (377-3, $3.95/$4.95)
He is a magician who likes hands. He likes their comfortable shape and weight and size. He likes the portability of the hands once they are severed from the rest of the ponderous body. Detective Lanark must discover who The Handyman is before more handless bodies appear.

PASSAGE TO EDEN   (538-5, $4.95/$5.95)
Set in a world of prehistoric beauty, here is the epic story of a courageous seafarer whose wanderings lead him to the ends of the old world—and to the discovery of a new world in the rugged, untamed wilderness of northwestern America.

BLACK BODY   (505-9, $5.95/$6.95)
An extraordinary chronicle, this is the diary of a witch, a journal of the secrets of her race kept in return for not being burned for her "sin." It is the story of Alba, that rarest of creatures, a white witch: beautiful and able to walk in the human world undetected.

THE WHITE PUMA   (532-6, $4.95/NCR)
The white puma has recognized the men who deprived him of his family. Now, like other predators before him, he has become a man-hater. This story is a fitting tribute to this magnificent animal that stands for all living creatures that have become, through man's carelessness, close to disappearing forever from the face of the earth.